ALL WATERS
ARE GRAVES

ALL WATERS ARE GRAVES

A HAZELAND NOVEL
By Matt Maxwell

A Highway 62 Press book

highway62press.com

Praise for *All Waters Are Graves*

"Maxwell's prose is austere and stinging. A character remarks that ghosts are "wounds in time" and that perfectly encapsulates the magical and mournful tenor of this novel. *All Waters Are Graves* is strong work. It will linger with you."

- Laird Barron, author of *Swift to Chase*

"*All Waters Are Graves* taps the idea of deluge upwelling through the zeitgeist, the threat of inundation, the erosion to total dissolution of our reality. Cait's neck-deep in a dark flood of intrigue; with her, we plunge into the weirdness of an eighties-noir LA landscape, submerge and swim breathless to a spectacular, kaleidoscopic ending. Another great read from Matt Maxwell. Recommended. Just don't forget your wetsuit."

- Jamie Delano, writer of *Hellblazer* and the *Leepus* books

ALL WATERS ARE GRAVES
by MATT MAXWELL
Published by
Highway 62 Press
www.highway62press.com

ISBN 9798327054028

All characters in this book are fictional.
Not a bit of it is real.

Other books in the Hazeland series
The Queen of No Tomorrows

Coming in the future
Fake Believe
The Missing Pieces
Asphalt Tongues

Previously

Cait MacReady was a forger of books who wanted to play a trick, so she made a book up. A book filled with secrets and power.

The Queen knew about the book before it happened and wanted it for herself.

The Queen used the book to make a thing that would have destroyed Cait and broke the world. She only ended up destroying herself.

Cait is still waking up from that.

ALL WATERS ARE GRAVES

A HAZELAND NOVEL

By Matt Maxwell

DEDICATION

For my mother who told me about laughing water.
For my father who taught me that they were all crime pages.

PROLOGUE

Cait's hand went straying. She'd been out of the hospital for months but the shakes still boiled up, unwelcome and consuming. The line around her eye went from modest to Siouxsie, flaring out in a short arc. Black and jagged on her cheek as she pulled the brush back and cursed. It wasn't that she was late or that this was the end of the world. She'd seen that already. She'd seen it and felt its breath hot upon her and everyone else in the junkyard that night. Few had walked away from that storm and whatever it revealed. Not the kids of No Tomorrows. Not Ariela who had instead found exactly what she'd promised herself and hadn't been seen since. Nor would she again, her tiny and fragile doll frame put through contortions that mocked conception. Not Alondra's sisterhood, though she'd gotten well-paid in return. Cait sometimes wondered if it had been enough for her.

But Cait herself had survived it. She went an entire week before collapsing in the middle of a job rebuilding the binding on a renaissance bestiary, pages peeling away from the whole, threatening disintegration. One minute, fine. The next, the scent of the parchment and glue hit her like a runaway train and she was obliterated by something from her own memory. Something about books. Everything about them. All of the thoughts put on those pages and how none of them had ever been real or true until she herself had made that book that Ariela had killed and died for. That Ariela had known before a single page had been written or drawn upon.

She came out the fugue a week after with a diagnosis of nerves and anxiety and no desire to return to anything from before. Everyone around her had understood. Rico had been murdered. And while they weren't close right then, they had been before. It hadn't been Rico's death that had tossed Cait into the hole. It had been marks on a page. If she'd ever told anyone the truth, they'd ever let her back to her life. Her life was radically pared back now, flayed. No books, no clubs, no life outside. Just head down and working. That wasn't the doctors; that was her. Time to move and move on.

The eyeliner mishap was a nothing. An everyday mishap that ballooned to fill her thoughts, crowding out any other with teeth bared and snapping.

She went back to what she'd talked about with the only doctor she'd trusted. Re-center. Fix on the moment. Breath escaped her, slow and steady. It wasn't even a sigh that she let out, more a futile whisper. Just another thing to endure.

The face in the mirror still threw her, hair short and the most normal shade of brown she could pull off the shelf, murky, plain. She'd colored it the first night home and every couple of weeks since. The purple that the dye had gone over still lurked underneath, only it was dirty and drab now at the ends. It might've been weird, if she'd ever allowed it to be noticed. She turned no heads. She caught no attention. Plain Cait.

The wayward line tugged at her, modest by her previous standards. There were nights where it felt like she'd brushed on the whole bottle, throwing her eyes into pools of black that couldn't be pierced. It was armor then. She didn't need it now. She needed comfort, normality. Cait fingered the string of pearls on her neck absently, toying with the idea of leaving the painted streak in place. Just to see if anyone would notice, if anyone would see her.

Then she thought about the last time she'd been seen. She'd been pulled out of a crowd, her anonymity stripped and the spotlight put on her. More than that, turned into a rock star, elevated. Who cared if it was only for a night or even just a moment before Ariela had chosen Cait for something bigger. Brighter stars become cinders quicker.

She reached across the neatly organized bathroom counter and grabbed at the jar of cotton balls, pinching one out of the flock then dousing it with baby oil. The swab went on like sandpaper so she just scrubbed harder. If it was going to roll that way, she'd just push more. That always worked. She wiped the eye clean and started over, drawing a perfect line, though she had to will her hand still. There were mornings she spent half an hour erasing and re-drawing, erasing and re-drawing, erasing and re-drawing.

It had to be right. She had to disappear.

She stood up and looked herself over without seeing the whole. Her collar was uneven, jutting out over the gray blazer like a broken bone showing through skin. She patiently put it back. Everything fixed. Everything was okay. That's what all the details would tell anyone who looked.

She was okay.

She opened the door to her apartment, heat from the morning blowing through the doorway and dry enough to choke on. There hadn't been any rain for a long time, none worth mentioning. She stepped out the door to a walkway she had to remind herself turned to the right, not to the left. This apartment was in a new part of town, new path to work. It would never be home and she'd never be welcome in it. She left it every day thinking that.

And every night, she came home and filled the bath, daring herself.

But not tonight. Tonight she'd pay her respects. Maybe a bribe to the dead would buy a little peace.

∽

Cait brought the Mercury to a stop on the sloppy clay and gravel of the industrial yard. The cold and rain had come unwelcome out of nowhere. If she'd done this hours ago, it would have been at least dry. She'd fought with herself all that time after work, torn between reliving every awkward interaction of the day and shrieking at herself for not getting up and doing what she'd promised this morning. That struggle boiled in her until the rain pattered on the window. She let the rain tell her to go to sleep, to pick another time. Instead of the day and its parade of mundane indignities, she fell into a locked groove memory of that night and the storm breathed out by what Ariela had called. What Cait had given her the power to call.

She shivered and hid, clammy as if she was out in that rain right now.

She couldn't shake it. But she didn't want to eat a couple Benadryl in response, something that had been going on for a while. Allergies were the last thing on her mind, but that black forgetting sleep she craved. Cheaper than valium. But nothing she in the house had was stronger than actually running towards a resolution instead of pursuing oblivion for a night.

She had to go now. She muscled the Mercury past Griffith Park and the skeleton trees thrashing along the riverbank. She drove until she was on the south side of the river, still contained in sloped concrete banks but drinking rain greedily and swelling with a speed that should not have been. It welled up in mirror of Cait's own heart filling her chest from within then threatening to burst and she wished it would to make this all stop.

Something broke and Cait just stopped with a lurch, unable to do anything else. She held her hand against the window, letting it fog. Mist danced sluggish and drunk, vapor on glass. A shape lingered there after she pulled away. It didn't look like a hand at all, more like something slipping beneath the surface.

The glove compartment door came open with a cold ratcheting. The five-shot .38 revolver the car had come with was gone and packed away somewhere that it would stay out of trouble. Cait didn't want to guess whatever crimes that thing could have been tied to. All that was left now was the pink slip and the gloves. Velvet, black. They'd been sewn for hands more delicate than Cait's. She wondered if they would fit but she'd never been brave enough to try them on. Tonight was no different. They had been Ariela's, just like the car. To the survivor go the spoils.

Cait wadded the soft fabric up in a clenched fist. Then she made sure the knife was still in her jacket pocket, only the third time she'd checked tonight. The process had slipped from ceremony to stalling.

"Enough," she snapped at herself. She jammed the gloves into the opposite pocket and killed the still-running car. It went down fighting. The rain pattered soft as distant gunfire on the roof and hood.

She opened the door and climbed out. Her sensible shoes sank into the greedy clay. Her feet went cold and had only risky purchase. She should have worn her Docs but those were packed away with her other old clothes, still unboxed after the move along with everything that she used to be. The chill of the mud brought her right back to that morning and the aftermath of what the news had dubbed "The Wyvrenwood Twister." The freak storm had set down here and jumped over a mile or two to tear right into the Wyvrenwood Apartments, ripping off windows and roof tiles, scaring a bunch of people half to death. The reporters only worried about that apartment complex and the residents they could interview, wide-eyed and holding onto children or cats or portraits of the Virgin of Guadalupe. No Tomorrows hadn't made the news. No Ariela and her blue eyes seductive over the embroidered veil that dared lifting. None of her crazy dream or desire or annihilation.

Everyone else had forgotten this place. Why couldn't Cait? The thoughts were stuck in her like birdshot buried in her skin. Anyone else's opinion didn't really register or matter. Not Anton's, not Alondra's, and least of all, not Ariela's. None of them would have held still for television interviews anyway. It's as if what happened here hadn't really. Maybe Cait was the only one who remembered now.

The metal plate hung from a chain suspended at knee-height. It said CLOSED — KEEP OUT in reflective lettering, dancing like afterimage. She stepped over the halfhearted barrier and the sign, catching it with her off-foot then pitching forward. Catching herself, she wheezed and her heart rattled, expecting jeers and mockery from unseen watchers.

The yard was quiet but for the wind whistling over the irregular shapes of the wrecked cars and other, less-identifiable, chunks of discarded industry. Everything was bitten and beaten. The sounds coming off the stacked metal were all hollow and minor key.

"Let's get this over and done," she said to nobody.

Wind whipped up around her with flashes of that hot animal breath that had hit her six months ago. Instead of buckling, she clenched her fists hard enough to ache.

Two streetlamps poured a bluish-white cast onto the middle of the yard, center stage. There was something artful in it, deliberate, installed, drawn out in the beams. Cait couldn't help but remember how Rico had been laid out dead in the middle of his own rented house's yard. Ceremony. Ritual. Purpose. It only seemed like a hundred years ago.

She fingered the knife handle and pushed ahead. Leather straps older than the city of LA and maybe any other city were smooth beneath her fingertips, seams between them as fine as hairs.

She walked towards the object centered in the pool of light. White shapes caught her eye, circular and oblong and trumpet-like all mixed in with darker organic forms of inverted hearts. All of it was overflowing, perverse in fecundity. She came to a stop when she realized what it was. Datura. A datura shrub just growing improbably in the middle of the yard. She kneeled and reached. It wasn't wild, rather it was a giant bouquet, wrapped and laid out in rain-spattered cellophane. The moon-white flowers faintly glowed all rain-beaded. No florist grew these blooms, both toxic and hallucinatory. Ariela had loved them, loved them so much that a tattoo of one had been inked into her chest, spanning from the hollows of her collarbones to the stem of the bloom between her breasts. Had it been the poison or the visions that she loved?

Someone else had remembered, Cait thought to herself, mouthing the words.

There was a card with the bouquet, elegant blackletter writing now running and melting, disheveled as tear-smeared eyeliner. Bluish rivulets of almost-meaning on the white. The only word was legible was one of salutation: Reina. Queen.

Cait would have dropped to the ground had she not already been kneeling. She braced herself with one hand and barely caught her breath, heart swelling to drive the air from her lungs. The hand with the gloves in it remained stuck in her jacket as if glued.

She stood slowly and looked around sure that she was surrounded by figures in black, not for mourning but because that was how they always dressed, even in the midday sun. She was sure that No Tomorrows was still here and still watching her, knowing what she had done to their queen, even if that throne was now occupied by her once-sister Alondra.

Cait counted breaths, lost to the wind howling on the metal. Seeing nothing but shadows, she pulled herself together, all the pieces mismatched in the process. She stood, feeling all of two feet tall in a world that was much bigger and much less stable than she'd known. The shapes of the junk and trash assumed the forms of titans above her. They waited for Cait to move so they could obliterate her, unmake her with a swat. Silhouetted against the gauzed halo of the distant city lights, electrical pylons stood like the towers of black churches, stripped down to the studs.

One of the streetlamps flared and burned out. The flowers still glowed before her. And something more above them, like neon signs unlit in the dark. Reflection and sheen revealed something there. The name of the queen's dark and beloved god, cut in half laterally. The echoes of those symbols hung there, just as Cait had carved their shapes out of the air that night. Carved then cut across in a desperate to make a thing real with words so that destroying the word might destroy what it named. She was probably the only person in the whole world still alive who could see the now-meaningless scrawl. She mouthed the sounds of the name but stopped herself before speaking it, knowing how to pronounce it without having heard it before. Hot tears welled up in her eyes, squeezed like diamonds from a pressure she couldn't imagine. She hadn't cried since that night; she'd barely felt. There was heat and shame that cooled as it met the rain.

"I'm sorry. Just let me be."

She unfurled the gloves, holding them both so that the fingers twisted and bent like there were hands within them still. They were bent and interlocked, digits bending forces that Cait couldn't comprehend but had named in her book. Ariela's spell had never ended.

"You're not real. You're not."

She threw the gloves into the pool at her feet. They hit the muddy water with just a whisper of sound. A black and velvety afterbirth of a nameless creature made of shadow and eating light. The wrinkles were as pattern-pregnant as a fingerprint or a hallmark left by a distracted maker. Carelessness.

That wasn't right.

That wasn't enough. Cait leaned down and demanded a more definitive erasure. She pulled the gloves out of the puddle with one hand. With her other, she loosened the knife in the sheath. Fear of cutting herself on it made her slow and careful. That edge was sharp enough to cut wood, glass, even those aluminum baking pans she'd tested it on. All as if they were insubstantial as smoke. As if the knife were the only real thing in the world. It left an edge so sharp that mishandling the tray left her sliced bad enough to need stitches. That was accidental. Who knew what it would do with intent?

"You have to go now. You have to leave me alone. Please."

She drew the knife through the gloves and cut them to uneven velvet ribbons, fingers becoming a rain of *O*'s. An unmaking, an undoing, a prayer of severance. The wind died, deflated. All the pieces fell into the pool and caught the light and looked like a door to another place, one made of radiance. She looked away and up, out of the junkyard. The walls of metal were built up like a crater, geology and astronomy mothering strange children in joining. Wind whipped around her and drove wetted hanks of hair into her eyes. She looked down and picked her vision clear. The remains of the glove now blotted the surface of the pool out, pushing out the reflection until only shreds were left, like moon-white tears wept and cooling. The place was still here and she was still in it. Whatever had touched down was something she carried inside her still. There had been no severance.

She turned her back on the pool and the flowers and the memory of Ariela. She felt no better but drove home anyway.

When she got there, she lit all the lights and drew a bath, neither hot nor cold, just warm enough that she could feel it on her chilled skin. There was no daring this time. She just slipped inside, clothed still, sensible shoes coming off her feet as they hit the water.

The surface ate her in and she closed her eyes for a long moment until her ears filled with water. All she could hear was her pulse and the roar of distant oceans right there with her. There was no outside, only inside. She held her breath as long as she could before opening her eyes.

Someone else was there. And she was no longer in the bath. Her fingers no longer grabbed the sides of the tub. She was underwater, only this water was cold as Pacific upwelling in winter. And it was clear. It was the water that was found in sunless caves where millions of years of sediment rested undisturbed. There was vaulted ceiling above her, but it wasn't that at all. Instead it was a crazy latticework of giants, structures sketched out in steel only describing the forms but leaving them empty. Electrical towers. Submerged in the same water that she was in. All of them, all civilization's power and industry and there it was consumed and forgotten beneath the dappling surface of blue and azure and the shades between with no name as the sun faded above. And then there was no light at all.

"This is what he wants," came the whisper. It cut through the roar of Cait's own blood and body, everything else falling away. She couldn't identify the voice, its source or anything else about it. It was a whisper across miles, like the voice that Ariela and Alondra had used, hands across mouth, obviating source and gaining power.

The surface was so far away, the sun even farther. And everything was underwater. It had always been underwater. As it had, it would be again.

Cait jerked upright with a scream that was muffled by the water before she broke the surface into a gasp that she could feel in the soles of her feet. She was back in her bathroom, pale lemon-yellow walls and white tiles and tarnished everything else. She was back there and breathing slowly as the water dripped from her. Licking her lips, it tasted salty.

She drained the bath and retreated to bed, still dripping. Her sleep was shallow as rain on the sidewalk.

CHAPTER ONE

Cait refused to reflect on the previous night. She'd slept in her clothes before. Normal people did that. She got up and changed into dry work clothes in her regular fashion. No wayward eyeliner. No other thoughts. Then she got yesterday's coffee warming on the stove and idled through the accumulated mail. She could do that much this morning.

Bill, bill, bill, stop. Her hands lingered on a big padded mailer addressed with neat black handwriting, spelling out Cait's address in a script that she recognized instantly from a lifetime of notes in lunchboxes and signed report cards and birthday greetings that came no matter how many times Cait had moved or how long ago she'd left home.

Mom.

Ripping open the package, Cait found a bound photo album, once bright red but now deepened to a duller and more indistinct maroon. The vinyl cover had split along one of the corners, revealing a chipboard foundation. It should have cheapened things but instead made them much more real. She knew where it had come from but not why it was here in her hands. A note indicated that it was supposed to go to her uncle, Vince Laurie. But here it was on her mess of a kitchen table. Addressed to her.

She cursed herself for letting it go so long but wasn't going to have done it any other way. And now she was backed into a corner by her own inaction. Mom would want answers. Cait wasn't in a mood to provide them. She hadn't freaked out about Cait being hospitalized, only asking the vaguest of questions. But not out of inattentiveness. Mom had kept her distance for a while. Now that time had burned down like it always had before.

Cait's fingers punched the buttons to a number that she was more accustomed to rotary dialing, but she didn't fumble. Two rings.

"Hello?"

"Hi. Cait? Well this is a nice surprise."

"Yeah, I was just getting ready to go out but noticed this package in the mail for me." Her chest went tight. She ran her fingers over the slitted cover by way of distraction.

"Package?" The surprise was close enough to genuine that Cait was reluctant to question it. "I didn't send you anything. And it's too early for Christmas."

"I come out for Christmas, Mom."

"You do."

"Anyways, it's a photo album, and there's a note here for uncle Vince."

She shifted the package around but did not open it. She could remember sitting on the plaid couch that still smelled like cigarettes even though her parents had quit smoking by then, looking over faded photographs while they talked about people she only sort of knew. It was like looking through *Time* or *People* but with faces that you knew personally. The few glamour shots were better lit and composed but they were out of place. Most of the pictures had been shot with little thought toward exposure or focus, simply grabbing a moment and these she remembered. Stutter-steps of time frozen in a flood now.

"Oh. Oh no. I must have spaced out and written your name down."

"And my address."

"Right." Not even a half-beat skipped. "Well, it's not such a big deal. Vince is just down in Santa Monica. That's not far."

"He lives in Venice, Mom. Totally different thing. That's like saying you live in Banning."

Her mother laughed and Cait un-clenched some. "That's silly. Everyone knows we live in Riverside."

"Since nineteen and fifty-seven."

"Yup." A long breath followed by "is there anything else, dear?"

"Uh, no. No." Cait's pulse thudded dully now, backing down from its previous roar. "I really need to get to work. It's a longer drive from the new place."

"But Venice isn't too big a drive, right? I promised Vince I'd have that to him by the tenth."

Cait thought a moment. "That's today, Mom. Tonight even."

"I sent it more than a week ago now. Are you just seeing it?"

Cait didn't answer.

Her mother continued. "Then it has to be tonight. You don't want to make me break a promise. I sent that with plenty of time to reach him."

"But it reached *me*."

"A simple mistake, my sweet girl."

"But you don't make mistakes, Mom."

"Only on purpose, Cait. I guess you better hurry to work, huh?"

"Yeah, I better. Love you, Mom."

"You know we both love you too."

The goodbyes were passed and Cait walked down to the carport, wondering what route she'd take. She'd dodged that bullet. She was doing fine.

Hours later, the workspace around her was nothing but weight and pressure, like she'd been dragged to the bottom of a sea trench and left there still able to breathe somehow. Her temples groaned with dull migraine. She took off her glasses, needing them now for fine work and not merely wearing them as decoration or distraction or as proof that she was an expert and maybe that you should just shut up and listen.

She took a breath then shifted her shoulders, trying to let it all go, just like the doctor said she should do. So what if she had to remind herself a hundred times a morning? The weight of her mask felt unbearable at times, neck locked into place, barely swiveling and that tightness taking root in her shoulders and jaw. The camouflage that kept her going through another day wasn't holding. It used to be okay, used to go okay. But that was before she'd broken the world. Not that she could tell that to her doctor or anyone else, not even the cops. Even Trager hadn't quite believed that story and he was better-set-up for that than most. He was just happy to know that No Tomorrows would be running a much lower profile from now on. The why wasn't qualifiable, didn't go on reports.

That thought ticked at her and made her heart press harder. She drew careful breaths for a moment, eyes closed, trying not to resort to another pill now that she'd restocked. They weren't habit-forming, the doctor had said. Besides, just pushing through another cortisol storm, as he'd so charmingly called her broken moods, was worse in the long run than taking another Xanax.

Her heart kept pounding as heavy as the bass and beats that had pounded her bodily at the club shows she used to go to. Only this wasn't freedom and wild abandon. It was being crushed down by boots from within and without. Nobody else saw them. She worked hard to make sure of that.

She reached behind her to her purse hanging on the back of the chair. It was nice if you didn't look at it too closely, a Coach, but the kind they only sold in Santee Alley. Sure those were legit and this is 100% real leather, just don't get it wet. Her hand closed around the unmarked amber bottle that rattled faintly as she did.

"Another research request, Cait," came the reedy voice, unfinished somehow, like it would never complete changing.

She jumped in spite of herself. Her heart didn't change its unrelenting beat, didn't go any harder. She was already riding those rapids. Her boss was just another rock on that river.

She caught hold of herself and her fingers released as she turned to acknowledge Robbins, her new supervisor. He never announced himself or greeted her. He just stood by her desk, somehow always able to move right up unheard.

"Didn't mean to scare you." His toothy grin made his shallow cheeks seem almost not there at all. His hair was unkempt and curly, but then he wasn't the one who had to work the desk out front, was he? He could dress however he damn well pleased except on staff meeting days.

Cait's shirt felt scratchy and dirty. Maybe it went deeper than that.

"It's okay, Bill. I'm just dealing—"

His smile lit up, but it was cold beneath. "We know, Cait. You're dealing with some stuff." The fluorescent overhead lights gave his teeth a gleam that came off wrong, like unearthed bone. But why shouldn't they be off?

Everything was wrong now. It was still here, that thing Ariela called. Cait knew it. The world had been broken, doors opened and never to be closed again. Because of her because of her because of--

"I'm sorry," she said as she took up the slim stack of printouts, tractor paper all marked up with lines of dots that assembled themselves into words if you squinted at them right. "I asked for this transfer and—"

"Yeah, about that. I've never seen someone take a step down like you." His eyes were wide behind his glasses for a second. Then the overheads made the lenses go opaque with reflected white oblongs, so you could only see glimpses of him. But he always saw Cait. Always interrupted.

"If you let me finish a sentence, you might learn something." The words were escaping her mouth before she could stop them. At least she kept them from having the bite they did in her head.

"Geez. rip my head off for being concerned."

"Sorry, Bill." She whipped her glasses off and rubbed at her temples. "I'll get right on these. Should be an hour." She turned back to her paperwork, not waiting on permission.

"Yeah, thanks. An hour!" he said as he wandered off.

She hated that he was giving orders. Not that she wanted to be the one in charge, but she shouldn't have to listen to an unfinished boy like him.

 formula

Day's end and she fumbled the ignition twice before the Mercury would start. She tried not to think that the car was actively against her. That was crazy. That would be crazy. It's a thing, inanimate and without volition. Even if it did have a personality.

She pulled herself together, wrapping the whole mess with twine so it would hold just for a night and another day. Get through this thing with Uncle Vince and then one more day. Then she could rest on the weekend, not do anything. She could just be.

Cait snapped the volume on the stereo and tape player. It was the only piece of the Mercury that had been updated, the rest being as the car had rolled off the lot nearly forty years ago. News words babbled out of the speakers, Cait only paying attention to that traffic feed, every six minutes whether you wanted it or not. Where was it damaged? Where was it clotted up, the rotten veins of LA. Dodge worst and hope for the best.

There had been a cassette in the slot after Cait had acquired the car, one side being punk and rock tunes, all teenage libido or despair and scratchy guitars, most in Spanish, but Cait knew enough to follow along. The other side was the hard stuff, some kind of heart-rending torch singing all in Spanish as well, which Cait had gotten a couple songs into before having to pull off the road and yank the cassette out. It was too raw. The tape was probably still back there behind the front, but she'd never gone looking for it. Rico used to speak to her like that, then he switched to English when their relationship became purely business.

She pushed the loaded cassette all the way into the slot—the last one she'd listened to, driving out to Ariela's funeral, as it was. Pause of waiting for the machine to load it with a thunk-snap that she could feel in her fingers.

"80 Times" by TSOL picked up and snarled. She wanted to feel the defiance and triumph that surged through the speakers. All she could hear was the undercurrent of rage-fueled despair. All she could feel was a flight from everything, an absence of feeling because they were too dangerous to be allowed. She punched eject on the tape and switched back to the radio. The knob turned under her fingers and she stopped when she could pull out a voice.

"Ghosts are, they're wounds in time," the voice said. "Like a scratch in a record if you will. A limited but powerful and jarring phenomenon, one that snaps us out of our routines."

"On that note, Doctor, let's hit station identification and give our audience a chance to digest. I'm Christopher Kent, and you're listening to a special daylight episode of *Exit Gate* on KRYC."

Not in the mood.

She drove in silence all the way to Venice, riding the crawl and jump of traffic down Westwood to Olympic to Ocean Park. The rain the night before had scraped the dust off everything. It all shone, brilliant gold sunset going down into the Pacific without even a fizzle. She parked on the street in front of a Thai place, realizing that hunger was clawing at her after not eating all day. Cait had learned to embrace necessity. Eat only when you have to. Sleep then too. Do the minimum. You get by.

She ate the chicken and peanuts and chili oil and noodles, not really tasting it, just noting a heat on her lips and tongue that the beer quenched. Crawl and jump, hot and cold, all just sort of blips on a long line of existence. Neither happy nor sad, she powered through things. Unstoppable force Cait.

A dimming band of pink and orange hugged the horizon by the time she got to Venice, the rest of the sky all black and inky. That's what Venice was. Inky. Sure, for the tourists it was colorful and wild, an unholy combination of sixties holdovers and the No Future Generation that followed hungrily. And money. Lots of that. Old houses being leveled and turned into modern concrete boxes with eight-foot walls and intercoms at enameled gates. But the old neighborhood wasn't going to go so easily.

Vince lived in a condo complex built in the seventies, abutting one of the last remaining canals that bled out into a small lagoon that trickled eventually into the Pacific just on the other side of a long sand spit. She parked in the cul-de-sac behind an old and beaten blue pickup of some American make with a mismatched red fender welded onto the car. That curved steel looked brand new. That red hung there like a sore.

"Whatever works, I guess," she muttered to herself.

Flipping the rear-view down, she reached into her purse with the other hand and took out her make-up one piece at a time. A little powder to even things up, touch of blush for color that the beer wasn't providing, fix her eyes, neutral but clean on the lips, just like she was going to work. She had to be regular, normal. Even for Uncle Vince. After all, Mom wouldn't be sending her to see him without a reason.

She stepped out of the car and looked down the canal, more a brown weed-and-reed-choked ditch, steep enough to be dangerous but not from drowning. Maybe from chemical exposure, judging from the multicolor slick snaking along the shoreline. A white art-deco bridge spanned the canal down a ways. If she squinted, she could see that it was the same one where the end of *Touch of Evil* had been shot, gargantuan Orson Welles lying in the ditch like a whale out of water, eyes all bulging and sad and lost.

She clutched the package and locked the Mercury and wondered if Alondra or Ariela had ever bothered. That car had belonged to No Tomorrows before and anyone who recognized it was not likely to mess with it.

"It don't need to be this way," a voice rang out clearly over the dull and distant roar of the ocean. The wet sea air did that sometimes, voices carrying further than you'd think. The words were weirdly accented, syllables dragged out and trailing off. She thought for a moment they were hallucination, like last night's near-sleep vision, the calls coming from inside the house. That's all it had been. Maybe that's all this was.

"It can't be another," came the reply, this one from a woman. Her voice was harder than river ice.

Cait went looking for the source of the conversation. There, on this side of the bridge. The woman was tall and blonde, almost ashen. The man who was maybe tall maybe dark-haired was sitting on the concrete sides of the structure, his back to Cait. He looked wrong in the light, blurry, standing in heat ripples all the way down the block on a summer day. Only little details made themselves apparent to her: the faded denim of his jeans, tears in his plain work shirt, pieces magnified and diminished somehow.

"Well, ya ain't said why. Not a reason that makes any sense." The woman had lost patience, arms crossed like a mother waiting for an answer from a kid as to why he was out until three that morning at a show in the city. Familiar.

Cait also knew it wasn't her business and looked away. The sense of distortion ate at her, shaking her as she thought about depths that couldn't be there. She all but ran.

The trickle in the canal bubbled and burbled and she retreated to Vince's building. There were voices in the water and she tried to shake that thought from her head as she climbed the stairs, surrounded by stucco and flaking paint.

The door opened, letting a bearded face and bleary eye to glance through the crack. "Kitty!" he shouted. "What the hell are you doing here?" The smile was bright under unkempt and sweat-locked hair.

Vince was tall and broad, more bear than man to younger Cait. His beard was always at five-days length, rusty-red stubble over sunburnt cheeks and bright blue eyes, even when he was perpetually heavy-lidded from beer or whatever else was in reach.

"God, uncle Vince, don't call me that. I'm not a kid anymore." She should have frowned but couldn't help a smile.

"Aw, you'll always be a kid to me. Come on, gimme a hug." He wrapped her like he was a second away from slamming her into a turnbuckle. He smelled like tobacco and cheap beer and denim that could've used a wash a week ago.

"Okay, enough funk. You smell like a whole biker bar."

"Funny you should say that. I've been on loan to the OC Sheriff's Department." He latched the door behind her and pulled to make sure it was closed.

"More undercover?" That part of his work had always fascinated her. Vince was a cop, but he never looked like one, not once he got past his patrolman rookie phase.

"Yeah, it's how I got this." He pulled down the collar of his black tee, one that just said "Waylon and Willie and fuck all the rest" in fancy white transfer lettering that looked hand-painted. There was a nasty gash with black nylon stitchwork all across it like a chunk of very delicate barbed wire sticking out of a misplaced bandage pad near the collar.

"At least you didn't ruin your good shirt." Cait's voice was teasing.

"Gotta dress the part. Yeah, buncha shit-kickers running crank out of the Swallow's Inn in San Juan. I guess someone took umbrage to my attitude problem."

"And it's only a problem—'"

"'—if you let it be one.' Yup. So yeah, the other guy was eating his beer mug when I was done. But they got me on Percocet and I'm supplementing with some Michelobs." He stared at her a moment, not sleepy-eyed but wider now. "So what brings you here to Abbot Kinney's nightmare-by-the-sea? You look…" he let his voice trail off as he struggled for something polite.

"Corporate?"

"That's nicer than what I was gonna say, but sure." He half-limped ahead of her through the messy apartment to a cubbyhole of a kitchen. "Hey, you want a beer? I still got some left."

"I find that hard to believe."

"You want hard to believe? I'll tell you about the days that the Scarman was in the news. Weeeird times."

"It was the seventies. Everyone was on drugs. Just like you are."

He scowled, wounded. "I'm hurting. This is *medicine*." He rummaged loudly in the refrigerator, which threw pale green light on the yellow lino- leum of the floor.

"Vince, you're higher than two kites stacked on top of each other."

"But I'm not driving. And that's what's important." He turned around with a beer in one hand, put the lip of the bottlecap on the counter and slammed hard with his opposite hand. The cold bottle was in her grasp before the top landed. It clinked and bounced around the floor like a lousy payout.

"Those are twisties. You're blitzed."

"Not... yet." He huffed as he sat down on the couch which groaned under him.

She leaned against the kitchen counter and the cutaway window, not wanting to get too comfortable.

"Sooooo..." his voice trailed off.

"So I think Mom wanted you to check on me, which involved her mis-labeling this package for you, if it is even for you, and then having me hand-deliver it."

He stared dumbly for a moment then broke into a smile. "That does sound like my sister, yes. She's sneaky like that." He brought the brown bottle up to his mouth and took a long pull. Then he fidgeted with the gold foil label. "Look, I heard about your... episode from her."

"It wasn't an *episode*." Cait breathed out hard. "It was a panic attack. That's it." The last part of that had come out shaky and she cleared her throat. She took as long a drink as he had then coughed at the end.

"You haven't had the practice I have. Takes years." He smiled with a brightness that made her feel like she was 12 again only without all the bullshit that had come with that.

Cait sat down on the ottoman, kicked out at an odd angle. She wasn't taking up residence just yet. "Look, I just... I got a little lost. Let things run away from me."

"After your boyfriend died?" He tipped the bottle and let it drain.

"Yeah, I didn't think it would hit me that hard, but it did." She didn't feel the need to add that she hadn't been seeing Rico for some time before his death or that he'd been killed after acting as a go-between for No Tomorrows and her. That would just complicate things. "Just… everything. It all added up. And when you put enough stuff in a basket and keep walking with it, well, that basket breaks." Cait took another swallow though the beer was too bland and somehow too bitter. "This is really terrible."

"Don't you be badmouthing my beer. Or changing the subject."

Cait felt the pressure begin to build in her temples and her wrists and her neck. "I took a couple weeks off and talked to a doctor and everything is fine. I just have to manage my stress. Took a lower-stakes job in my office. New apartment near Hollywood. Still… adjusting."

"Have you tried" he leaned in after looking around with suspicion "mari-juan-a?" He cracked a disarming smile. "Oh wait, shit, I'm not supposed to say that."

"You're the *worst* cop."

"Nah, I'm the best cop 'cause I look like I should be booked on general principles. But back to you."

She drummed her fingers on the weird wide neck of the bottle. "I know my mom wants the best for me, but she… This isn't something that she can just bull-rush and fix." She started another gulp of beer but couldn't stand it and smacked it down to the wood-grain plastic counter. "Goddammit, I'm getting up every morning and getting dressed and going to work. I'm doing that right."

"Yeah, a little too well." Vince dropped his empty into a metal wastebasket by his right hand, where the bottle clinked into what sounded like several others.

"What's that supposed to mean?"

He rubbed his eyes and scratched at the wound under his shirt. "You never were the straightest arrow, Kitty. I mean, not like me, who has to thank the Sheriff's Department of Los Angeles that he has gainful employment as fucked up as he is, playing a fuckup on the street so he can catch others, more fucked-up than himself."

"'There but for the grace of God…?'"

"I'd have made a pretty good outlaw, but yeah. Your mom, bless her, puts up with me. But I wasn't ever going to be quite so clean-cut as her or your dad." He paused and his fingers reached for a beer that wasn't there. "Oh, dammit."

"Here, finish mine." Cait passed him the half-dead soldier.

"That's the stuff. Yeah." He held it but did not drink it. "Your mom knows that whatever you are, you're not... This." He pointed at her business suit and fresh makeup and she felt like he'd seen right through her the whole time, felt utterly transparent.

"Maybe people grow up and change."

Vince pursed his lips and let his eyes go a little heavier. "Maybe they do." He then dropped Cait's beer into the trash can. "So..."

"What?"

"So what are we going to tell her? You know she's going to grill us eight ways to Sunday. Me, then you."

"Oh God, I don't know. Maybe that I'm just wiped, but I'm getting through things. I just need a little more time to..."

"Figure it out. Sure, kid. You want a Pepsi too?"

She laughed. "I wouldn't have picked you as a Suicidal Boy."

He smiled and shrugged in his denim vest so dirty it creaked. "You learn new things out on the street. Even old new things."

"Okay, so yeah. I'm pulling it together, holding together. And tell her that you and I will talk again and you said that if I wasn't back to better-better that we'd have a come-to-Jesus meeting or an intervention like they do on TV and everything."

She flashed and thought about how that would go down. That conjecture only brought up a black swirl, darker than the gunk at the bottom of the canals and twice as thick. Murder and crime and magic that broke the world, only halfway sewing it back up. They'd lock her up and throw away the key. Nobody would believe it. Cait hardly could, out in the sunshine and daylight. It crept up on her at night, dragging her out of sleep, robbing her of safety.

"Oh. So that's what we're doing?" His eyes were clear and wide open now as if he hadn't had a drink in his life. "Okay, so I'll do a well check in a few weeks, and that's where the rubber hits the road? Okay then."

"You're sober? Goddammit." She hissed out the last.

"Dirtbag don't mean stupid, Kitty."

"And I can see where Mom got all this. She learned it from you, right?"

"Only she's not as sneaky about it." He stood, still favoring one leg. Then he walked toward where Cait had set the envelope down. "Now let's take a look at this."

"Photo albums."

"Oh, you opened it?" he asked, heavy with mock disappointment. "Ruining my surprise. Terrible." He moved back to the couch with the album in one hand then patted the space beside him. "Sit by me and remind me who these people are."

"Sure. I can take a trip in the time machine. But I've gotta get back home soon."

Cait wanted to hate him for playing her so effectively, for looking right through her and getting her to say what he'd wanted her to. She felt like she had been in charge the whole time. That was what bit hardest. That she hadn't been in control. The worst part of the joke was laying out for everyone to see. She gets wiped out and sent home to the doctor. Poor Cait can't take it.

Vince was at least honest about it. Took him a little to get there. Everyone else? She was never sure about that. But he was a good head-check. Maybe it would even stick. She hoped it would, fixating on that as she went downstairs and out into the well-settled Venice night.

She took her time going back to the car, walking past the bridge again, coming the long way around the building. She stopped when she heard the couple still there, not arguing but not talking politely either. Sometimes people took a while to get to their point. She'd just marched past and let it go. Still wasn't her business, not at all, even if something had tugged on her hard enough to make her take this route back.

"I told you that I'd show you in time," the man said. His voice was different. Just as his image rippled through something like a heat haze, the sound did something similar.

Despite herself she looked up and everything was wrong.

The man was big, seen through aquarium glass at odd angles, ripples and currents making his outline snake and writhe. It wasn't regular, always shifting. In the glare of the security light he was a slowly pulsing, watery shape. Details and impressions she remembered from before were washed away.

The blonde woman stood before him, one hand at her side and the other in a sort of inelegant purse or bag hanging from her shoulder. Her dress hung just below the knee and looked kind of homespun as well. No way it came off a rack, not even one twenty years ago.

"I heard you the first time. You gonna talk all night or you gonna back it up?" There was a defiant bite in her voice that could have cracked sheet metal. Whatever it was, she wasn't about to back down.

"You asked for this, not me," he said.

The man gestured, making a slit in the air before him. Then there came a sort of seeping or bleeding sound. It came from everywhere, like time itself was being opened and examined then a piece found and removed and set down here. Something heavy hit the ground and glistened in the floodlights. It crouched there, an animal shape, crude and ugly. Its paddle-feet and tail wetly slapping the weed-strewn ground, gently exploring the moment it found itself in.

The gunshot snapped through everything. The blonde held the smoking pistol like she knew how to use it, confident, yet disappointment and shock still registered on her face as if she couldn't quite believe she'd fallen that far. Her eyes snapped to the lizard now but he gun stayed in the direction of the distorted man.

The sight of the creature transfixed Cait in disbelief. It was maybe eight feet long with a torso like a penguin: thick in the middle and tapering to a stubby tail at one end and a blunted lizard head at the other, all teeth and scales. It thrashed on four flippers at the end of vestigial limbs. The crocodile texture of its skin was moist and uneven, hot spots of reflected light against slouching dark. It appeared stunned, head lolling but now coming to attention with the sound and the light around it.

A second shot rang out. Not for the thing. She was taking a draw on her partner, just as the first shot must have been. Neither bullet reached its target. Or if they did, they simply didn't matter.

"Is that Daddy's?" he asked. "Wouldn't work on me even if you cut my name in each one. I'm past that now."

"You take his name out of your mouth."

The thing moved now, finally perceiving the woman in its path. It surged toward her. If the woman was aware of the danger, she didn't show it, still drawing on him. Useless gesture or not, she was going to go down fighting.

Cait caught herself for a moment, terrified not because of the thing but because she thought all this was behind her. Doors in the air, monsters, strangeness. It was supposed to be over. She'd almost convinced herself of that. All of this was buried with Ariela and the storm's aftermath. Even so, she wasn't going to watch the monster take an easy meal if it could be helped. She ran towards the blonde, faster than the lizard but not by much.

"Look out!" Cait screamed as she knocked her out of the creature's path. Cait heard the jaws snap once, teeth coming together hard as a bear trap.

Ache swelled across Cait's shoulder as she slammed into the woman's ribcage. The move took the woman off her feet and nearly away from the creature's jaws.

There was a second snap and hiss of breath. The jaws connected this time. A sharp jolt rolled through the woman's body and it receded into Cait before both of them hit the ground.

The woman hissed and muttered a curse but did not scream. Salty and rotten air blasted out of the thing's nostrils as it pulled its head back, taking with it a chunk of meat from the woman's lower leg. Cait saw that the wound was bad, wider across than the woman's hand, which clutched at but could not cover the damage entirely. Blood surged out from between her fingers. Cait looked for the gun, wondering if it could even do anything against the lizard. It seemed real enough. She could either fight or stop the bleeding, but if the thing wasn't put down, neither of them stood a chance.

Cait barely had time to get to her feet as the thing chewed on the morsel it had taken. It seemed to be transfixed, wondering what it was tasting. The creature looked oddly incomplete somehow, made of different and dead-end pieces combined haphazardly. Its eyes glazed as it gulped down the bite, an atemporal pleasure.

Cait's eyes went wide and frantic as she searched for the gun, desperate to drive it off at least for a little while. Maybe the gunshots would have gotten someone to call the cops. Maybe not. Venice could be a rough part of town. It could just be background noise.

"This ain't but the merest start to things," the man said. His voice sounded like it was echoing up from the bottom of a deep well, reverberation hitting before his words did. "They're all singing now and their song is terrible for a time before the assumption comes. Before the wanting ends. Before the having."

Something in the words lodged in Cait sure as a bullet in the brain. There was a recoiling from the language, a sensation of pressure and crushing and having heard this last night, from inside her but not her.

The gun was a leap away. The bitten metal shone between tangles of long-dead grass in a tangle.

The thing finished the snack and looked for more. It reared and then surged forward, ungainly and graceless. Whatever it was, it was unaccustomed to land, reduced to shuddering and heaving, strangely ridiculous as it was awful.

Cait lunged for the gun, hands closing around the metal. She spun to her back and looked back to where the thing had been. Instead of a wide profile, it was coming head-on. The creature had keyed in on Cait's motion, ignoring the motionless blonde woman. Flippers and belly digging, it angled hard toward Cait with an irregular and convulsive gait.

She squeezed off one shot, not ready for how strong the pull on the trigger was. She'd only ever fired her dad's .22 Colt Woodsman and this weapon was less refined than that. Her arm shook like it had been hit with a baseball bat, barely holding onto the gun at the same time.

The first shot went wide or went off the creature's hide.

"You're up for sport, I see," the man shouted. "Well give it sport then!"

You better hope there aren't enough bullets for me to put one in you, asshole.

Drooling and dripping, the lizard-thing came closer, mouth open and wide and ringed with teeth that were more red than white. Cait pulled twice more, aiming for the thing's maw against the backlit wall. She braced more, knowing how hard the weapon kicked now.

She couldn't hear the bullets hit over the reports but the thing shrieked, somewhere between a hiss and a roar, pain and outrage. It pulled back as if it had bitten onto a live wire and shook its head violently. Cait pulled the trigger more quickly after that, firing bullets into her panic.

"I do believe the demonstration has been adequate," the man said with some humor.

Gripped by adrenalin, Cait swung to the source of the voice and pulled the trigger again, only to get a dry click, laughable in its inadequacy. She scrambled to her feet, breath hissing between clenched teeth.

The creature turned away, no longer interested in prey that could bite back. It slumped and shrugged its way over to the canal, only pausing once to glare at her with something like recognition before it slid down the slope and into whatever water was there.

She looked over to where she'd heard the man but saw nothing, no strange rippling, no anything. Somewhere down the way, a car started. Its engine sounded old and throaty without a muffler to hold it down.

He was gone, but the woman was still there, clutching her leg weakly now, blood pooling on the sandy dirt and grass. Cait dropped the gun and began unfastening her belt and tried to remember her Girl Scout training.

CHAPTER TWO

Someone had heard the screams or the gunshots and had been bothered enough to call the cops.

Praise Christ.

It was all Cait could do to maintain pressure on the tourniquet on the woman's leg, using a sharp little leather belt she'd bought at Buffum's when she went about acquiring her new wardrobe. She'd never wear that again, even if it came through in one piece.

Thinking about these stupid little details kept her from losing her mind as she fought to keep the woman from bleeding out. The flow had slowed but not stopped and Cait wasn't sure if any of this was enough.

The blonde murmured, slow and in shock. Her words only resolved as a slurring with a question mark at the end. Then she tried to sit.

"Hey, hey," Cait said, loud enough to be heard through the haze. "Don't try to get up. You got… bit… pretty bad." The image of the reptile-thing still stuck with her, but damned if she knew what it had been or where it had come from. "I hope you've had your shots," she joked weakly.

"Did I hit him?" the woman asked. Her eyes were open but not tracking.

"The critter? Don't know. I fed it a couple."

There was a distant peal of a siren as it headed down one of the main streets at a good clip, coming closer now.

The woman's brow furrowed in irritation. "Not that. Him. Did I hit Lee?"

Cait swallowed hard at that. The blonde knew the guy and had tried to take him out, just like Cait had by reflex. "Maybe, but it didn't do much."

She grimaced in pain, every muscle in her face pulled tight. "Could you back that cinch off? Hurts fiercely." The accent was coming together now, Southern somewhere but not plummy. It was as lean as she was.

"This cinch is keeping you alive, so I'm gonna say no."

The woman's lips twisted and she hissed wordlessly.

"What's your name?" Cait asked.

"Call me Sue. That's enough for now." Her vision swiveled to Cait and pierced. "You a nurse?"

"Nope, just me."

"Well it's a good Christian thing you're doing here."

"Nope, just me," she repeated. "Couldn't let you bleed out, Sue."

Pulsing lights splashed across the space between the apartment building and the canal, all Hammer-horror red. Behind that was the red and blue flashers of an LAPD prowl car. The first must've been an ambulance.

Happy to see a cop. Look at me.

"What do I call you by?" Sue asked. "Your name."

"I'm Cait. Pleased to meet you."

"Likewise. You're the first person in Los Angeles I met who hasn't tried to rob me."

Cait let that roll around her head while the ambulance unpacked. Then the cops rolled up like they were in charge and it was all under control now. She repeated the story that she'd already figured out and hoped that Sue was delirious enough to get a pass.

Two people I don't know, arguing, some kind of wild animal maybe a puma or a rabid dog shows up, woman draws a gun, shoots at it, gets bitten, good thing I was here, can I leave now? No, I don't know any of them. I really need to get home.

The cops took the statement without interest, not caring about the wild animal, showing only perfunctory attention to the gun since it was right there and empty and there was no apparent creature blood, just some from Sue. They recorded it and called it in, watching as the paramedics worked her over with tubes and shots and lifted her onto a gurney.

Then another van rolled up on the far side of Ocean and stopped. It was plain and ordinary, one of a hundred news-type vans that rolled around on the streets looking for a story or out to shoot some b-roll. Cait recognized the vehicle, though she hadn't seen it in years. That stylized, part-techno logo still stuck to her. Eighteen months of interning there, too many pizza parties and goddamn Ken on top of all that.

Monsters are one thing, but this is something I'm not definitely facing tonight. Quest4 *is off the menu.*

"Oh, what the hell are they doing here?" she asked anyone listening. Then she made herself busy, pleading with the paramedics to help her friend. Not enough to make a spectacle of herself but enough to make casual approach embarrassing.

Sue was out of it now, blissed on a carpet-bombing of painkillers and anesthetics. An IV tube and blood bag plugged into her arm and the leg wound was swathed under plastic and gauze.

"She's gonna be okay, right?" Cait asked. She wanted to bite a nail to help sell it, but glanced down at her own hands and saw they were maroon and sticky, smeared to her wrists. She wasn't brave enough to look down on her work suit.

"Think so," the lead paramedic said. He flashed a smile, positive reassurance embodied. He was a handsome black guy with a high-top fade and quick hands that never stopped moving, checking the patient as he spoke. "She gonna live, Ramsey?"

"Yeah, Antoine, she'll be okay. Though that's gonna be one winner of a scar. Skin graft that baby."

Cait swallowed hard at those words.

"We got company. Talk nice." Antoine turned to Cait. "Excuse my partner's manners, miss. 'Cause he ain't got any!"

"'Scuse me. My honesty just gets too shocking sometimes."

"No, it's okay. Just. Yeah. It's awful." She stared at her hands, gummy with blood and sand and bits of weed.

"Here," said Antoine. "Clean up some." He handed her a couple squares of cloth soaked in something that smelled sharp. She scrubbed without thought.

The second paramedic fastened a belt on the gurney and locked it. "Yeah, we don't get a lot of bites down here. Ballistics, slashes sure. Not this. What'd you say did this? Dog?"

"I don't know. It was dark and fast. It didn't stick around. Looked reptile-y."

"Reptile?" Antoine asked. "Like in *Slithis*? That's wild. Our very own monster."

Cait glanced over her shoulder and saw the crew from the van making their way through the clumping crowd. Once people figured that the shooting was all over, they felt like it was safe to come out and gawk and gossip.

Her eyes focused on the man with the camera. It was a film rig, not video like a nightly news crew would run. And the big shape of a mountainous dude with shaggy brown hair and glasses.

That's Shrug. Yeah, I don't need this at all.

The two paramedics lifted Sue into the ambulance on a fast three count and busied themselves locking things in place for transport. Cait took a tentative move onto the vehicle's back step, lingering at the threshold.

"Can I help you?" Antoine asked the question with a smile.

"Yeah, I was hoping that I could get a ride to the hospital." Cait pointed at the woman in the stretcher. "You know, help check my friend in and all."

"We're not over capacity are we, man?"

"We're good. Hell, she can ride up front with me," Ramsey yelled back.

"I'll stay here if it's all the same to you," Cait said. She was dimly aware that she'd wrapped her arms around herself like a child left alone. She broke the gesture, though her hands came off only with effort. More clothes she was never going to wear again.

"Hey, hey. It's okay. Come sit down," Antoine said. "Pull that door closed behind and strap up. My partner drives like a bat out of hell."

"I'd do this job for free!" he crowed before flicking on the rollers. Bright lipstick red wash blinked in through the windshield.

The ambulance loudspeaker squawked twice like a robot being dismantled. The engine growled and the ambulance crawled forward, molasses-slow until it broke the perimeter of the crowd. Cait watched the *Quest4* crew and their gear and camera setting up in the growing distance.

Guess puma attacks made their list now. Scraping the bottom of the barrel for paranormal entertainment. But it hadn't been the same since the seventies, even Watkiss knew that. Still they hadn't seen her. So that much was good.

Cait laughed to herself when they passed the UCLA sign out front of the med center.

Kinda like going to work.

She'd take the jokes where she could get them. The weirdness and enormity of what had just happened started out fluid. She could move through it. Now it was hardening up, becoming solid, strong enough that she was stuck fast as a bug in amber. Everything from the distortions in the air around the guy to whatever it was that crawled out from wherever to attack, seemingly at his beck and call. All that was wrong. At least now there was cause and effect, not the other way around. It made a little sense, just not much.

She filled out the patient and incident information as best as she could, absently marking her phone number for a contact and the reason for visit as "Bite, Dog."

The duty nurse took the clipboard and set it to one side. "You want to freshen up?" she asked, taking a long look at Cait. "We got what we need."

"I cleaned off in the ambulance best I could. Unless you've got a set of scrubs for me to get into?"

"No, honey," the nurse said like grandma would. "It's just that you look a fright, aside from the blood."

Cait stood and held it for a moment, checking herself. "I'll be okay. Just let me get this done and check on her and then…" Her legs went wobbly and she staggered back for a seat in the crowded emergency room lobby.

"We don't have room for another one tonight." The nurse's name was Lupita, according to her nameplate, skin dark against the greenish scrubs. "Now sit down and drink some water. Maybe get a cookie in you."

"But my friend—"

"Is stable and will probably have a story to tell. Otherwise fine. She's gonna be sleeping for a while. Like you oughta be."

"Okay, okay." Cait squeezed the woman's hand and just sat there for a moment.

"I got to go, honey. This place'll fall apart without me."

The room went small and tight. Pressurized. People leaning on one another or pacing or looking like they wanted to claw at the walls in frustration.

Why the hell am I even here? I don't know her. I don't owe her anything. But she knew that man and well. And she wasn't thrown by a critter from nowhere, either. Or maybe that was just—

"You know that witnesses aren't supposed to leave the scene without giving a statement." The voice went right through Cait. The speaker was a woman dressed neatly in a charcoal suit jacket and slacks, yellow blouse between the lapels. She was a few years older than Cait, sharply featured and freckled in a way that just made those features more so. Her eyes were black and looked like they could cut stone. "I'm Moreno, LAPD. Open Door division."

Oh. Oh shit.

Cait froze, unable to come up with anything smart.

"This is my partner, Ruben Garfield." She pointed to a shorter, younger man next to her with a prominent Adam's apple and wavy hair combed back but not cooperating entirely. His suit was sharper than his partner's. They didn't really vibe as cops, not like the last one from Open Door that Cait had known. Not like Trager who was on the side of shabby rolling up to don't-really-give-a-fuck.

"Sorry, I… I'm just wiped. And I gave a statement at the scene. Ask the patrolmen."

"Sure you did," Moreno said. "But not to us."

"I didn't realize that I'd have to double up. Look, the nurse there just told me I should get something to drink and a cookie." The second the words left her, she knew they sounded weak and stupid, but time couldn't be rewound.

Moreno stared at her, expression hanging between disbelief and scorn. "Ruben."

"Trish?"

Without looking away from Cait, she said "Get her a cookie and a glass of water from the machine. We don't want her fainting."

"You bet. You want one?"

Then Moreno turned to stare right at him. "Yeah, that'd be great. Get one for yourself too. Cookie party, right here."

"You bet."

Moreno moved to sit down and flipped open one of those thin steno notebooks, half a sheet of paper in width with the coil of metal at the top to hold it together. "So that was a weird thing that happened back there, right?" She pulled a pen out of nowhere and rested the writing tip just above the paper. As if writing it down made it real.

"Yeah. Pretty weird, I guess. Not a lot of wild animal attacks in LA."

"That's true. Okay, so let's start with your name and ID if you've got it with you."

Cait knew that she couldn't dare give an assumed name even if she pretended that she didn't have her ID. She didn't think she could be compelled to and her skirmishes with the cops were all in the past. But she didn't want to be talking to Open Door just the same.

"MacReady. Cait MacReady." She reached into her purse, pulled out her wallet then slid the license out from under its plastic case. She grimaced at the hair color in the photo. And at the disrespectful, dead-eyed stare.

Moreno took the plastic card and her eyes went from the card to Cait and back a couple times. She smiled thinly and without warmth. "You sure this is yours? You're not young enough to need fake ID."

"That's… that's me. Just a little while ago."

"A long little while by the looks of it. What color is that?"

"It was bright red back then, I think, but the light and the flash gave it a weird cast."

"It's okay. I was a weirdo once believe it or not."

And Cait couldn't, looking at her. She was cool and comfortable.

"So tonight. You were just in Venice on a lark? That's a drive from downtown."

"That's my old address. I live near Hollywood now, but I came from work, UCLA. To visit my uncle. Vince Laurie. He's with the sheriff's department."

Moreno scratched out some words that Cait couldn't read. "And then?"

Cait told her what she'd told the patrolmen, trying to be as dry and straight as possible. There weren't any lies, but there wasn't anything particularly weird about it. At least until she got to the critter.

"Yeah see, that's what we're interested in."

"You as in Open Door?" Cait hesitated, drawing in a breath.

Ruben arrived with a small collection of packaged oversized cookies that had a picture of a cartoon grandmother on them and a couple translucent white plastic tumblers filled with water.

"Here you go, ma'am," he said, offering Cait one of the cookies and the glass. "Trish," and he did the same there.

Cait took the cookie and unwrapped it, making just a little bit less noise than a 737 taking off.

Oatmeal raisin. Nobody's favorite.

"So you're familiar with the squad?" Moreno asked. "You sure looked that way."

"I, uh, have read the papers."

"She read about us in the papers, Ruben. Isn't that funny?"

"Kinda."

"Why?"

"Because we don't like to be in the papers," Ruben said. "We're shy, right?" he asked his partner with a toothy grin that made Cait think of Rico for just a moment.

"We value our privacy," said Moreno. "But word gets around."

"More and more these days," Ruben added.

The woman cop shot him a look. He ripped open his package and took a bite, making a show of how he was going to chew with his mouth closed.

"Open Door does the, uh, strange crimes, right?" Cait asked. "Why are you interested in this?"

"Describe the animal that attacked you and the woman, the thing you shot a couple times but didn't end up dead."

"It wasn't a very big gun," Cait offered.

"It was an army issue Colt. An old one," Moreno added, narrowing her eyes. "You don't know much about guns, do you?"

"Not really, no."

"That gun was designed to drop men in their tracks, particularly the native population of the Philippines with whom the US went to war a couple generations back. It's not a *little* gun."

Cait was missing her uncle's misdirection right about now.

"I don't know. It was like a small dinosaur."

"What'd you say?" Ruben asked around a mouthful of cookie. Moreno smacked him on the chest with the back of her hand.

"I read dinosaur books as a kid. Who didn't?" She realized she had been holding the cookie hard enough to break it in half. She set the pieces on her lap, amongst the blood spatters and grass bits. "It was squat and short, but it had weird flippers for feet. Short neck, not like those regular sea monster dinosaurs."

"Like the Loch Ness Monster, right?" Moreno asked, pen hanging.

"I guess. I mean, not like it. Short neck, stubby head, but a mouth full of teeth. And its skin was knobby and scaly, like a crocodile, not like a snake."

"Have you been drinking?" Moreno asked with a bite. "Drugs?"

"I had a beer at dinner a few hours ago and half a beer at my uncle's place, just a little later. I'm a lightweight, but not enough to start seeing things because of that."

"And the drugs?" She indicated the purse which was open enough to reveal the amber vial floating at the top of the junk within.

"Just something for my nerves." Cait stopped. "I'm trying to wean myself off them."

Moreno's eyebrow rose. "Habit forming?"

"No, just they don't seem to be doing much to help. I had one today at work. It's just Xanax."

"Nothing else? You're not up on a possession rap."

"Yet, you mean."

"I'll be honest with you. There's only one street drug that we're interested in professionally. You either know it or you don't."

There was that something that Trager and Fellowes were talking about, blue something.

But it was nothing she could get a hold of, in memory or otherwise, so she let it go.

"No drugs. I saw what I saw. The guy said something like 'You'll get what's coming to you,' and then this thing showed up. I never saw either of these people before in my life."

"Have you ever had strange stuff like this happen to you before?"

"Excuse me, honey?" Lupita's voice was soft but firm. "I just wanted to tell you that your friend is out of surgery. They're taking her to recovery, but there's going to be more procedures after this one, they said."

"Th-thank you."

"You get your rest now. I'm sure these officers can see you need a break," she said then glared softly at Moreno in particular.

"It's okay. I want to help."

Lupita returned to her rounds and Moreno tightened a bit. "Is that woman your friend or you've never seen her before?"

"Friend at first sight," Ruben observed.

"Quiet."

"I overstated my connection to her to get on the ambulance. I just needed to get out of the crowd. I was getting all freaked out."

"Mhm-mhm." Moreno wrote something else. "Okay, fine. Is there anything you want to add to your statement?"

"Like what?"

"Like where did that thing go? You said yourself that it was 'flopping and surging' but not that it was fast like a coyote or puma or wild dog, right?"

"Yeah, sure."

"Then where did it go?"

"I heard it head down to the canal. I guess it just went into the water. I really wasn't in a mood to go after it."

"LAPD looked around for it, didn't find anything. Same with that film crew that came down. Who were those guys, Ruben?"

"*Quest4*. I never miss that show. Super cool to meet the crew."

Moreno let out a pained breath. "So there were some tracks, a little spilled blood, all human, but no creature. No mysterious dude either."

"I was *busy* trying to keep her from bleeding out."

"Oh, right. Your friend. What's her name again?"

"Sue. That's all I got."

Moreno flipped back a few pages in her notebook and read from it. "According to her ID, she's Lavinia Sue Whelan from Sevier County. Tennessee state ID but no other official documents, not even a library card. Did she say anything else to you?"

"She asked me if I hit him. With the gun."

"And *did* you shoot at this man?"

"Gun was empty after I took shots at the creature. Just a click."

Moreno blinked slowly then asked "And why would you shoot at a stranger?"

Cait was empty. "He looked wrong. Felt wrong."

"I'll ask again, have you dealt with anything out of the ordinary like this before?"

Cait's head shook and she turned it into a negative nod. "I'm done. If you have questions about me, go ask Detective Trager in your department. I'm sure he took notes."

"You know Detective Trager? Wait." Moreno's eyes widened in recognition. "Holy shit. I didn't put this together before. You know who this is, Ruben?"

Cait's heart sank to the bottom of her feet and kept going.

Ruben was swallowing the last bite of his cookie, brushing the crumbs off his fingers. He shook his head and mumbled "Nah."

Moreno turned to face him. "This is the girl who was at the center of Wyvrenwood. The case that took Fellowes off the board." Then she turned back to Cait. "I'm sure we've got a lot to talk about."

"Another day. I'm done."

"Wait. You can't just—"

Cait's voice came out cold. "Are you charging me? For what? Firing a gun in city limits? Shooting a dinosaur that's fucking endangered?"

Moreno stared at her for the space of a breath. "Fine. Do it this way. Fuck it. Fine. Come on, Ruben. Cookie princess here is done for the night."

He stared at her, eyes wide. "Fellowes? Really?"

"Really."

He pointed at Cait with intent. "That dude was a piece of shit. You did us a favor."

"Ruben, now. We're going."

Ruben looked Cait up and down and shook his head in disbelief then followed his partner out the main doors.

ආ

When she'd reeled her insides back up, Cait calmly called a taxi which then took her back to the Mercury at the end of Ocean Boulevard. She walked a half-block to get to the car and didn't look for evidence of what it was she'd seen and done earlier that evening. But she did stop near the canal and tried to gauge how something as big and ungainly as that thing could've slipped into the water and just disappear. Maybe the water was deeper than it seemed.

Cait knew it was.

She drove home and ran a bath and threw her dirty and blood-splattered blouse and slacks into it. She then climbed in and submerged herself for as long as she could, eyes and ears and mouth screwed shut as tight as her flesh would allow. She held her breath until things went black. Then red. Then black again.

CHAPTER THREE

"How can I help you?" Cait asked. She used her best voice, though it was well-frayed now, just an hour into window service. The public was exhausting today.

The client, a tall and statuesque blonde who wore form-fitting slacks and a V-cut blouse, turned to face her. She looked vaguely familiar, maybe somewhere on television or a magazine. It was rare such encounters ran long enough for the connection to be made past vague recognition and a brush with fleeting mundane fame.

"Yes, hi." The woman smiled. She was used to performing. Everything flicked on, and she lit up. Her makeup was muted, elevating features but not into glamor. She looked like she could have been reading the news, attractive but definitely unavailable. The recognition gnawed at Cait. Underneath it was a sense of loathing, moreso than a casual encounter with someone who could have better spent her time in Brentwood with two-hour and three bottle lunches on the westside. Cait's left hand clenched without thought.

"I was here to see if you had any information about the Wyvrenwood tornado."

Oh shit.

There was that cutting voice, only the last time Cait had heard it, it was badgering her about being slow on getting the morgue file for the Skullface Killer. She'd had a real thing for that story because it was going to make her famous, even if her episode on *Quest4* had not gone over well. Wrong vibe for the show. Those viewers wanted the weird, not the real. That had been several years ago, too long a time to stab like this.

Cait sucked in a breath and hoped the glasses threw her. Luckily she wasn't forced to wear a name badge here. That would have been a dead giveaway. "I don't follow you. This is a general reference desk. Media file is downstairs."

Her smile persisted. "I'm not asking for newspaper clippings, Cait. You are Cait MacReady, right? The pictures don't exactly match up. Your hair is more… subdued now."

Oh shit again. Time to play real dumb.

"I'm sorry. You are?"

There was the faintest marring of the perfect face as she scowled at being unrecognized. "Charlie. Davenport. I host a regular segment on *Watching LA.*"

"So you're on the news?"

Maybe she doesn't recognize me without the spikes and purple or was it green hair back then? She's acting like I don't remember her treating everyone in the office like an insect with too many legs, me especially.

Charlie kept the smile, sharpening it. "Twice a week and Saturdays."

Is she just messing with me? I don't get it.

"Between bikini-fitting and best pick-up bar segments, right?"

"We're the most-discussed and written-about segment on the show. Branching out to our own program next year. *Easy Streets.* Watch for it."

"I'm in the presence of greatness. You catch Bigfoot yet?"

Charlie's eyes widened for an instant, something unsettling there, something genuine and for a second Cait regretted the escalation.

She re-set her face to perfection and tossed the volley back, well-iced. "Bigfoot isn't a draw anymore. Or the Scarman. Our viewers are interested in something far scarier." She smiled and her nose crinkled endearingly, practiced.

"There's a line forming, Ms. Davenport. If there's a reference issue I can help you with?"

"We're not interested in newspapers, Cait. We're interested in that freak storm earlier this year. We have sources that placed you there."

"Your sources are full of shit." She almost believed herself. "I don't have—"

"Anything to do with it. Sure." The taller woman ate the space between them, right to Cait's skin. "But if you wanted to talk about it, we could make it worth your while. There's a lot of interest in the weird angle to this."

Cait locked her spine and wouldn't let herself back down.

"What 'weird angle?' LA has always gotten tornadoes. More often than Topeka."

"Oh, come on. Some crazy ceremony? Something about lights in the sky? Whatever happened to No Tomorrows and—"

Cait felt a flush rising from her heart to her throat. "I can't help you. If you want a book or old newspaper, then we can talk."

Charlie looked Cait down, drinking her in at a glance. "Not a book. Just a story. Consider it." She snapped a business card onto the counter. Her name was written out in tubular chrome lettering with a metallic hint along with EASY STREET in bold neon type and a street address and number. It all looked cutting edge for a couple years ago.

Cait left the card where it was. "Leave me alone."

"Don't lose this." She slid the card so that it touched Cait's fingers.

She took it up in her hand and clamped tight, corners dug into flesh. She wasn't going to let go, to give that woman the satisfaction.

"Have a good day." She angled to address the line and said, "Next!"

How did anyone else outside Trager and Open Door know my name? Sure, No Tomorrows knew, but they weren't the kind to be talking to TV tabloid reporters. Or were they? Ridiculous. If No Tomorrows wanted to mess with me, they'd wait in my apartment until I got home. They don't use Susan Anton lookalikes as cat's-paws.

She spent the rest of the morning focused very exactly on the reference requests and questions she got because if she thought for very long on anything else she was sure she'd start screaming.

ᘓ

"Cait. Office." Robbins' voice was clipped and tense.

Shit. She went from me to him. Guess I get to have the throw-down I was never in a position to have a few years ago.

She'd finally been able to dismiss everything piling up behind her, spending the entirety of her lunch break staring at a fixed point of nothing outside. She focused on that until she'd achieved motherfucking Zen or something close enough to pass for it where her heart wasn't pummeling and loopy. She'd banished any trace of the mayhem from last night and if Open Door came calling, then they did. She hadn't done anything wrong.

All this had been a welcome change from the usual gnawing of anxiety or pulse of pressure.

"Right now."

But Robbins had to go and wreck it. Everything whirled around her. Nobody else could see it but she could, like driving through a tunnel too small for the car. She could reach out, but it'd grind her fingers to the bone so she pulled in. She reached into her purse and grabbed the amber bottle.

"Okay. Sec."

This wasn't a research request. It wasn't going home early. It wasn't anything good. She'd have gulped a Xanax if it would have hit instantly and mattered. That reporter was going to have the last laugh and Cait would be out the door. Part of her laughed at that idea as she quietly made her way to Robbins' office.

"Close the door."

Robbins' office was coffin-small, so tight that the smell of his little pastille mints was smothering. She closed the door behind her and tried not to fixate on the finality of that click. She wondered if he was trying to make a pass at her, finally having built up the courage but safely out of sight of every other woman in the office. Not that it was earned, just something she had to take into account in situations like this. It wasn't fair but complaint never changed anything.

"Cait, I didn't want anyone else to hear this, but there's a detective out front in the main lobby. He's asking for you."

Just the cops? Thank god.

Robbins' eyes were dead-set serious, even if his curly mop of hair subtracted from that. Faint crunch of a mint being obliterated between his molars, though his jaw didn't move.

"Is there something I should know about. As your boss?"

"I was a witness at a crime scene last night," Cait said, fighting back the roaring in her temples. "That's probably it."

"You're not sure?"

"I can't look into the future or read minds, Bill. Why? Should I be worried?"

He half-spun in the chair and it whined, metal on metal. The sound made Cait want to take knitting needles to her ears. She pressed out a breath instead.

"We're all worried, Cait. I've asked around and there's nobody who disagrees."

"What is this?"

"We all think you shouldn't have come back to work so quickly, even taking the demot— Er, transferring to the reference desk." He looked like he'd swallowed a handful of rusty nails.

"Is my work unsatisfactory?" she asked with a point.

"Not *exactly*. But we can tell you're not really here."

"Are you telling me to take a vacation? Because I used up all my discretionary time after that personal stuff and my…"

"Your episode. I know. I only *look* like a freshman." He made to stand up but then thought better of it. He took cover behind the desk that was probably twice his age, a privilege knowingly unearned. "There was talk about you having potential problems beyond what you're telling us. It would explain things."

Cait snapped out a laugh and caught the deadpan stare frozen onto his face. "You think I'm on drugs and the cops are here to bust me? What is going on?"

He didn't have an answer to that. "We just want what's best for you. It may be that you just need to go on leave and—"

"I'm not *quitting*," she said. "You can't make me."

"That's not... just pull yourself together, Cait. Make us believe that you're not holding on by your fingernails every day, okay?"

She had ten answers to that bubbling up in the back of her skull. All of them ended in her getting fired on the spot.

"I know I suck at this," he admitted. "I'd rather work with books too. They're not so complicated."

Cait nodded. Then she thought of going back to restorations and the feeling of those old pages under her fingers may as well have been sticking them into roadside cadavers. Gooseflesh crawled up her arms and right into her insides.

He brought his hands up, palms to her, weirdly askew. "Take the rest of the day off. Just use this long weekend to get your head straight and we can talk about it on Monday, right?"

She nodded again, knowing that anything she said would either get her arrested or committed. She marched out of the coffin-room and went to the main lobby where a familiar figure waited, standing out in the sea of students and staff coming and going. He could've been a professor maybe with the tweed jacket and slacks, but his were a little too old, a little too worn. The Black man looked up from the copy of *Omni* he'd been reading, some slickly erotic future depicted on the cover, and smiled.

"Hello, Cait," Trager said. "Can we go somewhere and talk?"

He set the magazine down and stood, showing her which way to go.

Trager sipped from the Styrofoam cup and his face curled up like he'd swallowed bile. "That's bad even for decaf." His other hand rested on a thin manila envelope that sat on the table before him. He sat there in his jacket and slacks even though fall in LA was feeling more like a resurgence of summer.

Cait couldn't bear to drink any of hers. The thought of taking in anything made her stomach curl in on itself.

"Nothing? Come on, you had to expect someone to follow-on after you stomped out last night." He grinned to disarm.

It only made her buckle down more.

"I'm not here to bust you, Cait."

"I didn't think you were."

"Moreno thinks I should have let her drag you in to cool off in a holding cell. Teach you some manners."

"And why didn't you?"

He toyed with his cup, measuring his words. "Because I don't think there's much more to that story. It's just another weird thing that's happened. Add it to the growing list of weird things." He sipped and then sighed. "An unending list."

"Occupational hazard, right? You talk to any televisions lately?"

He smiled wide in surprise. "Oh, you remember that?" His fingers drummed on the pastel fiberglass tabletop. It sounded hollow. "No, I haven't. Hell, I'd welcome something as plain as that."

"What does this have to do with dinosaurs showing up in Venice?"

"So you're sure about that?"

"I don't know what I'm sure of right now." She breathed out and stretched her arms in front of her. The growing knots in her shoulders held, down to the marrow.

"You know, that night out on the street before you drove off with that woman from No Tomorrows?"

"Alondra. The new queen."

"Alondra, right." He looked as if he was making a mental note of that then continued his original thought. "I was pretty sure I'd never see you again," he said. "You were lost."

"And what makes you think I'm found now?" Cait drew back up and looked into his face. She couldn't read it still. As bad as Vince, maybe worse. Stupid cops.

"You're alive, for one. Though basically off the grid. I didn't even know how to contact you until I got the report this morning."

"You're a cop. You could've found me."

"Maybe so. But there once was a time, not all that long ago, that you wanted a thick stack of books back from me. You know, all that stuff I had to take in as evidence for the Fellowes inquest."

"Don't want them back."

"Which is intriguing to me. They look valuable."

"Only to someone who values them. I don't think I want 'em anymore."

"Okay. Okay. Fine. I'll hold onto them. Maybe we can talk about something else."

"It's something *weird* right? You're the second person today wanting that from me."

His eyebrows went up as he pursed his lips slightly. "Who?"

"Oh, that horrible reporter from *Watching LA*. You must have run across her. She and you work the same beat, just like my old co-workers at *Quest4*."

"Davenport." Trager sighed like the last air leaving a knifed tire. "Yeah. She's a pretty headache."

"More than that. She thinks I know something about that storm. The one that took out No Tomorrows. She mentioned them by name."

"But you *do* know something about it."

"Nobody is supposed to know that I know." She scratched at the tabletop and it gave a whispering shriek in reply. "Except Open Door and whoever reads your reports." Her gaze came back up to him.

Trager revealed nothing. "I can't help you with that. But I might be able to shake some trees."

"Thanks, for nothing." The urge to ask about the rest of No Tomorrows tugged at her, but she fought it off. She knew they still existed. The bouquet of datura flowers in the junkyard had told her that. Just not in what form. Which meant they could be anywhere, everywhere.

"Look, I came to ask you for—"

"I can't help you," she bit. "I don't do any of that anymore."

Trager weighed that answer but didn't question it. "You didn't let me finish."

"If it's not about what I saw and reported last night, I can't help."

"So you quit the life? No more books. No more hocus-pocus."

"I never did any of that before. Just faked it. Now I'm trying to just be… normal. I'll let you know when I'm finished." Cait was trying to disappear, will herself into intangibility.

He didn't blink, just waited her out. Not even sweating in the sun.

"Fine. What is it?" she asked, dragging it out as long as she could. Just to make him say something. Just to have him stop looking at her like that.

"This has to stay confidential. There's stuff in here that scavengers like Davenport and *Quest4* would love to get their beaks wet with."

"Why are you asking me? I said I was out."

"You might've quit the life, but it did not quit you. Last night happened. Moreno isn't convinced you will stick by it, but I figure you wouldn't have said it if you hadn't seen it. And if anything, well… I'll leave it at that."

"What are you even talking about?"

He flipped the manila folder open. The sun turned the photographs to glaring white.

"This. This weird shit."

Cait reached out and took the top photograph then stared as her eyes came down from the brilliance. She saw a strange fish-shape, no, two of them, conjoined and sitting in what looked like a curved specimen pan.

"Let's just start with this one. I don't know how strong your stomach is."

"It's fine," she lied.

"Look at this one and tell me what you see."

She looked at the next, camera pulled back some. Above the fish, sitting on the rim of the specimen tray was a strip of some kind, marked off in inch increments. The fish themselves were just under a foot in length. Their heads were blunted, not streamlined. Dotted with outward-pointing teeth, their snouts protruded from the skull in a way Cait hadn't ever seen. The scales were large and coarse, like a gar or a sturgeon. They looked wrong, unfinished. The thought nipped at her with needle teeth.

"Those are fucked-up fish."

"You don't know the beginning of fucked-up on this." He pulled out a third picture and held it for a moment. "I'm not sure I should show you this, so if decide to lose your lunch, turn to the side."

"What? How bad could it—?"

Cait stopped talking when she figured it out. Same lighting, same clinical setting. Only this one was of a man's body on a slab somewhere. She'd been in a room like that once, only it had been to see a different body just before everything went to shit.

She took a deep breath and focused on the photo in spite of feeling everything falling through her fingers. She latched onto the film grain and harsh flash, anchoring details, not the whole. The body had been cut, incision along the bottom of the ribcage and traversing the sternum. The skin and flesh were pulled back enough to reveal the slitted stomach. This alone was revolting but not enough to upset her. She'd seen worse before. Or so she'd thought.

The organ had been cut open and the incision was held open with sets of forceps. She thought of origami, strange folds of sheeted muscle and tissue falling against one another. The stomach cavity wasn't dark. Instead, it glittered with something like crumpled metal and unmistakably an eye to one side of it.

A fish eye, small and round and glassy.

"Little background," Trager said after clearing his throat. "Dead guy found by girlfriend, not wife, though he had both, out in the Hollywood Hills. Nice house. Nice neighborhood. LAPD checked it out, assumed it was a standard OD by way of mismanaging intake as there was no note. Ruled accidental death at the scene. That got revised."

Cait stared at the picture and tried not to imagine the eye was staring at her. She put her thumb over it and considered the canyon cut out of the man's chest and ribcage.

"How did that get *there*?" she demanded.

"Don't get ahead of me." He tried smelling the coffee once more to see if it had gotten any better with air and it had not. "What do you think cause of death was? Go ahead."

"I can't even."

"Drowning. Ambulance techs reported that his clothes were damp to the touch. Pools around his mouth and nose from drainage but he was still filled to the throat with water."

"Swimming pool or bathtub?" The memory of Cait's own long hideouts in the bath flashed over her like a black haze and then slipped past.

Trager shook his head. "No bathtubs, nothing drawn. There was a Jacuzzi in the backyard of the place but..."

"But what?"

"Bromine for a cleansing agent, so he should have been full of that. He wasn't. The water in his lungs and guts was salt water, but... wrong.

"Like I said, LAPD homicide had this until the examiner noticed the distended stomach. Someone drowns and gets moved? That's a regular crime."

"Happens every day."

"Right. But not with fish jammed into his stomach. And not just jammed but, well, what you see there. How big a thing do you think someone can swallow?"

"I don't know. Like a baseball maybe?"

He shook his head. "Those two fish are ten inches long apiece and big enough that, in the coroner's words, 'No force on earth could have gotten them down that throat without destroying them or the esophagus.' And there were others, smaller."

"Ships in a bottle."

"If you like. Now, you said those fish were fucked-up. How?"

She couldn't look back at the picture, covering the eyeball or not. "Just wrong. Unfinished. Unrefined, I guess."

"Like really old fish, right? Prehistoric even."

Dinosaurs.

"You're kidding." Her eyes flicked between Trager's and the pictures. "You think this is tied to… to that thing in Venice last night?"

"I didn't before. Hell, this case wasn't something that I even knew about until it arrived this morning when my homicide liaison delivered it to me more white-faced than usual and said that regular LAPD wasn't touching it.

"But weird stuff coming out of nowhere does seem to fit."

"Where are these fish now? I mean, you have experts to talk to for this, right?"

He nodded, protruding his lower lip in thought. "Talking to someone at the Museum of Natural History tomorrow. The fish bodies rotted fast. We had the coroner run impressions of them in the gel, but it's doubtful we'll get anything useful. And another thing."

"There's always."

"The body was just saturated with water, like it had been in it for weeks not minutes. But no decay."

"Had he been missing?"

"No. He was seen a couple hours before at his office. Big-time developer, projects all up and down the Valley, address in Glendale. There's maybe three hours between him at work and the body being found at home. He'd gotten into scrapes before, environmental and citizens' groups mostly, nothing serious outside a courtroom. Couple possession raps, quantities enough to get him up for distribution but he had a good lawyer. He probably just liked to party real hard."

"So you think someone is, what? Bringing stuff here out of the past and fucking with people?"

He shrugged, defeated. "I don't know what to think. Only that I got nothing that makes sense. And I wanted to talk to someone who'd seen something like this personally."

"You're bringing this to me because I've seen a weird old thing?"

"And maybe you saw the guy. Maybe it's something else and unrelated, but we don't know that yet. And the fact that you're still here after tangling with No Tomorrows leads me to believe that you at least have luck on your side. Or you're tougher than either of us think."

"That's over." She stood up uneasily, shifting her weight around the elongated kidney-bean shaped bench that was welded to the table. "We're done here." She turned away and took a step before he spoke up.

"Hey! Sit back down."

Cait took another, clenching her fists so her hands didn't shake. She heard a scrape of steel on asphalt as Trager got up and caught up to her.

He turned her around quickly, not roughly. "Listen. I took a bullet or two over this Fellowes thing. It was a mess and the only reason it wasn't a worse mess for the both of us, you *and* me, is that Fellowes was such a massive pile of shit that nearly everyone wanted the whole thing to just go away. But that stink still spread to me. Even though I was warning superiors for a long-ass time about him."

Cait wanted to fight her way out of it but didn't have any left in her. "It's not my fucking fault that he came after me."

Trager's glare softened but didn't let up entirely. "And I told you only to talk to *me*, remember?"

"You don't turn down a cop when they show up, right? Isn't that how things work?"

He released his grip on her upper arms. "I said I took a couple bullets for you. In the long run, I'm okay with that. I think you're worth it, 'specially since it took Fellowes out of the picture. But I need some help with this one, even if the explanation is gonna just stay within Open Door and we have to make up something palatable for everyone else.

"Even if we tell the news that he died in his hot tub and his pool crew moved him, we have to find out what really happened. That's the job. And I think you can help."

Cait breathed in and out sharply, aware that her mouth was moving on its own, but she said nothing. Too many things were happening that she was done with.

'You can choose to not believe in gravity,' Ariela had told her. But that didn't change what happened if you jumped off a building.

It was supposed to be over.

"I'll help how I can, but I don't want to go back to what was before, okay?"

"What do you mean?"

"I mean all this No Tomorrows bullshit. It's done. Ariela's dead and they killed Rico and that poor damn tech at the Coroner's office."

"Who's Ariela? You mean the queen?"

"No. Told you before. Alondra's the queen now. Ariela was."

"You knew her?"

"I'm… I'm not going there." She sighed with heaviness and let her shoulders drop with that weight. "I slipped up, okay? If you want my help, it'll be with boundaries. That's one of 'em."

"Oh, so you think you're in a place to dictate terms?"

"No, just warning you what'll make me walk. I'm trying to cooperate."

"Okay then. Okay." He pulled his hands away and stood, still in her path. "Then you can meet me at the Museum of Natural History tomorrow morning at 8 a.m. I need you there as an expert witness."

"On what?"

"On whatever comes across."

Cait fidgeted with her shirt sleeve, something she hadn't done since middle school. "Moreno isn't going to be there tomorrow, is she?"

"Yeah, she didn't care for you either," he said, smiling. "And no. Just me. I'm having to run this one even though I should be getting the new department office set up. It's a damn mess."

She let go of the fabric and with it tried to let go of the emotion. She could feel it running past her fingers like the river swelling in sudden rain.

"How is the other witness?" she asked.

"Oh, Ms. Lavinia Sue Whelan?" he smiled at the name. "Last I heard, she was going to be laid up for a little while but otherwise okay. We'll get to her in due course.

"So I'll see you tomorrow morning. You know how to get there, right?"

"Got my Thomas Brothers if I forget," Cait said.

Cait walked back to the office on auto-pilot, unthinkingly. Bill reminded her that she had the rest of the day off without making a big deal about it. She would have preferred to get back to work, to at least try to lose herself in something, to shake the image of the fish entwined in the corpse's stomach and whatever was portended from that. It was something else to think about that she didn't have to come up with herself, and now even that cold comfort was out of her reach.

She took her stuff and walked over to the Mercury and wondered what she'd do with a couple extra hours. She hadn't planned on anything. She never made plans, not anymore.

Aimlessly nosing the big sedan through traffic, window down and just hearing the endless changing, low-level chaotic murmuring of the street and shops as she passed. She was at peace for a few minutes. Norteñas blasted out of passing cars or storefronts, mariachi too, strings underneath rolling brass. Hair-farmer rock, like Gwynne had called it, came from scattered radios or motorcycles, from dudes clearly auditioning for the latest Crüe video. Rap, all scratching and boasts. All of these blended and became a kind of street howl, all of these people having lives and Cait just drifting past them in her dark red sled.

She realized she'd drifted her way to Melrose, which felt like it changed radically between visits. She hadn't been back there since meeting that fraud at the aquarium store a couple blocks down. Another memory from the Time Before. Nothing seemed familiar. Past and present collided and exploded, leaving gaudy neon colors splashed across one facade right next to another that had been there since the twenties and looked it. This street more than any other except maybe Hollywood Boulevard was constantly and restlessly reinventing itself, trying anything once or even twice.

Metal boys in tight jeans and bandanas with haystack hairdos and T-shirts slouched and joked with one another. There were a lot of them now, everyone latching onto the cool that had been sold to them in videos and on KNAC. Cait had no patience for that crowd, but then, she barely had patience for any these days. The freedom of what had been complete outsider punk had been homogenized into T-shirts and jeans and leather and studs after the hardcore jocks showed up. Then there were the goths: Victorian lace and black or Addams Family stripes and black or even black and black and more black. Cait was with the music but never fit the look past eyeshadow, never wanted to try that hard after her years of antagonism. She just wanted to be.

On the avenue, she knew what she needed.

She jammed into a side street and walked for a little while, not thinking too hard about where she was going but what she wanted to find when she got there. It was nearby. Not Aaron's. They were a good record store and all that, but she was in the mood for something a little less retail. And she found it in a few blocks at a store called Vinyl Fetish.

This place was it. After you'd searched the mall and Tower Records without result, looking for something breathed about or played once then submerging afterwards, you went there. She pushed the door open and the place smelled like clove-and-marijuana-soaked denim jackets. The guy behind the counter, not much out of high school if at all, gave her a once-over and kind of smirked to himself but didn't say anything.

I am dressed normal, so I guess I had that coming.

It was a small store, not much bigger than the loft Cait used to live in up until a few months ago. They only sold records and gear. And like the Freemasons, they only advertised by word of mouth or in the alternative press. You knew what you were getting into or you simply didn't go inside.

Just like Last Prayer.

And then she couldn't banish the clench of remembering that place.

The record playing behind the counter was weird, ethereal but with insistent and driving guitar, rising and falling like waves. Something about it was familiar, but she couldn't place it. This wasn't something from her collection; maybe something new on the radio. She'd been out of touch for a bit. But she felt as if she'd heard it before.

She tried to remember it while she flipped through the new used arrivals section. Current 93, Xmal Deutschland, a full run of Kate Bush's albums that probably had a story of heartbreak in the owner dumping them, a deep vein of industrial records all menacing block type on monochrome grain. She lingered on a copy of *It'll End in Tears* by This Mortal Coil as the song from the counter began to wind down, falling in on itself endlessly in a lockgroove which got pulled off after a moment. She was trying to remember where her own records were in the storage boxes still at her apartment. She hadn't even unpacked them or the stereo to even play them on.

A door opened behind the counter to the dark back room and another skinny and black-clad employee sauntered out.

"Damn, man. That Dreamless hits pretty hard." The new guy was dressed differently. Instead of the common panoply of band name patches on his jacket, there was just a single image with what looked like parentheses containing five mismatched dots in the space between. She'd seen this somewhere, something like it. Only this image was so abstracted, so boiled-down, that it could have been almost anything. Or maybe it was nothing.

Maybe I'm just losing my mind, everything spilling out behind me.

"Playing it a lot this week. Got that hollow weight."

"Weird that it's on SST, but they couldn't put out jock shit forever, right?"

The world rushed into Cait at that moment, an audible roar of white noise resolving itself into the familiar tune.

Of course. It's them. Dreamless. Just cleaned-up and not run through that overtuned PA at Last Prayer. It's the same band from that night. And the one that played…

Her strength rushed out, leaving her wanting to buckle to the floor. Her pride kept her standing. She held onto the record and walked herself over to the register. Just like a normal customer would and not like someone who was about to shatter at the merest touch.

"Fifteen bucks. That's an import," the dude at the register said. His hair was black and straight in front, teased out everywhere else. He wore a jean jacket the same color, marked out with band names in metallic paint and ink. Or maybe they were just artful squiggles.

She pulled the cash out of her purse.

"Doesn't look like your kind of record," he half-joked.

"Looks aren't everything." It came out roadkill-flat.

He brightened up, seeing that she could at least push back a little bit. "If you're into that, you might be into Dreamless. Last week's EP will make you flatline."

"No, thanks. I caught 'em live and it's just not the same."

She took the record and pushed out the door, sucking in the exhaust and food-smoke. Better than the drama club lounge in there. She shook herself off and set out for the car, no longer in the mood for adventures.

She walked back to the Mercury and stopped dead, almost dropping the record. Someone had vandalized the car. Not keyed or scratched it up or broken a window and run off. Cait wished it had been that. Something as simple as someone desperate breaking in to steal something to feed their appetite. That would have been far kinder.

Someone had instead written on the windshield in a sort of obscenely romantic and devotional script. In lipstick.

Siempre te amaremos, Ariela.

We will always love you.

Cait wasn't sure what part of it got her the most. It was the *always*, she decided. They were never going to let go of Ariela. Never going to forget her.

Just like Cait herself couldn't, no matter how badly she wanted.

She looked to see if they were still around, to at least know who it had been. But they came and went as they pleased, even after losing the queen and gaining a new one. They were like the haze, everywhere and nowhere, No Tomorrows and their lost children.

She drove home, weaving from lane edge to lane edge, never in a straight line. She drove home and sat on the ratty couch with *It'll End in Tears* sitting on her lap, not having the strength to root through all the boxes to find the turntable and speakers and hook it all up. She just looked at the cover, remembering the sound.

Until she fell asleep and dreamed of fish inside her, inside everyone.

Shrill ringing from the phone dragged Cait back out of sleep and the half-seen mountains and ridges from her childhood, but there was a wrongness to them, one that shed and melted as the sound rang through the bare walls of the apartment. The water was too high. There shouldn't have been water anywhere near them but instead it lapped around, girdling the hills and isolating them.

The record had dropped to the floor and her clothes were rumpled and stuck to her. At least they were dry. Outside it was the haze-choked light of the city nearby and faraway. She hadn't slept past her meeting with Trager.

That was today right?

She stood and shambled over to the phone, not letting the machine grab it, just wanting the sound to go away immediately so she could go back to sleep.

"Hello?" Her own voice was thick and strange to her.

"MacReady? Cait MacReady?" There was an accent on the other side that was vaguely familiar but she was too tired to place it. Like everything else the last few days.

Who even has this number?

"Yes. Who *is* this?"

"Thaddeus Khan. You agented the sale of some books to me… recently. I was hoping—"

"Oh, yes. Of course. Mr. Khan. We met at the, ah, aquarium shop. Do you know what time it is?"

'Cause I sure don't.

"I apologize for the hour, and yes, yes, that's me." His voice was silky with that indeterminate accent, perhaps Scottish but hinting at something even farther away, which convinced her that it was a put on, and not too deep a one. "You're very hard to get a hold of. And Soame's answering service was of no help."

Cait was surprised it had taken this long for something to snap back from that. She'd shut down the front for Rory Soame, bookseller and connoisseur, reclusive and utterly fictional. But there was always someone who wouldn't take no for an answer.

"I don't have anything for you, Mr. Thaddeus Khan. I haven't fielded any sales for Mr. Soame in several months. He values his privacy and him taking vacations is not unheard of."

"Oh, that is a shame. I, well, I was rather hoping to inquire after a potential purchase. Something no one else seems to have."

"How did you get this number, Mr. Thaddeus Khan? You don't know me, not personally."

"No, but Mr. Soame was able to obtain those books for me previously, you know the ones. And others had told me that it was impossible then. Perhaps *he* could pull the same trick twice."

Irritation pulled at Cait, irritation at being awakened and at this part of her past enterprises pouncing on her while she was on her heels. But it wasn't just anxiety this time. It was something else entirely. Like slivers she thought she'd pulled, only for one to become infected weeks later, erupting and inescapable. It wound up an anger in her.

"Are you still there?"

"I'm still here, yes. So what is it that you're after?"

"Well, I've heard talk of a book that surfaced less than a year ago, a translation of a much older work. From the new world."

His voice went from silky to sandpaper in her head. His gentility was condescension, and she was already tired of it.

Cait cleared her throat and threw the grit from that on her voice. "You know, Mr. Soame did mention, the last few times that I spoke with him, that he knew some of his clients were only interested in turning around books he'd sold them. That these men were nothing more than salesmen, dilettantes, un-serious.

"I'm wondering if that's what drove him to withdraw for a time."

"Miss MacReady, I assure you that—"

"You don't have to assure me of anything."

There was a creak on the other side as if someone gripping the phone handset in frustration. "Listen to me. You should tell Mr. Soame, should you see him again, that there are fakers out there, good ones. Good enough to fool even me."

Go ahead.

Tell him.

Tell him that you were the one who made those books that he wanted so badly. That copy of the Darrab Althabean*? That was me, and he had to depend on someone else to tell him.*

"Khan? Are you calling to ask for a book or to accuse Mr. Soame of selling counterfeits?"

"I'm asking for the impossible, is all."

Do it.

"Did your heart leap at seeing the *Darrab Althabean* before you? Because I know your answer."

"As much as it sank upon suggestion that it was not the genuine article."

"One of those feelings was more real than the other, I'd bet."

"One washed out the other, a sweet pill washed down with bitter wine."

Spare me.

"Now about the other book," he said.

"You'd ask after all that? You've got nerve."

"Desperation isn't nerve but will pass for it in a pinch."

"I can't help you. Try someone else. Anyone else."

"There are collectors out there clamoring for something, something new and unseen. I can get you in touch with them. Look, anything about the anvil or Blackrock or—"

"The name, Thaddeus Khan."

"It's called *The Smok—*"

Cait slammed the handset down before he could get the words out, hard enough to make the bell give a strangled ring.

She shook as she realized her whisper campaign had paid off, that she should have been ecstatic at this turn, that she'd arrived. But all those feelings had been rooted in the time before, before learning that everything in every page she'd forged might have had some basis in reality, no matter how fevered or strange. In truth, the whispers were hollow next to what the book had already done, what it could have done if Cait hadn't closed the door kept the unknowable locked away. But only barely.

She moved the handset to the table and left it there. No more calls tonight or this morning or whatever it was.

What would the book have done if I'd allowed it? What would Ariela have done?

She was too jangled and wired to sleep but too hollow and empty to stay awake. The flames of her career in forgery licked and grew, making her unable to sit still. She went to the bedroom, stacked with boxes that she hadn't yet unpacked and looked for the turntable and headphones, so she could at least play the record once more before everything collapsed on her.

CHAPTER FOUR

The LA County Museum of Natural History was housed in a beautiful beaux-arts brick-and-column building at the edge of Exposition Park, one that belonged to another time, where things were seemingly planned and executed with precision. Crafted for the benefit and lionization of a handful but with at least grudging accommodation for the baser public. Wealth and power tempered by refinement erected these monuments to knowledge and culture. Now the arches and decoration were merely a tasteful echo of that façade of gentility. The building was beautiful and severe. As much of it as Cait could see through the smeared lipstick writing on the Mercury's windshield. The rubbing alcohol had only removed most of it, leaving a half trace behind so that it wouldn't be forgotten so easily.

She parked at the edge of the lot and walked from the grubby asphalt to winding crushed granite paths that led finally to the building's east entrance. It was early yet, warmer than yesterday with the sun already burned through the marine layer. She tried one of the lobby doors, surprised to find it open. She stepped into a large, mostly dark atrium lit by the sun pouring through skylights in the roof.

The slanting beams fell upon a sculpture or fixture there, something large and square, maybe twelve feet by six feet by six again. It was monumental and somehow holy. The object itself was made out of what must have been polyurethane or Lucite, one of those almost-transparent liquid plastics. She remembered working with it as a kid in elementary school, putting flowers and leaves in it but never getting it done cleanly. Bubbles and streaks always marred her work and what should have been clear within was instead obscured and distorted.

This one, however, had been done painstakingly and it must have taken forever. A jumble of bones floated inside the block of plastic, big ones, longer and thicker around than any human skeleton she'd seen. There were shapes upon shapes, all near echoes of one another, shifting in detail but not in scale. The whole wasn't organized into any particular structure, rather into a chaotic midden. Sunlight hit and flared in the middle of the display, cleaving through and trapped by the material. All these bones were trapped there, stuck in time now. There wasn't one creature in there but parts of many, robbed of any sort of individuality or differentiation. Shoulder blades as big as a human torso, others stripped of context or relationship, unidentifiable pieces so large that they could have only come from titans.

The light occluded at angles, sifting incompletely through the media. Without thought, she put her hand out, fingers pressed against the flat plastic. She couldn't say why. She saw the suspension and wanted it, unable to let herself hear the reason.

She thought she heard a voice saying, "Yes," a child's voice. It must have come from a nearby family out for a day at the museum. But there was nobody there. She knew that. No families. Empty as a confessional on Saturday night.

The voice had come from impossibly within the ossuary, as clearly as any fact that Cait pretended to know. She knew that. It was true all the way down. The voice was right here.

Her heart pounded as she stood on some cliff that she couldn't even conceive of but which was nonetheless real. Light spun over the planes of the bones, rippling on imperfections in the matrix of plastic. She fell within it, soaring tiny over landscapes of bone and death, each piece as individual and unique as anyone she'd ever known. She slipped between spaces in time, years reeling away from her as the voice asked her to--

"There you are," a voice rang across the hard floor.

Cait startled not at the sound but the sudden return to her own body and perceptions, boxed in as tightly as premature burial. Sensation of sleep flying and falling as she jarred into her own skin and gasped.

The moment was lost. Any perception she had was gone now. The box before just held a bunch of jumbled bones. No mystery, no wonder, no being anything more than it was—a collection of old and dead matter.

"I didn't expect you to beat me here," Trager said.

Did he see that?

Cait turned away from the monument of bones and smile-shrugged. "Couldn't really sleep."

"When you work hard enough, you'll sleep wherever you can get it."

"If you say so. So we're here to get smart?"

"If that's even possible, in my case." His deadpan waited for Cait to crack first and she did not. "Our contact is up on the fourth floor. After you."

The workroom was big and well-lit, one wall entirely taken over by stacked flat-file and specimen drawers some three feet across and only inches deep. Entire histories compressed onto paper sheets and stacked like tree rings, all time cataloged to be paged through, reshuffled and re-organized. Banks of fluorescent lights threw their cold cast on the center table where a tall woman stood, ink-dark hair draped across the shoulders of her white lab coat.

"Dr. Gabi Wallis?" Trager asked.

Cait watched as the woman held up a hand with a single finger raised. Grasped in the others was a sliver of metal like an oversized dental pick. "Come on over. Just don't crowd my light." Then the arm went back to work.

The voice kicked something in her, sitting next to a dark-haired girl in drawing classes her first year at school, how she mocked the instructor and outdid her at every turn, how she held her pen when she was stuck a moment in thought or belaying distraction. Cait had to work twice as hard as that girl did. Cait had gone to parties held at her dorm with cheap beer, skunky weed and dudes hanging halfway out of windows like they were trying to French-kiss gravity. Wallis was that girl; Cait was sure. A real, living fossil of the time before Cait's time of breaking the world.

Dr. Wallis stood before a table on which was a large and irregularly shaped circle of sedimentary rock. Jutting from that was a collection of bones, half-exposed or less, some mere suggestion. She was carefully pick-ing at the meniscus of rock clinging to a curved section of skeleton, only recognizable by the vaguest of shape, not by function.

"I just wanted to finish this while I could see the rest of this *Thrinaxo-don* humerus in my mind's eye. Sometimes it's tricky, but I can talk while you're here."

"Well, I think you need to *see* this." Trager's fidgeting foot scraped on the floor. "Can't really describe it. Cait, how did you describe these?"

"I said, 'Those are some fucked-up fish.'"

"Charming. Why aren't you at Marine World?"

"Marine World closed down, Dr. Wallis," Cait said. "Little while ago."

The woman looked at her, trying to read the joke but came up with nothing. Cait waited for a glimmer of recognition and thought about beg-ging for it but didn't.

"Listen, you take point on this, Cait. I'll ask anything you miss."

"Okay, so you said something about fish, but they must be really old fish, or everyone's time is being wasted here." Wallis dusted her hands and pulled off the blue latex. "Skin oils, you know. Can't get 'em on the specimens. They'll etch."

Cait took the folder from Trager and flipped it open. "So this is gonna sound pretty weird." She handed the photo of the single fish in the tray over first. "What can you tell me about this?"

Wallis stared at the picture for about a second. She took the glasses off her nose and put them in the pocket of her lab coat and made a face of disgust.

"Why are you wasting my time with this? Is this a joke?" She handed the photo back to Cait, all but shoving it.

"It's not a joke," Cait said. "We're stumped too."

"Show her the other one," Trager urged.

"No, she's not ready for that."

"What other one?" Wallis' eyes narrowed at the judgment. "This is in poor taste. But at least I get the joke. This is publicity for some horror movie, right?"

"There's more pictures. But what joke are you talking about?"

"The *Xiphactinus*. That fish." Wallis tapped the picture with a black fingernail. "That's a very small one, barely fry. Okay, maybe not *Xiphactinus*, but something like it. Gimme that." She snatched the picture out of Cait's hands. "That's a ruler. When was this taken?"

"Couple nights ago."

"Where?"

"Coroner's office. LA county." Trager waited for it to register.

Wallis' face washed between intrigue and irritation and back again. "Where did you find this? Did it wash up on shore? And why the coroner? I have a lot of questions."

Cait warned, "Okay, you can't freak out at this. Promise?" She held out the third picture.

"Yeah sure, whatever." Wallis grabbed one with opened body with the fish head inside it and went pale. Then she returned to her chair, her stare switching between the two images. "This joke isn't funny."

"Nobody thinks it is." Cait rolled up a chair next to her and sat down. "How old is that fish?"

"It's impossible."

"Sometimes impossible is just something we haven't learned yet. Like the coelacanth, right?"

"It's in his *stomach.*"

"We're not parsing that yet," Trager said. "How old?"

Her eyes rolled up slightly, half-closed behind the glasses, focusing on him after a second. "Oh, I don't know. They go back before the Cretaceous extinction, but it's pretty likely they survived for some time after Chicxulub impact."

"Chicksa-what?"

Wallis sighed. "I'll tell you on background, but I will not repeat this in front of another member of the staff here."

"Oh, academic dispute," Cait said with a lilt of laughter. "I love those."

"I don't. Could be my job." She settled herself and inhaled deeply. "So this hypothesis isn't proven yet but has been kicking around for a little while. You know the dinosaurs, right? Ruled the earth and then got wiped out, more or less gone but for crocodiles and birds."

"Birds are dinosaurs?" Trager asked.

"Focus, detective," Cait said just short of a snap. "Okay, sure. But I thought it was all the climate changing and, you know, earth changing and the dinosaurs got left behind. I don't know—it's been awhile."

"Gradualism. Right." Wallis' eyes lit as she spoke. "Around the end of the Cretaceous period, we're talking peak dinosaurs, something hits the earth." She drove a closed fist into semi-open palm and then a slap. "Probably a really big meteor but we've never found it to prove that. It releases a ton of energy as heat and gas, and there's global fires. The sky is literally blotted out after, by probably *probably* toxic smoke. Doesn't work out well for our lizard friends. They might not have been fully cold-blooded, but life got real hard."

"Got it. Bad day for dinosaurs. So this fish times back to there?"

"Pretty sure. Paleoichthyology isn't my expertise. But back to sometime before Chicxulub. At least that's the theory."

"Is that a place or a thing?"

"Place. Southern edge of the Gulf of Mexico. Oil companies out looking for undersea petroleum reserves have a lot of money to do surveys that we could only dream of. Only they're looking for more money and we're just looking for fossils. Because who wants to learn something, right? So these guys, they're cruising around the gulf and they find what reads as a big ring in the stone itself. I mean, a great big one. Cataclysmic even."

"Like a volcanic ring?" Cait asked. She glanced over at Trager who was totally behind now, trying to absorb anything but only looking lost.

"Close, but an *impact* ring. Even solid stone, you hit it hard enough, you get a ripple or a wave. Hit it really really hard and it liquefies then acts like water, only we can see that stuff in time. Again, this is all by sonar, by feel."

The ripple in the water caused by the stone or the other way around.

Cait tried to let it go but the thought lodged in her like a barbed hook. More of Ariela's circular talk about magic and how after came before.

"It's not accepted yet. There's still a lot of research to do. But a few people in the field, including myself, think that Chicxulub is a good candidate for the end of the Cretaceous and therefore the dinosaurs. One of the most significant episodes in all of biologic and geologic history. It made the world what it is now."

"What does this tell us about that fish though?"

"Oh, lots of things survived. I mean, on an aggregate scale. Maybe this did. But larger species didn't, not in forms we'd recognize anyway. They kept evolving."

"So it's not…" Cait sighed, trying not to sound crazier than usual. "It's not like this thing just showed up here having been, I don't know, hauled out of the past or something."

Dr. Waller stared then broke into a smile. "Don't do drugs, kids."

Cait ignored the bait. "So is this an old fish or not?"

"It looks like a *very* old fish. I can't talk about the morphology too deeply, but look at how the head is shaped, the protruding teeth, the big scales. Those aren't markers for ocean-going fish now, but long ago, sure. Look, there's an easy way to settle this."

"What's that?"

"Just bring the fish here. You got pictures of it, so you can get the fish, right?"

Cait looked back at Trager. "Did the cast come out?"

He was dangerously close to putting his hands on some unidentifiable bone but Cait's sudden question made him jump. "What?" He asked, irritated.

"The cast. Of the fish. Did that happen?"

"It was melting as they tried it. Just came out a mess."

"It *melted?*" Cait asked.

"His words, not mine. I got the feeling he was glad he didn't have to mess with it any longer." He squared himself up. "Now tell her about Venice."

"I don't think that's a good idea right now."

"What about Venice?" Wallis asked. "More fish?"

"Bigger. And more teeth."

Cait told her about the thing that had attacked both her and Sue Whelan on the canal-side at Venice. She left out the mirage man and some other details and fixed on the idea that it wasn't just some zoo animal but something else.

At Trager's urging, Dr. Wallis pulled books off the shelf one at a time and pointed at various fossil creatures, some skeletons, some sculpted reconstructions, some ink drawings. Nothing quite came together. They were all too big or too fishlike or not quite demented enough.

"You said 'lizard head but short neck,' right?"

"Yes," Cait replied, staring at pictures one after another until they just sort of blended together. "But none of these are right. And it was dark, and who knows what I even saw."

Wallis rested her fingers on the bridge of her nose. "The closest I can come up with is *Geosaurus*, but that's not even really a dinosaur. It was, ah, a composite of other fossils just sorta jammed together by paleontologists who didn't know any better.

"You're sure you weren't high?"

"Even if I was, it took a bite out of a woman that night. *She* didn't imagine it."

"Maybe it was someone's pet crocodile. People do dumb stuff like that all the time. Keep animals they shouldn't. More likely that than, uh…"

Trager shrugged. "Seen all kinds of animals kept that shouldn't have been, that's for sure. Saw a guy once, kept an anaconda that slipped its enclosure and it took up residence near Travel Town. Ate coyotes and cats and whatever else it could until they caught it. Long as a semi-truck, or so they said."

His fingers snapped hard. "Hey, what about Bubbles?"

"Bubbles? What?"

"You know. Bubbles the hippo from that place in Orange County. Oh, what was it?" He snapped his fingers again, trying to summon the memory. "That's it. Lion Country."

"Oh, right," Cait said. "The hippo that kept escaping. Whatever happened with that?"

"Zookeepers shot it full of tranquilizer darts, and it rolled down a hill and suffocated to death."

"Poor hippo," Wallis offered. "People suck."

"You tell that to the housewives who were sure that a four-thousand-pound hippo was going to be roaming through their backyards."

"It wasn't a hippo," Cait said. "But it might've been an alligator."

Wallis pushed her chair back from the book-strewn table. "Well, if you see it again, take some pictures or better yet throw a net on it."

The beeper on Trager's belt chirped too loud for the workroom, reaching everywhere.

"Hate those things," Wallis muttered. "Like a leash."

"That's the job these days," he replied. "Thanks for your time and expertise, Dr. Wallis."

"Yeah, thanks," Cait said. "It's, uh, good to see you."

Goddammit. Goddammit.

The paleontologist smiled, only half-awkwardly. "It's, uh, good to see you too."

"What was the call?" Cait asked as the elevator doors closed.

"Office. Not critical. Hoping it's a background package on our stiff. LAPD is fucking things up passing records along since they originated the case. Everything's gonna be slow."

"I knew her," Cait said in reply.

"Excuse me?"

"The doctor. Went to school with her. First couple years anyway. Pulled her blitzed boyfriend out of a window before he could go street pizza on us all."

His glance went sideways. "And you didn't, you know, bring this up at all?"

"Nah. I was just hoping that she'd..." Cait shook it off. "It was a while ago. Lot has happened since then."

The doors opened and they stepped out to crowds of people coming into the museum, business hours having caught up to them. Cait's vision drifted back to the brick of time and bones. Only a corner of the bone monument was lit up now, a cold golden light just touching the greenish plastic.

"Hey, I'm starved. You want to grab something to eat?"

Cait looked at the landscape of it, surfaces in proximity but never quite touching, the whole of it making something entirely new with pieces decontextualized from the old. Stripped of the old relationships, it was open to unknown possibilities. It was—

"Cait. Cait." Trager cleared his throat. "MacReady!"

She turned back to him, and whatever thought was forming in her was lost now.

"You don't have to yell."

"You don't have to be a space cadet. I was asking if you wanted to get something to eat. Pann's ain't too far from here."

"No, I…" She stopped trying to hold the thought. "No. I'm fine." She squared herself up. "Are we done for now? I've got something else I want to check up on. 'Cause we're not the only ones looking for weird stuff."

The thought of even a remotely-shared intimacy like eating was too much to consider at the moment. At least not with Trager who was still just using Cait for expertise and as a weirdness magnet. She didn't take it personally, but it certainly put boundaries on where she'd go with him.

"Pann's is really good, and I hate to eat alone," he added.

"I'm sure you'll find other cops to eat with. Inglewood PD practically lives there."

"Oh, you know the place. Then you know what you're gonna be missing."

"Yeah, coronary disease later in life."

"Funny but not funny, MacReady."

Trager pulled out a card from his tweed jacket pocket and handed it to her. It was the same as the card he'd given her those months ago, only the address and phone number were crossed out by very even pen lines. She flipped it over to see the new address and phone numbers written in neat ball point.

"Cursive? I didn't expect that from you. Also, nice cards. Really sharp."

"Budgets are what they are. And the sisters at the parish school were sticklers for good writing. Still afraid of rulers to this day."

"That's a laugh."

"They weren't. They were good enough to not quite draw blood, but you always wished they did so you could have something to get 'em with." His grin cooled. "Anyways, stop by the office this afternoon."

"What if I have something better to do?"

"You really don't."

"Message received."

cRl

Half an hour and a take-out pastrami from Johnny's in Culver City later, Cait was back home going through her belongings one container at a time. Progress was slow as she'd stop and inspect the contents of the frantically-packed boxes, proximity rather than use or weight having been the primary consideration for what was put where. Greasy fingers left streaks on cardboard printed up with the Allied Van Lines logo that she'd stacked to window height in the apartment's main room. Her black book, her old one, wasn't on her any longer. She had a neat new one that she'd filled out the day she decided she was walking away from the old her. She'd had half a mind to burn it all but couldn't take that leap. Instead, it was in one of the boxes somewhere.

She knew she could have just looked up the *Quest4* production offices in the phone book. Or driven down there. They weren't ever going to leave that office on Lankershim, over in what people were trying to pass off as North Hollywood. But she wasn't remotely ready for a personal appearance.

She was barely ready to call them, but they had more eyes on the street than she did, and maybe they knew something about the current flavor of strange that she didn't. They were in the business of the weird. And they weren't out there running jiggle TV segments about it.

At least Watkiss took it seriously. Maybe too seriously. Better that than just running to lowest-common-denominator tits and ass.

If she called direct, she might reach Fabian. But he'd probably talk to her even if it'd been awhile. He'd been the smartest guy there. If she'd have listened to him about Ken, she might've avoided more than a bit of heartbreak.

Live and learn. Gotta get burned to know how hot the fire is.

By the time she finished the sandwich, bites were tasting half of dust and grime. She was most of the way through the boxes, at least an informal survey of them. Nothing had been marked as she'd hurried to get out of that old place, more so than she remembered. Bedclothes wrapped around an assortment of ink and perfume bottles, a handful of paperback mysteries dog-eared and cracking shuffled into a seam of cassette tapes, half-filled shampoo bottles leaking into a battered denim jacket marked in spiky magic-marker lines. The chaos was too much. Her head began to spin. Maybe she wouldn't find it. Then all those people would be lost. People move, they move on. They disappear. That whole part of her life would be gone, and suddenly she felt like she was gripping the sides of the bathtub in an effort to pull herself up but unable to.

Her heart raced as she imagined sucking in a breath of nothing but water, opening her lungs to it, about it all being over, and that's not what she wanted at all, not what she was trying to do. She ripped open the box before her, fingers trembling at what had been thrown away and how stupid she was. She tore into the clothes on the top, her old, beaten trench coat and a collection of black T-shirts, some silkscreened herself and just as many bought at sweaty merch tables or record stores. Under a shirt with IT DOESN'T MATTER IF WE ALL DIE written out in white block letters, there was her old blacking lamp, and beside it, in an octagonal green-glass ashtray that could have split a skull, there was the black book. The cover was smeared with cinders and burned along the page edge, but it was intact.

That wasn't even the book I'd really wanted to burn.

Then the phone rang like a bomb going off. She snatched up the receiver without thinking.

"Yes?"

"Cat MacReady?"

"It's *Cait*. My name's Cait."

"That's not what it says here. Okay. Anyway, this is the UCLA med center in Santa Monica. Your friend is well enough to take visitors now."

"My… oh, okay. Sue Whelan."

"Lavinia Sue Whelan according to this."

"She goes by Sue. So she's up and around?"

"Not quite. But you can come see her."

"Okay. Thanks."

Cait hung up the phone and wondered what Lavinia Sue Whelan would have to say. She could find out before heading over to Open Door's offices.

CHAPTER FIVE

The hospital room was painted sea green without depth. Cait still felt like she could fall into it.

Sue Whelan sat up in bed, sipping tentatively at a plastic cup of broth. She could have been forty or twenty: skin tight, crow's-feet tacked around her eyes and pronounced smile lines and creases. Her hands too, callused and skin rough from work. She looked for the world like one of those Okies in the pages of *Life* magazine, headed out west for a better life while the dust devils chased them all the way to California. All those people, anyone old enough to look around and to know what was going on, they were haunted by leaving the familiar and running headlong into the unknown. Sue wasn't haunted, nor was she at peace, just a very quiet wariness of everything she'd found outside of home.

She held herself with a quiet dignity and looked like she never bent a knee in her life, maybe only to God on Sundays. Not to her parents and not to anyone else because if mama couldn't get your obedience then nobody flesh and blood would.

She sat there for a long time before saying anything. Cait was feeling weird and self-conscious, but that was always now. She tried not to fidget with her purse or anything else while she waited Sue's wordlessness out.

"You're not with the law then." There wasn't a question there.

"No, ma'am," Cait said. Not knowing why she added the honorific.

"'Ma'am is my mother. Call me Sue."

"I'm not with the law, Sue."

"Good thing. I ain't ready for them again."

Cait let it ride. "You remember, right? I dressed that wound first."

Sue swallowed that hard. "I remember that well enough. I just wanted to make sure I could talk plainly." She took another sip of broth then set it down like it was still twitching. "This tastes more of the can than the chicken."

"I'll get you something else if you want."

"I don't need you to do me any other favors. I'm already in debt enough as it is."

"You don't owe me anything," Cait said. "I'm just glad I could help."

"It is the Christian thing to do."

Cait's face wrinkled in dry amusement. "You're new to LA, aren't you? Not gonna find a lot of Christ out here."

"Don't say that. Speak with respect or don't speak at all."

"Okay, I'm sorry. All I was saying is that you can't take being helped for granted out here."

"No, this city is not much on help."

"Maybe if you look in the right place." Cait flashed for a moment on her own isolation after everything and the endless nights she lived out now. The thought of who she could even ask came and went. She pushed it away sure as it had been a snake. She took a breath and tried to regain composure. All the parts of it were too slippery. "So I wanted to ask you, what you're doing out in LA. You're not from here or anywhere nearby."

"I most certainly am not. Sevier County in Tennessee. That's home."

"There's a place called 'Severe?'"

"*S-e-v-i-e-r*. It's in the east of the state. Cradled in the mountains." She looked over the rest of what lay on the tray before her: packaged saltines and orange juice and some thinly sliced apples going brown in the air. "How am I supposed to eat this? All this plastic."

"It's hygienic. What brought you out here?"

"You sure you ain't law? You wouldn't lie about that."

"Sue, I've punched more cops than I've saved the lives of women from Sevier County. But there's some in my family and I'm a nosy sort."

"I do owe you that much."

"You don't owe me."

"Debt's a debt." She took a drink of the juice, looked at the label and muttered, "All the way from Florida. Don't taste of sunshine though. But better a sickly wonder than none at all."

"That's just barely touching the surface. You should try a chili burger from Tommy's."

Sue's hands folded, fingers intertwined. "I came out here to find out what happened to my brother," she said after a long moment of reading Cait. "His name's Lee. He's a rainmaker. Best the family ever seen.

"But rainmaking's gonna end him. I'm sure of it."

"You mean, like rain from the sky?" Cait made falling motions with her hands and waving fingers.

"What other kind is there?"

"There's all kinds." The sensation of the storm bringing the Sightless Eye wrapped her in that moment, the industrial yard bathed in the hot breath of that weird and sudden rain.

"Water and Lee, they always had a special kinda shape. He could sing a storm out of a clear sky if he had a mind to it. But you understand, he was never boastful or vain about it. He respected that gift. Until he left home."

"And came here to LA?"

"Oh, eventually. He wandered all over the states near as I can tell. Driving daddy's old pickup and making money where he could, coaxing water out the sky. That's the secret, see. You don't *make* it happen. It's not your will. You're asking for these things to happen. You want to get the land so as it remembers the rain, and that helps. So he told me once."

The asking gives power. The same thing Ariela said.

Cait stared at her for a while, trying to figure out if she was using poetic language or was just plain around the bend. Or if what Ariela had been talking about was the kind of crazy that was being shared around. Or if it was even crazy.

"Why'd Lee go? Why come here? We got water year-round from the Colorado River and all the way from the Sierras. Hell—"

"Don't." Her blue eyes went dead cold.

"Okay, sorry. We have all the water in the Owens Valley. LA doesn't need a rainmaker. Well, not any more than any place in Southern California doesn't need one."

"Lee was a fool at some things, but he was good at sniffing down the tall green. Little too good if you ask me. That's a path that leads away from home and to trouble."

"Is he in trouble now?"

"I've a mind to thinking that Lee *is* the trouble."

Cait flashed back to their meeting on the bridge in Venice. Sue hadn't been standing like a lover or friend but as a sister and more a mother at that. Intimate but more than a little afraid at what had come out of a beloved relative.

"That *was* Lee at the canals, wasn't it?"

Sue winced, lip drawn back as surely as if a fishhook was pulling on the corner.

"Yeah, that was him. Only it wasn't him." Her face broke for an instant but she clawed the tears back and reached for simmering rage instead. "Why'd you leave, little baby Lee?"

Cait reached for her wrist and gripped it quietly. Sue shook it off.

"Look at me," she said bitterly. "Those pills took all my strength."

"You almost bled out. Takes time to recover."

"I wish we had time. I've got to get out of here and find him. Is that something you can help with?"

Suddenly she's gotten over her self-reliance. But then LA is an intimidating place.

"I've got a ton of my own troubles right now. What happened to you and me also happened to some rich developer out in the hills. Same night, I think."

Sue's stare grew distant.

"I mean, it wasn't a reptile thing but a fish. Something out of time. Millions of years old."

"Oh, Lee."

"Sue, what's going on? Did he make these things happen?"

"No. No. He only talked to the water. This is the water's doing." Her fingers had knit themselves in knots and she spent a moment undoing them.

"Gotta be honest, the police aren't going to like that answer. They're looking at that developer as a murder."

"It wasn't murder."

"You sound pretty sure."

"Lee wouldn't do that. Not by himself." Her face went stony, emotion and anything like helplessness evaporating like mist in the sunlight.

"Maybe I can help find Lee. While you're laid up." Cait wished she could take it back. There was too much already with just what Trager was asking about. But maybe finding Lee would get a quicker answer to the other.

"He'll be by the river. The sea is so strong out here. He would be afraid of it. I never imagined anything so big, seeing that ocean. How do you live so close to it? Ain't you scared?"

"I'm scared all the time. But not of the ocean."

"But you still keep going, right? Don't let up."

"I'm trying," Cait admitted. "Doesn't always work."

"Do you have a map of this place?" she asked. Her eyes flicked down to the tray in front of her. "I don't know nothing about nothing when it comes to LA. Biggest small place I've ever seen."

Cait went through her purse and pulled out the map she'd swiped from a Chevron station awhile back. The Thomas Brothers was too big to haul around with her, somewhere on the floorboards of the Mercury.

"I don't know that this'll work. But that line of thought never helped anyone. But you're from this place so maybe that'll help."

Cait handed her the map. Sue unfolded it on the tray before her, pushing the food items to one side. The broth tipped over as she did.

"Hey! It's okay. I'll clean—"

"Don't touch it. Not just yet. Here." She handed Cait a small paper envelope of salt. "Won't do if I spill this since I can't leave the room just yet."

The map lay upside down, south pointing north. Sue then dipped her fingertips in the spilled broth and waved them over the map. Drops flicked to the paper and beaded before soaking in.

Sue was murmuring something now in a low voice with a cadence that was old and from another place, not even so strange as Tennessee but farther away and older. Then she invoked the name of the Father, the Son, and the Holy Spirit, which Cait found weird and heavy in a way she wouldn't have thought.

"Open the salt and scatter it from about yay high." She indicated with her left hand where to work from. "Hurry, while I'm being heard."

Cait suppressed a shiver and tore the corner off the salt packet and let the grains fall to the tray below.

৶৶

Cait's hands shook as she looked for a place to park on South Mission Street, miles and miles away from Santa Monica. Anywhere in the industrial sprawl would be fine. She was still sweating from the creepy jolt that had hit her in the hospital room; indescribable other than electricity except alive. Her hair had stood up all along her neck and still felt like it was being pulled.

The salt had clumped weirdly around the bridge at Sixth Street. Grains had bounced down to the paper surface but migrated after they landed like they'd been pushed around by unseen fingers. Cait hadn't needed to be told where to go. It was right there. Unmistakable.

But she had no idea what she was going to find.

She sat there, gripping the steering wheel for a moment, just listening to the song playing from a tape she'd put together a couple of years ago.

She'd get up when "Dark Entries" ended, soaking in the memories that had been built up around this song, experiences as strong as brick and mortar. The tape had come out of a shoe box filled with them, all in cases, all labeled by hand and accumulated over the years. Sure they sounded awful, but they were a hell of a lot more portable than records.

The last chorus hit, and she felt it until there was a sound of crinkling and the tape winding around the playback head or some other nightmare. The music slurred for a mangling syllable or two then ground to a halt.

Or I'll get out of the car now, I guess.

"Shit."

She hit eject on the tape player and tugged at the cassette. It spooled out its guts behind like bursting roadkill. Irritated, she pulled at it, knowing that the tape would snap but not satisfied until it had done so. It dropped to the bench seat up front. The mylar ribbon shone unevenly in the midday sun. There was a lot of time wrapped up in it, a lot of experience and memory, and now it was just junk.

At least I have the sequence written out still. I can remake that. I can make it again.

Sure, Cait. When are you going to do that? When you get back to work? Your real work? When you climb out of the well? Forget it. You're fucked. It's all fucked. It was fucked the second you made that book and wrecked the world with it.

Then there was another voice, a whisper, hypnagogic and sliding in only around the edges of sleep. She couldn't hear what it was saying, or maybe she couldn't understand it. There was a lyrical quality to it, subdued, a murder ballad for the future itself.

Was it the voice from the museum? Is that me? Someone else?

She closed her eyes tight and tried to chase the sound in her head but there was nothing to find.

Great. Still hearing things. Maybe they were right. Maybe I do belong locked up for my own good.

Cait looked at the tape, label written out in a spiky and spidery script that was hers, probably drawn by the light of a television. She'd meant it then, meant it as much as anything she'd ever written. She wished she could reach that again.

PASTY GIRLS FOR PRETTY BOYS was written out on the tape label. Those days were gone now. She rolled the window on the Mercury down and sailed the tape out over the chain-link fence nearby, over the trash-strewn street and into the giant concrete ditch that contained the LA River below.

Cait climbed down the staircase that ran off the viaduct from the Los Feliz side of the canal. Faster to get down there, even though it was a short detour to cross. This was a space that shouldn't exist, technically public and open but unused. The river wasn't a place people visited, not here where it was just a huge set of slabs and planes.

What am I even looking for? Lee? The Mirage Man? His truck? Figure that pickup with the mismatched fender has to be his. Sue said something about him taking off with it. Enough of a coincidence for me. But what then? Tell him, "Hey, your sister's worried about you"? And what does he have to do with that developer? Or is it something else entirely?

Across the concrete expanse of the riverbed it smelled like equal parts trash and rain, piss and algae, the city and something much wilder. Water still surged outside the main channel, a wide notch cut in the bottom of the riverway. Most of the year that was a sluggish strip lined with green slime on both banks, even less impressive than the canals of Venice, just as artificial as anything else in the city. The river pulsed along with the last bits of runoff from the rain several days ago. It moved slickly, probably faster than it presented but she had no plans to get close enough to it to find out.

There were a couple of cars parked on the other side of the water, out on the flats. She stared at them for a moment, admiring how out of place they were. Cars on the riverbed was for the movies, an LA that didn't really exist. There was an older sedan, once white and now kind of vaguely smog colored. Beside it was a black van, the gloss long worn off, so it didn't shine so much as it just ate the sunlight. The last was a VW van painted in stripes of red and green and yellow, not psychedelic, but more uniform, like a flag maybe. Several people were out by the river, clothes laid out to dry in the sun.

Laundry day. Maybe they've seen something here.

The air in the riverbed swelled with water, the smell before a thunderstorm or when the first drops hit the dusty concrete and asphalt and made a sweet smell of dirt and rain and gasoline all mixed together. She wanted to get drunk on it for a moment. Instead, she walked to the river's edge.

"Hey! Hello!" she called. "Over here."

The people, talking amongst themselves or checking their laundry all turned their heads more or less to her. One who was fishing didn't look up at all, engrossed in the action of the bobber on the surface

"Hello there!" replied the one with the fishing rod, still in fixed stare. "I'm Missourah Marky! What's your name?"

"Just, uh, Cait," she said, caught off guard. She hadn't expected friendliness.

"Well, hi there Just Cait. That's Roger and Misty all the way from Jamaica by way of Manchester. And that's Lilah on the fine recliner there."

"Hello," Lilah said. She was older, maybe as old as all of them put together. She sat on a tubular aluminum beach chair with green and yellow nylon straps, faded and fraying. A shawl hung over her head and shoulders like a huge hood, leaving her face in the dark. She clutched a big green glass bottle with no label that she pulled up to the dark space where her head was and took a belt.

"Beautiful day, ain't it? Great day to be on the river."

"Good day to ya," Misty called back. "Pity ya be on the wrong side to come join us."

"Oh, that's okay. I'm out here just looking for someone. I was told he might be here. Well, would be here." She didn't feel in the mood to explain to these strangers as to how some kind of backwoods divination by way of hospital bedside brought her there.

"Nobody here but us chickens," Marky joked. "But we don't see too many your kinda folks down here. Seems as if they feel the river's off limits to 'em."

"My kind?" Cait tried not to take it as insult.

"You know... regular." He looked up and offered a cockeyed grin.

"This isn't my neighborhood, no. But I don't think my friend is a regular either." She tried to finesse describing the Mirage Man and failed at it herself. She couldn't have said whether he was young or old or bearded or clean-shaven. Just a sense of work clothes. So she said that, more or less.

"Hell, I ain't seen nobody like that. But I move around a lot," Marky said. "Pulled some weird stuff out the river day before yesterday, but it didn't stick around. Figured I'd try my luck at some other spots."

"What do you mean 'weird stuff'?"

Marky turned his lanky frame toward Lilah and asked her something. She shrugged, and he did too. "Pulled a bunch of history out of it. Ships and planes and monster movie costumes. Thought it might be worth something, but it all went to mist.

"I think the water's haunted, Just Cait."

"That's as good a word for it as any," she yelled back. "You folks mind if I look around a bit some?"

"Nobody owns the river, honey," Lilah said and took another drink.

"Well, thanks all the same," she said, feeling like she'd blundered into someone's backyard barbecue, and still they were gracious and invited her right over. That wasn't a thing she was accustomed to. When she fell in with the outsider kids at school and then the outsiders at the clubs, none of whom asked any questions, just took her in without judgment. This was something else. Over on that bank, that was a life that they'd made peace with. Maybe it was the same after all.

The walls of the riverway were wet, more than she'd have thought from rain a couple days back. Sun gleamed off the concrete that was now shining and water-splashed. There was no smell of the city, just a fulsome green scent, lush and inviting. Not clean but ripe.

How is this? It's wet? There's no rain, no river water this high up?

Graffiti covered the slabs, cut out in wide swathes of paint or skinny scratches of aerosol. The words lay under a slick of water that had come from nothing. The checkerboard beige and gray of erasure that would never be complete. Cait bent down to feel for herself, to make sure it wasn't some kind of strange mirage.

"Hey, Marky! Wh—what's happening?" Her own voice seemed shaky and shrill to her.

There was a sound from far up the river. It came out a distant roar, a terrible memory coming to the surface after years of suppression, grown so strong that nothing could hold it back.

"The river," Lilah said. She threw her shawl back and said "The river is remembering."

Cait turned to see.

An impossible cresting wave made its way down the concrete chute. She could see it swirling and seething up ahead of the 7th Street crossing, emerald waves with white tips, cascading off the bridge columns that sank into the riverbed. The thrum and crash followed seconds behind, deliriously out of sync with the sight of the water.

"Get out of here! Go!" Cait yelled to the people on the other bank. They scrambled, picking up their belongings and drying clothes and stuffing them into the waiting cars.

Car engines started up one two three, barely audible over the rush of water. They would at least be protected. She had to do the same for herself. She ran as fast as her flats would let her, wishing she'd had boots to track on the slick concrete as she headed back toward the spiral stairway that had brought her to river level.

The resurgent water sang as it spilled down the channel, high enough to be touching side to side at the bottom, even several feet above that. Water slapped up the diagonal banks and flopped back down into the main mass and motion echoed in on itself in strange triangular waves. It roared like a saltless ocean, maybe fifty feet away now. The leading line churned with foam and strength, sweeping up anything that had been left behind the rain swell earlier. This freak wave bore down on the Sixth Street Viaduct unbound as the wrath of some primeval god.

Cait leaped for the stairway, which she hoped would protect her from the worst of it. Pulling her body inside, she held on as the water slammed into the concrete and steel and she swore that she could hear the whole thing groan with the sudden weight and pressure. It was like one of her panic attacks brought full into the world and lashing out at anything in its path. The water smacked her left calf and foot with violence enough to smash it into the outer wall. Cloth and skin ground against the concrete as her leg wrenched, but she did not let go.

She sucked in and held her breath, feeling water rising up to her ribcage now. The river passed through the place, a mighty and smiting hand laying all time flat. Objects rushed past her feet just outside the protection of the stairwell. Unidentifiable fish and plant life, a horse and buggy and delivery van older even than the Mercury swept by. Bones and waterlogged bodies of people and animals swirled, dancing to the currents. She held on tighter, not letting go, no matter the jumbled past sweeping through liquified time.

Creatures that were long dead were swept up with the turbulence, bodies and parts of them. Shells and bones and other debris sifted into the concrete shelter and stairs, choking the rising water's surface with uneven and organic shapes. There were bodies of creatures that in silhouette looked even more primitive than those from the coroner's office, almost like insects. Cait's hand slipped from the rail and flailed into the water where it struck something hard and curved. Her fingers grabbed onto that reflexively and held. The liquid around swirled with green and brown and was mercifully opaque, sparing her the sight of what lay beneath the roar and eventual subsidence.

Cait didn't know how long she'd been holding on. Her fingers were swollen with ache from exertion. Her legs felt as if they'd been stretched, bones too big to stay in place just right. She looked down then hissed at the raw patch of road rash and bruised unfolding all along her calves. The surge had left her feet bare. At least she could put weight on them. She stood fully and stepped out from the protection of the concrete stairwell. Her right hand hurt, clutching onto something still. She turned it over and finally forced her fingers to relax some. The sound of water running off her in slackening rivulets and drips echoed in the tight space as her fingers unfurled, reluctant even against her own command. She had been gripping one half of a giant clam, almost as wide across as her hand, longer even than that. The shell had been worked, not by random action or the forces of nature, but by a guiding eye and will. Its edges were carved out and the whole of the etchings formed a set of interlocking curves, suggesting the shape of a galaxy, a whole made up and fed by uncounted arms or roots. Her eyes tracked inward from the edges and she found it difficult to pull her gaze from it, some weird magnetism fixing her. The underside of the curved surface was inlaid with a pearlescent sheen, and the topside was faintly brindle-striped in red and brown, like no shell she'd seen before.

It was an old thing, marked in a system that predated science and the culture that spawned that. Yet the work was fine and delicate, speaking a language that understood not vastness but rejected any sense of isolation or disconnectedness in distance. No matter the form of that distance, time or space. Cait's eyes traced the pattern over and over finding the center somehow fed back out to the periphery, though backtracking would show nothing, former path disappearing like a single fish into a unified and swirling school. There was a center and an edge. There was also no center and no edge. There were words for these things, better words, but nothing she could call up. Not even unity, not even infinity.

She put the shell into her purse, laughing helplessly at the water that drained out of the fake Coach bag, pleather peeling and flaking now. She cursed at all the paper that would need to be replaced. Driver's license, social security card, work papers; an entire identity. Maybe it would be better to let it go, as easily as that silver trickling pooling at her feet.

But you gotta live somewhere, be somebody.

Cait set her jaw and stepped away from the shelter of the stairwell. The sunlight dazzled in migraine gleaming on the concrete expanse, wet now to bedrock with the surge of river. Pieces of junk and litter were strewn behind, caught in weeds or greenery that sprouted between seams in the concrete of the riverbed.

Was that there before?

She looked down the course of the riverway but couldn't pick out exactly where the wave was now or if it had even been there. Maybe it was reunited with the Pacific now, displacing bathers and surfers, snarling fishing lines in an inexplicable moment.

Fish and less evolved things flipped in the rime of water on the concrete, eyes wide as mouths gasping and gills exposed with bodies jack-knifed and straightened in continuous motion, desperately returning to the narrow central channel that churned and sped to the sea. Cait toed an unidentifiable and glistening golden fish or snake or neither as it looked too weak to push itself the last inch to safety. The serpent was too delicate and refined to be mere accident, fins webbed with iridescent skin that glittered like a night full of hungering stars. This was something that had escaped out of dream or a zoo full of them, designed more than born. There was barely a ripple as it slid into the surface. Its body shone there in the muddy murk, scaling reflections burning impossible before flicking away and disappearing.

She looked down the river course and saw the three cars tossed together like discarded toys, all of them gleaming, seeming freshly painted. Cait ran to them as quickly as she could on bare feet unaccustomed to being bitten by concrete. Even though they were on the opposite bank, what had passed through was so frightening that what was left behind was easily crossed. The river lapped around her bare feet, chill in the November breeze. She gritted her teeth and crossed, trying not to think about how the water that had washed them moments before had been almost as warm as blood. Four open-spoked wagon wheels rolled past behind her, without axles or carriage to keep them aligned. Behind that, gloved hands seem to hold a rein and that horse it bode was the current itself. She tore her eyes from that.

"Marky!" she called. "Hello! Anyone?"

She approached the sideways-turned Falcon and smacked the driver's side window with the bottom of her fist. Something stirred inside and the window came down. The floorboards sloshed with standing water.

"Hey, Just Cait. You made it?"

"Mostly. I'm gonna go check on the others."

"I'll go see to Roger and Misty."

The black boxy Chevy van lay on its driver's side, half-tipped into the angled main channel. Cait made her way to the back doors and finally wrenched one of them open, exhausting her for the moment.

"Lilah! Come on out!"

No answer. At least not from inside the van. But there was one from the long slope of the main riverbank on the Los Feliz side where Cait had come from, upriver a ways.

"It's a beautiful thing, isn't it? All that life and energy?" It was the voice of the Mirage Man, who was maybe Lee and maybe not anymore.

Cait came out from around the back of the van and shaded her eyes to better see him. The swirling around him shone like molten glass cooling.

"Hey, asshole! There're people here! You could've killed 'em with that stunt!"

"What stunt? What did I do?" He stood there, air around him swirling, light bending through it as if he were underwater himself and maybe he was. Though his voice was clear enough.

Her arms went out to her sides. "Everything! All this! You're doing it, right?!"

"Not hardly." He shifted his weight and turned, hands going from hips to the top of his head, indicating himself as if he were unfamiliar and new. "But this vehicle is helping, even if it didn't want to."

She marched toward him, not sure at all what was supposed to come of it. She didn't have the gun or even the knife or half the backbone of his sister. She just had herself and her anger.

"What are you doing?"

"Kevin Lee? Whelan? That's you, right?"

"Who's askin'?" And in that question, his voice changed, taking on some of the lilt and drawl that echoed Sue's.

"Me. For your sister is who. You almost killed her!"

"Almost is a fine thing. Almost dead. Almost alive." He shrugged maddeningly. "Hey, you ain't seen a person I'm looking for, have you? You'd mistake it for a thing, you would. Wouldn't even give it a second look. Anyway, I turned this damn river upside down trying to find 'em."

Cait froze where she was.

He's asking. Either it's a game or he doesn't know. And he doesn't seem clear-eyed enough to be playing.

"What makes you think I'd even help you?"

"Oh, you look a trusting sort. I could make it worth your while too. More buried treasure in the water than on the land, y'know. Is there a bauble or a glimmering you'd be fixing to want?"

"Yeah, sorry." Cait breathed hard after.

He appraised her openly and let her know that she wasn't worth bothering with, a penny not worth making a wish on. "Hey. How long do you think someone could might hold their breath anyway?" He then pointed to the van. "She could be almost dead or alive right now."

"You son of a bitch."

He raised his hand as if to strike her from a distance but stopped himself. "That is not a thing for you to say."

"I did and I'll do it again."

"Go make yourself of some use to her or step to me. One of those ways will get you not killed. I guarantee it." He turned and walked diagonally up the steep concrete side, knowing the choice she'd make before she did.

"Goddammit," she muttered in an effort to block the feeling of futility that took her over as she turned and half-ran to the van. She clambered in through the half-open back door thankful that she didn't have to wrack herself against a second time. Inside, assorted junk and clothes and dishes were strewn hell to breakfast as Mom would have said. The whole thing had been upended and shaken until nothing was where it started. It all smelled sodden, never to be dry again. There was a weird oblong of light, reflecting off the water coming into the van. The water that Lilah's head was half-submerged in. She struggled and coughed, fighting for breath.

"Oh God, hold on." Cait stretched herself forward and tugged at her shoulder, trying to pull her back from the water. The woman felt like she weighed as much as a sack of feathers.

"Ow! Get off!"

"I'm trying to help you! Calm down."

"Okay, okay." She hacked up water, wet the entire way through.

Cait looked at her and wondered how she was still alive, skinny to the point of being bony, long iron-gray and black and white hair intermixed and thrown over her face. Lilah grabbed a handful of it and tossed it back, so she could get a good look at her rescuer. She shook her head slowly, somewhere between disappointment and disbelief.

"Wasn't sure you'd ever make it in time," she said but offered no explanation when Cait asked.

After that, the both of them sprawled out in the mess of the old woman's life in her van, gasping for air that was hard to come.

"You gonna be okay?" Cait asked. She felt stupid, all her words felt backward. "I mean, your van. That was…"

"Is just a van. Was a good one. It came to me from my son after he gave up his wild years. Took me months to get the smell of woman out of it." She slumped on the concrete near the algae-washed bank of the river. All the debris that she'd seen had been swept away. That must have been it. Things don't just disappear.

Flowers had grown between the concrete sheets of the riverway. Mostly yellow, dandelions and daisies and others she couldn't identify, bright seams of gold and white. There were so many that they burst and overflowed, insistent and cloying.

Cait was sure she would have noticed them before, but hadn't. They grew only where the resurgent river had washed through and nowhere else. The concrete was dry to the touch now, warm in the sun.

"He'd have liked you."

"Not a lot to like about me."

"Got that Ivory Girl look, under that mop." Lilah pulled Cait's hair back out from over her eyes and she was too drained to protest. "You'd have needed a baseball bat to stop him."

"I'd have used it." She pulled away from the touch, realizing it was too much now. Then she stood and dusted off her hands. "What happened here?" she asked, needing to talk about something else. Even a joke of desire was too much.

Who would even want this mess?

Lilah shrugged. "River stole my goddamn bottle is what happened."

"But it left you flowers."

"Better than my son would've."

Cait couldn't do anything but laugh at that. It was better than crying or screaming.

"It's okay. You've done enough, girl. I thank you."

The woman's skein of a hand lay over Cait's own, unthinkably light, almost insubstantial.

"Will you be safe? What are you going to do?"

"Don't worry about me. You already had your moment of that. Job's done."

If only.

The others waited by their cars, Roger and Misty holding one another, Marky eyeing the river like he was counting all the fish that were getting away.

"Going to have to do laundry all over again," Misty said. "What a thing."

"Looks like everyone survived?" Cait asked.

"We're all okay, but you look like a drowned cat," Marky said with a smile.

"You should see the other guy."

"And Lilah?"

"I don't know. I don't know her. Her van's a mess, but she seems like she's ready to walk away from it."

He jabbed a cigarette in his mouth, somehow dry after all this, and let it hang from his lip. "The river does provide, but it does the other, too. Even out here." Then he looked right at Cait. "You find the guy you wanted?"

"No," she said. "But he found me well enough." Weight returned to her shoulders in spite of survival and the profusion of manic yellow flowers like phantom spring. "You all take care of yourselves."

"It's what we do."

CHAPTER SIX

The Mercury came to a stop approaching Broadway under a brick fa-cade that had been painted in a giant woodblock-style image of human figures wearing suits and dresses, all of them with cartoon skulls for heads, both festive and mournful. A nearby billboard was printed up in blinding mustard-yellow with a strange, mirrored E logo that she didn't recognize, so bright that it hurt to look at in the afternoon sun. The slogan beneath it read YOU DON'T HAVE TO TAKE IT ANYMORE but nothing else.

What is it? Everything? If they can get rid of that, sign me up.

She needed some shoes and something to eat and to figure out what the hell was going on. She marched into the variety store next door to the LA Central Market and came out with a pair of high-top Converse that didn't match her outfit but would take a tornado to rip off her feet.

Then she sat down at a counter in the market and ordered enough tacos to get her stomach to shut up, suddenly not only hungry but starving. She tried not to think too hard. She'd been chasing something and instead it had come to her, so maybe that was a better approach now.

She took a big bite of carnitas and tortilla with salsa hot enough to make her eyes water and a gulp of sweet lime Jarritos. She let the burn settle all the way down.

Sue didn't set me up. But she didn't know what I was going to walk into. Neither did I. Just charged into it like an idiot. Just wanted to find him but had no clue what to do when I did. Dog chasing muscle cars and surprised when they get run over.

It fits.

She took another bite and chewed on that. A newspaper left open on the counter caught her eye: a picture of a couple, staring into their swim-ming pool. She was in a housecoat, he in pajamas, but they the clothes were old, not contemporary at all. In the water under the glass-smooth surface was a late-fifties Cadillac. Someone had parked it in the family pool. Weird.

The submerged Caddy, the one in the picture, that happened in '61. But the story was about Annabelle and Leo Mauritz, who thought they saw the same thing in their backyard at the same address, just a couple days ago. Saw it, touched it, screamed at it, saw someone in the driver's seat. Even called the police about it. But there was nothing when they arrived.

"It just melted," the story said, implying that there was something more but unable to prove a bit of it. The paper ran the picture of when it happened more than twenty-five years ago but didn't have one for today.

Because melted.

Cait didn't know what it meant but she thought about what she'd seen in the water an hour ago. It wasn't just a flood. Not a today flood. It was a flood from today and yesterday and something bit at her making her think about the golden serpent and how that was neither but more of tomorrow. More than one thing happening at once, collapsing as it did.

Horse and buggy. That's gotta be eighty, a hundred years ago? LA used to flood regularly. Fifty years ago or so, pretty spectacularly. Washed out bridges, marooned studios and houses. Frogtown got clobbered too. That delivery truck maybe.

And the bones. All those bones. Everything collapsed and happening at once. Even stuff that hasn't yet.

Aware she'd stopped chewing, she swallowed and took another pull from the bottle to wash it down.

Maybe what's going on isn't what it looks like. I was thinking water, but maybe it's not that.

Maybe it's time.

She let the afternoon crowd mill and pass all around her. When she unfocused her eyes, it all became one thing, not a hundred or a thousand people but all one thing, a presence. All the individual words were lost and became a gentle seethe of sound, barely more than noise. She breathed it in until the thought of her having to meet with Open Door surfaced and punched a hole in the stillness.

Now there was just the din, a thousand people all wanting something. Everyone wanted something. No connection. No unity.

Walking past everyone and the worlds they carried with them, Cait walked lightly in her new Chucks.

෴

Open Door's new office was in a nondescript shop front next to a Salvadorean restaurant and market near Third and New Hampshire. The building was an old-style block with businesses on the ground level and what could have been apartments above, but they felt too uniform, too regular to be occupied now, not by anyone with personalities. Usually there were flags hanging off balconies or barbecue grills or bikes or precariously piled junk. None of that. All drawn curtains and nothing else.

Yuppies or robots.

Cait parked the Mercury on the street and looked at the card twice more to make sure she had the right place, as much as she could read the marred and melting ink lines. Melting like Cadillacs. It was. The sign over the door said POLICE ANNEX with the second word crossed out by red spray paint, dripping at both ends. She hauled on the door and walked in, uneasy and at sea.

Guess this is a feeling I should get used to.

The place smelled like an old laundromat, mildewed and dully of detergent.

"Can I help you?" asked a smartly dressed Black woman behind a desk. Behind her was an open bullpen of desks, some shoved against walls, some against one another. Not so much in the interest of saving space but because it was the most convenient arrangement. Design by entropy. Most of them were occupied, some folks working, some bullshitting and without seriousness. The place felt cheap and piecemealed-together out of bureaucratic hand-me-downs and surplus but functional at least.

"I'm here to see Trager."

"*Detective* Trager?"

"Yeah. Cait MacReady. I was told to come by this afternoon and here I am."

"Indeed you are," she said after giving Cait a glance up and down, unimpressed.

"It's the Cookie Princess!" a familiar voice shouted from the back of the room. "Let's give her a royal welcome." Moreno's voice rang across the room and everyone else stopped what they were doing, heads swiveling to Cait.

"Hello, Cookie Princess," they sing-songed, like a schoolyard chorus.

Moreno stood there, hands on hips, taking Cait's measure, making her feel like something you'd step over on the sidewalk.

I can get mad, or I can take the joke. If I get mad, it never ends. Ever.

"Oh shit, was I supposed to bring 'em this time?" Cait clapped her hands to her pockets and patted herself down. "I thought you guys liked doughnuts."

"I like doughnuts," offered one of them, feet up on his desk.

"Shut up, Simmons."

"She's the one who—"

"Shut up, Ruben."

"Oh, let 'em talk, Moreno," Cait teased.

Moreno went from jovial ribbing to narrow-eyed glowering. "What are you doing here?" She walked right up to Cait and moved in a little too close. Her eyes flared for just a moment, daring Cait to take a step back or forward.

"Your *boss* asked me to come in."

"Then you better go see him." To the woman at the desk. "No need to ring upstairs, Wanda. I'll walk her back."

"Just leave her in one piece," she warned.

"No problem," Cait said before Moreno could.

"Feeling kind of invincible?" she asked Cait as they walked a central aisle between the desks on the ground floor.

"Not really. But I'm done with being walked all over."

They climbed up a set of stairs in the back that felt forgotten. This passage, at least, had been recently painted, but it came out uneven, bubbling underneath the corners from long-ago water damage. Every other stair creaked in an off-note.

"You're the walk-er or the walk-ee," she said. "You want to tell me what this is about?"

"I will if Trager says so."

"So it's not about the canals? You know LAPD didn't find anything, right? Just some tracks that they couldn't match to anything and then sent us the casts."

"Because that's what they do with anything that they're afraid of, right?"

"Doesn't take a genius to know that, so don't think you're a genius."

They came to the top of the stairs where there was a cluster of offices and a big wire cage in the back behind those. The area on the other side of the fence was well lit, stacked with metal shelving, boxes and books and unidentifiable things wrapped up in green hefty bags, all of them tagged.

"Yeah, don't go in the Cage."

"Got it. Evidence?"

"Just the Cage," she said like it was a rule. Then she pointed to a frosted glass pane with a wooden door set next to it. There was no name on any of it.

The detective knocked on the door twice. "Moreno. Someone here to see you."

"Come on in," came the muffled reply.

The door was held for Cait and she stepped inside, clearly hearing Moreno sniff once loudly as she passed.

"Swampy," she said, drawing out the *S*.

"Yeah, I wrestled the LA River this afternoon."

He watched them for a moment, tensing enough to make Cait think he was going to have to intervene. "Sit down. Both of you," he said without humor.

His desk was clean and Cait suspected that took a superhuman effort on his part. That or he'd just moved in and it was yet to be buried.

"Moreno, what else do we have on that thing in Venice?"

Her grin was triumphant. "Goose egg. Just the cast and that just looks like junk to me. No blood traces that they could come up with. Waste of—"

"Didn't ask about that. And Miss Sue?"

"She doesn't like cops," Moreno said with a growl. "She's angry that we went through her things. She says it's none of our business."

Trager scoffed at that. "Was that to LAPD or to you?"

"Blues won't touch her. They heard 'thing' and ran."

"I went and saw her today," Cait said. "She talked to me well enough."

"Do tell." Moreno looked deeply and steepled her fingers beneath her chin, daring Cait to misstep.

"I'm the one who saved her life. She feels like she owes me something. But she wanted to make damn sure I wasn't law before she opened her mouth more than a peep."

"'Law,' huh? We're deep south, are we?"

"Appalachia. Doesn't sound like she's from a big place at all. Well, not a big town but maybe a big place. Make sense?"

"Yeah," Trager said. "What's she doing out here amongst the heathen?"

"Looking for family. A brother named Lee. That's about all I got out of her. He was writing but he stopped."

Trager and Moreno hung there, waiting.

"I didn't say she talked *a lot*."

"Did she know anything about the thing that attacked her?" Moreno asked.

"No. I doubt she's even seen an alligator at the zoo."

"And yet motivated enough to cross the country."

"I didn't say it made sense."

"Of course, it doesn't make sense. That's why it's on us." His sigh was heavy.

"What about the man she was with?" Moreno asked. "You said you saw someone with her. Was that her brother?"

"She didn't talk like he was. I mean, maybe? But they didn't seem friendly. No joyous reunion, and that's what she crossed the states to find."

"Maybe she crossed the country to do some revenge. Hate would make you do something like that," Trager said.

"No, it wasn't that. She seemed, well, disappointed. But it wasn't hate."

"Can you describe him any better?" Moreno asked, maybe too eagerly.

"No. And…" Cait struggled for the best way to say it, but it kept slipping through her and escaping like runoff.

"Go ahead."

"This is going to sound weird and dumb."

"I can't imagine," she said.

"She did, like, a little magic spell to help find him. Right there in the hospital room. And it was weird."

"What *isn't* weird with you?"

"Moreno."

The detective lifted her hands up and away from the desktop and she pushed back in her chair some but did not ease down past that.

Cait wrapped her arms around herself, aware that she could still smell the river in her clothes and it wasn't reassuring. "It felt *real*."

"Real?"

Cait nodded.

"That's bullshit," Moreno grouched. "Are you going to listen to this—"

Trager held a hand up. "I said *quiet*. Cait."

"Yeah?"

"You know we're not a usual police outfit, right?"

"Sure. It's like *Barney Miller* meets *The Outer Limits*."

"Right. Well some of us think there's something weird or are at least open to things we can't explain immediately. And some of us are here because we're excellent cops and sometimes you need to be grounded. Detective Moreno is one of those. She takes a lot of convincing to look past things sometimes."

Moreno smiled thinly. "I don't believe in bullshit."

Cait let go of herself. "Well this particular bullshit worked."

"I don't follow you."

"I wasn't just down at the river because I wanted to get my feet wet and maybe my leg broken," Cait said. "I went down there because Sue said I'd find something valuable down there. Something useful anyways.

"So I went down there, middle of the day, sunny day, right?"

"Sure."

"And I'm looking, not sure what for, when without warning a wall of water comes flooding through the canal way. Not a cloud in the sky. So it's not rain."

"They let out some water upstream," Moreno suggested. "After the storm a couple days ago."

Which explains the things I saw in that water, right? Or how the concrete was wet before? Or the flowers? Or none of that.

Cait just stared. "Forget it."

"Maybe you tripped over a bigfoot."

She clenched her fist but didn't get up.

"Or scraped your leg getting into a flying saucer?"

"Moreno," Trager warned.

"I'm not going to listen to a strung-out basket case. That's a waste of time."

"And every witness you ever talked to was one hundred percent composed and perfect, right?" Trager was pointing now. "You know we throw those out. Nobody's that cool unless they're making things up."

"Listen—"

"Enough. Go on back downstairs and keep Ruben out of trouble."

Moreno stood and walked out, composed and cool, every fold of her skirt suit perfect and clean. She was everything Cait was pretending to be every day she went to work and Cait hated it and hated herself for wanting that. It boiled in her heart like blackest crude.

"I'm sorry," Trager said by way of apology. "That was a mistake. I should have figured your style and hers would clash."

"It's okay. I'm a big girl."

"Not sure you're big enough to keep pushing Moreno's buttons like that, so maybe back off." He tapped a pencil on the desk as he tried to string his next question together.

"What?"

"Sue is, what, a witch?"

Cait shifted in the chair, anxious. "I don't know what she is. I've never met anyone like her. Super-intense, just sitting there. Even after having a bite taken out of her, super-focused. Touchy about Jesus, too."

"Who isn't?"

"Don't tell me that…"

"No, just had a firm upbringing. Though what I've seen has made me question that something fierce."

Cait held her tongue. "There was something wrong in the river today," she said finally.

"Wrong how?"

"I don't have a word for it. I saw stuff in the water, shooting past, being carried along. Old trucks, bones, even critters. It was all wrong."

"You're going to have to be clearer. First rain of the year always cleans out weird leftover stuff from the dry season."

"It wasn't like that. Here." She pulled the folded-up newspaper from her purse, damp but still readable. "You see this?"

"Someone had a hell of a night. That's a sweet ride too. What kind of fool puts that car in the water?"

"That happened in '61," Cait said. "But someone just a couple days ago said they saw and touched the same thing. Down to the driver behind the wheel."

"But when the police got there, there was nothing to see or to touch, right?"

"Sound familiar? It's happened to me twice now." She left out the vision in her bathtub. That was just an anxiety freak-out. She was already unreliable as it was. Didn't need to push it any further.

"The thing in Venice and this river wash? Cait, the big thing in front of me is a murder, not this craziness."

"But it was a crazy murder, right? And where are those fish now?"

"Digested. Coroner suggested that stomach acid did a number on them, made 'em dissolve completely."

"I'm sure Moreno believes that."

"I said that I was open, not that I'm a wild-eyed believer." His lips tugged down.

"Which leaves me where?" She demanded. "I *know* what happened to me."

He brought his hands up flat, soothing. "Okay, settle down. I appreciate your assistance this morning and I'm glad you came by today. And if you can get Sue to cooperate with us, that's even better. But right now we have to get on this developer thing and get something to appease everyone."

"So someone murdered him by stuffing fish that are millions of years out of time, fish that should be fossils, down his throat? And you think *I'm* crazy." The chair shifted back and scraped as she stood quickly.

"He drowned, and that's all anyone else needs to know for now. Hell, we only have half the files that the original detectives pulled together. It's a goddamned mess. This other stuff is just muddying things."

"Or it's all the same thing." She dragged out the space between the last three words.

"We just have to figure out what that is."

"Yeah, I guess. Fine. Can I go now? I've got some stuff I want to go check out."

"Anything you want to talk about?"

"Nah, it's just gonna *muddy* things." She stood up and felt like she'd been out in the rain all night long. Looking down, she caught the sight of the clean white rubber on her sneakers and that much cheered her for just a moment.

"Don't go messing around in things you shouldn't," Trager said.

"Like what?"

"You'll know."

"One hopes," she said as she left the office and marched down the stairs.

She got out of the building and saw a tall and skinny brown-haired man checking out the Mercury admiringly. A cigarette burned between his fingertips. He was exhaling a cloud of blue smoke, lazy and careless.

"Excuse me," Cait said, walking past him to get away.

"Hey, that's a beautiful car," he said. He was younger than Cait had first guessed, maybe twenties. His eyes were green and he smiled like it was a good way to get out of or maybe into anything, well-practiced.

"Thanks."

"Where'd you get it?"

"Uh, a friend left it to me." That was mostly not a lie.

"Yeah, don't see many like this one anymore. Is that a Mercer?"

"Mercury," she corrected.

He hissed a breath in-between his teeth, wincing. "Yeah, sorry. Mercury. Of course."

"Are you with them?" she asked, tilting toward the Open Door office with her jaw.

"Yeah? That obvious?"

"You don't look like you're here for the pupusas next door."

"They're awful good. I've eaten there for lunch a couple times a week since I got transferred here."

"Huh. Where from?" Cait popped the door open but wasn't in a hurry to jump inside just yet. "If that's not too nosy."

"It's not." He took a draw off his cigarette. "Keaton Memorial Station." He looked like he'd sent all the dishes flying instead of simply whipping the tablecloth out from under them. "I mean Rampart. Yeah."

"Keaton?"

"I said Rampart. You heard me." He stubbed the rest of the cigarette out on his shoe. "Hey I gotta go. Back to work."

"Well, don't eat too many pupusas, else you won't fit in those slacks anymore."

"I'll take it under advisement. I'm Joe. Parker. By the way."

She smiled. "Smooth. I'm Cait, but don't expect to see me again, not here."

"You don't like cops?" he asked, shoulders sunk just a little.

"They don't seem to like me all that much."

She slammed the door and left it at that.

CHAPTER SEVEN

Hollywood Boulevard lit up, an unwavering line of candy-color gloss on trash left out in plain sight. Fifty years of reputation covered enough to keep people coming back, hungry for glitter and loss. Tourists gawked at old theater marquees and drunks passed out in the gutter before the cops came and kicked them out of sight. Faded glamor of old names and facades splashed with incandescent lights or the red of rollers, scraggly perps spread-eagled on stucco or brick for nothing more than being the wrong intensity of weird. Freaks still walked the street, eyeing their luck-less kin because that was what the place demanded. Liberty spikes two feet high and years out of date, mohawks or braids with chains interwoven. The manufactured history of the dream industry collided with outsiders and weirdos and people who didn't have a place anywhere else, leaving beautiful and hostile debris. And places like the Last Prayer club, where what was left of No Tomorrows still held court, even if their Queen was not what she once was.

Creeping until she could find parking, Cait slid up a side street. She missed setting the brake and the car rolled back onto the curb then jarred enough to throw her in the seat. Cursing, she jammed the brake and slammed the dashboard.

"Don't you fucking start on me now."

I shouldn't be here.

The sun had plunged and was out, leaving only the writhing club lights on the street. This was always the worst time, knowing she was going to be surrounded by the dark and everything in it. Anticipating and imagining. She struggled to push through, just like going to see Vince. Just like work. Just like everything. Even nighttime wasn't downtime. It was hiding time. Wait everything out time. Running on defense until exhaustion.

But she had to be out now. The club was never open during daylight. Nor did it close at 2 a.m. like a respectable dive might. Only when the sun scraped itself over the skyline to the south did the place clear out and lock up. People would be there now.

Her hand shook. She just stared at it.

"Don't you start either."

She sat and breathed but the feeling didn't go away. Being in the moment only made it worse. Maybe it never would stop. Events and blame and consequence all swirling around her as hard and strong as the water that had run her leg against the concrete earlier today. Rico and Ariela and the book and—

Cait closed her hands and slammed them repeatedly into the steering wheel, long and hard enough to feel something, anything, to cut through the nerving grip on her. Red pain throbbed dully in her hands. She focused on that. That was real. Not the imagined stuff that she tortured herself with, not the guilt and weight that came with that.

She grabbed the mirror and pulled it down to get a look at herself. What looked back seemed as ludicrous as a cat pulled out of a bathtub: fur plastered to limbs and frame too small and thin to be threatening, head too big to be anything but pathetic. Passing lights of a cop car painted her red and blue, colors never mixing. She broke the stare.

Fuck it. Just fuck it. I'm gonna find out who's haunting me with this Ariela shit even if I get some broken bones for the trouble. At least I'll know then.

The door slammed hard enough to rattle her own fillings. Clothes still rumpled from the river and unruly tangle of hair on her head, she at least had new Chucks to carry her there. All she had to do was follow the sound, that insistent and metallic beat that used the buildings around the club as resonators, loudspeakers, air-raid sirens. It was war on the floor there every night, No Tomorrows and all the other outsiders against everyone else.

Down to Hollywood and a block of street vendors and lingerie-clad mannequins in glittering metallic wigs, dudes wearing just enough leather to keep from being arrested. Then up Cherokee, just like last time. Only Link had been there with her. Even if he refused to step inside.

Shit.

The girls were still working the door. She'd never learned their names. This time, one of them was dressed head to toe in something glossy and poreless, either rubber or vinyl, that wrapped her better than her skin ever had. Banks of lights under the marquee raised a pair of matched and streaking highlights, bright white parallel lines that wrapped to every bend in her flesh. Beyond that, she was featureless and flattened, clothing squeezing identity out. She wore makeup, a broad swipe of black across her eyes and temples, with two black circles on each cheek and black lipstick that curled down like fangs at either corner.

The other one wore some kind of deranged princess outfit in pink and white leather, looking like cotton candy and cyanide. Taffeta and ruffles hung around her shoulders and hips, like half-torn and useless wings that advertised a kind of brokenness. Her face was white and without expression. Her hair was so blonde that any texture or depth was lost, an immense flatness.

As without, so within, huh?

"Dress code," the one in black warned. Her voice was empty, bottomless in contempt. Cait wasn't worth notice.

"You two remember me?" she demanded. She had cleared her throat five times on the way up, making sure she wouldn't crack.

"What's there to remember?" said the princess.

"I was here before the Queen died."

They looked at one another and smiled with a twist that would have wrecked the Pope.

The one in black spoke. "What are you talking about? The Queen's inside. Her reign never ended."

"Ariela's dead."

"But the Queen lives on." Her fingers drummed up and down on latex kid gloves that reached nearly to her shoulder. The flesh still showing made snow look dirty. "Go on home, whoever you think you are. You're not dressed to be received."

"But the sneakers are a nice touch." The princess pursed her lips.

Cait took a step forward. "And what if I go in anyway?" There was no weight in her voice. She sounded hollow even to herself.

"You might sucker punch one of us."

"But you can't be in two places at once? Or can you?"

The giggle at the end felt like broken glass under Cait's tongue. She curled up her aching fist but didn't raise it yet.

The twins stepped closer as if sharing a body, simultaneous. "Whatever you think is in there is not worth the new teeth you'll need after you eat shit on the sidewalk." They both pointed down with their left index fingers. "And you'll eat it. Right. There."

They pointed to the same place before them. Perhaps it was a trick of the shadow and light, but Cait could see the stains of blood there, sure as the lipstick that hadn't come off the windshield of the Mercury. Someone had been humbled there and it would probably happen again tonight.

"I'll come back. That's a promise," Cait growled.

"We can't wait to see what you'll wear." They waved to Cait's back but did not take their eyes off her.

She drifted back to the Mercury with her guts feeling like they'd been scooped out for autopsy or maybe there were fish in there. She opened the door and slumped across the steering wheel, just listening to the engine purr, waiting for release. Something rustled between buildings ahead of her, up the street. Something that glittered and caught light as it turned in the shadows and watched. It moved on four legs with furtiveness, not stealth, as if it were unaccustomed to anything but strolling down the middle of the sidewalk. Like its strength had been taken away and it would never hunt again.

Tired. Seeing things.

Gotta go home.

After she gathered the strength, Cait drove but not to home. She followed Hollywood Boulevard out of the neon and freakshow all the way down to Hyperion and the freeway sludge up to Glendale Boulevard. Maybe she'd even be there before the place closed. It was the only thing that made any sense now. She couldn't go home. That apartment wasn't home. It was a collection of boxes in which there were more boxes. She hadn't made a life there, barely a subsistence.

She had to go somewhere real. Do something real.

Cait nosed the Mercury up the concrete grade to where it leveled off, just into Silverlake. She kept her eyes out for the strip mall, breath tightening as she imagined the lights were off and she was closed for the night. Night was settling in hard and would just get worse all the way until morning. She wasn't sure she could take that, not now, not alone.

There. The pink neon sign is still on.

DISTRESS.

She pulled hard left across oncoming traffic and came to a lurching stop then exited the car. One foot dragged after another, marathon miles tailing off behind her. She pushed against the door and it scraped on the tile like it always did, jagged asphalt-black arc torn in the floor for as long as she could remember. The air inside was a blinding mix of cigarettes and perfume, ripe cosmetics and the sour crinkling of dyes underlaid with bleach. Cait had spent too many hours here, feeling half-high upon leaving, whether it be from the results or the fumes didn't matter. It felt like home too-long gone from and she wanted to just sink to the floor and take it in.

"Sorry, hon. We're closed." Trace had her back to the door, sweeping up a dustpan full of bright arterial-red hair and debris. Getting no response, she turned slowly in warning. She was teenage skinny but radiated palpable menace, figuring she'd have to fight to evict whoever wandered in. She wore boy's jean shorts tight and low across her hips and a sleeveless tee that said SOLID GOLD BITCH in flowing script silkscreen that glittered like a shattered rainbow.

"Can't you hear? We're *closed*. I got plans tonight."

Cait stood there and didn't move. That was it. There was nothing else. No reserves to draw upon, not more force of will to keep going.

"Trace."

Trace's eyes narrowed, and she stared as she stood there, holding the red clippings. "You know me. Do I know you, girl?"

"It's Cait," she said without breaking. She was proud of herself for getting that much out. "Cait MacReady."

"Cait?"

"I'm sorry. I haven't been around for. I had to…" The words tumbled out of her without meaning and in fading strength. "I had to move."

Trace dropped the broom and pan and crossed the room in a second. She held Cait tight and Cait wanted to run from it but was unable to break away.

"What happened to you, Cait? Who fucked up your hair like that?"

"I did. I fucked it all up."

A moment later, Cait was in the chair and faced away from the mirror. Anxiety filtered through her, but a different flavor of it than that she'd been dining on for months.

"I was going to ask you what color you wanted," Trace said. "But you look like what you find at the wrong end of a long chain of bad choices."

"No good ones made themselves apparent."

"Sorry."

"Don't be. I didn't aim for all this shit, but it just kept happening to me. I held it off for…"

How long? Months? When did things stop being weird? Did they?

"It's okay. We all run into bad patches. Sometimes we drive ourselves there, you know?"

"Living it."

"Honestly, girl. What is this crap? Clairol mousey brown? I think it's gray cover and not actually color."

"I don't know. I did it a while ago. I just wanted to be normal."

"You fool anyone?"

"Doesn't seem like it."

Cait settled in to the chair further, letting gravity hold her down. With Trace's gentle needling, she relaxed. Strong fingers gripped and worked her scalp and she felt it all the way down to her hips and past. The last time she'd been here was where a lot of the crazy felt like it had started, but maybe it could be short-circuited. It didn't have to happen again and again.

Rinse, no repeat.

"Okay, sleepyhead." Trace waved fingers in front of Cait's eyes. "If I get a little dye on your blouse, well maybe that's just my way of telling you that you should burn it.

"I was gonna do that anyway. Took a bath in the river today."

"You really need adult supervision."

After the dye set, Trace's clippers danced all around Cait's hearing, at the edges of her eyesight. She didn't know how long, but just long enough.

"Okay, let's get you to take a look at this." Trace spun her around fast and caught her, stopping her just as hard.

Cait looked at herself in the mirror. She still felt pale and drawn, eyes sunk in dark circles without foundation or eyeliner to hide them. Her hair was a coppery red, maybe just a shade brighter than what it would have been naturally had she not spent half a lifetime dying and messing with it in a hundred different ways. None of them had ever felt right so she'd just kept looking. This felt like something she could work from, finally.

"Yeah, I don't know what was going on with your right side. Looks like it got cut kinda close then just left to grow out."

"That's a long story." Her hair was longer on the left, framing her face unevenly but not without character. "You fixed it." She brought her hands up to just below her eyes to hide her face breaking.

"Hey. Hey. I didn't do anything more than clean things up some. You know you can get heads to turn still."

"I don't feel like it."

Don't want to feel like it.

Trace pulled up the stool and sat down then took Cait's hand in hers. "I heard about Rico. But I can't believe this is *all* about that."

"Big part of it," Cait said. She sucked in a heavy breath.

"You wanna talk?"

Cait nodded. "No."

Trace squeezed the hand and set it back down. "I'll call Marcela. She'll understand."

"Oh no, Trace. I don't want to intrude."

"You're not getting out of it that easy," Trace said as she dialed home. Then she called another number and punched in the salon's callback.

Cait stood up and admired herself in the mirror, not hiding for the first time in a long one. "I'll drive."

"No, you won't. I rang Link. I'm not getting in that devil car."

Cait didn't fight it.

Link's piecemeal fifties/sixties Cadillac rolled into the lot and idled rough enough to strip old paint. The window came down and he smiled upon seeing Cait.

"Good god, woman? Where you been?"

"Out of commission."

"But I brought her back to life," Trace joked. "You wanna earn some money and take us to dinner, maybe a drive after?"

"I'm all about the money. Wilmington Slicks got a slot opening for Los Lobos and some band from Ireland I ain't never heard of. Need a new jacket by Tuesday to look my best."

Cait and Trace slid into the back seat. "Thanks for coming, Link. I'm not allowed to drive."

"You were sittin' on that car like it was yours. The Mercury with the cloud of bad vibes."

"Yeah. It was a gift."

"Some gifts should be lost and never looked for again."

"It would just find its way home."

"Peruvian-Italian, Link! Don Felix on—"

"Yeah, on Sunset. It's there or the Nayarit for you. Or home after."

The Caddy went down Glendale like a slow landslide of metal, streaming Jerry Lee Lewis through open windows and off tarnished chrome.

Cait picked at the strips of beef and tomatoes mixed with slivers of fried potatoes, hungry but not. Talking had taken it out of her. Trace and Link took it pretty well, hearing that Cait had made up the book that ended the world. Or would have had she not doomed Ariela to being consumed by whatever it was she called or created. And the bad cop. And Rico. And freaking out after, being exhausted by hanging on by her fingernails during the daylight and only half-wanting to survive it all most nights.

"Look, Cait," Trace said. "I can't address all the *Twilight Zone* stuff. I know something happened. And it must have been wild for you to go anywhere with those No Tomorrows vampires.

"But lemme talk about something real." She took a long drink of Tecate from the can, her third or fourth. "The only real thing I know in there. Rico went and got himself killed."

"I killed him," Cait said.

"Knock that off." Link gestured with a glass of ice water, slopping some.

The liquid glittered in the Christmas lights inside the place, cycling through the many colors as it hung too long in the air. Cait was able to watch it changing shape in the arc of gravity and wondered why she could.

He continued. "Rico wandered into a thing that he couldn't get out of. He'd been hungry and pushing things as long as I've known him."

"Listen to him, girl. Rico stuck himself in business that he couldn't get out of. He shoulda known better."

"But won't ever get a chance to learn," Cait said.

"This other girl, this Ariela?" Link asked. "What was her angle in things?"

Cait shrugged and finished the beer she'd nursed since getting there. "I guess she saw something in my work, in this thing that I made."

Wasn't any point in telling them that she knew about the book before I'd even finished it. They're just trying to help and having them figure out which came first will just mess things up.

"She was like your first fan," Trace said. "Right?"

"Yeah, I guess." The feeling that phrase evoked was uneasy-making.

"And she ran into something she couldn't control either. She just got caught up in this storm or whatever it was that happened. That you *think* you made."

"That I made possible. She called it."

"My head hurts thinking about this," Link said.

"I haven't hit you with the real brain-melter either," Cait teased.

"That doesn't matter," Trace said. "You're eating yourself with guilt for something that isn't your fault. Rico was a nice guy and a great dancer and probably real good in bed if you like that sort of thing."

"I did," Cait said with a half-smile. "A lot."

"And he threw that all away trying to chase down the score that got him killed and almost got you." Trace took Cait's hands in her own. "Don't feel guilty because you survived and he didn't. Go ahead and mourn him but what you've been doing doesn't do him or you any good."

Cait swiped at the welling tears and nodded, finally adding a weak "Okay."

"I don't nothing about nothing but cars and guitars, Cait." Link's eyes went dark and serious in the strange rainbow light of the place. "But anyone who coulda walked away from you isn't worth the tears."

Trace laughed. "You're not sweet on our Cait, are you?"

"Nope. Just stating the facts."

Trace cajoled Link into driving them out to Griffith Park to look at the lights of the city and to help her sober up some with fresh night air. It hadn't been so hard.

Lights glittered in a vast grid cut through by rivers of vehicles, red and white eyes teeming in the hundreds, all frozen into arteries of color. The skyline of downtown jabbed up like spines made of jewels, all sharp enough to cut by sight. Smog and haze and streamers of fog pushed through it all and the whole place seemed like it was breathing. The rhythm was uneven and palsied, sifting through layers of atmosphere, the twinkling of earthbound stars.

Cait just watched. It wasn't a place any longer. It was just vast seas of color and life and energy. Electricity was the water now.

"You feel better?" Trace asked. She fanned herself with the collar of her T-shirt, face still flushed and gleaming in the cooling air.

"I guess," Cait said. "Probably not as good as you. Marcela's going to give you hell for getting drunk without her."

"Well we're not going to tell her, are we?"

"Secret's safe with me."

"Good." Trace leaned on the concrete railing of the observation deck, half-supporting herself. "You know there're people you can come to anytime, right? That you don't have to do all this alone?"

"I was just surviving," Cait said.

"That isn't enough." Her grip went tight and she was strong as steel.

Cait wanted to borrow some of that, just for a little while.

The night air hissed hard and she looked out at the expanse of blue and white and yellow light, the entire city at her feet. Something shifted and the air went dead and cool, the whole world's breath being drawn in and down. She reached for her own breath and couldn't find it.

The lights of the landscape went out block by block, starting in different places, different neighborhoods. Every moment there were fewer lights, empty black spreading out like fast cancer, eating the jewels, eating the city.

Then the waters rose. Roaring over the sand spits of beaches and out of the concrete channel of the river, black water gushed out and up, consuming architecture, lapping at buildings and houses for a moment before erasing them, submerging them. The worst part of it was there was no sound, not of gasps or of screams or even people trying to breathe. They were just gone beneath the spreading slick surface that eddied in the city's disappearing.

The black water filled the basin that Los Angeles had sat in once before. And Cait couldn't even breathe to scream now. The Pacific reached in and drowned the city, smothering it in its sleep with water that was opaque as obsidian. Only a chunk of Palos Verdes stuck out above the surface, amplifying the isolation by its presence. The water lapped all the way to the San Gabriels and Santa Monicas, the Whittier Hills and Montebello and as far south as she could see was only a faintly-disturbed liquid surface.

The risen moon now reflected on the shimmering stillness and the city that had been silenced. The only shapes beyond nature were isolated bits of building tall enough to still be visible. In the water, things moved. Things without name or shape recognized. They rippled lazily at the surface, having all the time they wanted to live in this new world.

Then she heard the chorus, all those who had drowned before and those who would yet be. She closed her eyes and clapped her hands to hear ears but could not stop it. The sound was within her and they were crying and wailing, lungs being wrung of every breath, poured into the last pleadings of a population.

Los Angeles was underwater.

Cait heard a child's voice apologizing but no more than that as the world tumbled out from under her.

CHAPTER EIGHT

Cait felt the water calling the entire drive back. But she couldn't face a filled tub, not now, not yet. Sliding under the surface and never coming up and..

No.

She stood under the shower, cold then hot then cold again, anything to try and wash her clean. The river still stuck to her, smell following her like cartoon stink lines, even after washing for what felt like an hour. She threw on some extra Chanel from the bottle her mom had gotten her years ago, the first bottle of perfume she'd found in the midden of her boxes. It took her a little longer to find clothes that worked with her new shoes. The musty threads at least distracted from the underlying notes of swamp that she couldn't shake. She stared at the blinking light on the answering machine for a long time, finger resting on the playback switch. She'd been out most of yesterday and enough of today for something ugly to land. Maybe a couple.

Beep

"Yes, Miss Mac-Ready," the voice mispronounced the name. "This is the discharge nurse from UCLA Santa Monica. Your friend Sue Whelan is ready to be discharged. So if you could get down here shortly."

What?

The machine said it was from just an hour or so ago.

"I should have never left my number."

And maybe I can still make it over.

Cait walked the room hard enough to wear a new track in the carpet. She didn't know Sue, not really, and could barely take care of herself much less anyone else.

But then I'm not the stranger in town. She's the one who went off across the country into unknown territory. I can put her up on my couch for a couple days at the worst, right?

She depressed the pause button and the machine continued.

"Cait, it's Mom. Wanted to make sure you got to see—"

No, not now.

Cait went back to the bedroom again and sifted through the pile of clothes she'd dumped out some time ago and had already forgotten when. She pulled out the denim jacket that almost matched the jeans she was wearing. She didn't have to be in the office until tomorrow. She could backslide some, fashion-wise.

The jacket went on and even felt loose over her shoulders now. She marched down the stairs and to the garage so she could get to the hospital before they turned Sue out on the streets on her own. They weren't running charities anymore.

ঌ২৴

Sue's face pulled tight every time she put weight on that leg. There were only a few steps between the wheelchair and the car but watching her try and swallow the pain was agonizing. Cait winced in sympathy but dared not say anything. She didn't know Sue all that well, but figured empathy would not have been welcome, much less pity.

"Let me help," Cait said, approaching her from around the open door to the Mercury's passenger side.

Sue batted the hand away with a biting slap. "Day I can't make two steps on my own is the day I should throw myself in the river and sink."

Something tugged at Cait, not just the mention of drowning but the stubborn pride that was keeping this woman going. She didn't know how to approach the conversation and it felt like letting go of the side of the pool and being unable to swim quite on your own.

She hauled herself onto the seat and used the crutch to help pivot herself into a forward-facing position. Ragged breaths between teeth clamped tight followed. The brow above was damp with sweat, a single trickle running down her temple.

"Hey." Someone tapped Cait on the shoulder before she closed the door. She turned to see a thin and focused Asian man in hospital-blue scrubs. He was holding out a small amber vial. Recognition and almost reflexive need kicked up in Cait at the sight of that.

"What's up?"

"You tell your friend that she has to take her painkillers or she's not going to heal up." He smiled but there was an aura of burned-out patience beneath it.

"Yeah, I don't think she has much use for modern medicine." Cait took the vial, which was filled with large white pills like small footballs.

"Pain and stress go hand-in-hand to really mess you up. Let her let the pills do a little of the lifting, okay?"

"I'll try."

"Yeah, you can tell that one, but you can't tell her much," he said before walking back into the hospital, shaking his head slowly.

Cait turned to look at Sue who was watching her from the front seat. Blue-eyed stare bit harder than a junkyard dog.

"You made a friend," Cait said, indicating the orderly.

"He bothered me. Always askin' about how I was *feelin'*."

Cait laughed as she crossed around to the driver's side. "It is his actual job." She climbed inside and buckled up. "You too," she said.

"You don't trust your own driving?" Sue asked. There was something in her look that reached down into Cait and she didn't care for it.

"It's not me but all the other crazies out there." She waved her hand as if to indicate the entire city.

The Mercury's motor turned right over the first time.

Sue reached across herself and fumbled with the belt. "This an old car?"

"Nineteen and forty-six or so it says on the registration."

"Older'n daddy's truck but not by much."

"The one Lee drives?"

"The same. Did you find it yesterday?"

"Are you asking me if your divination found him?"

"Never called it that. It's just sight."

Cait pulled out and made the hard left onto Ocean, heading back to LA proper. Sue just stared straight ahead as if she was trying not to look down off the edge of a cliff.

"You okay?"

"Now *you're* doing it," Sue growled.

"It's my job now. Just like it'll be my job to get you to take your pain medicine so you can sleep."

"You're gonna need a switch or something stronger."

"I'm sure I can find a willow by the riverbank." She laughed. "Look, your body needs time to heal. Medicine's just going to help you do that."

Sue said nothing. "Pain's a fact. You erase that and you're losing something."

Cait sighed hard. "It's nothing worth holding onto." She drummed the wheel while waiting at the light. "He was right where you said he was going to be."

"You didn't believe me, did you?"

"I don't know what to believe." Cait accelerated gently off the green, pacing the bright, metallic-silver Starion on her right. The driver was getting an eyeful of Sue, hanging out his window, beckoning.

"Roll the window down," Cait told Sue. "Please. And hold the wheel straight."

"Am I in a position to argue?"

"Hardly not."

She did and Cait leaned across her into the breeze of the late morning air. "Hey, buddy! She's taken!"

"By who?" asked the hefty and bearded driver, sunburnt and sweaty.

"By me! Now fuck off!"

Cait re-took the wheel. The Starion dropped back as if it had hit a spike strip.

"Must you?" Sue asked, acid curl to her lip.

"Sorry about the swearing. But some dudes only understand the most direct approach possible."

"And the other part?" Her eyebrow shot up. "Are you…"

Cait laughed. "Oh, that. I prefer guys, sometimes even boys. I'm sure that's a great disappointment."

"I'll never understand this place. Everyone pretending to be something they're not."

"And you don't? What are you, Sue? Something like a witch?"

She considered the question for a long moment, dragging herself from a different thought. "Not like you use the word. But I'm not afraid of the gift of the spirit. I think that's what you're talking about."

"Yeah, I guess so. How'd you know that Lee was going to be there anyway?"

"I didn't. I just asked a presence who might."

"And there he was." Cait weighed the thought before letting it go. "You know that Lee's a danger, right? I don't know what else to call him."

She nodded in silence, jaw set. "I've prayed and asked for help but I'm afraid that my first thought was the right one. I wanted to be wrong."

"About what?"

"My brother's lost, Cait. I'll never see him again." Something in her was breaking but she kept it almost entirely buried. Only a faint limning of tears and tautness of lip betrayed any real feeling.

"Hey. Hey." Cait reached over with her right and took Sue's hand. "I can't help if I don't know it all. Maybe let's get something for you to eat and you can tell me what you really know. And since I've seen what he can do now, you don't have to make up anything or lie."

Sue nodded.

"Believe me, I know what it's like not being able to tell the whole story because, well, because people will think you're crazy."

"I'm *not* crazy," Sue said.

"Neither am I." Cait let go of her hand and put both on the wheel. "Now what can I take you to eat that won't scare you to death?" she mused aloud.

"I'm not scared of anything."

Cait laughed. "Tell me that in half an hour." She laid the accelerator down and drove toward Hollywood.

જી

Tommy's Burgers was a red-and-white enameled stand that was as old as the Mercury, over on Beverly and Rampart. Weekend nights were a parade of kids in cars or on bikes, hanging out and joking with one another, stopping only long enough to inhale chili-cheeseburgers or take gulps out of soda cans. It wouldn't be so bad this time of day.

Hopefully not too crazy for Sue, though.

Cait set the cardboard baskets down on the bench seat of the Mercury and tossed a pile of napkins beside.

"Here, take this." She handed Sue a can of root beer, almost bitterly cold. "I didn't know what you liked best, so I just guessed."

"What is that?" she asked as she folded the yellow tissue paper back to reveal the chili-covered mess.

"You said you weren't scared of nothing, so you get to prove it. Chow down." Cait sat back down in the driver's side and opened up a bag of chips. "No dawdling. It's no good if it gets cold. Believe me."

"Then we best say grace," Sue said.

"I haven't… I mean, not since visiting my grandma. I was still a Girl Scout."

"I'll lead it then." She took Cait's hand in her own. "Lord, we thank you for making this food and bringing us here safe in this hour. And even if some of us aren't speaking to you as often as we should, we thank you for listening. Amen."

"Amen," Cait said quietly.

She's not just talking about me.

Sue braced herself and brought the burger up to her lips then took a big enough bite to get to the meat underneath the slathered chili.

"Don't watch me," she said with her mouth full, all slurred.

"Sorry. Just, you know, this is a special moment. First Tommy's in LA and all."

Sue finished the bite and wiped her face. She sighed as she realized her fingers were a mess and would be until the burger was done. "It's pretty good."

"Finish up and then we can talk this out." Cait ate her own, trying hard to keep things contained to the box and not all over the front seat.

Sue drained the soda can and lay it down in the debris and napkin-strewn box.

"That was good. A fright, but good."

"I'll take it. Now can we talk about what the hell is really happening?"

"That's a real place," Sue said with a scowl. "Don't take it so light."

"Okay, sorry. I'll try to develop some better manners around you."

"You'd do well to develop them in general, even when I'm out of sight."

"Okayyy."

Her gaze softened a little but didn't let go of its fierceness. "What was Lee like? Was he well? Down on the river."

"You're not supposed to start by asking me questions."

"Just tell me."

Cait rubbed at her temples and took a breath. "He slipped in and out of being Lee. It's like he was a couple different people. Only one of 'em wasn't people. He stood differently and carried himself differently. Seemed to change a couple times. Like someone was pulling his strings."

"That's the spirit moving in him."

"That's not the spirit you were talking about though, is it?" Cait asked. "When you talk about you and your gifts, that's the Holy Spirit, isn't it?"

"What other would it be?"

"I won't pretend to know enough about that to understand, Sue. But Lee and you are running on two very different frequencies, I think."

She nodded while she worked her hands together as if washing. "You asked me if I was a witch."

"I didn't mean…" Cait rushed to say.

"No. It's all right. I understood you. My grandmother and before her, they were well enough witches. It's not a word with that kind of weight where I'm from."

Cait's face scrunched up. "I don't get it. You're a pretty devout Christian though. The handmade, modest clothing. No makeup. Baptist?"

"Pentecostal. Not at all the same."

"Okay, sorry. But *Pentecostal* and *witch* don't seem to go hand in hand. Or I don't understand one of 'em."

"Maybe you don't understand either," Sue suggested.

"Ouch."

She stared ahead out the window, past the haze of lipstick traces and to the row of white stucco and soda coolers with stainless tops gouged and scratched by forty years of kids declaring themselves to the world on this corner. It took a moment for her to speak.

She's respected for this back home, it's a source of pride but not now. It's failing her.

"All the things that I can do, find lost things, undo charms and hexes, healing and doing a little to make life better in the world, all those things? Those are gifts of the Lord.

"Just like my women-kinfolk knew this. I was brought up to use these same gifts." Her eyes were wide and somehow innocent now. There was no judgment, no sternness, just a wonder and a gratitude for something that Cait didn't have a name for.

"So they're just you?"

"It works through me. Only because I've practiced them. They come from something else, everything else. At least they do at home. Out here, it's harder. This is… this is not my place."

"LA does take some getting used to."

Sue groaned faintly. "No, that's not what I mean. I grew up learning the names of everything between Whalen House and town. Every ripple in the landscape, every copse of trees and even the stragglers between. It was a place I knew. This place. It's something else."

"You can say that again. And you've just been here a couple days." Cait shifted in her seat, aware of the smell of the river again, but it wasn't really there. "What about Lee? Did he have the gift of the spirit, like you say?"

"Lee? No. He was different. He asked gifts *of* the spirits. You were right when you said we were not the same."

"Different wavelengths, yes."

"Whatever you mean by that. Lee had in himself a tremendous desire for these gifts. He sought them out. He'd have wrestled Samson himself or worse to get them."

"What gifts *does* he have?"

Worry creased her forehead now and she frowned without realizing how much she was giving away. "Whatever he has given himself over to. He asked things of the creation and the things within it."

"The rainmaking."

"Yes, but not rain-*making*. More rain-*remembering*. He would bend himself and dance and sweat so that the drops would hit the ground and remind the land what it was to receive rain. When he could."

"So he lost the ability?"

Sue shook her head with bitterness. "Not lost but not found so much as he wanted. He kept asking.

"And whatever he found out here has given him that. Not a gift but a power. A terrible power."

"What did he have to offer in return?"

"All he had," she said.

⌒⌒

Cait took the turn off Playa in Culver City just before it became Overland and wound its way back up to Los Angeles. The neighborhood was a mix of condos and older detached homes with a Catholic cemetery not far off in the distance. It was pleasant enough, but growing long in the tooth with construction that wasn't meant to last forty years pushing past that. They were there to visit a trailer court, itself a last vestige of a Los Angeles that was all but gone now. Putatively mobile homes up on blocks and frames parked there since World War Two, even as the rest of the area was moving towards stucco dingbat apartment buildings or the weedy remnants of tract houses.

I should not be doing this. Not without Open Door being involved. This could be a crime scene. Or evidence.

That's if Lee was involved, which Sue hasn't confirmed.

But who or what else could it be?

"You're sure this is okay?" Cait asked as they pulled up to the oblong box painted with the word OFFICE and brought the car to a stop.

"They're my things, and it's my brother's place. Why wouldn't it be? I know y'all have all kinds of rules and regulations out here." She unbuckled her seatbelt as if to get out of the car. "But what's mine is mine."

"Sue. Hold on a second." Sue's shoulder was drawn tight to the point of quivering under Cait's touch. It was more than anxiety to get this done.

"What's the matter?"

"You aren't fond of the law, right?"

"Not when they stick their noses into something they don't got a right to."

"Well, you'll find they think they have all kinds of rights to whenever they want."

"Oh, I know. But this isn't their business."

Cait sighed hard, trying to figure out how best to frame this. "Sue, there was a death, the same day you came to town to find Lee. That night, a man drowned at his home. *Before* the alligator or whatever it was attacked us. You remember that, right?"

"Of course. Flesh won't let me forget that."

"The police are calling that drowning a murder. Only the victim wasn't found in the water." She read Sue's blank expression as hard as Sue usually read hers but found nothing. "It wasn't just a drowning."

"I'm sure I don't know what you're talking about."

"If not, then it's an awful damn coincidence."

"Your language."

"Hang my language! Did Lee murder that man? Fill him full of water and then some? And don't 'He can't,' because I've seen him do it twice.

"Now tell me what happened before you and he had your falling out." She had to keep herself from pointing at Sue, barely keeping her tone civil out of frustration.

"It wasn't Lee," she said with some urgency.

"I'm not the one you have to convince. Eventually."

"But it wasn't him. He had ambition and a temper, but he wouldn't kill a man over a sum like that."

"Sum like what?" Cait asked. "He worked for that builder?"

"Not exactly. He'd had a contract with that man. To bring rain, which he did. Then he was to be paid for it. But that part didn't come to pass."

"Pay him? For rain?"

"That's all what I gathered. Lee wasn't but partially in his head when I got out to Los Angeles. He'd already fallen."

"To… whatever he'd asked for power from?"

"Something like that. He wasn't clear on it to me. He spoke in riddles when it was him speaking. He talked about a chorus, a multitude, a unity."

"Of ghosts? Spirits? What?"

"Something about time," Sue said. "Something about water in time. That was its secret."

"And now he can—"

There was a sharp rap on the window, something metallic hitting the glass twice. Cait and Sue started then turned to the source of the sound. It was an older man, sway-backed and drawn all in denim and lazy curves almost rubbery. He had a quarter between the first two fingers of his fist, which he'd knocked on the window.

Cait rolled it down with irritation, glaring at his easy smile.

"What?!"

"I was just wonderin' as to your business. Seein' as you've been parked here for a bunch of minutes." He sounded like he and Sue were neighbors.

"Hello there, Mr. Crews," Sue said, strained but pleasant. Probably not the first time she'd put manners over emotion. "Remember me? Sue Whelan? You helped me find my brother's trailer a couple days back."

"Well, hello there, Miss Sue. I didn't expect to see you riding in such an *unusual* automobile as this." His gaze flicked over the car, not with approval.

"This is my friend Cait and we were hoping you could let me into Lee's trailer, so I could get my suitcase and other belongings?"

"Your brother's not here?"

"No, we called ahead. He didn't pick up."

"I don't know," he said, mulling things over visibly. "This seems like a police trick to get in without a warrant. Not that any of my clientele have ever had trouble with the law, you understand."

"Heavens, no," Cait said.

"Please, Mr. Crews? I got laid up by an animal bite. I've been in the hospital for several days, and I just want a fresh change of clothes."

He scratched at the dark and rusty stubble on his scalp and temples. "Okay then. Lee's an unusual client, so I guess I can be unusual in my generosity. Follow me."

"Is it okay if I drive her down? Sue's leg is still bothering her."

"You can follow me in the car. Just don't run me down. Wouldn't want to scuff your chrome."

He ambled off slowly and Cait kept him in sight, trailing him at a near-idle with lots of clutch in to coast back to Lee's trailer. Each of them were unique, personalized. All were in surprisingly good shape, no sense of a dead-end but rather a celebration of a road few traveled. Apparently Mr. Crews didn't brook any nonsense when it came to keeping his court tidy and cleaned. None of them was quite the same color. Each had their own bicycles or barbecues or tiny little gardens or graveyards of flags marking them as personal islands, sovereignties.

Crews fiddled with the door and opened it for them. Sue let Cait help her up the stairs, but she was stiff the entire time.

"You could make this easier on yourself."

"It'll come in time."

"Here you are, ladies," Crews said. "I'll just wait here a moment whilst you get your things."

"Oh, could you please carry them for me?" Sue asked. "I'm not in a state."

"Yes, of course."

Lee's trailer was single-wide, wood exterior staircase and tiny porch, leading to the living room door, kitchen and plumbed rooms off to the right, bedroom to the left. Everything was tight and close and musty. Sunlight filtered through cotton pattern-print window shades, where it died an unnatural death before even getting to the other side of the room.

"I can only ask people to maintain the exteriors, you understand. I'm even happy to help spruce things up. Inside, well, a man's home is his castle so long as he makes his rent."

"It's okay. I grew up with him. Mother would beat him raw and he still never learned to clean things up."

"Is Lee good with his rent? No trouble?"

Crews looked at her closely. "Well," he said, drawing the last part of the syllable out all the way to Hollywood.

"Cait's a friend, Mr. Crews. You can tell her anything you'd tell me and I'm his family."

"If you insist. He used to be real poor about paying regular. And even though he's not from Arkansas, I gave him a measure of trust. But that patience got tested."

Cait looked over the collection of newspaper clippings and photographs and drawings that had taken over one of the living room walls, sprawling nearly the length of the room. Water and rivers and seas ran through all of them but that seemed the only link.

"So he was late with the rent?"

"He was for a time. Until a few months ago maybe. But then he presented me a new problem."

"You were getting paid, so what's the problem?"

Sue sat down on the couch opposite the wall, grimacing. "I thought I was better enough to do this."

"Let me get you a glass, Miss Sue. You rest here." Crews marched over to one of the kitchen cabinets. He came out with a green, pebbled glass, pinched out to a little pedestal at the bottom. He filled it with water from a bottle in the refrigerator. "I always tell folks not from here that they gotta get their water from anywhere but a tap. It's not like home. What they got coming out of the faucets here should be a crime."

He handed the glass to Sue, who took it gratefully.

"So he paid you, but he didn't?"

"It's more a matter of what he paid me with. Go ahead and open that box there on the table. Seein' as you're almost-family." He pointed to a Red Wing boot box that was cleaner than just about any surface in the house, only scuffed at the corners a little. "Go on," he added when Cait hesitated.

"Is this okay?" Cait asked Sue. "It's your—"

"Do it. Though I've a notion as to what's in there." Her face was drawn, losing the battle of willpower against the pain.

Cait lifted the box and it slipped through her fingers at first, dropping back to the table with a solid thud.

"Heavier than it should be." She grunted and lifted it off, cradling the box against one arm and working the lid with the other.

Light caught on the faces of scattered coins and flattened ingots. There were dollars of both gold and silver, dimes and quarters, coins that Cait couldn't recognize at all, some that was barely recognizable as currency. And the ingots all different weights, different measures, all gold or silver.

"What the—" Cait cut herself off. "What? I don't know much about coins, but I'm guessing this is enough to buy the trailer outright."

"Might be buying the whole park," Crews added, dancing the silver quarter over his knuckle bones, up one side and down another. "Now it's a bit of a fuss to get the payment converted, but it spends. Eventually."

Cait glanced over at Sue. "Did you know about this?" Getting a non-response, she then returned to the box. Pushing aside a flurry of still-shiny silver slugs, she saw a string of pearls that showed a dancing sheen of color.

Sue shook her head sadly. "I knew he loved money. That's a fault in all the men in my family. It sent some of 'em chasing all over creation when they'd have been happier back at the house."

The box went back on the tabletop with another thud. "None of this is contemporary."

"And why should it be?" Crews asked. "Buried treasure's supposed to be old. At least that's what your brother hinted at."

"You said this started around a couple months ago," Cait asked while gazing at a gold coin with a man in a long wig on the head and a crowned coat of arms surrounded by a chain and Latin writing on the other. It was rough, uneven, stamped out by hand, not by a machine. She mused at that similarity to the knife back at home.

"Sue, when did he stop writing?"

"Nearabout that time. His last letter was September, late."

"And then Lee started paying his debts in old cash, not cold cash. Which he never had."

"No, Miss Cait. He was often short. Until then."

Cait dropped the coin back into the box with the others, though there was no way it would have been missed in the mess and jumble. "That was a doubloon. Date said 1797, and I don't see a reason to doubt it."

"Pirate treasure?" Crews asked.

"Maybe but certainly lost. Lost in the water, I'd bet. Just waiting for someone who knew where to look for it."

How much was out there to be picked up or pulled out of the water if only you knew where to stick your hands?

"Spanish? You mean Mexican?"

Cait shook her head. "There wasn't a country of Mexico back then, but there were people. Spain came in and claimed all their land as part of their empire. California, too and a bunch of other stuff that would later become part of the US of A. After a war or three."

"Have you seen Lee lately?" Sue asked. Her knuckles were bunched and white around the glass.

Crews shrugged in a motion that seemed to take all his strength. "Can't say as I have. I mean, I did once, coming and going, maybe three nights ago."

"The night we were in Venice," Cait added.

"If you say so."

Cait went back to the papers and photographs on the wall. They'd come from a hundred different sources or had been copied from them. Most of the images had the weird grainy look of the cheap xerox machines she'd seen at the public library. The pages had been duplicated sloppily, in a hurry. Huge swaths of faded blacks and haloing around the images made some of them nearly unreadable. But there was enough to see that it was all about water, events taking place within it or because of it.

"Was Lee a bookish sort, Sue? Did he read a lot?"

"Not hardly. He put his nose in them when it was the only way to avoid Mother's wrath."

"Looks like he's changed his habits of late."

"What are all those?"

"News clippings, historical records, maps. He liked the water. Does any of this sound like him?"

She shook her head negative.

"Okay. Well, let's get your stuff, Sue. Then we'll get you some rest."

"We're not staying here?" Sue looked as if moving from the couch was only barely preferable to having her teeth pulled without laughing gas. And that maybe this was all somehow Cait's fault.

"We are not. I have a perfectly usable bed you can rest on and I'll just sleep in the bathtub or something. What's your suitcase look like?"

She pointed to it and Cait hauled it out with some effort, determined not to spend any more time here, less Lee actually show up and show what he could really do.

"Anything else?" she asked.

Sue shook her head again, teeth already set.

"Right. Let's get your feet up." Cait found a scrap of paper and a pen and scribbled out her number, which she pressed into Crews' palm.

"What's this?"

"Just call me if he comes back or if anyone else comes looking around."

"You're sure you're not the law?"

"If I was, she wouldn't talk to me."

"That's the truth," Sue added.

"You're sure?" Cait asked as she helped muscle Sue up the stairway to the lobby of her building.

"Yes, you win. I'll take some of your damn pills." Sue was wet with sweat and her whole left side was clenched tight enough to bounce bird-shot. "I felt fine sitting in the room."

"Language," Cait said with a grin. "And that's because you weren't doing anything."

Cait pressed the elevator button and waited. Sue's face was tight with apprehension, aged out ten years since this leaving the hospital.

"Don't tell me you're afraid of elevators," Cait joked.

"No, not that. Just that I don't recognize Lee anymore. Nothing he's doing makes sense."

The bell rang. Cait dragged the suitcase across the threshold and helped Sue in, bracing her on the handrail. "Have you ever heard of spirits or whatever taking over someone who calls them?"

Sue shook her head for what seemed like the hundredth time that night. "I've seen preachers gripped by the spirit and the gift of holy speech."

"Speaking in tongues, right. But that. That's more ecstatic, right?"

"You could use that word."

"I was thinking something more maybe calculating and of a longer duration. Unless Lee's been in a service for several weeks now. Okay, just a little farther." Cait fiddled with the door, working the sticky lock and punching it open with her shoulder. "Welcome to home." Only she hadn't quite convinced herself of that.

"I really shouldn't…" Sue trailed off, drifting.

Cait knew what was coming next and dropped everything, dashing to keep her from sliding off the door frame to the floor. She went down like a heavy bag with a snapped chain, and Cait barley kept her from wiping out on the living room floor.

"You really shouldn't try to bully pain. It'll knock you right out."

She brought her in and set her down as gently as she could on the couch. Then she pulled one of the back cushions down and jammed it under Sue's legs, elevating them.

"Smells like cigarettes."

"Yeah, sorry. Goodwill special," Cait called from the kitchen. "Cheapskates can't be choosers." She came back with a glass of water and a hand full of small crackers in an unnatural shade of yellow. "Speaking of which, time for dinner. Come on and sit up a second."

Sue looked around bewildered. "Your house?"

"Apartment. I couldn't even afford a house in Pacoima." Cait watched her take the pills and gulp down the water, making a face. "Oh, come on. It's got minerals. Good for you."

"I see Mr. Crews wasn't lying about the water."

"Culver City's got water contaminated by the old oil wells. I'm sure that's worse than this."

Sue munched a cracker and nodded weakly. "Oil?"

"California, Southern California in particular, used to pump more crude than Texas. There're still rigs standing, lots of 'em hidden behind warehouse façades and the like. But that money never sleeps." She pulled up a chair next to the couch, keeping an eye on her the whole time. "Now can I get you anything else?"

Sue's face was cracking, like the duress of existing in this place was dragging her to pieces, shattered by LA's strange gravity. "Get me settled with Lee, so I can go back home from here."

"I can't grant wishes. But I can get you some soup or something?"

"I'm okay. Better now that I'm not moving." She half-smiled. "Your place is nice."

"You don't need to be polite. It's a box, much like the other thousands of boxes you can find in buildings like this. I don't even have a balcony. He—" She looked, but Sue hadn't noticed. "I've barely even unpacked." Her glance shot over to the bedroom filled with half-emptied boxes, and she groaned at how much work it was going to take to make the bedroom usable by a guest.

"It's a nice box, nicest I've ever been in."

"Thanks. Can I get the TV for you? It's not a big one but I think the remote actually works. Even got cable, thanks to Yusuf who wired the whole place, under the counter of course."

"I don't watch television."

"Well, I don't either mostly. Usually videotapes when I do, or…" her voice trailed off as she looked for the remote.

Sue stared, her intensity's corners ground down by exhaustion. "You're not understanding. I don't watch television or go to movies. None of that. Radio's fine for Sunday programming though."

"Comes to Los Angeles and doesn't watch television or movies. You're full of surprises. Most people come out here *because* of that."

"I came out for family."

Cait found the now-unneeded remote and sighed, putting it on top of the tiny Magnavox. The once-white plastic had yellowed to the color of old teeth only marginally-tended.

Sue was heavy-lidded now, tottering.

"Stick a fork in you, huh?"

"What's that?"

"You're done, honey. I was gonna invite you to a genuine television studio, but seeing as you don't watch television. Guess my friends at Quest4 will have to wait to make your acquaintance."

"I can't stay awake. This is why I don't like these pills. But I can't sleep yet. Not yet." Her hands grasped at the air, at something unseen.

"Why? What's going on?"

"I need to teach you to do a casting, like I did in the hospital. I need you to do one for me."

"I don't understand."

"I've tried reaching out to get a hold on Lee and where he might be, but it's like grabbing… grabbing a whole river. I can't. I think he knows I'm looking now. And he knows me, knows how to hide from me."

"But I *can't* do that."

"Ain't you ever been asked to do something you didn't think you could? And then you find you did? You've never been asked to do this is all."

The asking grants the power. That was what Ariela had said.

Cait froze in place. "You couldn't know."

"Know what?"

That wanting something is better than getting it and I wanted to make something magic. I wanted that kick and maybe even that power. Getting it was the worst thing that happened.

"Forget it," Cait shook the chill off and stood, hands on hips. "What do I need?"

"Get the Bible from my bag," she said, dragging each word out.

Cait fumbled the latches on the suitcase and only hated herself a little for rifling through Sue's clothes, underwear and all. It was all plainer than she could have imagined, without ornament or embellishment. Just what anyone could need to get by.

"I'm sure I have a Bible around. I can find it."

"No, no. It needs to be mine. Maybe you can borrow some of the power, sneak up on him."

Her fingers brushed against something hard. She pulled the book out like it was an unexploded bomb. It was unremarkable, sort of a blue marbled pattern on a cardboard cover with uneven and worn brassy embossing that read "Holy Bible, King James Complete." Cait had seen hundreds like them on bookstore shelves or at Goodwill or even in crates on the street. The only thing unique about it was that it was Sue's.

"Okay, got it. Now what?"

"Don't open it. And don't let me touch it. Set it down on the table, not a chair. Treat it gently."

Cait placed the book, cover facing up and waited.

"Okay," Sue gulped a breath. "Do you have a knife? Not a kitchen knife. A pocketknife or one used for hunting but not cooking."

"I don't carry a knife," Cait said with dread. "I don't…"

"This ain't gonna work then."

The thought of unsheathing Tácito's knife made her hands go cold. But there wasn't time to do much else.

"Wait. Don't go to sleep now. I'll be right back."

Cait dashed out to the kitchen, slid a chair into place before the cupboard then stepped up onto that. Reaching back over the dusty sill, in the space between that and the ceiling, she took out the old steel cashbox she had hidden, far out of sight and easy temptation. She unlocked it with the tiny sheet-metal key on her key ring and opened the lid. Along with an envelope of mixed cash and some loose jewelry and ticket stubs from shows she'd been to, there it sat.

The knife waited in the wrapped-leather sheath. She picked it up like she would a still-burning coal then slipped the handle free. It hadn't broken or shattered or proved itself to be a bad memory. It was there and wanting to be used. But any wanting was only on its part. Whatever was reaching to her, whatever she was chasing down, she wasn't going to be caught or catch it without something sharp in her hands, beyond just this ceremony or whatever Sue had planned.

Cait ran her eyes over the edge, faintly uneven against the dark material of her jacket sleeve, like a mountain range or rock face in miniature. It didn't possess bland simplicity or perfect cleanness. Instead the roughness described complexity and depth. She snapped it back into the sheath, else she keep staring at the ragged edge.

She stepped back into the living room and saw Sue sleeping, or almost there.

"Hey, hey! Get up! We're not done yet."

"Oh, whuh?"

Cait patted her cheeks lightly. "We were going to look for Lee, right? Only you can't, so you asked me."

"Oh, okay. You have the, uh, knife?"

"Yeah, it doesn't have to be steel, right?"

Sue looked at her blankly as if that wasn't even possible and Cait took the blade from her pocket. She removed it from the sheath, light glinting along the flinted infinite edges, catching in the flakes and scalloping of the bevel out to where the fuller lay flat.

"Sure, that will work," she said sleepily. "Now think about who you're looking for, what you're looking for. Hold that image in your head and your heart, your heart mostly. It's your heart that's going to do the finding."

Cait closed her eyes and tried to grasp an image of Lee Whelan but she could only see ripples and figments and fragments. There was nothing complete to hold onto. So she imagined sinking into that moment, being surrounded by the aftermath of an event she could neither understand nor explain away.

"Ask for forgiveness for what you're about to do."

"What?"

"Better do as I say."

"Who am I asking for forgiveness?"

"Me. That Bible before you was given to me by my mother on my tenth birthday. She went all the way to Gatlinburg to get a nice one. I have had it with me every day since then." Her words were slow and deliberate, not sleepy at all, as if something else gripped her.

"I won't… I don't want to desecrate this."

"Gonna take more than that to desecrate it, but the sting of sacrifice might make it more real."

"Okay. Sue. Forgive me for what I'm choosing to do here."

She nodded with satisfaction. "Now think back to Lee. Once you have that, I want you to hold the knife over that bible, my bible, as if you meant it harm."

Cait had always hated anyone who destroyed books. She remembered crying when she heard about Nazis burning books in school. And the good Americans who burned books when she was a child and how that never changed. Both were just as bad. Yet she stood here, set to plunge a knife into this book. There'd be nothing left. Bibles weren't made of steel. This blade had cut through hair and creatures made of smoke and magic all the same. Those pages wouldn't survive.

"You don't understand, Sue. This knife will go right through that book and the table and maybe to the floor if I push hard enough."

"Then I give it gladly. Be mighty with it."

Cait took to her knees before the coffee table, all formica veneer and sawdust and glue and worth maybe three fifty if nothing so heavy got put on it. She held the image of Lee, whatever he was now, in her mind so much that the image overflowed to her heart and everything else. And something else was there. She couldn't see it but that didn't stop her from feeling it, the vast and terrifying suction of a whirlpool, all things moving in the same direction and that direction was down and down and it would never stop because there was no bottom.

She thrust the knife down rather than feel that any longer.

Cait felt the point pierce the cover and push in slowly as if time itself were congealing. It moved at a pace of glaciers scraping out new canyons and gorges, inexorable but oh so slowly. Moments trickled and she felt tired. She kept pushing with the image in her mind, the sun on that medallion and his ratty work clothes and how he was only partly here.

Something broke or maybe snapped together as strong as magnets the size of planets held apart until unseen forces collapsed them into one thing. Both women gasped in unison. Cait from exhaustion, Sue from something else, surprise or shock.

The knife's point dug into the Bible but not even halfway through. Cait couldn't believe it. She'd used it to carve up sheet metal and monsters and the blade treated both like they were no more substantial than air. Real, unreal, it hadn't mattered.

"It's done," Sue said. "Open the book like the blade was a handle and keep to mind the last page. Don't lose that."

It's not a Bible any longer, is it? Simply a book.

Cait grabbed the impaled page with a thumb and forefinger and moved them as one. Then she pulled the knife free and opened the book wide. She still couldn't understand what had happened, what force could possibly have held the blade back. There was no answer that comforted.

Sue whispered. "The last page. It'll have a mark on the first line of a verse. It may be the front of the page or the backside. Let's hope it's the front."

Cait looked and frowned. The front of the page was marred, but it was in the middle of a chunk of text, not the first line. "It's on the backside." She swallowed and it tasted like milk gone bad.

"Read it anyways," she said through a bitter grimace.

Cait turned the page over and dreaded the outcome.

And I'll have screwed it up like I screw up everything.

"I'm waiting."

Cait read. "Job 41, verse 31. He maketh the deep to boil like a pot: he maketh the sea like a pot of ointment.'

"I don't know what that means. Sue?" Cait asked.

But Sue was already asleep, breathing deeply and untroubled.

Cait's heart was beating like a beached fish, struggling and slackened. She went and found some paper and a pen to write with, trying to keep her hand from shaking the entire time. Her arms and hands only partly listened, connected now to something else. She copied the words neatly and accurately once she got going, but it took a few tries to get there. It still didn't make any sense to her. Just words, no real meaning.

What was I expecting? To hear that Lee's downtown at Broadway and 2nd at the Criss-Cross Club? This stuff never works like that. If it ever works. Sue herself said that her own gifts were broken or not working properly any longer. Maybe it was a misfire.

Cait kept thinking that until she heard the first drip of water. It wasn't coming from the kitchen or the bathroom but somewhere closer. Her heart quickened as she looked around but she still couldn't find the source. Then she turned her attention to the book on the table. It sat in a growing puddle of water, only a little bigger than itself. The water welled out from inside the book, between the pages.

A feeling creepy-crawled down her arms and through her chest like direct current, a flow from some place outside herself yet rippling through her flesh. Hand shaking, she flipped open the book, verses all waterlogged now. Water gushed out of the cut in the pages as sure as blood out of an artery.

The Hell?

Liquid cascaded from the tabletop to the carpet in a spreading blot. What issued from the book was warm to the touch, which made it worse. The book was bleeding out and that thought made her want to scream.

"Oh shit! Oh *fuck!*"

She grabbed the book off the table and carried it out of the room, its issue running down her and onto the floor where it left a trail with every step. Hitting the hallway, things tilted and it seemed too long, too many steps, doors in front of doors. Her breath went short as the pulse of the water surged.

After what felt like running a mile she rounded the corner to the bathroom and dropped the book down into the white ceramic tub. The flow swelled to that of a stunted fountain, an unfunny joke or magic trick going wrong, all humor bled from it. The water was faintly green against the smooth white and Cait was appalled to see things swimming in it. Bits of plant matter, leaves and fronds she couldn't recognize, darting insects like tiny origami of folded chitin, fish that swam to her fingertips as they hesitated on the surface. She checked her hands to make sure nothing had stuck to them, nothing that wriggled or bit.

I found Lee, alright. But maybe he found me back.

She went so tense that she felt like snapping a bone. The tub filled as the water churned inside it. She waited for something to manifest itself, something bigger than the tiny critters, the lost life that was finding its way here through a hole in a book.

Nothing. Nothing yet.

She dabbed her hands off with a towel and watched the rippling surface, eddies near the source of the water, the book itself. Then the child's voice again, the one on the edge of sleep from those nights ago. Words but no meaning in a maddening jumble of near-sense, as significant as the babble of streams or the roar of waves.

A small group of clam shells tumbled out of the book, pushing pages and cover aside. They were banded red and purple with a zigzag triangle pattern, almost too planned for nature but rougher than one executed by human hands. One she recognized instantly.

The shell from the river.

There in the curls of the shells in the bathtub were the echoes of a similar pattern. The same or close enough but no clue what the significance was.

"The chorus is whole but muzzled," came words from somewhere, everywhere. "The cup fills slowly but will overflow."

"What?" Cait asked. "What are you telling me?"

She reached for one of the shells, but the action of the water kept it from her fingers. The bathtub filled and she felt a pull. It was fluid. Every time she thought she had a handle on it, the attraction shifted and reappeared from another direction. The currents beneath that surface were stronger than they should have been, dragging like riptide with a physical force that streamed past and moved her hand simultaneously. She was gripped by a chest-clutching feeling of anxiety, her self-manufactured fear. There was no mistaking that. The claw-to-stay-holding-on-until-morning blind fear. It was the thing in her heart that kept it beating. To let go of that would be to die. She ripped her hand from the water but that did nothing to interrupt the force pulling at her.

With both hands, she pressed against the bull-nose rim of the tub to keep herself from throwing herself in. This was something Lee had brought, something calling her in. Muscles tight across shoulders like

Atlas dead-lifting the whole of the Earth and all of that was falling through her, filling her, shaking her frame.

Sweat burned across her brow and shoulders as she pushed herself away, whispering the chorus of "Gimme Danger" as a catechism, as a lifeline. Over and over as she tried to move what she could only describe as the weight of the world. Muscles strained, her bra strap and clip cinched to welting on her skin. Her shoulders locked and shook with futility. But she would not hurl herself into that water. It was the same water that she'd seen that night in Griffith Park, the water that would drown an entire city and more. She would not yield.

And then it lifted. No voice. No pressure. Only a sense of frustration and rejection. Drops fell from Cait's face to the still surface and she told herself that they were sweat, not tears. The water went still now but for a splash as if by a child's hand, insouciant and surly. That cast drops on Cait's face and she couldn't help herself from tasting it.

It was blood-salty.

Fish hovered on fins and eyed her for a moment before turning belly-up. She couldn't remember their name, but they were the same species as she'd seen those photos of, fish that had welled up from the insides of that poor bastard. They floated on the surface of the tub, flesh shedding from translucent bones which themselves disintegrated before too long. All of the life that had flowed in was now ebbing into death and decay, time accelerating but the water remained. There was a feeling of abandonment in this, that the gift hadn't been accepted so she had to watch it die.

She slumped against the side of the tub, exhausted and tumbling into a sleep that had neither dreams nor memories.

CHAPTER NINE

Cait awoke and felt like a rag that had been wrung so hard it had worried down to threads. Her muscles were spent and stiff from her neck to her abdomen and thighs. Standing was a long process of assimilating pain in one part of her body until she could flex another until the whole thing was upright. She hadn't felt this bad since collapsing in front of the toilet after one of Wynne's parties where she had thrown up until there was nothing left but green stuff that looked like poison in the bowl.

She stood uneasily and investigated the tub. She expected an extinction event, a carpet of bones and putrid flesh so she prepared for sickness.

Just the book.

Reaching in, she found the pages were wet but not sodden. There was no trace of the fish or clams or other life, just a faint feeling of grit on the ceramic. She dragged her fingers across it and they came up with a faint white residue. She knew it would be salty and felt no need to test that further.

Then she went to check on Sue who was up and hobbling around the kitchen. The sun wasn't even up yet.

"No chiliburgers for breakfast?" Sue asked. She stretched her leg out on the diner's red vinyl-cushioned booth, laid out in a semicircle. Eight by ten glossies, mostly in black in white, of the famous and the not-quite, smiled out from the brick walls behind her.

"Something more conventional. Figured you'd be starving. I know I am."

The diner was more midcentury rustic, masonry interior and cheap stained glass lampshades, more Hollywood-adjacent than of Hollywood itself. Glamour wasn't evenly distributed.

"Those crackers don't have a lot of staying power."

"Neither do I. I'm sorry I wasn't a better host last night."

"So you gonna tell me what happened and why you were as white as a clean sheet this morning?"

The waiter filled their coffee and took their orders. He was nice-looking boy who looked too much like Rico with big almost-black eyes, fine features, bright smile.

"Biscuits and ham and eggs, no gravy please," Sue said with her fine lilt.

"Never heard someone from the south asking for no gravy," the waiter replied.

"Never cared for it."

"Pancakes and bacon, please," Cait said. "And leave the pot if it's not any trouble."

"I was gonna."

Sue stared as Cait took a sip of coffee.

"It's part of the meal," she warned.

"Oh, sorry."

Sue said a quick grace, asking again for lenience on those who should know better. They'd learn soon enough.

Cait grit her teeth at that, but knew it wasn't going away anytime soon.

"Okay, last night." She leaned against the table, suddenly uninterested in coffee or anything else. "Do your castings ever, I don't know the word. Do they backfire?"

"I don't catch you. Did you not get what you wanted?"

She shrugged. "I wrote it down. Remember it was on the backside page, not the front." She passed Sue the folded page from the notepad.

Sue grimaced like she'd taken a slug of gasoline then took the paper and read, paling as she did. "Job is a very heavy book."

"That verse itself is pretty nebulous."

"Leviathan," Sue said.

"The sea monster?"

Sue flexed her fingers slowly and curled them against the side of the table. "Not that simply. But a thing of the depths, unknowable, eating."

"We asked where Lee was."

"*You* did the asking."

"Right. Fine. I did. If that's the answer we got, then…"

"There is nothing to like in it." Sue's jaw set and her eyes narrowed. "What else happened. What did you feel?"

"Feel?"

"Were you alone or were there other… presences?"

"There was something else. I could feel something. And after you passed out, the book started… leaking, I guess."

"Leaking?"

"Then it was gushing." Cait went on to explain everything in as much detail as she could recall, which was all of it.

Sue's expression was utterly blank.

"We went looking for Lee and maybe he figured it out," Cait said.

"I've never heard of something pushing back on a casting. Not unless you were looking for someone else with the gift, but even then."

"Something roused when we did."

"You, Cait. I just told you how to do it."

The sound of that made Cait uncomfortable again. That thought had nagged at her all morning. She'd done it just like what she'd done before with Ariela and *The Smoking Codex*. How it was all her fault. She clutched her own hands on her lap and found the reassurance weak at best.

"The voice wasn't Lee? Not any of his voices?" Sue asked.

"You mean the different ones that he talks with? No. None of them. It was familiar, but..."

"But what?"

"I heard them a while ago when I thought I was maybe going crazy or actually was. Everything was just so fucked up."

"Where's my *soap*?" Sue asked of nobody in particular.

"You're gonna need to curb that instinct, or I'm going to have to leave you back at my place. The guys in the bullpen all swear like sailors. Creatively."

"They sell soap out here, right?"

"You'll turn heads, Sue. But ain't a one of 'em wants to be schooled in upright and moral behavior."

"I'll bite my tongue as long as I can."

Breakfast arrived and Sue grimaced at the biscuits on her plate. They were the size of hubcaps.

"Something wrong, miss?"

She handled one, checking its density. "These just aren't the way I'm used to 'em is all. Thank you. I'm sure they're tasty."

"You two have a good breakfast. I'll be right over there if you need anything else."

"I think my time of knowing more than you about this has passed." Sue buttered a chunk of biscuit and looked around.

"What do you need?"

"I'm looking for a bit of jelly."

Cait tapped the wire basket of individually portioned jelly containers between them on the table. "You were looking for a jar, weren't you? Yeah, those would get stolen out here. Or you'd need to go to a nicer place."

"I've never been to a nicer place than this," Sue said. She ripped at the plastic top of a pouch of blackberry jam.

"You mean that?"

"Only the Howard Johnson's in Gatlinburg and I was young then."

"No, no. About you knowing less than me."

Sue set her fork down with some gravity. "This isn't my place. You need to stop asking me what you should be knowing. I taught you that cast, which is only gonna work the one time, unless you can think of another book you'd want to sacrifice. And I wouldn't know how to interpret what was said anyways."

"That one was hard enough."

"You have to take up the knowing of this place if you want to ask for that kind of help."

"I thought that, well, you know."

"Yes?"

"That He was everywhere. Capital-*H* he."

"Oh, that's true. But the spirit is of a place as much as it is the Presence. Why would you expect it to be other than that?" She laid a very modest amount of jam onto a chunk of biscuit, as if too much were sin. "Whatever I could do is done now. Whatever is with Lee has quieted my ability to search for him. It's for you now as much as that pains me.

"I'm not one to ask for help lightly."

"I'll do what I can," Cait said. "I mean, I can barely keep my life together, but why not?"

"Good because you're my rock right now."

That answer gnawed at Cait. She tried to bury it for the moment with pancakes and bacon dipped in syrup.

"Is that what Lee did?" she asked. "Asked for help he shouldn't have?"

"If you want to think of it that way. He went to fetch water from a well but didn't realize how deep it was."

"Leviathan."

Sue nodded. "Whatever you think that word means."

"Do you think we can get him back?"

"We?"

"You can barely cross a street without help right now, not to put too fine a point on it."

"I'll manage."

"We don't even know where he is. Last night didn't exactly work. Well maybe, but we don't know how to read it. I'm assuming Leviathan could be the whole of the seas."

Sue nodded. "We'll just have to narrow it down some then."

"And once we find him, what then? He'll drown us both."

"Not me. Maybe."

"Reassuring."

Quest4 kept their offices out on a stretch of Lankershim, not too far from the towering neon clown over on Vineland and Burbank in North Hollywood. The place was layered with low brick and stucco buildings, occasionally dotted with larger and newer towers, contemporary and monstrous architecture ripping up the old and digesting it. Cait had weighed going there all morning and figured it inevitable. She didn't have much of anything more to go on and they were out there scaring up weirdness twenty-four seven. It could be that they'd found something that would at least tell her where to start looking, if she could survive the weird homecoming that would present itself. She could probably put pride aside and—

Cait gasped then jammed the wheel, all but careening into the sidewalk. The car came to a wrenching stop.

"Fuck," she whispered. "Fuck fuck."

"This better be good," Sue said with a withering hiss.

"My work. It's Monday. I'm supposed to be there now." Cait snapped her wrist around and stared at the battered watch on it. "An hour ago." She held her head in her hands. "How could I even…" Nausea whirled around her guts like an hour in the teacups at Disneyland after a basket of corn dogs.

"You have a job? I thought being an investigator or what all you're doing now— I thought that was your job."

"Ha. You aren't made of money and the police strong-armed me into consulting on this. Then they blew me off. I have to call in. Wait right here."

Cait leaped out of the Mercury and almost into traffic coming up from behind. Honk and screech of Lincoln swerving on the pavement followed by a dopplering stream of obscenities.

Sick and adrenalin-wracked, she caught herself on the fender and looked around for a pay phone and wondered what the hell she was going to say. There was one just a bit down the block in front of a corner convenience store, dingy in the sunny morning.

She picked up the handset and shakily dropped a quarter in the slot. It fell into the guts of the machine like the bottom of a well. Her pulse roared in her ears.

I'd been doing good work. Stable. Not a fuckup. Just a regular person clocking in and clocking out. Sure, things were rough a little while ago, but it's all smooth now.

The line rang twice before pickup. "Robbins," came the voice.

"Bill. It's Cait."

There was only an aggravated sigh. "What is it now? You know that you had three days off, right? Not four. Three."

The river tried to eat me, and I'm driving around a witch from Tennessee to find the guy who's responsible and he's her brother and I still don't know what's going on. Yeah, that'll hit him as well as it would hit Trager.

"I'm really sorry. I'm helping out a sick friend and I just got wiped out last night. Lost track of what day it was. I can be there in a couple hours." She traced the scratched-out graffiti as she waited for the reply which was long in coming.

"Cait. Listen."

"Wait, Bill. I'll be down there and—"

"Look, everyone here has seen that you were swimming with too much chain, and you kept tripping over it. People were stepping up to cover, and I just can't—"

"Bill, please."

"Please what? Don't fire you? I can't. That's my boss's call but they will make it."

A diesel truck roared by, trying to beat the light. Black smoke coughed out of the pipes and hit Cait full in the face. Her voice went dry.

"No more screwups. I promise."

"You can't not right now. Get help, Cait. Nobody wants to believe the rumors, but you're making it very hard not to. Go get cleaned up."

"I'm not on fucking drugs," Cait said, her voice rising without thought.

"It would've been a good excuse. You should have used it."

"Dammit, Bill. I've tried—"

"You've tried. That's it. Tried. You're not fooling anyone." Bill let it hang for a moment and added "Just come in and clean out your stuff when you can. You'll have to sign some papers. Maybe HR will be more forgiving."

The nausea was gone. The fear was gone. Something had eaten it over the course of the conversation, something strong and hungry and hot.

"Bill, if any one down there had the faintest fucking idea what I'm dealing with right now you'd throw yourself off the top floor and scream the entire way down."

"Your desk will be cleaned out by Friday whether *you* do it or not. Be at least that together."

"I'll be that together."

"Sure."

Cait didn't say goodbye. Instead, she inverted the handpiece so that everything would go right to Bill's ear. She took the hard plastic and smashed it against the face of the phone until she heard yelping and then finally didn't hear anything at all.

Panting, she felt a hand on her shoulder. Whatever energy had driven her rampage was gone now, and she just felt empty but not shaky. She could stand.

"Y'all okay?" Sue asked. "You were gone for a while. And then I saw you wailin' on that machine like it killed your mother."

Cait panted in place a moment. "I'm not okay. But at least I've got some more free time now."

"Your job not understanding your situation?"

Cait smiled like a razor slash. "Oh, they understand just fine. They just understand the wrong thing. They think I'm a junkie."

"Junkie?" Sue asked. "You're a drunk?"

"Pills. Or heroin. Not that it matters. They just think I can't do my job anymore. And maybe they're right."

"I don't understand. You seem like a good enough person."

"Wasn't in the job description. They wanted dependable and sturdy and maybe I wasn't that at all."

"Why would they?"

"Later. We'll talk about it later, Sue."

There was no way she could go back to the *Quest4* offices. That would have to wait until later in the day. She wasn't unhappy about that part.

CHAPTER TEN

Cait pushed the door to her apartment open and let it slam into the opposing wall.

Sue set herself down on the couch, nearly evenly but her lips were pulled tight. "Have to take some more of that darned medicine."

"Language!" Cait chided as she looked down at the blinking light of her answering machine. There were three messages there.

Weird. I've only been out a couple hours. Maybe Bill called here first?

She pressed the button and waited.

"Cait, this is Detective Moreno. The captain and I need you to come down to our offices at your earliest convenience."

Well that sounds like not gonna happen.

She went to pour a glass of water and got some crackers for Sue as the next message ran.

A loud beep and then "Cait, this is Trager. We need to talk to you and Ms. Whelan as soon as possible. Call me. I should have figured that you and Trish don't get along and called you myself. I'm sorry for that. Please call."

Cait handed the medicine to Sue.

"The law again?"

"Afraid so. And trouble comes in threes."

Beep. "Cait. Trager. No screwing around. This is very serious. We need to question Ms. Whelan as a material witness in the murder we're investigating. Call me the instant you get this."

Cait shut off the machine but didn't erase the message. "Sue."

"Yes?"

"What is he talking about?" Cait pointed at the machine.

"I suppose he's talking about the man Lee drowned." She bit a cracker and chewed thoughtfully, not looking at anyone.

"See, this sounds like he has a witness to *your* being a witness." Cait slumped into a chair that creaked as if it would give way any second. "Ohhh f—"

"It's not his affair."

Cait stood up hard and fast enough to knock the chair backward. "No! You don't get to play that! Not now. I'm going to be swearing my fucking head off, and you're going to take it. Do you understand?"

"You sound like a child." Sue's blue eyes went wide. "But yes."

"Good. Now why don't you tell me the parts you've been skipping over. We're out of time for evasions."

Sue was silent with her teeth were clenched, jaw working slowly in practice for what would come next.

"Like what?" she asked finally.

"Like when you and Lee visited the developer's home way out in the hills. I suspected that Lee had been there but I didn't know it had been *with* you." Cait shook her head slowly. "We are dogmeat if we don't show up there real soon."

"It's not their business," she said flat as a fresh grave.

"Look, if it was just about him calling up a thing to take a chunk out of you, sure, that's between brother and sister, right? But this? Uh-uh."

"It's not their business. It's mine."

"And that's not even including whatever Lee plans on doing. He's not just treasure hunting. Nobody who can do what he can just sits back on that."

"It's not Lee. I keep telling you that."

"And let's say that I believe you, right?" Cait pulled the chair over and seated herself directly in front of Sue, staring her in the face. "Fine. I believe you. Lee started something, and it took a hold of him. Now there's something walking around using Lee to operate in the world."

"That's as good an explanation as any."

"But the police are never going to believe this. Hell, not even Open Door will. Their job isn't to deal with this stuff but to serve as some kind of vault to lock it away where it's forgotten."

"I keep telling you that it's not Lee. That Lee would never do these things."

"But something that looks like Lee is doing them. So tell me what all happened and let's start there." Cait tapped her feet, waiting.

"I think it drowned Lee in himself. It took him over."

"What did? Leviathan? A ghost or a demon?"

Sue laughed at that. "I've seen spirits but they don't tinker with the flesh like that. And while there're demons and temptation plenty in this world, it wasn't that. And Leviathan, that's like a layer over what we see here."

"You're going to tell me that it's the holy spirit? That Jes—"

Sue's face wrinkled into a scowl. She slapped Cait across the cheek with a report hard as a shot. She sat up tall, breathing heavily.

"I have heard quite enough out of you. Now you can mock my ways, my beliefs, but I won't have you take his name in vain."

Cait felt the red throb in the shape of Sue's long and elegant hand, almost to the separation of the fingers. "Dam—" she bit the curse back and hissed out a breath. "I'm the only one who believes you because I've *seen* Lee. A couple times now. Nobody else in this big, crazy city will, okay? The law will mash him into whatever shape they need to clear this case. And you."

Sue's face was impassive, but there was a faint quiver in her lower lip.

"If they can, they will lock him up, Sue. Or a lot of 'em will end up dying trying. If you want to help him, you've got to tell me."

Sue let it out, but no tears came with it.

"Lee is gone. I been fighting it and fighting it, hoping that the dream that brought me out here in the first place was wrong. But I'd seen Lee drowning in black water, blacker than coal sludge, blacker than oil. I came out to save him and thought, even after seeing him with a hundred different someone elses behind his eyes, that he could be pulled free."

"It's more than one?"

"They are legion. But they're not demons. They're not ghosts either. It's an unholy thing."

"Why did he kill the developer, the Toretti guy?"

Sue's eyes went moist but no more than that. "It wasn't a debt. I thought it was at first. I thought it was just money. But it was, what did he call them? Trinkets."

"Like what, artifacts?"

"I suppose so. I didn't understand at the time, but they're attachments, you'd say. They're a way to speak to those who held them."

"The chorus?"

"The what?" Sue asked.

"Just a thing in my head is all, something Lee gave a name to. Voices, not one but many." Cait thought about what else she'd seen in the box in Lee's trailer. Just gold and silver and metal. Just money for debts or whatever else.

Or was it people themselves? That's what he said. That he was looking for someone, but I wouldn't see it as that.

The shell. That's—

"What about them was important?"

"I don't know. He just wanted them very badly. He said something about assembling them, but it didn't make sense…" Her voice trailed off. "That poor man. I tried to save him."

"What?"

"The developer. When he was choking, I struck him, right here." She pointed beneath her diaphragm. "I thought I could make him cough his wind out and that would make him get rid of what was drowning him."

"If it makes you feel any better, he wasn't a good guy."

"That does not. It wasn't right for Lee to do that. Put more than breath in him."

"You said yourself it wasn't Lee. Maybe it was the chorus. Whatever they are."

"Not Leviathan then?" Sue asked, somehow disappointed.

"Not like you understand it, no matter what the book said."

"It's never wrong," she warned.

"I'm not sure it matters what we call it. What's the attraction between it and Lee?"

"I couldn't tell you." Her eyes were hollow now with something Cait never thought she'd see in her: doubt.

"Maybe there's something here they, they, whatever. They want." Cait thought about the shell but didn't know what to do with it. Another calling? If it was anything like what she went through last night, she wasn't up to facing it.

"We have to find Lee."

"How? Wait for him back at his trailer?"

"I don't know he'll be back there."

"We have to start somewhere."

"Do something, even if it's useless?" The doubt was blooming into something larger now.

Someone rapped at the door twice, hard as a gun barrel. "MacReady! It's Trager! Open up!"

Sue's eyes went right to Cait and they were wide.

"You got any prayers handy?"

"No time for a charm to make the law kind," she whispered back.

"Just a minute!" Cait called. "Geez, you sound mad." She unlocked the door and opened it enough to see who it was. She kept herself from shaking for the moment. "What's up?"

This could be played okay. Maybe.

Trager's whole body was a scowl, tensed under the neat yet worn jacket and slacks. "What's up?" he grated. "That's how you're gonna start this?"

"Look, we just got back from breakfast and visiting my old job. Was just showing Sue the sights."

"The sights? North Hollywood is 'the sights'? Nothing there but the clown and that Thai joint on Magnolia next to the Greyhound station."

"When you're from where I am, anything out here is amazing," Sue offered.

He pinched the bridge of his nose and grimaced, sour and toadlike. "Do you not check your messages?"

"Messages? I forget I have that thing half the time. Were you trying to reach me?" She feigned casual even as her legs felt like she was riding out a seven-point-oh right beneath her feet.

Trager wandered around the apartment, taking its measure. "Yes. Messages. As in the one officer Moreno left and the two I left because for some reason I thought you might listen to me if I asked nicely." He stalked the living room to the short hall and bedroom, eyes always scanning. "Nice place."

"Thanks. Any more and you're going to need to show me a warrant."

"Jesus, MacReady, did you not unpack? How long have you been here?"

Sue glared in his direction, but Cait held a hand up. "Last thing we need is you setting him off," she hissed.

"He can't talk like that."

"Cop," Cait continued in a low voice. "He can do what he pleases and you will accept that." Then to Trager, much louder, "Couple months or so. I wanted to get out of the old building."

"Mhmm-hmm." It was weighted with approval and disdain at once. "Better neighborhood."

"Fewer midnight visitors." Cait found him impossible to read. He was here to pick up Sue, but now he was casting line to see what else he could drag in.

"Your bathroom smells like a sump. You have a line break?" he asked as he strolled back into the main room.

"I'll talk to the super about it."

Trager drifted over to the answering machine and its blinking light. "Oh look, you have messages. Wonder how many." His finger paused over the playback button.

"Warrant," she growled. "Otherwise it's what you see in plain sight."

"Would be easier if I could trust you."

"So the law is what you like? Come on, Trager."

He sighed. "This would have been easier if you'd just called back."

Cait's hands went to her hips, knuckles in. "I'd have to have fucking known to. Don't act like I haven't danced to your tune ever since three days ago. If you want to *employ* me, then pay me."

"Are you looking for a job?"

"No."

"Which is why your supervisor told me he wrote you off this morning."

"Oh, he wrote me off months ago. Just didn't have the spine to tell me until today. But no, I'm not looking for a job."

"Funemployment runs out sooner or later." Trager paused at the other end of the couch. "May I sit? Let's start this over." He dropped the tension as easily as setting down a cup of coffee.

"Fine. But hands stay out from between the cushions."

He sniffed the air once. "You couldn't pay me."

Cait took the chair over to Sue so she could stretch her leg out after turning to accommodate Trager.

"Miss Whelan," he started. She practically glowed at the proper–to–her-ears honorific.

"Detective."

He pulled out a look of disappointment, a dog being left on the porch and staring through the front window. "You left a few items out of your statement."

"Such as?" Butter wouldn't have melted for her.

"Such as your activities before being attacked on the beach at Venice. You made a little tour around town, didn't you? Taking in the sights."

"I was only asked about being mauled by that creature. Not what I was doing there."

"Not entirely true. You were asked if you knew the man you'd been seen with. Which we only knew about from Cait's statement."

Sue stared blank. "'Twasn't your concern."

"It is if he attacked you. Or if you were recorded in his company earlier that evening. Say, up in the Hollywood hills."

Cait wanted to sink through the floor and disappear. Sue remained impassive as a granite mountainside.

"Only hills I know are the Great Smokeys."

"Don't be cute. LAPD screwed up and retained the CCTV tape from Toretti's security. It only showed up on my desk this morning. Needless to say, it opens up several lines of questions."

"C'mon, Trager, let her be. She was a wreck and where she comes from, nobody trusts the police."

"Thank you, counselor. I'll enter that into the record." His voice was about as pleasant as stepped-in vomit.

"Hey! I'm trying to help out here!"

"Help out? By sitting on this? What the hell were you thinking? This is goddamn serious, Cait."

"Don't you do that," Sue warned.

"Excuse fuckin' me?"

"That, Trager. The swearing. Though it's the blasphemy that really gets her."

"I didn't realize you were devout," Trager said. "I'll try to watch my fu—freaking language. You Baptist?"

"Pentecostal."

"Snakes?"

"Not my church."

"Okay then, just wanted to know where I stood." He shifted and smiled. "My family's Catholic, but it never really took. Saw too much operating to the contrary. How about you, Cait? Since we're all talking of the spirit and not the flesh. You got religion?"

"Not as such. Too much time in LA."

"Don't you know nothing about anything, Cait? Pentecostalism was born here. Asuza Revival. Angelus Temple."

"Sister Aimee?"

"The very one."

"She knew good business when she saw it."

"And had solid PR." He smiled widely and let it hang. "And this is all fine and good, but I think we all need to go down to the office and straighten your story out. Don't you?"

Cait watched the slow blink of the answering machine out of the corner of her eye and said "Yeah, I suppose we should."

"I'm going to have to ask to drive you both."

"Come on. Where am I going to go in this city that you couldn't find me, Trager?"

"Don't push it."

"I'll go," Sue said, flat and straight. "Let Cait stay."

"Oh, I think we need to make sure that she didn't leave anything out of her statement, being you were a wreck?" He stared right through her.

"Cops," Cait muttered. "I'll follow in the Mercury. You can put an APB on it if I fall off your rear-view mirror."

"Fine."

œ2ʋ

The video was black and white, mealy from erasure and re-recording over and over. Save a few bucks by recycling tapes but you lose clarity. The images were fidgeting, flickering at times but more so whenever Lee was in the frame. Watery.

Animal or Fabian could tell me how to get that look on video, how to fake it or mess with it or read it however you wanted. Wish they were here.

Wish I had a lawyer who spoke crazy.

There were three figures: one a middle-aged man in a white suit that was too tight, pretending to be twenty years younger than he was; the next a weirdly distorted figure, only button-down shirt and jeans and work shoes evident and the last was Sue. The two men argued for a time and the rippling man gestured to end it. Lee pushed at the air with both hands and something happens on the tape, a flaring or burning where the signal went to overload and then faded to white that left only skeletal suggestions of everyone but him. When the camera came back, white suit reached for his throat, clutching and grabbing, trying to get something out that simply won't come. Water runs down his chest from his open mouth and nose, black holes on the playback. Sue seemed to shout at Lee and turned to the man in the suit, striking him cleanly and sharply under the ribcage.

He coughs out water, but it doesn't stop.

Trager's finger swiped over the pause button and the frame locked to one of the suited man on his knees and unmistakably dying.

"What am I looking at here?" he asked, tapping the doubled-over figure with a ball-point pen.

"It's—" Cait started to say before he snapped his head around to scowl at her.

"I'm only asking witnesses."

"Fine."

"One summer, my cousin Roberta June Whelan, she was swimming and she got herself stuck, trying to get what she thought was a watch stuck between some rocks. She spent all afternoon on it. Anyways, she got some water in her lungs and flopped to the surface. We, that's me and my cousin Viola Beth, dragged her out of the water and onto the shore and she couldn't cough all that water out of her. So Beth went out and struck her, just like that, right 'neath the ribs. You never saw so much water come out of someone. Saved her life for certain. She's got two kids now, even though her good-for-nothing husband ran off with that nurse from Georgia."

Sue smiled sweetly and watched his reaction.

"You're saying you were trying to give him the Heimlich?"

Sue blinked.

"Trager, she doesn't…"

"Okay, fine. So you're telling me that you were not trying to strike to injure him but in fact trying to save him."

"Yes."

Trager assumed the seat behind his desk. "I'll ask this once, and please, less than a hundred words. Save him from what."

"Drowning," Sue said. "Wasn't that clear from the television picture there?"

"Drowning from what?"

Cait tapped Sue on the shoulder. "Just tell him."

"Yes, just tell him, Miss Whelan."

"He was drowning because of what that other figure on the television was doing. He was callin' up the waters as far as I can tell."

"I'm sorry?"

"You heard her," Cait said. "But you don't want to believe her. Just like you didn't want to believe that someone tried to drown me in the LA river channel a couple days ago."

"The same man?"

Cait glanced at Sue, eyes already on her, and she nodded slightly.

"The same man," Sue said.

"Okay. That's something. And I'll get back to *you*," he said, pointing at Cait. "Now, Miss Whelan, who is this man."

Cait winced, waiting for the inevitable, watching a plane missing the landing strip and plowing straight into the ocean instead.

"That's not your concern." You could have balanced a knife on her words.

"It very much is."

"Not from where I'm sitting, right here."

"You don't get it. This isn't you talking to your local sheriff, the one who's making sure that the man you shot was actually on your land when you opened fire."

Sue's eyes went a little wider.

"I didn't grow up in the deep south, just Louisiana. But I know how it can go way out in the hills and hollers."

"Then you understand—"

"But we're not there. You can carry your home with you in your heart, Miss Whelan. You can well and truly believe that you're there when you're anywhere else. Out here, the law does get involved when someone is killed."

"But—"

"And unless you own 11061 Beechwood Drive in Los Angeles, you and that man are actually trespassing in Toretti's home. You have no standing."

"It's a blood matter," Sue said and left it at that.

"I need more," Trager said. "Help me to help you out. You said yourself that this is the same man who let the animal loose on you in Venice."

She said nothing and took her time doing it.

"Is this the same man you saw in Venice, Cait?"

"That tape's all fu— er, messed up," she said. "He could be George Washington, and I couldn't confirm it. Was pretty dark by the canal."

Trager's fingers drummed in sequence, tightly. "And on the LA river?"

"He was hard to look at, you know? Hard to see even in the sunshine."

"So that's not just the tape freaking out?"

"No, he looks like that."

"Okay, so who is he?"

"I couldn't pick him out of a lineup if that's what you're asking."

"You should have been a lawyer."

"No stomach for it."

"I'm asking if you know who he is. Look, your friend is stubborn and prideful."

"I am not prideful!" Sue said with a snap that could have sliced through a brick.

"You got a funny way of showing it then."

"It's not your matter to solve. It's blood. I said that. Repeating it seems necessary for you, though."

Trager slammed two open hands onto the desk and it shook from that. "That's it. I'm done dancing around. Tell me who he is or you're both going to get booked for obstruction. We'll hold you in the cage if we have to."

Sue looked over to Cait and whispered "Do. Not."

"We can't do anyone any good if we're behind bars, Sue."

She said nothing.

"I said 'both,' and I meant it, MacReady. I'm tired of this screwed-up case and so's LAPD. Tell me so I can tell them. If you cooperate, if you two *finally* cooperate, then I'll do whatever I can for you."

Sue stared straight ahead as if Trager wasn't even a thing of this world.

"It's definitely the same guy from the river."

"You're stalling. Tick tock."

"Come on."

"No, *you* come on. We don't have anything on this other than that tape. His financials are a nest of snakes that are going to take weeks to cough up anything. We know Toretti was dirty. Illegal digs, lots of trouble from everyone from the Sierra Club to the Malibu Surf Association and a couple tribal groups. But he didn't deserve to die for it.

"Magic bullshit or not, I need to know."

"His name's Kevin Lee Whelan," Cait said. "He can do things with either water or time or both. I don't know." She watched Sue's reaction but there was none.

"Who is he?"

"Her brother. He rents a trailer at a park in Culver City."

"And you *knew*?"

Trager's incoming wrath was nothing to Sue's utter silence.

"I knew he was her brother. I didn't know that he was involved in Toretti's death until a couple hours ago. Had to drag it out of her."

Sue grated her teeth. "Shoulda never said nothing. Wish I'd never come here."

"That's two of us," Trager said. "What else."

Cait fumbled for an explanation of the events on the river or any other part of it, the gold, the artifacts, all of it. "He's been pulling up buried treasure, hauling it out of the water."

"But he still lives in a trailer park."

"I didn't say it made sense."

"What for? What's all this for?"

He plans to drown Los Angeles? He's going to flood the basin? What's he going to believe?

"I don't know. Sue doesn't either."

"Not another word," Sue said.

"We're out of options, Sue. If you have anything to add, you better."

"I'm going to need a full description of him and more than 'hard to look at.' Vehicle, habits, hangouts."

"Red pickup truck, fifties maybe. Mismatched red fender, the rest blue and beat up. That's it, honest. He seems to like the Venice area, but I don't know why."

"Where the river hits the ocean maybe."

"Yeah, I thought about that, but I don't know what he wants. Other than it's not good."

"Fine. Complete your statements and then go back home. Stay there. Do not leave town. Do not pass go, do not collect two hundred dollars."

"I'm not going with *her*," Sue said flatly and Cait felt a stab at that. She should have seen it coming. Instead, it went in from behind and out her chest, point glinting and red.

"Come on," Cait started.

"No," she said. "You'd best lock me up," this last directly to Trager. "It's all the law wants."

"Prideful to the last. But I'm not sure I can accommodate." He set his pencil down, making it clear that he wasn't preparing to move on anything official just yet. "There's nothing to charge now that one of you has started talking."

Sue stood up and walked without crutches over to the television sitting on the cart beside Trager's desk. The screen was still half-frozen and flickering on Sue trying to save or smite the man. Without a word she hauled out with all her strength and overturned the cart. The television hit the ground with a crash and a hiss of escaping vacuum from the imploded tube.

"That sounded valuable."

She put her hands on her hips and stood as straight as her pained leg would let her. "Arrest me now. Or is destruction of police property outside your bounds?" She dared either one of them to do something, anything.

"Goddammit," Cait whispered.

CHAPTER ELEVEN

Cait swore out the rest of her statement, flatly and without emotion, not having the energy to embellish or suppress. Sue's dead-eyed stare, not even worthy of a scowl, hung over the room even after she'd been escorted out. Cait finished by being prodded by the sketch artist, who was really just another cop who had to moonlight. His hands were unsteady, as if he didn't even trust himself. The drawing he came up with could have been anybody. But then Cait herself couldn't pick Lee's face out of whatever distorted the air around him like twisted glass.

And maybe nobody else could really see Lee as he was.

Sue was marched past, not cuffed by anything other than her own anger. She stared ahead as she was led upstairs, refusing to acknowledge Cait's presence. She had become an un-person, not even a thing to be avoided. She couldn't leave fast enough, pushing the front door so hard it shook.

The skinny cop was out there, skinny ass planted on a steel and concrete post out front not meant to be a bench but he almost made it work. He had a lit cigarette in one hand and a can of Dad's root beer in the other. One more sat at his feet unopened, boots dangerously close to setting it rolling through the parking lot. She stalked past to the Mercury on the street, which he was looking right at.

"I thought you said I wouldn't see you again here."

Cait kept going.

Not now. You're cute and you got some pretty eyes, but this is not the right time for a cop to be making a pass at me.

"Hey, come on. I got some root beer. Dad's even. I usually don't see this stuff."

She stopped and hissed a breath out. "Not in the mood, Officer Parker."

"Detective. I don't have to put on blues. Nobody here does. Weird department."

She turned sharply. "Look. I already said—"

Parker cracked the can open with a snap. It sounded right in the late afternoon heat. "Just take a minute. You look like you could use a drink. Cait, yeah?"

She took a step toward him and then another.

Weird, lanky, plain kinda charm with this one. I am in a dry spell, dammit. And that's the first time I've even had that thought in months or more.

"Okay, just a moment. I've got stuff to do." She took the can, careful to avoid his fingers which were spread wide over the cool metal.

"I'll take a moment if that's all I can get."

"That's all you can get."

"Okay then." He released the can and watched her take a sip. "Your, ah, friend seems to have made an impression."

"Don't think she's my friend anymore." She looked the soda over. "Don't usually drink this. Too sweet."

"Oh, I love it. Can't get this back home. Not for a long time."

She left the invitation where it lay.

"Do you really have a holding cell here? I didn't think this was an actual police station."

Parker frowned. "Can we not talk about work? Something more fun?"

"You opened that up by asking about her."

"Okay, okay." He turned back to look in the shop or office or whatever it actually was. "We can hold folks overnight. I've never seen it go past that. But I haven't been here so long either."

"Maybe she'll come to her senses by then."

"You don't believe that, do you?"

Cait shook her head and took another gulp. Traffic rolled past, coughing out a thin veil of exhaust that caught the sunbeams and made even the trash look good.

"Not for a second." She rattled the can, all but empty now. "Hey, thanks for the soda."

"Anytime."

She caught herself giving him the once over with her eyes. "Nah," she said finally. "But thanks."

A door behind them slammed open, and Trager strode out into the parking lot with a purpose. "Hey, MacReady!"

Cait tensed to her toes then spun to face him.

"What is it? Haven't you got enough out of me yet?"

Trager stopped and shot a glance at Parker. "You. You know *better*."

"But sometimes I forget."

Trager's lips curled down into what would have been a sneer had it gone any further. "Inside. I'm sure you've got paperwork."

"I do at that. Good afternoon, Cait."

"Not for anyone I know."

Trager watched Parker amble off, stubbing out the cigarette on his sole before yanking the door open, tucking the remainder behind his ear. He then turned back to her with an air of spoiled-milk sourness.

"What the hell is wrong with you?" he demanded. "I know. You're not a cop. You don't know procedure, but—"

"You can't arrest her! She doesn't even *belong* here!"

"And if you'd come to us with any of this earlier I wouldn't be backed into a corner."

"I didn't know that Lee was in it for murder. I thought it was just the sort of usual weird shit. That *you* tapped out on."

"I handed it to an expert."

"What part of 'weird shit' was unclear to you? There's no easy path through this. No goddamn checklist for these crimes."

"You thought he was involved earlier. You suggested so."

"And you and Moreno both blew it off. Just crazy fuckin' Cait."

"That's not what…"

"Sure it is. How much did my boss have to say, huh? You know they all think I'm on drugs or whatever? That I'm some kind of goddamned junkie flake."

"Look, Cait. You're hard to read. And I'm pretty good at it."

"Maybe you're just not?"

"And maybe you're not good at fitting in." He tried to settle back down but his strained breath gave him away. His voice came out tight, controlled. "Normal doesn't suit you. I saw that the second I met you at your job. Something's eating you and I don't know what it is."

"Fuckin' *everything*. That's what."

"Maybe you need to slow down. Take some time off. Just rest. Just—"

"Get my head, right? I don't even know what that means anymore. Not since Ariela's death and the book and Fellowes." She tore at her hair for a moment then ripped her hands away and tried to control herself, feeling like she was pinned under a rollover wreck.

"Don't you mean Rico?"

Cait caught her spinning heart in her hands, turning so fast that it burned her, charring them to stumps. But it stopped finally.

"Yeah, I mean Rico. Of course. Rico."

"Your job's done, Cait. We have an APB running and I'm sure that Sue will be released as soon as we get a lawyer down here. I already called for counsel even though she hasn't."

"But you, you need to *slow down*." He was stern and solid, not out of meanness or superiority or worse, pity.

"If I slow down, I'm gonna drown," she said. "Sure hope you send your guys out with scuba gear if they're gonna try and take that guy. He'll fuck their shit right up. Or don't you believe that?"

"I believe that we'll get him under observation and we'll figure out a way to get him under wraps. Anything else you wanna add?"

"No, just lemme go so I can see what else I can fuck up."

"Don't make me suggest protective custody."

"You'd have to find someone who cared enough to throw me into it. Goodbye, Lieutenant."

"Where you going?"

"Someplace where I can seem sane."

She got in the car without waiting on a reply.

৫২৴

The blinking red light on the answering machine was the first thing she saw in the darkened room. She pressed the playback button hard enough to make her thumb hurt.

"Hey, Kitty. It's uncle Vince. I know. It's not even a week yet, but your mom was working on me and—"

Next.

"Cait, hello. This is John. Watkiss of Quest4. I know it's been a long time and—"

Why am I so popular now? Next. Be good.

"Ms. MacReady, Thaddeus—"

Cait wanted to rip the machine out of the wall and smash it. She thought about the act, the satisfaction of watching it shatter into junk. Just like everything else she'd done. Little pieces, impossible to put back together. She only had the energy to press the END button.

Nothing had gone right. Not since I wrote that goddamned book and got Rico killed, yes Rico, him first. Not Ariela. Who was she anyways? A crazy witch? A crazy witch who valued something I made. And maybe me. Even if it was just to feed that all to—

Cait locked up for a moment remembering staring into the space within the storm where it was all eyes and beyond that some kind of damned machinery, a system without a name or a purpose other than being everything, investigating everything, consuming everything. It pulsed and roared like an hunger given shape and Ariela was there to bring it into our world. Cait had just told her how to do it, somehow.

Or was she going to close it off? Was that the circuit?

It doesn't matter. It is done. She is gone. Rico is gone. The world is broken now. Things are being let in one by one. And Sue's brother is just another of those trickling horrors.

Cait wanted to draw a bath and throw herself in it. It would at least be over then.

Maybe that's all I really wanted this whole time.

She gathered herself together. That wasn't it.

Answers. Those she wanted.

She went back to the bedroom and started tearing apart boxes until she found what drove her. Then she dressed and put on warpaint severe enough to get her through even the doors of the Last Prayer Club. The muscle memory was right there where she'd left it. Months of going straight and narrow hadn't withered it. Her mascara lines were strong and bold. The black dress hung a little bit in places but there wasn't any time to do anything about that.

Cait paused for a moment, looking at the steady amber light on the machine as she got ready to leave.

I better.

She fast forwarded for a second to pass Khan's message. Then a hiss of tape before the next one.

"Miss Mac-Ready?" Heavy drawl, thin voice. It was the trailer park operator, Crews. "Yeah, I wanted to tell you that, Lee, he was back. And you told me to call if he came back. So I am. He asked after you and his sister and I told him. He didn't seem unhappy about it. But he wanted to talk to you so I gave him your number. That's all. Good afternoon."

Cait stood there a moment, wondering about that. It seemed like he'd have already known, what with the water and the bible and that strange compulsion. That was magic. That was something reaching back and shutting down a connection.

That has to be Lee, doesn't it? Or could something else have been listening?

She took down her black handbag, the weird vintage one that had a clasp done up with fake gold and pearls and curling like a spiderweb. She put the knife into her ratty black trench coat with its long, hidden pocket up front. Then she got in the Mercury, threw the first tape she could grab from the shoe box full of them and listened as the heavy drone that opened "A Forest" flooded the car like a black wave. Then she drove to Hollywood. Maybe she didn't have the answers. Someone else would.

The kewpie dolls at the door gave Cait no problem this time other than to say "Different outfit next time. We remember that one."

Cait let them eat a flipped bird and she passed into the red and dark loudness of the club. It was early yet so the PA was brutal and hollow. Without a couple hundred bodies to soak up the sound it reverberated crazily everywhere. It was scattered and without focus, percussive but empty, slicing without injury. The lights were low and set in the floors, casting up the walls so everyone was a black shape against a red or purple background that was suggestive of meat and bruises.

The club was subdued, funereal almost.

She regretted not asking the girls up front if the Queen was even in, but there was no way she was going to go back and check. A total expenditure of any face earned by passing through the doors in the first place.

Maybe the bartenders. They know everything, right?

She moved deliberately. If she didn't own the space, she was going to get hauled into someone else's, made into points scored by someone else. Best to be impervious and bulletproof. Maybe the answer would come to her if she just flowed with the room hard enough.

The man behind the bar was wiry to the point of being flayed, muscles fibers like fingerprints over his entire body with a ruby sheen of baby oil or sweat in the red lights. He was bald down to his eyebrows and the eyes beneath were green and penetrating in their vacancy. His front teeth were steel and he looked like a machine when he spoke.

"You drinking?"

"Yeah," Cait said. "White Russian."

"Okay. First night here?" he said as he grabbed the vodka bottle, Cyrillic characters in white on a red label, constructivist in layout.

Rocket fuel.

She shuddered at the coincidence but pocketed the chill instead of giving in to it.

"Why?"

"Haven't seen you before. You got a nice mask. Good legs too."

Cait rolled the shudder off. Uninvited and unwelcome. "Came in before. Months ago," she said. "When Ariela was still queen," she added.

He nodded, light playing off his gleaming skin. "Another era." He poured the Kahlua, just enough cream to put a white halo on top of the drink and slid it to her.

"What do I owe you?" she asked.

"You don't. Just watch yourself." His eyes indicated someone near and to the left but said nothing else.

A hand closed around her upper arm. Cait didn't look to see who it was. Beneath notice.

"Back off," she growled like chunks of asphalt buried in raw skin.

"Just tryin' to be friendly," said a gassed male voice.

"I'm not interested in making friends."

"Then why you dressed up like this?"

Cait turned to see a dude her height only because he was wearing lifted boots. He had scraggly-dreadlocked hair that ran down to his shoulders, bony as they were, rickety as a farm torn down to beams after a tornado. There were trinkets and little bones and junk woven through his hair so it glittered in the club's lights. His nose was biggish and his eyes were sunken as the dead. Cait keyed in on the patch on his ratty outerwear, curves with circles between like a compound eye, like a fly's eye. Like the one that clerk at Vinyl Fetish had worn, though she didn't know its significance. Things came and went overnight, so it was maybe nothing more than that.

"Because I respect the goddamn dress code. Now buzz off."

"Pare, leave her alone. She's not here for you. She wants to see the Queen." The voice cut right through the club noise, pure as crystal glasses being rung.

"I saw her first, Cut," he growled, sour as a kitten.

"I saw her a long time before you."

Cut stood tall, a little more so than Cait, but thinner, slighter, balanced expertly between he and she. They wore a black bodysuit with razor slashes through the fabric. Exposed skin radiated white in the club lights, shown by cuts that looked like open and irisless eyes. Over all that, they wore a blouse or something that was stitched together out of too many T-shirts with band names blazed across them in silkscreen. Only pieces were recognizable, brought together into a whole that was a kaleidoscopic nonsense, syllables strung together into a babble.

"So pleased to meet you at last," Cut said, extending a hand as if they expected a kiss.

"At last?" Cait took a hard sip of the drink, trying to soften the edges of the conversation sure to come.

"Ever since you came through the door, dearest." Cut must have been a dancer, fat melted off, leaving only lean muscle now streamlined as a sidewinder missile or an art deco skyscraper.

"I didn't come looking for a date."

"But you came looking for something." Cut melted onto one of the ratty leather-and-chrome barstools, ripped with razors and knives over time, so it was more rough than smooth.

I can't read them. Are they No Tomorrows or just a club vampire? Waste of time or a good line?

"Yeah but not for you. Though I like what you've done with the shirt. Burroughs wept."

"How dry," Cut said before grabbing a drink off the bar. Maybe it was even theirs. "Are you sure you should be out playing with the wild boys, tourist?"

"Please. I was in clubs like this before you were in middle school."

"But now looking for something more royal?" Cut sipped from the thin black straw into thin black lips.

"Sure. I'm here to see the Queen."

"The Queen is dead. You killed her, right? I recognized you, even with the square haircut and color. So Lady Clairol." Cut's smile was as charming as a face through a windshield.

"Ariela killed herself chasing something. Found it too. I'm here to see Alondra."

The back of Cut's hand brushed against the side of Cait's head that had been cut short. "Alondra may call the shots but not everyone recognizes her as the Queen."

"That's not an answer." Cait finished her drink and flipped the glass over, thinking about breaking Cut's nose with it. "But she's Queen all the same."

"And you think knowing that gives you any kind of leverage, hmm?"

"We could ask her."

Two more black and white vultures, pasty and thin, drifted in line behind Cut. On the street, either of them would be unique. In here, they were just wallpaper.

"Trouble, Cut?" One of them asked, hair haystacked up high and shaved on the sides. The tattoo on his scalp said WITHERING HEIGHTS in straight razor slashes.

Cut's eyes went to Cait's glass and flicked back to her face. "I don't think so. She's here to see Alondra."

"And you tell her I'm here," Cait growled.

"Why?" Cut's eyebrow shot up and was *Vogue*-perfect.

"My business, not yours. And I'm getting tired of thrift-store weirdos putting their faces into it."

"Testy. But I'm still going to need a reason."

"Someone's following me," Cait said. "Someone from No Tomorrows. Someone who still loves Ariela."

"Of course we *all* still love Ariela. Some more than others." Cut smiled without mirth and leaned back to the Mohawk-do then whispered, coming back with a cat-cream grin. "Expect nothing tonight and you might not be disappointed."

"Maybe I'll do to you what I did to Ariela if I don't get what I want."

They looked her up and down in dreary appraisal. "I *love* a good magic trick. You wait here."

A few more clubgoers filtered through the doors. More total weirdos than not. Some folks street-legal and wouldn't get stopped by even the most bored beat cop. Lots of people with something to prove. Leather and plastic, piercings and stainless steel, all pretending to be cold and distant as Cut but each having a beating heart within, one that had to be hardened, or it might be bled dry. Cait could appreciate that. That's what she'd been doing. Pretending. Shielding. Petrifying. And the best way to do that was to withdraw so you didn't even exist.

Something moved out of the side of her vision. A girl's face, powder-pale and blue-eyed and those set wide, making her nose seem small and an afterthought. Her hair was pulled back in clumps and fixed with mousse or egg whites, like Cait did more than once, wild as the Bride of Frankenstein. She was staring right at Cait. She was just a kid, probably too young to even drive much less be in a place with a liquor license. She wore the same Siouxsie shirt that Cait had been wearing when everything went to hell, when the world broke.

What's the world for déjà vu that's already happened?

"How'd you get in here? Don't they card?" Cait yelled to her.

The girl turned to disappear into the shadows of the filling crowds as the beat cranked up. Bone-dry rattling snares on a machine track over throbbing electro drones filled the place. Cait wondered how long it would take for the vocals to come on and ruin everything.

"Hey! I'm talking to you!" she shouted.

The girl stopped and turned back, shy as a Bambi in the woods.

"What's with the stare? I know I don't fit with the crowd."

The girl's eyes seemed to eat her. "Why are you here?" she asked. "You don't come here."

"How would you know?" Cait thought about going to a place more than a couple times a week and reading the crowds, seeing the familiar faces, who to greet, who to avoid. Before, that was a game. Felt more like a minefield tonight.

A woman's voice wailed low on the music track, warning and beckoning at once in a language she couldn't understand. It implored coldly.

The girl didn't answer and she'd pulled her gaze away from Cait, standing near but distant.

"You got a name?"

She turned to look back at Cait and started to speak.

"Well, hello, Grace," Cut said. "Why did I think you would be sniffing around?"

Grace looked like she stood about two inches tall.

"Talking to her, not to you," Cait growled.

"Why would you talk to a groupie? One of the *subjects*." Cut's voice flayed in derision.

"What are you talking about, you ridiculous scarecrow?"

Cut's lips pursed as they indicated Grace with a kiss-off. "The subjects. Diehards. Like her. They think Ariela is coming back, that she never died. Isn't that right, sweetie?"

"I'm still allowed to be here. I'm not leaving."

Cut moved in until they were close enough to breathe one another's words. "Not as of to-fucking-night. Your extracurriculars—"

Cait could smell the fight, adrenalin going sweat-flared on skin. "Hey, Cut!" she snapped. "Is Alondra here or not?"

"Not for you," Cut said, not looking her direction. "Come back another time."

"Where is she? Upstairs?"

Their head turned slowly and locked onto her as if she were an idiot. "There is no upstairs. Nothing is upstairs."

"But the last time…" Cait's voice trailed off.

There was. I was there. I was there with Ariela. And she talked about the mirror and the pool and the rock and time. It was like what, like nothing I've seen. And then it was my kitchen with the curtains and that table, that god-damned table.

There is no upstairs.

"But what?" Cut demanded.

"Nevermind."

"Look, you want to stay? Fabulous. But not everyone here is so nice as me."

"Home room was more threatening." Cait said. "Thanks."

"As for you," Cut went to say to Grace. "You can—"

Grace stomped her foot down hard and Cait imagined she could hear something crack beneath it all. Then she shoved and sent Cut backward, off-balance and comical.

Their fall threw everything askew, arms swinging madly. Cait jumped back to avoid it, throwing herself into the bar. She heard a clink and clatter of glasses and ice and her eye was drawn to the sound.

Spelled out in vodka or water or both was the word GO in messy capitals that only held together for an instant, but Cait saw it clearly enough for it to take.

What the hell?

"This is my place too!" Grace's cheeks flushed and maybe there were even tears streaking her dark eyes.

"Not anymore," Cut hissed. "You two, take her out back where I can take some time with her." Their voice thickened in anger and pain.

The two scarecrows moved to grab Grace by either arm. Cait flashed to a moment where the same had happened to her on Alondra's order and she had thought for a moment that it was going to be her death or worse. Nobody should get treated like that.

Cait's hand shot inside the deep pocket of the jacket as fingers curled around Grace's upper arms. By the time the knife came out, she was held tight and wasn't going anywhere.

"Hey!" Cait shouted. She turned the knife so it caught the club lights, glittering in red and purple and it made the air itself bleed color. "Let her go!"

If Cut's eyes went wide at the knife, Grace's went wider.

"You think you can wave that and—"

"Shut up! You know what this did. Sure as hell Ariela does." Cait tightened her face and hoped she wasn't going to be pressed into actually using it. She didn't think she could avoid inflicting a fatal wound just about anywhere a blow landed. Cut was far enough at the end of her reach that things would have been impossible to control. She jabbed the tip of the blade a little anyways.

"Okay!" Cut hissed. "You two, let the brat go."

Grace ripped her arms away from both at the same time and smiled grimly.

"But don't ever come back if you want your parts where they started out."

"You can't—" Grace started to say.

"Not me. The Queen," Cut said. "The actual, real Queen, flesh and blood. You and anyone else in the fan club are not going to be tolerated."

So she is here. But I'm not getting to see her, not on my terms, probably not ever.

"But Alondra wouldn't do that!"

"Go and ask her if you want to try."

Cait sank a little at that but knew that she couldn't just show up on royalty and expect anything but a snub. Queen's got to be treated like one. Even if she's just a regent-in-waiting.

Grace looked as if she'd been kicked out of heaven.

"Don't feel bad," Cut teased. "Maybe those poseurs at the Veil will take you sad little creatures in." They pursed their lips and blew, making a wish for her to disappear.

The knife flashed as Cait pulled it back then slipped it into its sheath. "Come on, Grace. I'll get you a ride out of here."

She nodded, but her face did not brighten.

Cait took a step to the door when she felt the rumbling beneath her feet. Something rattled and built up, pressure increasing below the floors. Enough people's heads turned to look and see what was going on for her to figure that she wasn't imagining it. The air went soggy electric as the first pipe burst somewhere in the bartender's sink. Water started gushing out of it and Cait's hair stood on end.

It flowed uphill, out and over the bar, only to cascade down as if it was being run through a tight channel no more than a couple feet wide. The bottles on the shelves rattled and broke, bottoms all giving out at once. A hundred different kinds of alcohol all blended and mixed in the air, astringent and biting. That undrinkable mixture, it too flowed up and joined the weird channel, pouring straight out the door and onto Cherokee street.

Color and light swirled in it, club lights and different densities of liquid: the stream was a hundred things, and it was nothing.

Cait and Grace had no choice but to walk through it as they went out through the doorway. Grace ate in the wonder of the drunken river flowing of its own accord and Cait could only think of what and who was directing her out.

CHAPTER TWELVE

"Nice, but kinda old," Grace said when she heard the music playing in the Mercury.

"'Tonight' by Iggy Pop. From 1977. Not too old." Cait turned it up a little. "You know, you could walk." She tried to figure out if the girl's age but couldn't grab hold of it. That young and Cait's life was maybe UCLA and parties she didn't have any business being at; people she hardly talked to now.

"Sorry."

Cait made the left turn to loop back around to Hollywood Boulevard. This felt more run-down commercial and mundane than the neon-washed candyland a couple blocks behind them. They had left the strip that bordered dreamland, crossing into that which was more workaday, more concerned with balance sheets and invoicing and customer service than trafficking in the imagined.

"Can we do the radio instead?"

"You're a picky one for someone who just got saved a curb-stomping. But I guess."

"Thanks." The girl looked at the cluster of push buttons and frequency indicator like it was an alien artifact.

"You can pick."

"What, are you afraid to touch it?"

"I don't want to break it. This car's special, right?"

Cait drew a heavy sigh and wondered how much of this she'd have to put up with. "I think I could drive this car through a concrete wall and it'd be fine. You won't break anything. Go ahead."

Grace shook her head. "Sorry, I'm just a little messed-up. It's been a long…" she drifted off, as if calculating an impossible length of time. "A long time since things have been normal, particularly lately."

"Hanging out with No Tomorrows will do that to you. What's a nice kid doing—"

"I'm not nice."

"Not sure I believe that for a second." Cait punched up KROQ and gritted her teeth expecting to want to change it immediately. Instead it was the opening strains of "Cities in Dust" and she marveled at her luck. Though her passenger hadn't picked up on it, Siouxsie tee or not. "So where are we going?"

Grace's big blue eyes ate the road and landscape absently and without thought. "I'm hungry. Pie."

"I can drop you at House of Pies. It's close." She tried to figure out what to say next but could only fumble with it.

The thing with the water was certainly the kind of thing that Lee could do, but why? But then why did he do half or any of what he was doing? Maybe it was a warning, maybe just play.

"So that thing with the pipes was weird, right?"

"Mhm-hmm." Grace went from watching the road to watching Cait plainly, not leaving a chance to pull out of it. "But not the weirdest thing you've ever seen, right?"

She left that invitation unopened. "Was what that weirdo had to say true? That you're, I don't know, waiting for Ariela." The question itself left her queasy.

"Cut? They don't know what to say half the time. Are you going to answer my question?"

"When you answer mine. And maybe one other."

"I just want to make sure she's not forgotten. Alondra is a good shot-caller, but that's it. She can't do what Ariela could, though she'll never say it. But you've got to be better than Ariela. You beat her, right?"

"Mhm-hmm," Cait said with a faint mocking tone. "So you know who I am. Hence your question."

Grace's eyes went up and down Cait, pulling her apart. "You look different. I was around then, but still pretty new to the place. I know who you are."

She went to laugh it off but that felt as fake as a Halloween mask that cost her all of a quarter. "You don't know anything. You just know I was around when Ariela died in that junkyard. Were you there?"

"She didn't die." Grace's eyes filled with regret then and she pulled away. "And I couldn't be there. Last night in my old place. Had to set it on fire."

And you might not even be kidding about that.

Cait punched it hard enough to make the Mercury shake in order to catch the yellow arrow onto Franklin. Siouxsie chant-sang in time, a dreamy backing track to the physical sensation of being thrown around by a huge metal bullet.

"Wheeee," Grace said with her arms hanging out the now-open window. "Beats walking." She pulled herself back in. "And I do too know who you are. You wrote the book. The one Ariela wanted."

It didn't sound so bad, so earth-shattering coming from her, this kid who was playing at being tough. Cait wondered if this was how she'd come off back then, back when she had been that young.

"And why did she want it?" she asked, not knowing the answer herself.

"Magic. Power. Both." Grace's expression was blank as the brake lights ahead of them painted her face pink and carmine. They were words repeated without meaning, without knowing what they really were.

"And what do you know about the black rock? Piedra negra?"

"It's something about time, I think. I don't know. I didn't understand her talking about magic."

You and me both.

"You seem sharp enough, but I don't think you know what's really going on."

"And you do?"

"I thought I did. And then I lost everything for a while. It's beginning to maybe come back. But Ariela, what she was chasing killed her. It'll do the same to you."

"It didn't kill you. You're stronger than she was."

"I wasn't running toward it."

Cait saw the tall sign for the restaurant, something seemingly time-lost now, more of thirty years ago than today. She breathed a quiet sigh of relief.

And this is why I never sold to true believers.

"I don't think anyone was stronger or more determined than her. For all the good it did." She pulled to a stop but didn't crank the brake.

"She was real, Cait. The realest." She looked like she wanted to say something else, but the words escaped her.

"She was real, but I don't know what she was. You believe that she was doing magic?" Cait didn't even know what to think any longer. Everything she'd seen in the last week felt more real than what had happened before the hospital and her breakdown. But Ariela had nothing to do with that.

Then why did I go looking for help the last place I found her? Water and time and Ariela was doing something with time. But who knows what. Or space. Or both. Things happening in and out of sequence and across distance at once. Was that magic or something else?

Grace looked at her with eyes that were too deep and wide.

"Are you coming in?" she asked after waiting out the song on the radio.

Cait realized she hadn't eaten since North Hollywood this morning, which only felt like a week ago.

"Okay," she said as she cranked down on the parking break. "But not for long, and you gotta find your own way home."

"I can make something happen."

Cait followed the smaller, slighter girl who walked through the door with insouciant assertion in her slim hips and black tights. She stopped at the sign that said PLEASE WAIT TO BE SEATED and began scanning the room. Cait recognized because it was something she did back not so long ago, having a ton of friends and thinking they could be anywhere at any time. Grace pivoted on her right and waved at someone in back.

"Lilah is here!" She turned back to Cait, enthusiasm barely contained. "We should go back there. She's really cool."

The name rolled around Cait's head unmoored for a moment until she saw the woman sitting by herself in a booth in the back. It couldn't have been the same figure that Cait had pulled out of the water in her van a couple days or weeks or months ago.

But it was definitely the same Lilah, dry and rested, sitting wearing an off-the shoulder dress and threadbare lavender shawl over that. Her long hair was pulled back neatly and she looked over the menu spread in front of her in the pool of light cast from overhead. She looked more substantial, but who wouldn't after having been half-drowned.

"Hi, Lilah. Didn't think you'd be here."

"I get hungry just like everyone else, Grace."

"I brought a friend. A new friend."

Lilah didn't look up from the menu, finger in the middle of the column listing different pies both hot and cold, fruit or cream, nut or berry.

"I like key lime myself," Cait said.

Lilah stopped and craned her head upward. The light from above made her eye sockets seem hollow but for a faint glinting.

"Well, I'll be damned. Ivory look. I hoped I'd see you again sometime."

They both slid into the booth and Lilah watched Cait warily. "Your hair is fixed and you're dressing more like yourself."

Like you know me.

"I was just getting comfortable again. Took a while."

"Hell of a thing to lose yourself, isn't it? Sometimes you don't get to find that again. Slippery like a woman get with a good man—or woman, I don't judge."

"I found her at the club."

"That's not a place for you, girl. They do the rough business there. They think they big, working in the shadows."

"Cut threw me out. Cait saved me a beating. Pulled a crystal knife on Cut and made them cry." She glanced at the menu and set it down just as quickly.

"That was fast," Cait said.

"Coffee and a piece of pie doesn't change."

"Ah to be young enough to survive off that alone." Lilah's eyes went from Grace to Cait then back. "What kind of knife?"

"Like glass. You could see through it." Her blue eyes went narrow as she faked a jab into the air.

"I didn't see you as the type," Lilah said.

"For what?"

"Don't hear too much about glass knives. White obsidian. I thought that was all gone like the golden bear and red wolf, never to be seen again. Old Califia stuff."

"It's real enough," Cait said. "Did you want to see it?"

"Oh, very much. That's a thing I'd like."

The waitress, a tall woman with a high dome of bouffant blonde waited at the edge of the table. "Speaking of what you'd like, what'll you like?" She cracked a smile at her own joke.

Everyone ordered and the waitress disappeared with trim steps. Cait made to pull the knife out of her pocket, curious as to what Lilah knew or if it was the same kind of stuff that the undergrad dudes who read Castaneda tried on her when the joints and candles got lit.

"Such a hurry," Lilah said as she put her hand on Cait's arm. "We can wait a little while, can't we? Waited this long."

Cait finished the burger in short order, not even caring that it wasn't great. Then she waited for Lilah to pick through her pot roast, which felt like the passing of geologic time. Nobody spoke. Grace made an epic poem out of her apple pie and coffee.

Lilah pushed the plate away and cleaned up with some degree of ceremony.

"Now we can talk. Hard to talk when you're hungry. Get impatient. Snappy." She held a hand out flat, faintly curling the tips of her fingers inward. For her apparent age, there weren't so many wrinkles there, just a tightness of skin as if there wasn't quite enough to go around. "Now let's see this."

Only the question wasn't about the knife so much as it was about Cait. She was the one being drawn out of the sheath to be examined. The knife was a pretext. Back on the riverbed, that was someone else, a skin to be shed. What remained behind was on the menu now.

She pulled out the blade and left it on the table, still encased.

"I don't have X-ray vision. I'm not Superman," Lilah teased.

"Yeah, Cait," Grace the girl said with tease.

So you don't want to touch it? Interesting. Or scary. Or both.

Cait wiggled the handle a little bit and pulled it free. She paused when it was only partly loose and the light from above was caught and trapped inside like a swarm of glowing sparks in rippled glass.

Drama. Partial reveal. I'm selling this like it was a book. Why?

"Where did you get this?" Lilah asked.

"Scary dude in No To—" Grace started, excitedly.

"Quiet, child. Watch and learn a thing." Lilah's hand took Grace's, gently but without chance of escape.

"It belonged to a man named Tácito, a kind of magician with No Tomorrows."

"This doesn't belong to *anyone* any more than the sun does."

"I'd have thought you were gonna say the moon," Cait replied. "Seems more that kind of power."

Lilah laughed. "So you're the expert now?"

"I didn't come here asking for knowledge." Cait's pulse quickened some, not quite a lie but not the whole truth.

"Which is why you're out messing around with No Tomorrows in their home, yes? Why you lost yourself? When you can use the right words, because those are the ones to use, then I'll believe you."

"Such as?"

"Tácito wasn't a magician. A magician entertains children with rabbits and card tricks. He wasn't a curandero because curing was not his business, yes? A better word is sorcerer, one who trades with powers.

"So it was held by Tácito. Did he simply hand it to you and then he asked you to enjoy it?"

How did she even?

Cait fully drew the blade out now and held it in what she felt was a neutral position but low enough to not attract attention. Lilah's eyes balanced between the edge of the knife and Cait's own. She laid out a brief story of what had happened, relaxing because she felt like she could have said anything and not be ridiculed or laughed at or suggested that she was cracking. Though she left out the book that she created and wondered how much Lilah would be able to guess at.

"A sad story for some, less so for others." That was all she said for a moment.

"So yeah, that's how I broke the world and ended up with this and the car outside and a total inability to have a normal life." The last came out more bitter than she wanted.

"I didn't say who the story was sad for. And why do you say you broke the world? Like that's a thing that can happen."

"It feels like, like that thing that Ariela let in, even just for a bit, like it's not really actually gone. It's just underneath things or casting a shadow over them. Polluting them."

"And that's all your fault, hmm? Because of the book Ariela wanted? Or because it makes you feel important?"

Cait felt the prickly blush of shame but couldn't give it a reason. "What, what about the knife? It's glass or obsidian, right?"

Lilah held Cait's eyes for a moment and went back to the knife, tracing its edge and the complexities within. "That's not a knife."

"What is it then?"

"A metaphor. That's a good enough word."

"How is that? How is it language?"

"Everything is language. Everything is energy." Her hand reached out but not quite touched the blade. "This a metaphor for working within both."

"I don't understand."

"This, the white glass, is a knife that was coaxed and carved by a girl who was a boy from a piece of a fallen star. It is the shinbone of the great father of the mirror wolves. It is a surgeon's tool and killer's toy."

"More metaphors."

"No, facts. But it is what will be done with it." Lilah's eyes were dark but with a gleam within. "That is all I can tell you. It will make sense, or it will not.

"What have you used it for since it came into your life?"

"Well, I cut my hair with it, to save myself. And that thing, whatever it was, the Sightless Eye. I tested it on a metal tray, sliced through. Banished a thing that Tácito had called to maybe kill me." She swallowed hard, leaving out the fact that it had used Rico's body as a tether. "Oh, and sliced through the name of Ariela's god. I uh, I stabbed a Bible with it." That last one came out harder somehow.

"Now that's an interesting use. Did it work?"

"It did what it was supposed to. That was part of a casting, looking for someone."

"Oh, so you *do* have an idea as to what this is."

Cait shook her head. "Only by coincidence. I was being directed by someone who knew more than I did. She needed a knife that was not used for cooking."

"It's a wise woman who knows which knife to use when. Cross purposes will set you on the wrong road."

"Yeah, I just wish I knew what the right one was."

"Maybe don't think about that so much."

Cait pushed the fork on her nearly empty plate between her two hands, flicking it so that it scraped as if on bones. "And what if the one you're on gets people killed? What if it gets everything killed?"

"Everything is a tall order. Flood and disaster and things like that?"

The image of the black water swallowing the city flashed behind Cait's eyes and she went cold for a moment. "Yeah."

"Now we're back to breaking the world. Specifically you breaking it."

Cait said nothing. Grace watched her with eyes that took in everything and revealed nothing.

"That's *pride*. You know that, right? Nothing but pride."

"But I—"

"You didn't do anything. Maybe Ariela did. Maybe the Sightless Eye did. The mirror surface made the rock fall. You've already been shown these things but maybe you failed to learn anything."

Something churned in her guts, burning with acid. "I don't need this."

Lilah took the half-empty glass of water before her and held it at an angle so the liquid was right at the lip of the glass, a meniscus just visible on the edge threatening to fall but never quite. She held it there for a while.

"You think this is you, right now. Just a perfect balance. It'll all hold. No matter how far things tilt, right? You wore the right clothes and thought you said the right things, but this thing inside you, it wants to spill. It's going to and you're afraid, so you put all your strength in holding it. You know what that gets you?"

Lilah held the glass and waited for an answer. She did not shake or flinch.

Cait felt herself wanting to reach for and right it, to keep the spill from coming. The feeling passed and weariness welled up in her, the same that had her doing nothing but surviving, nothing but being half-alive, unable to listen to the record, just staring at it in her lap and knowing that there was more to it but unable to summon the strength to do anything but that. But watch.

"Tired," she said, and she felt like she'd been dragged up and down the boulevard, barely holding onto the bumper of the car dragging her, wanting to let go to do something else, but that was unthinkable.

"You damn right." Lilah kept turning the glass until it was all but inverted, water and ice still tilted at the lip. "Takes effort. Maybe it's better to be a thing than fight being it."

"So I should be crazy?"

"Crazy is this force that I can't see touch but can feel that draws this stuff down, all to the center of the earth. But if you know the right way, well you can trick it for a time."

Cait watched the glass for too long a while. It should have dumped out. It should have.

Nothing worked for a moment, not time or the pull of weight.

Then the water sluiced out onto the table, too much of it for just the little glass that Lilah had been holding. It was almost a physical relief for Cait to see. Runnels splayed out and seemed to breathe, like an anemone or a flower unfolding in time-lapse and then it drew back upon itself as impossibly as it had been suspended outside gravity.

"What do you see? Quick, don't think," Lilah asked.

Cait stared at the liquid on the table, reflecting the overhead lights so that it almost glowed. The words GO HOME were written out in uneven but clear letters, faintly quivering but maybe that was just Cait herself, feeling her hands shake with the pulsing blood that roared within her. The water was moving in time with her blood. It was all the same.

"I have to go home."

"But not until you paid the bill," Lilah said with a grin. "Knowledge never comes for free."

"I'm sorry, Grace. I have to go." Cait pulled out a couple rumpled bills from her purse, not counting them, just tossing them on the table as she shivered out of the booth.

"I'll figure something out," Grace said. "The Palomas house is never too far."

Cait didn't ask what it meant marched out to the Mercury, cranked the key and the stereo then drove home like she was water running downhill, like she heard a voice telling her where to go before it happened so that there was no resistance, effortless.

↺↻

The single light on the answering machine blinked orange in the dark room. Cait saw that and only that before she flicked the room light on and the adrenalin ran right out of her. Probably just Trager yanking her chain or worse, Moreno being unleashed. All the cop stuff had been handled about as badly as Cait could manage and she hadn't even been trying. Just screwing it up at every at-bat. She punched the button and gritted her teeth.

Nothing. Just line noise.

It couldn't be anyone professional. They'd have started yammering the second the line opened.

"I never know when these things're on." The voice on it was Lee's, or whoever it was that lived in him. Something in it crept through Cait's bones like a child-killing disease.

At least he's not on his way here.

"I ain't even mad about things. Crews let you in and that's between me and him. But I know now you do have a thing that's mine, that I need back. I wish you hadn't lied to me at the river. Maybe you were too ignorant to know your lie. Maybe you and I can still work a trade."

Shit. He wants Sue and thinks she's with me, not in jail.

No. Not Sue. Something else.

"Keep waiting for an answer like I'm talking to someone. Anyways, that shell that you saw fit to steal from me? It's more than you know and I got a father who's anxious to see his daughter again, so whyn't you bring that to me so that my work can be done and you might live to see it so. Midnight sounds good. Midnight. The Sep-ul-ve-da Dam. Bring that shell. Don't not bring it."

The shell? I don't even understand. He's talking like it's alive. Didn't even ask about Sue.

The machine stopped with a thunk and the light went out.

He didn't say anything about not calling the police or anyone else.

She glanced up at the clock, just under an hour until midnight. It might take her about a half an hour to get there.

Cait punched up the number and waited for someone to pick up.

Cops work late, right?

"Trager. What." His voice was strained to near breaking, whether it was irritation or fatigue was anyone's guess.

"It's Cait. I know where Lee Whelan is going to be."

"I'm listening. So long as it's not magic bullshit."

"Not unless AT&T is magic in your book."

"Go ahead."

"He wants to meet me. The Sepulveda Dam. Midnight."

"Ooh. Dramatic."

"Be serious. Or do you not want him still?"

"No, I want him. This just sounds like a setup. What's he want?"

"Something I have. A thing he's developed an attachment for."

"Not his sister?"

"No he didn't even mention her. Sounds like he's just expecting me and nobody else."

"They all say that. What's the trade?"

"Not a trade so much as 'gimme this.' But maybe I can get some answers out of him."

"You're not going *anywhere*. Got it? I see you up there, I'll put you in stir myself."

"Then you better get a move on," she said as she slammed the receiver down.

CHAPTER THIRTEEN

Cait leaned up to the wheel, driving it hard from the shoulders down, every muscle tensed. *Phantasmagoria* by the Damned played as loud as it would go as she roared down to Sepulveda and up the pass. Couldn't depend on the 405 being clear, not even near eleven on a Monday night. The permeable border between LA and Santa Monica was riddled with fancy houses, glass and steel and concrete, clutching at a germ-free future. Others were less than forty years old but falling over, built with money that had been bled from the state or the land or even dreams and imagination. None of it felt real anymore. It all felt strange as that night she'd spent in the back seat of the Mercury with Ariela as they both read the book, the one that Cait had written. The one she'd been asked to write.

Dave Vanian croon-roared about the shadow of love and Cait sang along with it because that much at least felt right. She jammed through the tunnel, going around a car that was at least as old as the Mercury, all deco curves and chrome and driven by a ghost for all she knew. Those good old days were never gonna let go, not gonna be buried so easily. She flew out the other side and kept rolling hard.

The Sepulveda Dam had been built for flood control in the forties but was a useless concrete barrier most of the rainless year. Surrounded by sprawling bracken and willows, it was more a wetland than river up the backside. The worst thing that you'd find out there would be a really hungry coyote or a homeless camp. Still, Cait had to work to keep her pulse from racing. She nosed the Mercury through a ripped-out section of hurricane fencing that normally would block off the access road. It'd be a good place to run a beat-up truck through.

And it beats walking.

The earthen wedge of the dam rose up on the car's right side, headlights bouncing off it, and on the left, there was only flat land leading to the dam itself. A few days ago, this place would have been soaked with the early winter rain, but the land had sucked all that dry already after the long summer. The river channel was maybe ten feet wide here, flowing under the main dam structure. Cait drove past the largest part of the structure, the curved wall and flying buttress towers that gave the place the sort of past-in-the-future looks that made it a prized location for car commercials and weirdo science fiction flicks ever since it had been built.

Above the bouldered dam wall the sky was starless, just the churning high clouds reflecting the light of the city like staring up into the surface of an implied ocean. Cait didn't like the thought and put that one away.

Crazy. This is crazy. I should just let Trager and Open Door deal with him.

Sure. Deal with a guy who can make the river rise up and call things out of time, and they're gonna say "stop or I'll shoot," and that didn't work before, so why should it now?

She stopped the car and waited for herself to calm down before getting out. It was early still. Plenty of time to just sit and think. Or wait for backup to arrive and maybe put an end to this whole dumb thing. Then she could go get a job and just go back to normal. She wouldn't get tired. She was okay with that.

What the hell did Lilah know anyway?

The curves of the dam were lit at the ground level, the rest of it falling into darkness outside the limit of her headlights. It looked more like a moonbase than flood control.

At least it's dry ground here. He can't pull a river surge that far.

She turned the lights off and waited in silence for moments that dragged on like splinters under fingernails.

The sound of an old and only serviceably-tuned engine echoed off the concrete. It seemed to come from the side of the river and Cait didn't ask how that was possible. It was not going to be an answer she liked.

She turned the headlights back on and there was the truck, wet to its fenders, dripping water that seemed green in the headlights. It sat there in the center of the concrete plain that marked the dam's spillway. Cait felt sick and empty like she was standing on the shore watching a tsunami build in the distance, shattering power just growing and growing. There was the faint hope that it was so far away that maybe it would weaken before it came and smashed everything to bits. That was all that kept her standing there and not running as hard as she could away.

The truck jerked to a stop and the door opened. Lee stepped out, tired and stiff-seeming, back bent in the hefting of some unseen weight. He was swirling and reflective in the Mercury's headlights. The waters were with him and he wore them like armor.

He waved and smiled. "Come on out. I ain't gonna bite ya." He waited for her to listen, standing still but the waters around him moving eerily hinting at swarming currents below the surface. If Cait looked hard, she could see faces in them, just for a second, melting and re-forming, never the same twice.

"You don't look the type," he said.

"What type is that?"

"To be hanging around Sue. She's so godly, and I can tell at a glance you aren't. Where is she, anyways? I knew I said to come alone, but I'd have been glad to see her. Save me a trip."

"Maybe she was afraid to," Cait snapped. It wasn't much, but she wanted to put down her shame at having broken her word to Sue, leaving her with the police.

Which should be safer than here.

"Oh, she's safe enough from what's coming. I'd never harm her. Never really harm her."

Which of you? Her brother or any of the other voices in you?

"And just what is coming?" Cait gripped her hand around the handle of the blade, even though he was fifty feet away. There was no way she could hope to cover the ground in time. But it was at least some reassurance.

"Nothing that wasn't here in the first place," he said with a plummy note, as if it had been eternal wisdom. "Ain't you figured that out yet?"

"Sure. You're pulling stuff out of the past, bringing it here. Those fish in that guy you killed. The river. The thing you tried to kill Sue with. Wouldn't harm her, my ass."

"Hell, if I was trying to kill her, she'd be dead. She didn't understand is all."

"And what didn't she understand?"

"What's rolling now. What always was. The chorus is warming up, getting ready to sing this all into the way that, well, the way that it is wanted. The singing, it woke a thing. The wanting woke a thing. You might say it's all wanting now."

"You're gonna kill a lot of people to do that, flooding the LA basin. You want that?"

Lee shook his head with humor and modesty. "I don't want anything. I'm just here to help. The Thing That Wants…" He shook his head again, like he'd known what to say but it slipped away from him. "I don't think it's a nameable thing. It's too big for that."

"Leviathan?"

"Haha!" The laugh came out like water gurgling from a corpse's mouth. "That's for Sunday school and keeping sinnermen in line. Hell ain't like that. Neither is heaven. Neither is being dead for that matter."

"Because Sue came out here to end you."

Lee stopped as if he'd been struck and the waters around him went still and smooth which was somehow worse than the teeming glimpses it had been before. Whatever force rippled through them went quiet and flat like it was coiled up and waiting now.

She could see his face clearly and without the distortion of the water he wore as clothing and shield. Without that, she could see that Lee was dead and drowned, but there he was, walking and talking with another thing's voice. His flesh was white and bleached, wrinkled but intact enough to hold his features. Maybe he was between, coming and going.

"She wouldn't tell me that," Cait said. "But I thought about it for a while. That's what Sue's task is, the one she can't hand to anyone else. It's blood, and she wants it cleansed."

"Dead isn't what you believe it to be, girl." His eyes watched her through the still water, bulged and distorted by liquid refraction. Sediment and bone swirled now, veiling him. It should have been his shroud, but it was incomplete. The sight of his vacant yet lit eyes would never be something forgotten.

"You're being used. You could stop this."

"I could stop this no more than prevent creation. But maybe it can be made right this time."

"You can fix it?"

"I'm just what you'd call a facilitator. They can speak to me and I can listen, but pretty soon, everyone'll hear. I won't even be needed. Just so soon as you give me that shell for starters." There was a chill in his voice, bone-eating.

Everything now reminded Cait that Lee was un-alive. Even Fellowes had at least that, in the moment that Tacíto's servant had not yet killed him, just made him an idiot and destroyed his mind. There was still a presence there. Lee was an absence, animate and consuming. An un-thing.

"You stop this. I'll get you what you want."

A lie, but I have to keep him hooked. "Be right there, Cait," my ass.

He took a step toward her. "It ain't for you to interfere."

"And the thing that wants, he gets to?"

The curtain of dust lifted from him and Cait saw a stiff tongue pulled across teeth as if before a meal, an unholy grace.

"Ain't a *he*. Ain't even barely an *it*. More like a weight. Maybe you'll get to understand, should it be wanted. But I really must insist that I have that shell back. Things must be complete."

Cait put a hand in her other pocket and if Lee was worried about a gun, he didn't show it. She pulled it out slow and held it to the side, so he could see the shape of the carved shell in the light.

There was a wanting smile on his face but the expression was uneven and wrong, like someone else forming it with their fingers from within.

"Daughter," Lee said, but it was not his voice. It sounded like stone, something ancient. Primal. Every father.

"What do you mean?"

"That is her house," the thing in Lee said. "She hides there. We made a place for her in everything. She must join the song. Give her over."

The girl's voice. In the bathtub and the observatory. It's her.

The realization hit Cait bodily. She tensed like she'd kissed a high-voltage line.

"No."

"It is not yours," Lee said with another's voice.

"And she isn't yours." Cait wrested the knife free of the sheath, fumbling it, so it cut through the jacket pocket as it pulled free, no harder than cutting air. "Not another step."

"Not yours," said the stone voice. "Now you're just stepping where you may not," came Lee's voice, a change as sudden as a rogue wave sweeping up. "I get it. You want something for something. That's fair. This is America. We can deal."

"I don't want anything you have."

"You got no idea what I got. What I can get. Those trinkets and coins? That ain't even half of nothing." His voice pretended envy and desire, but only the memory of it, a rotten and degraded bouquet buried a lifetime ago.

Goddammit, Trager. Where the hell are you? I can only keep him going for so long.

"What do you think water's for? Just for drinking? For fighting over, out here in the west? Water is what you might call a medium, like paper or magnetic tape or radio waves." He took another step and it was stiff and staggered.

"Being dead makes you crazy, huh?"

"You know what's crazy? You're drinking the same water that dinosaurs drank. The same water that life crawled out of, not no six thousand years ago but further back than nearly everything can remember. Ain't that a kick?"

A chill crawled down from the base of her skull as if the whole of it was ice now melting and falling falling falling. A childhood memory of science class and how humans were mostly water and the planet was mostly water and that never seemed strange until this moment.

"I hadn't thought about it." Cait kept the knife to where it could slice the shell and hopefully not take a finger with.

"Anything that happened, the water remembers it. And I can bring it back. I've been granted that much. Now, sure it helps when I can hold a piece of it, helps me talk. But it don't always need that."

"I don't believe you."

"Don't believe? Ha! You've seen it!" The smile that had hung on his face, visible but obscured, washed away. "Give me the thing and I'll give you a treasure. I'll pull the song of it out of your blood. I could do it now. I am." The voice shifted several times, different timbres melting and running through it, so there was not one voice but several. "You were never safe here."

The chorus. But that can't—

She thought she heard the crush of tires but couldn't tell if that was real or wish.

"You don't have power over me."

"Hell, *you* don't have power over you. That's a sad song I hear in you, but more'n that, it's… well, it's pitiable." He reached into the swirling waters around himself and pulled something out. "You think the water is all outside of you, but the blood, that's within. All that's got to be done is to bring it out." He lobbed the thing he'd found in the water, letting it land with a wet slap at Cait's feet.

"Go ahead and look. It'll still be there. And I won't even move. Promise."

Her eyes flicked down, not believing him. She only meant to look for a second or less. She couldn't pull away. It looked like a flat, black sea creature of some kind washed up on shore and left to bake in the sun. A flower of broken unfairness. Splatter of water around it already drying but the shape remained. Cait could make out the fingers and thumb, splayed out at angles that bones wouldn't allow.

But that was impossible. She'd cut the gloves to ribbons in anger and sorrow. She'd left them in the puddle there by Ariela's memorial marker but then picked them up and cut them into a state where they could never be reassembled, replaced, remade.

But the water had remembered.

"Time ain't what you thought, huh? Takes some getting used to." He sounded like he was right next to her now.

How long was I—

His voice tore her out of shock, but that trailed behind her, like a burning fuse that she couldn't outrun. She swiped at him, his voice anyway. Maybe it would be enough to throw him off guard so something, anything else could happen. She felt the thoughts boiling at the back of her mind. That rising surge of despair and desperation was there because it had never left, no matter how hard she'd wished it away.

The knife met only air, hissing as it cut an arc before her. She looked but there was nothing.

"You thought you were safe here. You brought the seas with you. And so long as that heart of yours beats blood, I'm gonna have the advantage."

She felt something wrench the shell from her, leaving her hand wet and empty. Whatever gripped her wrist was frigid with a chill that went past skin and all the way inside.

"The river's right there," he whispered as big as the ocean itself. "You can wash those sins away or at least try." Maybe the voice was inside her, just like the blood that went sluggish in her veins now. She wasn't dirty so much as she felt like she wanted to dissolve. She'd had so many chances before to do that but hadn't let it happen.

She could do it now.

Lights flashed behind her and a sound like screaming, but she couldn't tell what it was. All she could think about was falling, falling into the river and clawing through the bottom, clawing through time, going back to when things hadn't been wrong and starting over there. Every cell in her sang that song, not of destruction but of chasing what could not be caught, not here on the land or in the air but in a world that was so much older.

He brought the glove back. He undid time. He knows. He knows how to go back and undo things.

It could be found in the water. If she went deep enough. She felt herself taking the first step toward it.

"Oh, ya brought friends. Little late." He glanced over Cait's shoulder as she passed him. "Little little little lit-tle late. I've no need of trinkets any more, no attachments for what was wanted is now had."

"Get down on the ground!" came a clipped and metallic voice off in the direction of the headlights, but for all of Cait, they were a million miles off.

She was walking to the river. Nothing would stop her.

Then she fell into it and hoped there would be no bottom.

CHAPTER FOURTEEN

The water was black and green and blue around her, sunless but all those colors within. Water rushed into her ears and for a moment she heard the collapsing rush of her pulse and then she heard music and song. A voice, a child's voice begging for release and tears lost to the water and then nothing for a time, a long time.

Then another voice and a second, and they were singing a song that could only

CHAPTER FIFTEEN

Cait came to in an unfamiliar and antiseptic room, unbearably parched. The last thing she remembered was the cool comfort of water and never needing to feel thirsty again and this was the opposite. Cold mint-green walls with the blandly-planned abstraction of hotel paintings hanging on them. The beeping of a machine that she was vaguely aware of being in time with her heart. The dry tang of chlorine from scratchy sheets.

Hospital. What happened.

"Good, you're awake," said a curt and clipped voice from somewhere just outside her vision. "I'll go get your friends."

Her throat hurt, rubbed sandpaper raw. The taste in her mouth was green and cloying, unmistakably algae.

"What friends?"

"The police are everyone's friend," said the nurse with more than a little irony. "Don't get up."

Trager plowed into the room a moment later, Parker following him a couple steps behind. Trager was unreadable until the scowl twisted across his whole face.

"I told you to stay home. Pretty sure I remember that."

"I heard you," Parker offered. "That's what he said."

"Not now." He held up a pointed finger and waited to hear nothing for a moment. "What the hell were you thinking?"

Cait didn't have an answer. She had a hundred answers. "You guys were outclassed."

"A guy in a pickup truck? Come on."

"Did you catch him?" she asked. "Did you throw him behind bars and get him injected into the judicial system?"

Trager's scowl faded back to something more like mere disappointment. "He disappeared into the river. Right where we found you, trying to drown yourself."

"I was trying to put that part together. Didn't have enough pieces." She sat up in the bed slowly. Her chest and back spiked pain as if she'd been dragged over an unending river of rocks and stones. "You're lucky he didn't reach into your head like he did me."

"Uh-huh," Trager said.

"You don't really believe that I wanted to kill myself, do you?" Anger welled up in her, flushing her cheeks.

Or is that shame? I couldn't control what was going on and it was exactly what I wanted.

She bunched up a fist, wadded in sheets and not entirely visible.

"Maybe not deliberately." He sat on the bed without asking permission because why would he need to? He tried to shake off the fury that he'd shoved below the surface but liked the feel of it too much to let go entirely. "Look, I read your files from job and from your previous hospitalization." Any judgment there was tempered enough as to disappear. "You had pills that you didn't get at a pharmacy. Need I go on?"

"Yeah."

He took a heavy breath for a long time. "Your house."

"So I'm lazy. And those pills were prescribed for nerves six goddamn months ago. Just refilled them for cheaper elsewhere. I took like two last week when things were coming apart but haven't since. Make me piss in a cup if you don't believe me. It'll be mostly coffee."

Trager brought his hands up, trying to hold her off. "All I know is what I've read and what I've seen. You're not who you were six months ago. Whoever that was who faced down half of No Tomorrows and told me they were gonna do it alone? They're gone now. I don't recognize who's left."

"I didn't either."

"Enough to make you try to cash all your chips in?"

"Fuck off. Lee did something, reached in my head and threw a switch. I just needed to…"

"To what? Turn down the volume on the voices in your head? You know that sounds like a not-well person talking."

"Says the guy who talked to a television to solve crimes."

"A television?" Parker asked. "Oh shit, that was you?"

"Yeah, 'oh shit' that was me," he growled back. "You keep shutting up now."

"Look," Cait said as she finally let go of the sheets, tension of the fabric still pressed into her skin. "I feel like shit, like the worst dentist visit ever. But I'm not, not sick in the head." She smacked her temple a couple times with her fingertips and regretted it instantly.

"You said *not* twice. Double negatives don't work like that."

Cait bit her lip just to slow herself down a second. "So I'm crazy. And Lee just disappeared into two feet of water so you couldn't find him. Is that it?"

"Something like that." He sighed and turned his irritation inward. Lee getting away was eating him as much or more as it was Cait. "Did you at least learn anything on your damn-near-fatal misadventure?"

"No judgment. No matter *what* it sounds like."

"My lips are sealed," Parker said.

"Dammit, kid. You are gonna feel my hand before this exchange is through. Do your talking at the station." He turned back to Cait, eyebrows raised, flat-lipped in expectation. "Hit me."

Cait told him, carefully at first, what she thought she'd figured out about how Lee wasn't really Lee any longer and that whatever had a hold of him made all the weirdos in No Tomorrows seem like second-raters, the chorus of voices and the treasures from the water and how he could maybe use them to talk to the dead or whatever else was happening and it sounded so crazy as she said it. But there was no way to take it back. She waited for him to pull out a straitjacket and fit her for it.

"So what's the dead man want?" he asked. "To send us all back to the Flood?"

"At least Los Angeles. Anything on the Pacific side of the Hollywood Hills. Probably more."

"This whole thing used to be a big sea, you know?" Parker spoke up, half-wistful, half-grave. "Everything from Malibu to the hills and south almost to Anaheim. Under a hundred feet of water."

"But what the hell for?" Trager asked.

"You're asking for a reason? Because that's what was before," Cait said. "It'll be a flood in time as well."

"And do you know what the fuck that means?"

"Not a goddamn clue." She flopped back on the pillow and wanted to disappear into it. "But that's what I heard."

He pinched the bridge of his nose as if migraine-wracked. "I know I'm going to regret saying this, but 'heard' from who?"

"The drowning chorus."

"And they're, what, ghosts?"

"Again, not a goddamn clue. You pulled me out of the water before I could get an answer."

"Before you could kill yourself, you mean."

"If I really wanted to kill myself, I'd have done it by now."

"I'd rather the psychiatrist on staff tell me that."

"And then maybe we could turn around, have you answer some questions with the one hundred percent truth and see how he treats you. Come on, Trager. We both know how that will turn out. I'll get locked up and Lee or the chorus or whatever else gets their way."

"And Hollywood goes beachfront," Parker said. "I dunno, boss. We could make a killing."

"You stopped being funny the minute you came over, Parker. You know that?"

"Now you're just being hurtful."

"Not enough. Cait, how long have we got before everything goes bad? And don't say, 'I have no goddamned idea.'"

"Okay, sure. I have no fucking idea. Other than soon."

Trager left Cait with instructions to stay the fuck there and get better. The nurse told her that she was being kept under observation, which was somehow less kind. The room got very small, walls pressed tight as a cave-in. She became acutely aware of the IV needle in the back of her hand, of fluid flowing into her. The liquid looked clear but she suspected there was something in it, something aware and watching her as much as she was watching it seep into her veins. Nausea settled in her insides like a spoiled jelly. Anything she'd need would be a button away, but there was nothing she wanted nearby.

And what could she even do if she got out and found Lee again? He'd just wiggle a hand around in the soup of her brains and pull out something worse. Whatever was coming was already here and she was helpless to stop it. She wished for the right words to convince Trager that she wasn't a flake or a junkie or whatever he thought was going on. The truth was that it wasn't even as dramatic as all that, just that she wasn't worth listening to. She wished for a river to sleep in. Maybe the water would wash it all away if it just roared in hard enough.

Her eyes closed for a moment and what followed was black. But not black enough.

The room was unlit when she awoke. Impossible to tell what the hour was, only no-time. The curtains were drawn on the dark so she couldn't see if it was the flat grid of lights of the Valley out there or the crazy patchwork of Los Angeles with the rivers of white and red that were the highways cutting through the landscape of irregularity and planned chaos. Day or night, it didn't matter where or when she was.

She could see that there was a dark shape at the foot of the bed, sitting on a bench there, back to her. Cait tried to pull the shape together in the half-light of the instruments and monitors and when she did, the heart within her clutched ice and stopped pumping for a moment that seemed to last forever.

Ariela?

Eyes adjusting to the dark, she saw the twin noose braids hanging down the woman's back, sketched out in green and washed lights. She was too large to be Ariela, shoulders too broad and taller. But if you'd have asked her, she'd always stood in Ariela's shadow. Only now she was out in the spotlight.

"The Queen visits," Cait said.

"Don't use that title. It's not yours." Alondra tensed underneath her leather jacket and it creaked quietly as dying breath. She did not turn around.

"Which should I use?" Anger and fear pulled at her in changing measure, claws from all sides. It was one thing to stupidly go chasing after Alondra at Last Prayer, another entirely to have her appear in a place that even Cait didn't know the name of.

"You know my name. Use that."

"Fine. Alondra. How did you find me?"

"You should ask *why* instead."

"Maybe you should ask the questions since you don't want to answer mine." Cait scratched at the IV needle and the collar of her gown. Everything was dry. She looked for a glass of something to drink then saw a cloudy plastic glass half-filled with something that could have been water, but what was in it past that? She shuddered at the thought, dry sheets scratching.

"Nothing is hard to find if you know where to look." Alondra stood up and pulled a chair over to where Cait was sitting up. Marred fiberglass back facing the bed, Alondra straddled the chair and hunched her back, less regal and more predatory.

"Great. More riddles."

MATT MAXWELL

Alondra stared, features exaggerated in the half-light, eyes bright and dark, cheeks and jaw confident in line even if her lips betrayed preoccupation and not just with Cait. For that moment she as common as dirt, nothing royal about her. She watched, earthy but not ageless. Time had weighed heavy on her since Ariela's passing. Or perhaps being made Queen did not suit her as much as she thought it would.

"I'm sorry. Am I wasting your time? You seem so very busy."

"You want to be mysterious. I get it. I've just had a really awful week on top of the last awful six months. I'm a little worn out on patience."

"You sound fine to me. You... bite. Better than the last time I saw you."

"Well, it got worse after that. If this is recovery, I'll take being unwell."

"I found you because I have friends. The reason why I found you is that you left quite an impression on Cut and their crew."

"I wasn't interested in fighting everyone in the club to get to you."

"Wise." She stared. "Whatever it was must have been very important."

"I thought it was at the time. I thought someone was following me. Apparently the car that you gave me makes me easy to find."

Her face twisted in a boil of regret but that passed. "*Anton* gave the car to you. That was my punishment for handling things... inelegantly."

"You can have it. I'm getting nothing but the wrong attention from that thing." Cait clenched her fist hard. "But I do love driving it."

"I did too. So did Ariela, but that's been a long time." Words tugged at her lips, but she didn't let them go. "As for being followed, that was not my doing."

"No, it's that sweet, crazy kid, Grace, isn't it? She's not big on boundaries. Or someone like her. Groupies, I guess."

Alondra's eyes went sadder now, but dry and sharp. "It's Ariela's own fault for being so beloved. Or mine for allowing it. Everyone in the family felt for her in their own way. Some have difficulty in letting go of that emotion, letting it turn to grief. They want that love to be eternal. Nothing is."

"Except being in her shadow?"

Alondra tensed again beneath the jacket in a flexing of barely-contained anger. She took a long breath and a longer time to answer that. Her dark eyes read Cait and right through her.

"Who could?" There was a faint sigh, more defeated than wistful. "I am not the Queen she was. She could be both the Queen and Bruja and she was very good at both. I can barely manage one." There was a confessional note, one clothed in the fact that Cait could have told this to anyone who'd understand but would never be believed.

"So you don't do the magic or fortune-telling. You don't throw the lotería, big deal."

"It is a 'big deal' because that is all we have now. Reputations can be tested and when they do not measure up, no amount of sleight-of-hand will help."

"Grace and kids like her won't accept you, so you're throwing them out?"

Alondra tilted her head slightly, eyebrow raised. "That wasn't me. We need all the hands we can hold on to. As for Grace herself, perhaps you should--" She caught herself and went tight-lipped. "Who told you any of this?"

"Cut, in not so many words as that."

Alondra nodded slowly, weighing out measures only she knew. "I heard nothing of this."

"Then Cut was lying. You should have a talk."

"Cut is ambitious. Favored by Anton."

And "I am not" is the unspoken part here.

"I'm fine with Grace," Cait said. "Just so long as she doesn't touch my, ah, the car. Or come bother me anywhere really."

Like I have anywhere to be.

"If she is even the reason you feel… stalked. Honestly, this doesn't seem like her at all. She's a child, mischievous and what's the word?"

"Precocious."

"I was going to say 'precious'."

"You know her well?"

Alondra set her jaw then relaxed it, though the subject was clearly sore for her. "Grace's faults are many. Subtlety isn't one of them."

"Like a landslide."

Alondra nodded and stayed staring at Cait long enough to make her squirm. "So, then you have no reason to return to Last Prayer." This was not a question.

"I didn't say that. You did. I still have questions."

"I'll answer what I'm able. But I don't have all morning."

"Did you get what you wanted out of this?" Cait asked without hesitation. "And don't say you don't know what I mean."

Alondra's stare was black and bottomless. "If you were anyone else, this conversation would be over."

"But I'm not. Don't answer me if you want. I know what happened to me, and no matter how Ariela framed it, I was not interested in being sucked into this horrible goddamned world that you live in."

"You were more interested in making money from it."

"Damn right I was. And I was good at it. Now I can't hardly look inside a book without getting the shakes. I haven't copied or made anything in months."

"Sounds like shame."

"And you would know that. You put your 'sister' up on a plate for Anton at least and whatever that thing, the Sightless Eye, was. You knew what was coming."

"*Nobody* could have seen what was coming for Ariela. Least of all her. Nobody believed…"

"*She* sure as hell did. But hell, I guess she got her answer. Right before it all ended."

Guilt welled up like black water from between floor slats in a rising tide of dark and sickening emotion. Cait could all but see it building up around the bed, surface eating everything it came in contact with. Worse, she could feel the room go cold, the dank smell of it filling her lungs, tasting it. It wasn't outside her at all.

"Turn the light on, Cait."

Cait fumbled for the control bulb on the bed frame. White-green fluorescents flicked on behind and overhead, giving Alondra black hollows for eyes. The jacket creaked as she slid out of it, making a noise like a snake crossing over itself, sliding and black. She turned her hands upward, palms to the sky, forearms exposed all the way to the elbow.

On her left arm was an exquisite portrait of a woman, unmistakably Ariela, drawn out in black and gray-wash tattoo ink. Her face was downcast with stylized tears from her eye, running down her cheek to where the veil draped, covering her nose and mouth. Cait was thankful it was there having seen what was under it once. Ariela's hair pooled out behind her, radiating in countless directions. Every detail was etched into Alondra's skin, razor-precise down to the jeweled threading of the corseted dress.

On Alondra's right arm was a bouquet of datura blooms, a galaxy of them, mirroring the tattoo that Ariela had worn on her chest. There was scrollwork with lettering that Cait couldn't read past her own eyes that were misting.

She couldn't imagine the hours it must have taken, meticulous needle-work and design, a hundred hours of penance and tribute, but what was time in measure to devotion?

"I miss her every day and every hour in those." Alondra's voice was wracked with sorrow but she offered no tears, as if they were too expensive even for this.

Living in No Tomorrows, no tears, no regrets, only strength.

"So no, it was not worth what I paid. What I made Ariela pay. I can tell you this but no one else. Though I think the new Bruja knows. I cannot hide long from her."

"I'm sorry too, Alondra. But neither of us could have stopped Ariela from chasing oblivion."

"And neither of us had to make it so easy for her to catch it." She pulled her arms back to a more neutral position and pulled her jacket back on over her shoulders. She was protected now. "So what are you going to do? My understanding is you're enjoying a free vacation, even if the accommodations are bland." Her vision scanned across the room, taking in the mundane and drab then rejecting it.

"More like solitary with free psych evaluations. They're not gonna like what they find. Or I'm not gonna like it."

"Perhaps you should just leave?"

Cait held the hand with the IV up. The tube glowed green in the fluorescent light. She felt green to her skin, soaked through with sickness and weariness.

"Look at me. I wouldn't make it five steps before I got tossed in a straitjacket."

Alondra's face soured like milk left out. "Shadow and silence, Cait. We can move through both." She stood and squared her shoulders. "But you'll need to commit to a course."

Cait's feet hit the floor, cold and flat but not like the chill she felt earlier. She raked her fingers across the IV plug and ripped it out without thinking. If she paused, she'd lose her nerve. The needle flew free and clinked against the stand.

"Ow! Fuck!" Red hurt jabbed into her arm, but the pain put her right in the moment.

"Pain is better than numbness." Alondra crossed the room to the plastic woodgrain wardrobe and opened it.

Cait pressed a thumb into the IV wound to give her something else to think about. "I dunno. Valium is sounding pretty good."

"I can get you some grass if you prefer."

"What I really want is something to put my feet in. And some clothes. This gown isn't even fit for July."

Alondra tossed Cait's new yet muck-soaked tennis shoes and bundled clothes to the bed beside her. Then a plastic bag filled with her effects. "I have friends who work here," she said without looking. "Long hours. Hard work. The brown healing the white." Cait saw her shake her head at that.

"How did you know I'd go?"

"You were the only one who ever told Ariela no. Even Anton wouldn't do that to her face." Alondra's frown could have broken glass. "I knew."

"Well I sure didn't." Cait pulled her jeans on, still feeling tacky and grubby from the riverbank. Everything she wore was so brown now that it could have passed for fatigues. "Dammit. I just bought these shoes."

"Don't be so attached to things. They make so many of them." Alondra moved the curtain aside and early pink-peach light radiated into the dark room. She peered out the window to the sun that was rising, gold sky in the east over the flat haul of the valley to the San Gabriels. "You'd best hurry. Our shadow will not last."

"Okay. Ready." Cait drew the belt tight on her hips. The jacket crackled with flinders of mud as she put it on. "Geez, I'm never going to get clean again."

Alondra dropped the curtain back and turned to Cait, backlit orange but still sallow fluorescents before her, softening her conviction. "Let's go."

Cait froze. "Wait. The knife."

Alondra paused, cocking an eyebrow. "Tacíto's blade?"

Lilah's warning about possession flashed, but Cait didn't dare correct Alondra.

"The same. It's not with my stuff?" She dumped the contents of the bag onto the bed and rifled through them with frantic fingers, making sure it hadn't fallen under a fold of the sheet or somewhere else. "It's not here."

"There was nothing else in the cabinet."

"Trager must have it. And my car probably. I'm going to need them back."

"That will be your problem to solve. After this, I have no interest in seeing you. And you me. Yes?"

"Pretty sure the bartender would punch me in the mouth if I showed up again. What good's going to a bar if you can't get trashed?"

"If you wanted to go back, you shouldn't have blown those pipes."

"I'd tell you that wasn't me, but it wouldn't matter, huh?"

"Tell me, if it makes you feel better. But it changes nothing."

Cait gave the last of her river-soaked cash to the cabbie. She felt bad about it but Link wouldn't be rolling this early and the guy behind the wheel was glad for the tip, stashing the bills immediately and flicking off the meter.

"You sure this is it?" he asked in a voice that had been spent on cheap smokes. "Hear they put a police squad in that old laundromat, brought the smell to the place."

"Yeah, end of the line. Thanks for the ride."

"Thanks for the scratch. Be careful."

"Always," Cait said as she crossed the parking lot to the dim lights on behind the glass at Open Door's private station. The smell from the pupusería made her stomach growl and she wondered when the last time she ate was. More than a day now? There was a line of construction workers out the door, all Mexican or Central American in work clothes, some grim, some laughing and passing coffee around while they waited to get breakfast. While this was their place, something was up and they glanced over to someone in the storefront as much as they spoke amongst themselves.

A tall and lanky white dude in dress shirt and slacks with cowboy boots underneath made his way past, nearly a head taller than everyone else. They moved aside grudgingly for him and didn't look at him directly. He knew better than to try throwing pleasantries at them and instead kept to himself. He was only tolerated.

Parker.

He held a big paper bag in front of his chest and balanced a cigarette on his lip, drooping almost comically.

"Hey, Parker!" Cait called. "Working overtime?"

He stopped and glanced her over, surprised but not shocked. "Night desk because I'm a screwup." His grin widened. "You're not supposed to be here. Or anywhere."

"Yeah, I figured that." She shrugged.

"So why're you where you're not supposed to be?"

"I need my car back. And that knife you guys took from me. I sure hope you didn't mess with it."

"Why? Is it cursed or something?"

"Jury's out."

He took a step toward the office door. "Look, I gotta put these down before they burn my hands off. Can you open this for me?"

Her eyes flicked to the doors and stayed there. "Who's in there right now?

"Me and a few others. Trager hasn't come in yet."

"And Moreno?"

"Yeah, Trish's off today."

"Good. I don't feel like being recognized right now. How long do I have before Trager gets here?" She pulled the door open for him and stepped aside. The ghosts of bleach and gray laundry seeped out from behind it.

"Little while. Come on. I'll let you have a pupusa or two. You look like you could use it."

Three pupusas later, Cait took a sniff of the office coffee and let it pass. "Never seen anyone eat anything so fast."

"No manners. I was raised in a barn." She brushed her hands off on her dirty jeans, abandoning any worry of grime. She looked around, eyes settling on the door.

"Relax. Trager was here late last night. LAPD chewing him up one side and down the other."

"Toretti?"

"Yeah, nobody liked how that one turned out. This in particular is a shit job."

"I think you can still get the guy, the one who's responsible for it. You know that Sue wasn't involved, right?"

He shrugged, more futile than defeated. "She has made precisely zero friends over here. Nobody shed a tear when she was walked out. She's in LAPD custody now. I talked to her a little, much as she would let me. She's a lot of things but not a liar."

"Just good at withholding the whole truth." She grabbed a sip of the coffee after all and put it down. "You like coffee with your sugar?"

"Only way I can drink it."

"Look, if you get me my knife and wheels, I can maybe pull something together out of all this. I think."

Parker rolled an unlit cigarette between his thumb and forefingers, scowling. "I'm already *a lot bit* on thin ice around here. I'm gonna need a little something in return to tell me that this is a shot worth taking."

"I sure hope you're not using this to get a date out of me."

"Though that is a thing I would not mind, it would be a gross abuse of my station in doing so."

"A conscience?"

"More like a nuisance but yeah." He put the cigarette to his lips and struck a lighter. "You?"

"Gave it up in my teens."

He lit the smoke and took a deep drag on it. Cait found a faintly off smell about it, maybe lavender or some berry fragrance.

"I didn't take you for the type to smoke cloves," Cait said.

"These? Nah. Brought 'em from home." He reached over for the pack on his desk and palmed it, sticking it in his shirt pocket. The wrapper was red and black and purple, one that Cait didn't recognize.

"Okay, so what do you need to know?"

"Was that bullshit about the ocean coming home to roost? Back in the hospital yesterday?"

"Nope. Can't tell you how or when, but it's gonna happen. Soon. Today. Now." Cait wrapped her arms around herself, imagining the upwelling.

"What can you do to stop it? 'Cause it seems to me that you've got more than enough of a mountain to climb and too much pack for it. You aren't any kind of junkie, 'cept maybe on misery and those are just people who can't see a way out, so they dive deeper in.

"Wow. Look at me using that sociology degree."

"I wasn't going to hold it against you. And thanks for not calling me a junkie. Beginning to take offense."

"Sure, but the point stands. What are you going to do if you don't know what needs to be done?"

"I was thinking about it and I think I know who to ask."

"Well, go ask 'em." He tilted his head back and exhaled, blue smoke uncoiling.

"Trick is, they're all dead."

"That would be a real impediment."

"But I also learned that dead isn't quite so dead as you might think, at least in this case. I need Lee Whelan's truck. I'm guessing you impounded it the night you took my car."

"After we hauled you out of the river."

"I said, 'Thank you.'"

"Nice to hear all the same. Though you did require mouth to mouth as crude as that sounds. Didn't think it could wait." Parker was deadpan, almost apologetic.

Cait stared, trying to read if he was joking or not. "Yeah, I don't like that. But it's done. And I'm here, so again, thanks."

He nodded and took another long drag. "And you can talk to these dead folks and get them to help?"

"I think they've already been trying to talk to me, maybe to stop it. It was them, one in particular, trying to show me what was going to happen." She wiped her eyes, tears welling up.

She was so scared. I thought it was my fear, but she was the one who was scared. And now she's stuck in there.

"I sure hope this doesn't sound crazy," she said, knowing it did.

"A little, but a believable kind of crazy." He stood up and pulled his jacket off the chair, pulling it over slim shoulders. "Now to be clear, if this gets back to Trager, you got my gun from me and you made me do all this stuff I'm about to do."

"What's gonna make him believe me now? He didn't before."

"Well, I am, according to him, a *legendary* dumbass." He smiled. "Besides, I think this assignment has worn thin, which presents its own problems. But one day at a time."

Cait reached out and grabbed him around the upper arm. "Thanks." She let go almost as quickly, realizing what she'd done, though he hadn't started of barely even paused. Maybe he was as surprised as she was.

"You're welcome. Now let's go charge headfirst into this thing that we're gonna regret later."

They walked past the empty desks, all but Simmons who just slammed his phone down and yelled. "We got another one, Parker."

"Another what?" he asked without slowing.

"Dead dude. Like the last one."

"Which last one?" Parker stopped for a moment. "You'll have to be more specific."

"The halo jobs. You know the outlines. We need to get someone down there."

"I got shit to do, man," Parker said. "Cover it and I'll get you a whole box of Doughnut Prince."

"And what's so important?"

"Impound."

"Impound, my ass!"

"And the end of the whole damn city," Cait added.

The tow place was an industrial yard in a loop off of Alhambra boule-vard just east of the city. Nothing out here but low sheet-metal buildings, housing everything from import/export to plating companies to ware-houses that only seemed to showcase rust. The sun was full up and gold poured beneath the dome of clouds that was gathering, not just from off the coast but from everywhere.

Parker pulled the unmarked sedan out in front of a cinderblock wall and three spindly magnolia trees that either didn't get enough water or got too much sun or a devastating combination of both. A sheet-metal sign read BEDDOE TOWING AND IMPOUND — ALL DAY/ALL NIGHT — CASH ONLY in neat red enamel lettering.

"I'll talk," he said, lingering at the door for a moment.

"Fine by me. You're the cop."

"Don't remind me."

A wizened woman who looked older than the city itself sat in an of-fice chair, listening to music from big plastic headphones. She twirled the coiled cord like she was queen of the dance floor, eyes closed in reverie.

Parker waited a moment, trying to get her attention by waving his hand in front of her still-shut eyes. She hummed in bliss, fingers still dancing. Cait followed the cord back with her eyes and reached across the divider to dim the volume knob.

The woman's eyes shot open, idyll denied burning in them. "Who the hell is messing with Ruthie's tunes?!" she shouted as she bolted upright, chair spinning behind her.

Parker held his badge out where she could see it. "Parker. LAPD. Open Door. Need a car and access to an impound."

Ruthie took the headphones off and set them on the table. "Just so long as you don't try to fob off a PO on me. Put the money down. Sixty bucks." She patted the table as gently as she might a baby's bottom.

Cait was already shrugging when he shot her the glance. "Do not look at me. I burned my last cash getting to your office."

He growled and reached back for his wallet. "I better get this back."

Cait watched him count out an assortment of bills, nearly everything in his wallet.

"Someday, I hope."

"The old Mercury. Came in the same night with that pickup," Parker said.

"Oh, that beautiful car?" She pronounced it *cah*, some vaguely northeastern accent coloring the speech. "I was hoping you'd forget all about it and I could take it up the boulevard."

"I'm attached to it," Cait said.

"I just bet you are, sweetie."

"Do we need the keys to the other?" Parker asked as Ruthie pulled Cait's keychain down from the wall.

"No, I just need to... look at it, I think." Cait looked over to the lot attendant. "That won't be a problem?"

"Nah, you go do what you need. Just no funny stuff."

"Great, fine." She drummed her fingers on the countertop before asking "Hey, do you have running water over there?"

"You gonna wash?" which she said as *warsh*.

"Kinda."

The hose was green and cracked with bleached fabric showing through the gaps in the plastic. Water began running out and filling the bed of Lee's truck. It was going to take some time. Now the flow felt sad and inadequate, nothing to be afraid of no matter what might be lurking in the water.

Parker walked back, jacket hung on one finger over his shoulder, sweating even though the sun had gone up and behind the clouds.

"Warmer than usual for November."

"There's no *usual* where Southern California is concerned." Cait stripped out of her jacket, dropping it to one side. She thought about it a second. "Maybe this'll get some mud out." She then laid the jacket to one side of the truck bed. Flattened daylight glittered over the collection of junk there: bones, trinkets, clothing, tools. Every piece had a history, a life before becoming just another thing lost in the river or the sea. Time had been collected there, ordered into something grander.

"You sure we have to do this... submersion thing?"

Water pooled now on the bottom of the truck. The whole bed had been covered with some kind of black rubber or plastic, something that could hold liquid, at least for a while. Cait wondered how long Lee had been at this and what else he might've had in mind. She put her fingers below the surface and it was almost as warm as skin. The holding tank must've been right near street level. That had to be it.

"It's the only thing that's worked before. I was hearing them when…" She turned back to look at him. "When you pulled me out of the river."

"But you weren't asking back then, right?"

She shook her head. "I think that was despair. Lee showed me some things that I didn't like so much." She shook it off. "This isn't that."

"Trager thought you wanted to kill yourself. He was kinda busted up about it."

Cait shook her hand off, scattering droplets. "Really? He wasn't acting like it."

"You think he gets to wear his heart on his sleeve?"

"I guess not," she said. "And no, I don't really think I was trying to end it all."

"How about now?"

"Well, I gotta do this. It's the only thing that makes sense. Then we'll see what else makes sense."

"Hope you're right."

"Yeah, me too. I like Los Angeles. I mean, it's fucked-up and weird but I love it. And hopefully I can pull Sue out of this mess."

"What about her brother?"

"That's not her brother. Least I don't think it is. She didn't either. That's what she was willing to go to jail for. It's her job to save his soul at least. Only she's locked up."

"So you're gonna do that?"

"It's not real high on the list, but let's see what I can see."

They both watched as the water grew to a depth that Cait could lie down in. It took some time. Flat white reflection of the clouds whirled and surged on the surface. Beneath it, uncountable lifetimes bound up in objects and the water itself, the drowning chorus, waited for someone to listen.

"What do you want me to do?" Parker asked. He was a shade or two paler than before, seeing that the game of chicken that had been talked about all morning was not a game at all. "I should pull you out if you look like you're in trouble, right?"

Cait didn't say anything.

"Hey. Awaiting further instructions here." His fingers closed firmly around her wrist as she climbed up and over the wall of the truck bed.

"Don't disturb me again," she said with a chill. "I'm trying to get in a mindset. I don't know what to expect. Last time this happened, I was almost half-asleep, total relaxation. You know how when you're drifting off to sleep and you hear voices talking right in your head? Not your ear but your head. And you hear music you've never heard before?"

He looked at her like she'd started speaking in tongues. "I know you're not crazy, but…"

"Then don't say it."

He pulled back, not wounded but anxiety-bitten.

"You didn't let me die last time. Just do the same this time, only give me a little longer."

She stood in the truck bed, water up nearly to her kneecaps. The different textures under her bare feet were confusing, metal and bone and wood and cloth all blending into a feeling that was all and none of these.

"Okay, don't say anything. Just let me talk," she said without looking at him. "If I need to be pulled out, I'll just squeeze your hand really tight. Or if I go totally limp, I guess."

"Not cool."

"Stop talking. Just say you'll do it."

"Yeah."

Cait closed her eyes and pulled out the knife. "You reached out to me before. Now I'm asking you to do it again." She removed the sheath, holding it in one hand. The blade looked like a shard of the sun dimmed and cooled. "You know that I could come armed but I come defenseless. I'm only drawing a way for you to come through."

She carved out the shape of a door in the air above her, neither circular nor square but an uneasy compromise. Reflected sun cut off the blade and seemed to be split into its component colors, a rainbow haze that followed like drunkenness.

She put the knife back into the sheath and held it firmly.

"I'm asking and the asking gives you the power to answer."

Cait pushed out every other thought, every anxiety, every memory, every recrimination that had been left like a collection of splinters in her soul to fester and boil. All that weight was left behind as she breathed slowly and regularly. Her heart was steady. She crouched as gracefully as she could and kept her breath calm and regular as the water surrounded her more fully. It was colder now, but she didn't know why.

This was not the black water welling up from before. This was something she called, that she had made, that she if not controlled at least was prepared for. There were no other thoughts, just the feeling of water wicking into clothes and on her skin. She breathed again and again as she lay back and breathed for the last time.

Cait surrendered to the water, eyes closed, mind open, surrounded by black, bloodred at its edges but expanding outward slowly until even that tentative perimeter was gone, obliterated. She kept in her mind the sense of the sea, close by but daily forgotten. The blood in her veins was the same as that sea. Lee was right. He'd said so himself. The water began to sing its song and she was the only one there to listen.

Other voices rose out of the quiet roar, lucid and not dreamlike. The black expanse turned blue and sunlit or emerald green or churning and silver-bubbled. The water was salty and fresh, fouled and pure beyond imagining. She could catch words in this and with each word came associations, feelings, memories, not hers but from others. The bravest to step forward felt old, confident, or else those who had not been old enough to even learn fear before the waters took them.

Flood and surf, drunks drowning in puddles, children wandering into pools, and suicides from bridges. The water was both the giver and taker and in all of them, it watched and remembered.

All waters are graves.

It became a torrent, so much that there were no individuals any longer, no more than the winter storm had namable drops of rain. There were sheets, waves, oceans and they surged through her. She didn't try to catch them whole, only to let the impression pass through her, holding the bits that she could here and there.

"I'll never—"

"Thank god it's over—"

"They'll never find me—"

"Alone—"

"Can't I can't I can't—"

"Beautiful quiet—"

And in a time another presence revealed itself. It unfolded and unfurled like a banner flying from a sinking ship, declaring dominance over nothing as it roared to a bottom that would never come. There was a sensation of weight and compulsion, of pressure but directed and channeled. The image of a whirlpool came and went but a whirlpool of time and energy itself.

She felt the first tightness in her chest and fought it, locking her arms and legs.

All the voices and impressions and sensations, all of them flowed past her and were drawn into this weight. She herself was. She refused to fight it, only to keep herself from surfacing. Her body felt like a nuisance, something to be forgotten. The weight was all consuming and could take her that much more quickly if she'd just be shed of her skin.

The waters went darker and darker, light attenuating from silver and blue and green to deeper colors, a blue beyond blue but not black. Ultrablue. Deepest blue. The bluest. Blue without cool or warm but consuming. And in that, the slowest of colors, was something that waited. It was down there and its patience had come to an end. It wanted.

It was ancient when the first thinking being drowned. Ancient when there was life to extinguish or to flourish. It would persist until the light went out of the sun and then it would wait in the ice as it had waited before. It was not alien, but it was not us, not of her or anything she had known.

The weight was terrible and crushing now. There was no escape from it, no more than light could escape a collapsed star. She saw herself reflected in time, just as she had in the face of the thing that had been Rico before she had cut it to ribbons.

It was terribly lonely. It had collected all those who had died by water and it was making something, preparing something. But piece in whatever was being constructed was done so out of isolation and fear and a crushing sense of being close yet always apart. Cait flashed on Grace's expression on hearing that she was thrown out of the Last Prayer, youthful and innocent wonder and acceptance turned into the pain of denial.

Cait's chest jabbed, a million miles away. She felt sheet metal biting her arms and the midden of the dead pressed into her back as she fought the urge to break the surface. She reached back into the lonely, the isolation, the weight. It felt like every night after the storm and Ariela and Rico, every night she couldn't sleep and couldn't stay awake and instead was afraid that it was all real, that it wasn't some terrible dream and that she was the only one in the world who understood it. More even, that it wasn't ending, that it was all unfolding like a terrible black flower and in that flower were a million stars of impossibility. She had seen the truth of things, that everything she lied about with her books and her fakes, all of those were real and living and breathing.

She was the only one who understood it, utterly alone. She was un-tethered, adrift, subject to the same horrible gravity that was collecting all the dead and drowned here, feeding their singular voices into a whole that couldn't even be conceived of above the water. She couldn't imagine something as big and as old as this.

The blue was everywhere, flat yet infinite, as pure as the atmosphere on the edge of space before it yawned into black. As above, so below. Something within it moved and always had been moving, an intricate song on multiple scales at once, from molecules to drops to currents to entire oceans but the whole of them so large that seeing it was impossible. The carving on the shell which she imagined she could feel in her fingers now but couldn't dare to look and see for herself. The all, the one.

For it, all time was simultaneous. It knew the footfall of insect titans and their predation, birth and extinction after extinction. It wanted. It wanted the whole. For there to be no division between water and land. What she had seen before was the merest, slightest step. It would not end until mountains were islands or less even than that. It would have all things and maybe then would find completion. Only then would hunger cease.

The voices of the drowned coruscated though her as they spun forever down. Snatches of whispers, a cascade of phonemes, partial sounds that were not even parts of words but assembling into something like them. She pulled herself back, navigating in the blue abyss on instinct, and things resolved. Sound became word became—

My name is Chelen. I was a girl like you, and the waters nourished me, my family, my people, but they could not wash the stain from my father's heart, Yussh's heart. He became consumed by it and asked Thing That Wants for power, power to break law, power to take, power to keep me.

My father led others to the water and he sent them below. And those who found the water on their own, no matter where or when, for time is nothing now. He sent those to Thing That Wants. Every piece has made it stronger and hungrier and more and more alone.

"What can I do to help?" Cait asked.

Nothing. The waters will claim. Thing That Wants will become Thing That Has. All will become Thing That Wants.

"I refuse. You wouldn't… you wouldn't spend so much time trying to reach me if not."

We are not Chelen but her echoes. Those who have not joined in the weight. We did not call you. We only remember the calling. All time is now. That is how you hear us.

"Show me where he is. Lee or Yussh or Thing That Waits. Show me and I will stop him."

They cannot be undone.

"Then I'll make sure it stays Thing That Wants. Please!" Cait felt impossible tears burn down her cheeks at the thought of the erasure, the obliteration, the weight becoming everything and leaving only this blue emptiness in its place.

Ghosts floated past, sinuous reptiles as long as a building, jellyfish trailing uncounted tentacles behind them in a maze of stings, ships and planes and people, so many people, skeletons and bleached-white flesh and those who looked still alive. They all swam down to the deeper blue.

Thing will be on the water yet cannot touch it. He will be dry on land and still in the salt water. He is there now. He was there. He will be there.

Time is your prison, but not for Them.

"More! I need more!"

The river meets the sea. The—

YOU WILL NOT BE DEAD IN THE PAST
YOU WILL BE ALIVE IN ME
I AM WITHOUT TIME
YOU WILL NOT END
BECAUSE ALL WILL BE ENDED

Everything shook, every part of Cait felt it. Something immense moved, dragging atmosphere and gravity behind it. It shrugged and in that shrug was seaquake, waves that rippled through bones and souls.

The cascade of life and death that fell around her snapped and was ground to shreds by some unnamable force. Bones shattered to clouds of shards, jelly liquefied, flesh was stripped from bone and it all hung in a murking red mist. All names, all identities, all things were reduced to component. The voice that followed was a sound only the whole world could make. It was the sound of everything being consumed, loud so that volume lost meaning.

Thing That Wants turned in the depths and silenced the chorus and Cait felt it turn its attention to her.

She screamed and broke the surface of the water, screaming still. It was absolute. Her heart roared stronger than the Mercury's engine at full throttle. The scream went on until she ran out of breath. She was afraid to close her eyes now.

Afraid because she'd only see blue.

CHAPTER SIXTEEN

"Cait. Cait. Come back." Parker's voice sounded like it was coming from somewhere deep beneath the everything, only the vaguest sense of word and sound present in it. And the urgency that drove his words, those stuck sure as a stepped-on nail.

She shook uncontrollably, but this was not like before, the anxiety, the worry. This was an outside presence being visited upon her. She drew her knees up to her chest and put her arms around those, trying to quell the tremors. The water in the truck bed surrounding her moved in time with her, waves crashing in miniature. Everything felt like a resonance of the feeling being passed through her. The only thing solid and real was the shell that she clutched in her hand now, not realizing when she'd picked it up or even had found it.

"I saw it." She had to drag the words out like pulling her own teeth.

Parker's face went screwy. "How could you have seen anything? You were down there for maybe twenty seconds. Maybe."

She looked up at him in disbelief. "I don't understand. I was… it felt like an hour… longer." Cait clenched all her muscles just to try and be still, which only made her ache.

He put a hand on her shoulder, slow and tentative before pulling it back by reflex. "Jesus. You're ice-cold. Come on, out of the water."

She was aware that the water felt warm around her but not of her own chill. Her whole body locked stiff as she stood up and tried to clamber out of the truck bed. Parker caught her and righted her. She just kept looking ahead as she stood there, shaking of cold on an eighty-degree and overcast day.

"Okay, let's, ah, get you dried off. Maybe they can help you inside." He took her by the shoulders and turned her gently, marching her to the lot's offices.

She went to shivering now, not quaking from fear but from exposure.

"What'd you see in there?"

"It was flat and endless. So… big. And bones and dinosaurs. And it doesn't live in time like us. It's… so heavy."

They turned the corner to the office, oil-stained asphalt giving way to gum-spattered concrete. A car had just pulled up beside theirs. A squarish, basic, bureaucratic, bought-in-the-hundreds kind of unmarked cop car.

Trager stepped out from behind the wheel so angry he was shaking with it.

"Oh, hey. Hey, Trager," Cait said.

"Shiiiiit," Parker added.

"Yeah. 'Shiiiiit' is right."

Cait sat in the office chair, wrapped in blankets that smelled of mothballs and cigars, bare feet next to a square heater with glowing red coils that still wasn't enough. She'd only just stopped shivering but was still cold even in the stuffy room.

"Are you okay, dear?" Ruthie asked.

Cait nodded her head and said, "No."

"Drink the coffee." It came out *cawfee*. "It'll warm you up. And if that don't work, I've got some Glenmorangie in the back. My son thinks I don't know where it's hid, but I do."

"Just the coffee, thanks."

Ruthie tugged the blanket tighter around her shoulders then marched off in search of the promised whiskey.

"How'd you find us?" Cait asked.

Trager sat in a chair on the opposite wall, sagged from defeat or anger's passing or both. "The dumbass over there had to get directions from Simmons. And Simmons told me for a doughnut."

"Goddamn Simmons," Parker growled.

"If you knew this town as well as you pretend to, you'd have gotten away with it."

"I made him do it," Cait said over the coffee cup. She was just holding and smelling it now, letting the aroma try and rouse her. "It was me. I got his gun." She took a tentative sip and it wasn't too hot so she took another.

"Hell, even Parker doesn't believe that."

"Dumb story was his idea."

"Dumb story from a dumbass."

"Look, I'll take the heat for it. And you gotta let... let me finish this. It's way too big for you."

"Way I see it, you couldn't menace your own shadow. What did you hope to pull with this stunt anyway?"

"She was—" Parker started.

Trager's pointed finger promised a beatdown. "Not. A. Word. Or the next call I make is to Lancer."

Parker said nothing to that, just played with his lighter.

"It's not just LA," Cait said, barely above a whisper. "But it's gonna be LA first. Don't know how long it'll take either. Doesn't matter."

"What will? This bullshit flood story you're peddling?"

"It's not a flood. It's not even *the* Flood. It's something else. Like… god, words are so hard to find for this."

"Better work hard then."

"Okay. I'll try." She took a gulp of coffee and felt it simmer like alcohol all the way down. She was colder inside than out. "There's something out there in the water, and it is the water. It is just so goddamn big you can't understand it. It's so big that it lives out of time. Or not in time the same way we do."

"This sounds like No Tomorrows bullshit."

"No, this is way worse. They were, Ariela was, *calling* something. This, the Thing That Wants. It's here. It's always been here. It's gonna outlast us all so long as there's a drop of water on the planet for it to live in. And yeah, we're fucking made of water."

"I passed science."

"I think that this thing is lonely. No wait. It's like, it's like everyone who's drowned, or will, but they're trapped in this moment of death. So imagine that each of them becomes a little piece, but that piece becomes part of something else. But they're still alone. The more it takes, the worse it makes itself. It's not lonely so much as it's just a giant crush of need."

"You're sounding positively Zen."

"You asked and I'm trying to do this, so listen or lock me up."

"Someone's feeling better," Ruthie said, filling the coffee cup again.

"So I think Lee mistakenly found a way to tap into this thing. For a while. Only now it's tapping into him, using him to walk around and set things in motion. Which is why you couldn't catch him when he was right under your nose. He could have waited for you to save me and still gotten away. He was fucking with you. And me."

"So what is this all adding up to?"

"It's the Thing That Wants. That's going to end. It'll become the Thing That Has, and that'll be everything. No division between the water and the land because it'll all be water. Nothing alive because it'll all be… that."

"And you're going to stop it?" Trager was somewhere between laughter and despair. "You did a number on No Tomorrows, for which I'm thankful."

"They're not gone, Trager."

"But their Queen—"

"You're not getting it. All I did was shut the door then." She slapped an open palm on the arm of the chair and it sounded insubstantial to even her. "It's too late for that now. This thing has woken up. It's being directed. Last time I was just… keeping something out."

"Then what's there to do?" Parker asked.

"This thing, it works in time differently. Only I've had some… exposure to this kind of thing. I can see it at least. You guys couldn't, right? Lee just looked like a dude to you."

Trager nodded. "That's a long way from stopping it."

"I don't know that it can be stopped. Maybe it can be talked to or, I don't know, redirected. But I'm not going to sit and wait for it to happen."

"And here you'd almost convinced me you didn't have a death wish."

"Remember what I said last time I had my back to the wall? Or rather your back? Alondra would have happily run you down or put a bullet through you if you'd stopped me from getting in the car with her. And what'd I say?"

Trager only had to think a second, as if that memory was always close by. "That it's about your size. And you really believe that? Now?"

"Well, I'd ask Sue for help on this, but I'm pretty sure the only words she'll have for me would be the polite country equivalent of 'fuck you.'"

"It's 'bless your heart.' Gotta say it with a tight smile."

"I'll take that chance. Maybe I can learn something from her before I head to the shore."

"You know where to go?"

"I'll just look for the weirdest shit I can find on the shore."

"You said something about being out on the water," Parker said with a snap of his fingers. "But not in it. That's gotta be the Santa Monica Pier."

Cait stared and tried not to get slack-jawed as she did. "Parker, there isn't a Santa Monica Pier anymore. Fell down a couple years ago. They're all fighting about rebuilding it or not. I know you don't get out much, but…"

"Yeah, Parker. *Dumbass.*" Trager stared, and there was a glimpse of a dead snarl beneath that.

"Oh. Oh shit," Parker groaned. "I didn't mean—"

"Just stop talking," Trager pleaded.

Cait watched the exchange but didn't know what to make of it. There was something else going on, but it wasn't about to get answered now.

"He might be dumb, but he had kind of the right idea. Gotta be close to the river mouth. So that's what, Marina Del Rey maybe." The memories were already jumbled in her head like too much had been poured in and things slopped out and around.

"There's the jetty there," Trager said. "Boats can get through, but there's that final breakwater. It's a little swim."

"No, that's no good. He can't go in the ocean. Or won't, not sure. There's the pier in Venice. That little one. End of Washington I think."

"Yeah, that sounds right." Trager made ready to stand and his beeper went off with a repeating electronic chirp. "Oh, now what." He looked down at the unit and said, "I need a phone." He looked stricken.

"Bad news?"

"Emergency code. Call in right the fuck now. Excuse me." He took the headset off the desk phone without asking permission and punched in a number lightning fast. He stiffened as he waited a moment and said, "Trager. Hit me." His face slackened in shock to whatever was said. "What? Say that again? Yeah. Okay." Then a big sigh. "Yeah, I get it." He hung up the phone and just stood there.

"What's going on?"

"Sue Whelan is gone. Her cell was flooded out by some kind of freak water-pipe thing. The door came right off and she's gone. So I hope whatever you were gonna ask her wasn't that important."

Cait pulled the blanket around herself tighter. "Oh, not Sue. Goddammit."

"There's an APB on her and Lee for what it's worth."

"You don't want any cops getting in his way right now," Cait said. "He's close to what he wants and will probably forget his manners. What happened to Toretti was nothing."

"That isn't all," Trager said. "Weather departments all up and down the coast are freaking out about some extreme low pressure system. Storm surges, winds, all that bullshit. Nobody wants to say hurricane, but that's what it sounds like."

"It's not bullshit. It's Lee."

"Yeah, well, we're supposed to be on standby for traffic control and emergency support. All of us. Even the weirdo squad."

"You okay to get up and move around, Cait?" Parker asked.

"I feel like I want to get under the biggest rock I can find and hide out."

Trager stood there, not defeated but resigned. "What do you need in order to do what you're going to do? Because it's ask now or forever hold your peace."

Cait thought about it a moment. She was still cold and achy, but the worst of it had moved on. "I'd say a fresh change of clothes, but I figure I'm going to end up getting wet to the bone even if any of this works. You got a pass that can get me through traffic control down in Venice?"

"I can write you a note and make a call, but the odds of it mattering are pretty puny. Anything else?"

She had the knife. She couldn't think of anything else that would have mattered short of an aircraft carrier. And even that would've just been swamped with the merest effort. She needed something that made her feel a thousand feet tall.

"If there's cops down there, just let Lee do whatever the hell he's doing. No need for them to get hurt."

"That sounds like retreat. Regular cops aren't going to like that."

"They should start getting used to it."

Trager crossed the room and opened the office door. The wind that blew in was wet and hard, jagged drops spitting across the threshold, heavier than even the most savage monsoonal rains that lashed the basin.

Trager shook his head slowly. "This is some shit. Hey, Parker! You too. Even dumbasses are being called up."

"Can I have a minute here?" he asked with some sugar.

"Son, you've already climbed into the vat of shit up to your chin."

"Then what's a little more?"

"And can you sign my car out?" Cait asked.

Trager laughed. "Sure. You want it washed?"

She threw a glance up to the sky. "Yeah, not necessary."

Trager laughed long enough for it to stick then pointed dead at Parker's heart. "If you're not five minutes behind me, I'll have Lancer come shoot you herself."

"That's a thing she'd like to do, yeah. Okay, five."

"MacReady?"

"Yeah?"

"I sure as hell hope you're right."

"Right there with you, Trager. Be careful out there." She saw him go with a little sadness. There was so much he thought he knew but he never let himself realize it until cornered and by then he didn't know anything at all.

"So, ah, Cait." Parker looked like he'd eaten all the butterflies and they were down there jostling into one another, a flurry of wings and colors. "I wanted to…"

"I'm listening." She could hardly believe this.

Tough cop turned into tongue-tied kid. Bad, bad timing though.

He brought his gaze up to her eyes. His were green which she was somehow just noticing now. "I really want you to come back in one piece. Maybe get a chance to get to know you better."

And here I was feeling adrift and unloved. Unlovable. Just lost. Drowning. Even worse, drowning on my own, in my own thoughts and every time the lights went out. And here this man is falling over himself talking to me.

"Me too."

"You too what?"

"I'd like to get to know me better. Been lost on that for a while."

"And me?"

"You seem pretty nice for police. But your timing is really godawful."

"Yeah well, we don't get to choose these things. They sorta happen even if you'd never have seen them coming."

"Especially then." She stood up and let the blanket drape over her shoulders. "Look, no promises on anything," she said as she extended her hand.

"Limited time offer."

"I'd say 'raincheck' then, but that's a crappy joke."

"I'd have laughed at it." He took her hand and held it gently a moment.

It was warm against her cool skin and she'd have been okay staying there for a while were it not for the weight of the air outside and the sad magnolia trees dancing hard in a wind that wasn't there an hour ago.

"Take care, Parker."

"You too."

CHAPTER SEVENTEEN

It was barely two in the afternoon but already was dark enough for the Last Prayer club to be open to all its vampire clientele. Clouds solid as blackout curtains killed off the sunlight, not a silver lining to be seen. Cait had driven home for boots and clothes that didn't smell like primordial ooze. She even took a moment to do her eyes. Her hands were still and the lines went thick, just like she'd wanted them to. She looked and felt right for the first time in a long time, aside from the hollow nerves. But those were barely nibbles compared to what had been eating her before. Maybe the real end of the world was less than the one she'd been imagining.

She gave a thought to anyone she knew in the lower basin who might be in danger or would need to know to get the hell out. Most of her friends were up in the hills or on the other side. Call the newspapers and say what? Surf's up forever? She called Vince and left a message. He probably knew already that it was time to clear out with weird weather like this, but it at least made her feel better.

Why not?

She placed a call to the offices at *Quest4*, telling them that the story of the year was probably happening right off the Fisherman's Pier in Venice. She didn't have an explanation as to why. She owed none of them anything, but if it gave them a leg up against the jerks in *Easy Street*, then it was worth it. She was still remembered, unless Watkiss had called just on a random whim a couple days back.

Cops probably won't let them within a mile of the water anyway.

She left a message for Bill. It wasn't even rude.

Cait pushed the Mercury through the curtains of lashing rain spilling all over the westside. Water sluiced off the split front window faster than the wipers could keep up with it. The world melted by half and then went silver smear over and over. Even when the rain stopped, the sky was lead-plate gray, erased by mist and scud. That was somehow worse because she knew it would just come harder the next pass.

LAPD tuxedo units had set up, blocking intersections and routing her around, though she persistently kept rolling west even against their advice when she slowed down long enough to hear it. She wove past lines of black and whites with miserable men in raincoats that were insufficient yet overwhelming in numbers.

More cops than Black Flag shows used to draw.

I'm gonna need a police radio if this shit keeps up. Would be good to know where they're gonna be ahead of them being there.

Coming down Washington, she was one of only a few cars heading toward the water and the others were losing their nerve with each passing block. Everyone else was pushing the opposite direction running from the freak storm. Jammed and lurching bumpers all but kissed over and over. Police didn't seem to be doing anything to moderate eastbound traffic, just trying to herd it along.

Then she got to Dell Avenue and saw the two-car police team, blocking any further progress towards the water. A slow stream of cars headed away, hunkered down in a new band of rain and wind that rocked vehicles on their shocks. The police officers outside with flashlights and slickers stood ungainly and robotic, just hopelessly pointing while stand-up drowning.

Shit.

Cait was only a few blocks out and could barely see past the next street, much less to the ocean that she knew was right there. She watched for weird stuff in the wind and rain, but there was nothing more than a steady stream of palm fronds and trash. No dinosaurs, no detritus of the past. Just the lashing of the storm of all storms, the one you'd see if you looked up the word in the dictionary assuming the page would stay in place long enough.

She stopped at the end of the street on the other side of Dell and wondered if she could nose past the cop cars blocking the road but put that thought aside. The units were a little too close together as it was. She wasn't interested in trading paint with the LAPD while on the way to the end of everything.

Tink tink came the rapping on the driver's side window.

Cait kept herself from jumping when she realized that she'd been stuck there for too long trying to get around. A traffic officer stood there, leaning on the Mercury, flashlight beaming into the front seat in the dark afternoon. She rolled down the window and turned the cassette player down. Runnels of water pissed off the brim of his cap and into the Mercury.

Cop is not going to appreciate these tunes.

"Hi, officer. Nice day, right?"

He stood stone-faced and flashed the light into her eyes. "You high? Road's closed this way. Turn around and get out of here."

She couldn't tell if he was bemused or frightened or angry.

"But I have to get through. My grandma. She's all alone. Her cats."

"Sweetheart, the cats are going to have to learn to swim."

"Okay, okay," Cait said. "Can you get off my fender and maybe move one of the cars, so I can turn around without hitting you? This old car doesn't turn as well as it used to."

"Hank!" he yelled to someone unseen though he might have been just five feet off. "Push your unit back a little. We need to clear a turnaround for her!"

There was a door slam then a car turning over. One of the tuxedos pulled back just enough that she could punch through without scratching anyone up. She hoped that they weren't interested enough in chasing an obviously crazy woman once she broke the line.

The cop started waving the light like a runway controller, pointing out the clearest path. Cait peered ahead at the route and drummed the fingers of one hand. The low industrial buildings on the other side of the street looked like they had a parking lot that ran all the way around. Maybe. It was tough to see that far. Maybe she could just disappear.

"Now," the cop growled.

"Can you hold oncoming traffic for a second? This car is sometimes cranky."

He made a face like he'd bitten into half a mouse in his morning dough-nut. "Okay, hold on." He turned to look at the eastbound flow and chose a moment to step out and halt them.

Cait judged the turn and the wet road and the hope for the route.

Think I can do this without flipping. Maybe.

"Thanks!" she yelled as she popped the clutch and slammed the gas. The Mercury heaved forward, slipping on the wet pavement before grabbing and biting down on it. She turned the wheel and felt the slickness of the road, letting the Mercury slide with its own weight and sending rooster tails of silver behind. She saw the cops start to run after her, but eastbound traffic pushed after the gap closed. There was a clamor of horns, all out of sequence, just honking for the hell of it. There might've been a couple cop voices, but their hearts weren't in it.

They're not gonna want to work that hard.

I hope.

The Mercury wheeled around the building and slowed ahead of the turn. She cranked the wheel and accelerated gently this time, not wanting to fishtail and lose control so close to the first of the canals. This was a big and heavy car, weight high off the road. The weather wouldn't do it any favors. If she ended up on her side, it was going to be a long walk in heavy weather. Another glance back to see if there were any rolling red lights behind and she saw none. Just the insistent patter of raindrops as big as bumblebees.

Nothing between her and the coastline now, just the rest of Washington Boulevard slick with standing water and a growing collection of debris floating out of storm drains and gutters, off roofs and front porches. Junk skittered along sidewalks like living things, uncatalogued undersea species both weird and beautiful. Palm trees bent as if to giant and unseen hands, howls shrieking ragged through the fronds, trailing vapor and drops behind.

Cait could feel the wind heaving on the Mercury's windshield and she leaned into it, pressing the accelerator a bit more, engine reassuring underneath the dissonance.

Not much farther. Road's just about out.

The weather let up and the whole world held its breath for a moment. Wipers pushed aside water and twigs and cigarette wrappers and the window cleared. What she saw ahead brought her heart right up into her throat and she gagged upon it. There was enough of a break in the clouds for just a moment, for the sun to shine through. For an instant, it was mid-afternoon again. Only it was the wrong color.

It was all blue, cold and aquatic, no silver-white sun.

The road ended and the ocean began and the water no longer lay flat. It wasn't wind-whipped and choppy like she'd expected. Instead, it rose into the sky, high enough to filter the lower quarter of the horizon through a curtain of shifting green and blue. Things swam through it, streamlined shapes of whales or schools of fish merging and shattering over and over. Gravity was wrong, suspension until shattering, that lip of water in Lilah's glass hanging but never falling. She was looking up at the sun through a mask while snorkeling, through the surface of the water above. Instead of a white disk, it was a fractured shimmer, irregular and fluid, changing from second to second. Life was in the clouds, it was the clouds swirling and breaking and reforming in acts of consumption and reshaping.

I'm looking into the ocean. It's not where it's supposed to be.

Between the land and the sun lay a standing wave, hanging and held by who knew what force or how long it would stay. She tried to think about how high it must be in order to what it was doing, but the thought just made her want to turn around and drive until the wheels came off the Mercury.

There's no running from this.

Fisherman's Pier lay straight ahead on a junk-strewn road. If she squinted, she could see something standing at the end of it, though the light was failing, attenuated with depth until it was just a lingering blue glow. Standing at the perimeter was a weird phosphorescence, as if glowing dust swept up in the shape of something like a man. It had to be Lee.

She accelerated toward it, not knowing what she'd do when she got there. The Mercury shuddered as if in protest.

"I'm not wild about this plan either," she muttered.

Maybe it's as simple as knocking him into the water? He said something about not wanting to touch the ocean. Could he not or was it something else?

The wind picked on her approach, enough so that the car shook from side to side, forward speed reducing and leeched away. Unmoored debris slammed into the windshield and front end, an unending stream of wet slaps and thunks and clawed scratchings.

I wouldn't last ten seconds out in this. Thank god for Detroit steel.

She floored it and the car responded with a surge of power through the frame that came on but produced no forward motion. Wheels spun on the wet pavement, gripping and failing and gripping again.

"Come on!" She slammed the wheel with an open palm in frustration.

The back end bucked and slipped and she eased down for a second, afraid that she'd flip the whole mess. The resistance followed in turn.

Finger trap.

The car idled heavily for a moment and the wind seemed to wait for her next move. She nudged the gas just a bit, enough to push forward slowly like she was trying to sneak up the street without waking her parents. The Mercury made slow headway into the veiling rain and wind. As she cleared the end of Washington, her ears popped, only the sensation passed through her whole body and even the air inside the cabin of the car. She found herself through whatever membrane of pressure had been in place. Her ears rang like she'd been face up to the amplifier stack the night before, but she was free to move now.

Lee stood there clearly at the end of the concrete pier, arms raised to the sky, sheathed in the water and submarine phosphorescence, glowing weakly in the muted blue daylight. The wall of water was pulling in upon itself from the north and south, becoming a column that rose impossibly out of the ocean. She stared at it open-mouthed for too long, finally willing herself to do something about this unreality that was about to collide with everything she knew.

He hadn't noticed her yet.

He's too far gone, conducting this thing, controlling it. Now or never. Put him right in the water. Hope I'm not going to get in trouble for running down a dead man.

She took in a deep breath and curled the fingers of one hand around the steering wheel. With the other, she turned the tape player back on, forgetting what the next song was. Piano notes rang and then the guitar line, drenched in echo and chorus and that grand, hollow voice. She waited until the chorus kicked in, needing that power to push her forward. It was all part of the ceremony, part of the asking.

She dropped the hammer and called everything the Mercury had in it. The car lunged forward, wheels grabbing and weight throwing her back into the seat. Its wheels went over the curb before the transition from parking lot to pier and walkway. Concrete walls were close on either side, not allowing for any mistakes or shaky hands. It forced her forward. There was no other way, no bailing out now.

It might not have been the best plan, but it was all she had. She drove all two tons of steel and glass and power right at Lee.

The Mercury ate distance like a tyrannosaurus, all greedy and gulping. She kept her eye on the undersea glow that sketched out Lee's form, undulating slowly and meltingly. Her hands were as steady as they'd ever been, harnessing velocity and anger, anger at Lee and the Thing That Wants, how they'd take everything away just when she'd decided to stop her own suffering, anger at everyone being snuffed out and smothered, anger at the black seep that was going to flow up and become everything anyone ever knew or remembered.

Lee must have finally heard the engine's roar. He spun on his heel, quickly enough so that Cait could look clearly into his eyes as she bore down on him, instead bringing to him what he would bring to the world.

They had both run out of pier. The Mercury's front end hit the waters surrounding Lee or whoever he was not. All Cait could do was keep her teeth clenched so she didn't scream and somehow break the spell.

Sensation of motion stilled or rather suspended. She went weightless and the Mercury's wheels must have somehow left the ground. The instant stretched and she felt like she was holding her breath but it had run out already. Like everything had.

Had the car stopped? He just waved his hand and ended gravity?

Lee was still before her, looming huge in the windshield, eyes so dead that she wondered how she might have once seen life in them.

That was easy. Seeing the reality was too terrifying, so I made something up.

She could move freely but the Mercury itself was stuck, lodged not in the landscape but something more fundamental, something deeper. The water in the column behind Lee was no longer rippling but frozen. The music on the tape player stretched out into a long and continuous tone, the segments between notes becoming a huge and awesome expanse of sonic and geologic time.

Lee's hands were outstretched before him, fingers splayed and close enough over the hood that Cait could see them for what they were, puckered and wrinkled and blue. He'd been in the water forever.

"Do something!" she screamed at him. "Finish me or give up!"

Lee's dead eyes said nothing, just reflected the green of the glow around him.

I can just crawl out through the window or door. Not a lot of room, but I can clear the car at least. Then figure something else out. Maybe I can cut through that stuff around him and shut this all down.

She tried not to think about how she had all this time to think.

Water and time. The Thing That Wants. It's fucking with time.

It wants me to think I'm outside it and safe.

Cait cracked the window, unsure of what she'd find. Her fingers closed around a droplet of rain suspended in the air. It yielded to touch but would not completely disappear, a little diamond heart inside its center. She couldn't have crushed it for anything on this earth.

She fought the desire to just climb out the window and take the knife to him directly. That's precisely what he wanted and then time would snap back and momentum would wrap her around the front of the Mercury or the edge of the pier. And that would be that. She unbuckled the seatbelt anyway and withdrew the knife from its sheath.

The playback stretched to the point where she could hear vistas of sound in the hiss of tape noise slowed to where the song became something else entirely.

Cait put the tip of the knife against the front windshield, etching it. "I'm really sorry, Ariela. I'm really sorry, car."

She pushed gently and started cutting a crisscross pattern in the glass, putting into it the thought of exploding outward, glass cut by magic so that each edge was razor sharp, sharp enough to cut through whatever protected Lee and the Thing That Wants. Once done with the shape, she put the knife back. The tone on the playback rose, steep as a jagged mountain peak carved out by time itself over uncounted years. She focused her thoughts and asked anyone or anything who would listen for the strength to do what came next. She put up her right, her good hand, the hand she drew with and did her face with and if that had to be sacrificed, so be it.

She struck the windshield with all her strength.

Pain streaked across her knuckles and wrist and forearm. Shards exploded outward in some uneasy compromise between frozen time and instantaneousness. They tumbled in slow and dizzying motion, cutting edges catching the light like the white obsidian blade itself did. Like makes like. A thousand shades of blue and green coruscated around the cabin of the Mercury and around the front end of the car as she threw herself back into the front seat then down into the passenger footwell. If time resumed, she was going to be unmoored and hitting a concrete barrier at almost fifty miles per hour, according to the speedometer needle frozen there.

The shards all of them sapphire- and emerald-toned in the weird and conflicting lights, rained into the water that Lee wore as armor. They cut through it easy as steel-jacketed bullets through gelatin blocks.

There was an instant of screaming, not of a human voice either but one strangled by water and pressure and weight and so much time that it could not be counted. She was thankful that there was just an instant before the speakers started pouring out her music again.

The Mercury, unmoored by time and control now, rocketed forward. There was a surge of contact as Lee's body hugged the front end of the car. Immediately after that was the more definite reckoning of steel and burning gasoline hitting concrete. The car jarred and lurched for a second.

And then it kept going like judgment.

There was a sickening sensation of weightlessness but inside time, so it was knowable, and in that knowledge was terror-making. Cait used the song's beats to count the moments before the car hit the water. Sinking would follow not long after.

Guessing nobody made these to be seaworthy.

She tried to go limp as gravity dragged them both to the ocean and farther down. The car came to a second, barely gentler stop this time. She was thrown into the front of the bench seats and felt stars burning under her shoulder and neck. The surface held and the car's weight rocked to something approaching horizontal, undulating slowly. Then water poured in through the open front windshield. She looked up to see a curtain of green-tinted sea flowing in and over the dashboard. She clambered up to the seat and unrolled the passenger window as quickly as she could, trying to keep the pace even so it wouldn't stick.

The engine's idling was drowned in a sick gurgling and the stereo cut out like the tape being eaten.

Even if I was beginning to believe everyone else thinking this was a bad news car, I'm gonna miss it.

Cait didn't look for Lee as she went to the passenger window, now fully open. Water slopped in unevenly with the rippling of the ocean surface. She pulled herself through before the whole car filled, sucking her and anything else around down with it. The ocean couldn't have been that deep here just out past the pier's length, but that didn't mean it was safe to stick around.

She spat weirdly-warm salt water from her mouth as she kicked off from the listing car. The curves and dark-red, glossy finish went under with awful inevitability. She took a few kicking strokes away, feeling the undercurrents swirling around her feet as she did. She splayed through the water, trying to keep her cool even as she felt the pull from below, just strokes above panic now.

Lee was nowhere to be found. Even the flickering green swirl he'd been encased in, that was gone too.

Good riddance.

Close enough to shore that she could almost feel bottom, she treaded water for a moment, looking out at where the standing wave had been. There was nothing. Just the hammered-pewter light of the sun, crashing through the dome of clouds.

Cait wanted to laugh at it all but couldn't, not until she got out of the water. Looking around and behind her, there was no way out of the sea here, no ladders for divers, no wharf for a boat, even a dinghy. She was going to have to finish it under her own power.

The tide was absolutely slack, no ebb or flow, as if the whole ocean had forgotten the tides or any other motion. There was no surf to ride into shore and her clothes and boots weighed her down as much as chains. By the time she hit the gray sand, she was panting from exertion. The raw back of her throat flared hot and burned. She was both sweaty and chilled. Fish flopped listlessly amongst the kelp and debris-strewn shore and she felt that for a long moment.

She lay back on the sandy and gently sloped shore, smelling the ghost of the rain and the wet saltiness of the ocean, the stink of the dying sealife. When her pulse got under control, she looked back out and wondered where the hell Lee had taken Sue, if she was around here or just back safely at his trailer or something much much worse. She stood and nudged a couple still-alive-seeming fish back into the water where they just lay gulping.

He probably wouldn't have put her on the water, but he might have wanted to keep her close by. No way to know, and I'm not even sure I could have summoned up the energy to ask.

Away from shore, the water surged and recoiled like a living thing away from a hot wire or a knife blade. It boiled, and Cait could see the ripples of fish and every other kind of creature, swimming away from whatever was coming.

What emerged was green and glowing dully and pulsing with eerie light. The sun itself hid behind the clouds as Lee or whatever lived in him crawled out of the sea, seemingly rejecting him. He stood and calmly walked across the rippling surface as easily as down a sidewalk.

"That was a right neat trick. I'd ask you how you did it, but I don't think you even know." It was Lee's voice but slurred by liquid-filled lungs and throat. "I think you just got a little kind of lucky."

Cait stood in the sand and cold wind that kicked off the chopped and angry ocean before her.

"Only one way to find out!" She fished the knife back out of its cover and held it before her.

"You know that's right."

He kept on coming.

CHAPTER EIGHTEEN

The ocean behind him drew inwards then heaved. A cylinder of the water and everything in it rose slowly. It started small and then grew, pulling the mass of the sea itself and climbing far past the natural surface. Swelling quicker now, it sprawled and grew, maybe the same size around as one of those industrial gas tanks along the freeway, but the motion of light through currents made any guessing foolish at best. Cait could see that it now towered over the horizon and showed little sign of slowing.

Shapes were distorted through it weirdly as the water refracted more than light, bending and reorienting time itself. Inside it were creatures like those that attacked Sue that first night, soaring through the water with all the grace that the land had robbed them of. Something about that tugged at Cait and she was glad that she hadn't met them in their element. Larger things, the size of whales with grotesquely misshapen jaws and protruding teeth pursued anything within reach, maddened by swarming prey. Shoals of tentacles reached and twisted in helical forms, impossible to separate one from the mass. There were too many of them to be an octopus, each of them bigger around than a human and with bleached-white suckers. Ships dove through that glittering column, veering the wrong way, cutting through volume and not along surface. The bow of something that looked like a galleon jutted out and the rest of the ship followed slowly, teetering in a way that made Cait sick to her stomach before it left the column and fell many times its length to the ocean surface, slamming and shattering with towering and misted fingers of spray all that remained of them. Plants without name spun and danced to a current only they manifested. Broad and gelatinous green leaves entrapped uncounted masses, all held fast by loving tendrils.

There were so many skeletons within the column, so many bodies, so many lives that it had stolen and built upon, a horrific collection of misery and loss. She couldn't bear to look at it anymore as the column kept rising toward the sky.

"Don't look away," Lee said. "You oughta look the future right in the face when it's coming."

"Stop right there!" She slashed the knife again, holding it up and between herself and him. "Where's Sue?"

"Nuh-uh. That's a matter for family."

"Family? You're not even Lee anymore! She figured that out and tried to shoot you. Don't pretend to care about her."

The thing in Lee's body stopped, standing uneasily on the last several feet of water before shore. "Of course, I care. I care about *all* these souls you see, all these and more!" He pointed to the column and demanded, "Look to it!"

Cait's eyes flicked to the spire of water and epochs in spite of herself. For all the world, it looked like that slab back at the Museum, the one of time frozen in the bones of titans. This one though, this one was alive or was an echo of life or the ghost of it, thousands of little wounds in time adding up to something far, far more.

"You see it now, don't you? It ain't even one ghost or what I thought was the drowning chorus. It's so much more than that. All waters are graves. You said it yourself!"

Good Christ how did he know?

He swept his hands across it as if to embrace the whole. "I thought it was a thing I could hold, and instead..." The voice trailed off and something like pity flooded into it. "I found something that could hold me! There's your god! There's your holy spirit!"

"You tell me where Sue is and I can get her and show her."

He looked as if he was actually considering it but let it fall away. "She'll see soon enough. Then she'll know which of us was the stronger."

"Speaking of which, why aren't you trying to psych me out like you did at the dam? Or can't you?"

"This is a stupid game you're playing, Cait MacReady." His voice had changed again: this time it was the fatherly voice, the stone on stone of certainty, one that could even end his own daughter if he deemed it necessary. "You stand in the way of a thing you couldn't possibly understand."

"I understand well enough that even you don't know what it is. So here we are." She shifted her weight, and her legs felt like lead still. "You're stuck with me. And I bet that as bad as the windshield cut you, this will do a hell of a lot worse." She twisted the knife in the air like it had already sunk into him.

Lee rubbed his face as casually as if he were testing the closeness of his shave, clammy flesh touching cheek. "Like I said, anyone can get lucky once." There was teasing in his voice.

He took a step toward her and she broke into a foolish run at him.

It's close enough that the water won't slow me that much. And surprise should count for something.

Lee braced himself as she swiped the knife down in front of her. She came up short. It wasn't going to reach him, but it would cut into the waters he surrounded himself with. For a moment there was a tug of resistance, like when she stabbed the bible, like stitches being pulled. The waters cleaved from the narrow slice just across his chest, following the curve of his ribcage.

"Knife don't do much if it don't cut flesh." He grunted, and it sounded like a wave slapping the shore.

Cait felt something hit her. She'd been in the surf before and eaten a wave she didn't see coming. This was like that, only more concentrated, packed into a smaller space. All the air came out of her in a sigh and she caught a mouthful of water laced with sand before she tumbled backward. But at least she held onto the knife.

She sat there bent over in the shallow surf, breathing heavy until she could get a hold of herself again.

"I got no fondness for striking women," he said by way of apology. "But that don't mean that I won't. So stay down and out the way. Or stand up and take your medicine."

Rage pumped through her veins as she stood up, shin-deep in the water that Lee seemed to float just above. She'd been told what to do and been pushed around by men but never like this. She knew she was just two steps away from derailing him or he wouldn't even bother with her. But she wasn't sure how she'd get close enough to do it.

She took a lunge toward him, held back by the water more than she thought. Instead the knife sliced through a heap of gelatinous matter, amethystine and pulsing. It had been thrust out of the water an instant before the knife came down. The thing took the blow meant for Lee, sliced so cleanly that it held for a moment before the top half of it slid off and sloshed into the water.

"Gotta keep your powder dry, girl. Can't just cut whenever you want. Gonna get tired."

"Every minute I keep you tied up is another minute that the Thing That Wants loses patience." She smiled weakly. "I can do this a while longer. But can you? I mean, even a dead man has to keep a schedule."

Lee nodded. "You got me there. Maybe we should just wind this up then? Lemme ask you, you wanna be alive when this all comes to pass? Or you wanna drown now and join the chorus?"

"If you think you can take me." Cait slid back half a step so she could jump if needed.

"Lee! Lee!" called a voice from further up the beach. It was Sue. "Kevin Lee Whelan, you cease your doings right now!"

He didn't have her at all.

Cait couldn't afford to look but Lee evidently thought he could.

She didn't stop to ask how this was possible. So much had happened that possibility had become much more malleable than she ever thought it could be.

Lee's dead eyes turned to the sound of Sue's voice. There was no light in them, dark as the depths that he'd called up.

"Sis?"

The thought that this was the wrong thing flashed through Cait's mind, elusive and slippery. She didn't even try to hold it. Instead, she fully leaped at the now-distracted Lee. Maybe it was a sucker punch, maybe it was a dirty move, but fair fights were for idiots. Vince had taught her that much.

And Cait was done being an idiot.

Her feet left the water and she went right for Lee, his one arm reaching toward Sue up the beach, half-defiant and half-pleading. The posture left his chest completely exposed. Cait brought the knife down in a single arcing sweep, a slice that seemed to catch on bone but only for a second.

Lee didn't see it coming until it was too late. He was able to counter only falteringly. Cait's face fell numb as her vision blurred and she sucked in half a breath of weirdly fresh water suddenly encircling her face. She coughed, but nothing came out, no sound, no air. Blindly, she slashed in front of her, knife and hand passing through a wave that hung somehow in the air, breaking the thing that had grabbed her face and smothered her.

She felt it drip away as she dropped down to her knees and coughed out what felt like a gallon of water. It tasted like Lake Arrowhead in summer, then it tasted like a chlorine-soaked pool.

"Lee!" Sue shouted.

"Stay back, goddammit!" someone else yelled but only half-heard and unclear.

Fuck. Helpless.

Cait kept coughing until it became retching, being squeezed until empty. She struggled to sit back on her knees, to at least get her arms free and put the knife between her and him. She shook sand and hair out of her eyes and tried to see what was going on.

Lee clutched at his chest. He staggered like he was one drink away from oblivion and a moan was dragged out of him, pulled bodily, not human. There was a richness to it, voices layered upon one another so that timbres bled across and gave the sound a depth and dimension that Cait had to fight from getting lost in. It was the voice of the chorus, but it wasn't just in her head now. It resonated through the air, through her body, across the water.

"Let me go!" Sue yelled and there was a sound of an open palm hitting flesh. Cait knew what that felt like.

The scream bubbled down to a whimper now.

"Don't think I'm ever going to feel bad for you," Cait said, holding the knife in Lee's direction.

He stood there and let his arms drop. The slice in his chest bled out the flickering green teeming but its glow died before it hit the water at his feet. He was too tired or beaten to stop it. But he wasn't done, not yet, limbs shaking as he tried to step towards her.

Sue stopped at the water's edge and Cait got a good look at her. She must have been in agony, sweating profusely and favoring her bad leg, bent like a tree in a storm but refusing to yield to the wind.

"Stay back, Sue. That's not really Lee," Cait said as loud as she could manage. "It's just walking around in him."

"He's still in there!"

"The whole chorus is in there. If any part of him is alive, it's in that."

Words boiled behind Sue's lips, but she couldn't bring herself to speak them, not even as filled with fire and sorrow and loss as she was now.

"You knew it was over when you saw him. But you never told me."

"My baby brother." The tears streamed down her face in place of the curse she withheld. "I failed him."

Parker walked down the beach a couple steps behind Sue, rubbing a raised red handprint on his cheek. He shrugged at Cait and she half-smiled in return.

The sea around them all slackened as if exhausted. The column shimmered and turned slowly. Life within it swam suspended but did not diminish.

Then Lee started to laugh. "Y'all think it's done. Y'all want to believe in triumph." It was his old voice, as if that gave him power over Sue at least.

"No more," Cait said as she walked toward him, staying just out of arm's reach. Mercy and rage fought inside her: one side shrieking that she cut him down where he stood, the other demanding her response be tempered. And the both refusing any easy compromise or alternative to the other.

"Still holding that place in the chorus for you." He rolled his head up and looked at Cait. The hollows of his eyes were dark with a depth that could not have been. They ate the sight of her. They revealed what was coming, and that thing was consumption. He pulled his lips back in a smile that made a wave of nausea rise in her.

"And you and her and him will be part of it. Hell, you'll be cheerin' it on. You won't be happy until it—"

Cait swiped up with the knife, catching the swirling waters at his crotch and bringing the blade up in a smooth arc that curved off and cut over his heart before slicing past his shoulder.

Hope that was not too shallow, not too deep.

More green fire seeped up, millions of particles teeming and weltering. All of them given release, they fled the body that held them and swarmed to the laceration. The magic that kept them in place now bleeding out and paling. Like summer campfire, the sparks flared and then burned out, unable to survive.

Cait clutched the handle of the knife with three fingers and hooked her index under one side of the cut, her other hand under the opposite side. She pulled with whatever strength she had left. The swirling and cleft waters parted, exposing everything beneath to the air.

"God almighty," Sue sighed with a broken reverence.

The magic or whatever it was shucked off him like a split skin, plain as a cocoon being opened. As it did, voices rang in relief, in song, fleeting past the three of them on the beach insubstantial as breath.

Lee stood before Cait, bleeding from a very long but very shallow razor cut in the frontmost part of his ribcage where the blade had actually reached skin. His clothes split, and the skin beneath was pink and healthy and warm. He breathed easily, as if nothing had happened, and perhaps that was even true for him.

Who knew how long he'd been trapped in that?

"Holy shit," Cait whispered.

"Oh, thank God," Lee replied before he spilled forward.

"Shit! Parker!" She tried to hold him up but couldn't and they both top-pled backward into the chattering surf. She did her best to roll him onto his back but struggled with the weight of it.

"I got you." Parker dragged him up onto the beach, just enough to keep him from drowning.

Sue was slow to kneel to Lee's level and still remain in control of her-self. Cait slid over and tried to help lower her down, so she didn't have to push the leg any further than she had. Her eyes locked onto hers once and Cait read both rage and relief in them, both feelings absolutely pure in that instant, inextricable and fiery.

Sue held Lee's head to her breast and the water lapped at them both.

Cait turned to see what was left of the thing that had held Lee. It lay beside him like a hundred pounds of beached jellyfish, gelid semi-solids quivering in the foam and sand.

The column still waited there, filled to spilling with its impossibility. Behind it, the storm boiled in the sky, sun all but eaten away.

Lee couldn't remember anything. Not for weeks before. The wide and sad-eyed responses he gave couldn't have been faked, not even by the flat-test sociopath mimic.

"That's a mercy," Cait said.

"Is it?" Parker asked, tossing a dead cigarette up the shore. "LAPD still gonna want him for that homicide."

"You're LAPD."

He bobbed his head back and forth by way of reply, half-yes and half-no.

"Doesn't change anything. They'll find him, same as finding me."

"I don't get it."

"I'm not supposed to be here, Cait. I'm supposed to be running crowd control along with every other cop in the city. Instead, I got the bright idea to go find Sue."

"And how did you?"

"Looked at maps of where she was being held and found Pentecostal churches in the area of where she was being held. First one I looked at. Just had to sneak out."

"And why would you go and do that? Trager's gonna eat you alive."

The wind turned bitter and Cait felt it in her bones.

"You don't know the half of it."

Cait tried to remember the other name that Trager had brought up, Lancer maybe. She didn't feel it right to ask right now. "Still, why?"

"'Cause it sounded like you needed her help is all. I didn't think you should go charging in all alone."

"Sue probably would have been happy to push me face-first into hell. Probably still does."

She was dabbing at the cut on Lee's chest with strips that she'd torn off his shirt. Messy work, red sopping up like swollen creeks.

"Is he okay, aside—?" Cait called.

"No thanks to you," came the chilly reply.

"And we both thought he was dead no matter what," she hissed back. "Little gratitude."

Parker's hand rested on her shoulder for a moment, slowing her down.

"She's been through a bit. She told me that her getting out of that cell was an intervention. Holy spirit type."

"I'm not so sure on that call. But I got no evidence to argue it."

Those burst pipes and the liquid spilling into words? What was that?

Cait shivered again and turned to look out over the water.

The column had grown. She was sure of it. Everything within it seethed and turned, all of time churning in the waters there. Things lost or hidden or forgotten were now revealed. If the water kept secrets, it was giving them all up now, all at once.

"So what the hell's going on in there?" he asked. "Thought it would have, I don't know, gone away since you put the kibosh on Lee."

"It wasn't Lee starting it. He might've been helping it, even if he didn't want to at first. It's always been there. Just we can see it now. And now that it's moving, it's harder to stop."

The feeling it stirred up in her was a slow and strangling dread, making everything as heavy as time brought to a standstill.

"We're not out of it?" he asked, begging for one answer.

Wet wind pelted them in a hammering sheet, thousands of tiny needles on skin.

"You want the comforting lie?"

"Yeah."

"We're just now getting to it."

"You don't know a single thing about comfort, do you?"

Cait leaned on the door of Parker's squarish Dodge. The window was dotted with uncountable water droplets all glittering in the parking lot lights that had flickered on in the premature night.

Lee sat in the back seat and his eyes were all but empty, sights he'd seen drained out of him, hollowing him. Sue's glare had settled to a slow burn but still could melt glass.

"We don't have a lot of time, Sue," Cait said, just shy of ordering. "And right now, I don't care about anything other than that." She pointed at the restless surface of the ocean and the column's aquatic glow. "I don't care whether you think that's Leviathan or the devil or even some fu… some manifestation of the holy. It's got to be stopped or redirected. Let me talk to Lee. He's closest to it."

Sue refused to meet her stare. She ate at herself, waged war on herself, relished the act of self-consumption rather than yielding. Cait understood it intimately.

She eased down into a crouch, trying not to loom. "Look, you did this all for Lee, right? Well, you won. You got him back. But you're only gonna have that for tonight if even that long unless I can get something I can use."

"Haven't you done enough?" The words came out angry as spit.

"Not by half," Cait said. "And if you're demanding honesty, I'd have done what I did even if it cut him in half. 'Cause that's what I thought was going to happen. Just like that's what you thought was going to happen when you brought your daddy's gun all the way from Tennessee with you."

Sue said nothing, chewing on the substance of her own soul.

"Lie to me if you got to." Cait reached a hand toward her.

"She was only doing the necessary, sis." Lee whispered. "Let it go."

"What he did was unholy and what you're going to do is worse. That can't be spoken to, only excised."

"I don't think there's a force you or I can name that can remove that," Cait said. "If there was one that had any interest in doing so why is that thing still standing?"

Sue didn't have an answer, her face twisted like taking punches. "What do you want?"

"I just wanna know how to talk to it."

"You listen is how," Lee said. "I went looking and looking and I only found those voices, the chorus. I just entered the stillness for a time, and it spoke to me.

"But it spoke so loud. I couldn't hear nothing else, couldn't even think for myself. There's no room for self when you touch that."

Sue looked like she envied him in that moment.

"What did it want?"

"It wanted everything with it. That's all. Only everything. All that is not it has to become it. That'll be the grand chorus, the drowning becomes drowned and things can end." Tears limned his eyes, catching the dashboard lights in amber.

Cait stood slowly and with some ache.

"Maybe we shouldn't stop it," Sue said.

"And maybe it doesn't even want what it thinks it wants," Cait countered.

A pack of black and brown birds, upright and waddling, shuffled past the car and away from the lapping surf. They were bigger than pitbulls. Cait had to suppress a giggle as they moved by like something out of a cartoon she'd seen as a kid. Seals, big and feral with clawed flippers and protruding tusks, picked at the body of something primeval all blubber and bone. An anchor that had been coughed out of the sea lolled half-hooked into the slope of the sand like it was tackle meant to move a continent.

"Hey, Cait. Why do we have time?" Parker asked.

"So everything doesn't happen at once"

"Oh, so you've heard that one."

"I'm living proof of it."

Someone fell from the fishermen's pier, just hitting the water and thudding to the sand. Cait sprinted over and rolled them face-up. Young, Chinese girl, weird and unrecognizable clothes, pretty, glasses that were not in style anywhere. A silver box about the size of a cigarette case only thinner lay next to her hand, attached to something that looked like earplugs, only hanging by a white plastic-coated wire.

"Hey, hey, you okay?"

The woman shook her head. "Dude, what the fuck? I was just—"

She swatted at the wires connecting her ears and the little box. On the back side of it was a picture of an apple, bite taken out, etched into the steel. Cait tried to figure out where she'd seen it before.

A helicopter roared overhead, whipping sand everywhere. It wasn't a shape that she recognized. Not a cop chopper but something else, more slender, sinister in profile, way quieter than she'd expected. It looked like the future. Following its traverse, there lay something on the sea that looked like chromed spires and billowing teardrops made of gossamer, more a city than a ship, rippling as the sea beneath it did.

The woman's mouth opened in an *O* of surprise as she took in the scene. "I gotta get out. Out of here." She took to her feet and began to run from the shore, pushing away from anything and anyone in near-panic.

Cait's hand reached for the box she'd been holding, and she yelled. "Hey! Wait! You dropped… whatever the hell this is." She turned it over, heavy in her hand. A faint light like a weak television flicked on when Cait pressed the control button on the top. There was a screen not any bigger than four postage stamps with words that she couldn't read. The fall had cracked the screen, but it almost halfway worked.

The woman was already up the beach or maybe she'd just disappeared in a screen of sand.

"Things are happening faster," Cait said

The sea was alive now, less a surface and more an arena. Dorsal fins and breaching dolphins or fish undulated through the water, seeming without aim or direction. All of them bigger than anything she had seen without glass in front of her. Knowing there was nothing but air and distance between made her want to retreat up the sand.

She pressed the metal thing into Parker's hand. "Give her that back if she comes back around."

"Feels like it's made of bullets. Heavy."

"Who knows, maybe it is."

Her vision fixed on a pilotless boat not far from where the Mercury went down. It was turning a big slow circle out in the animate sea. Not a figure walked along its deck.

"I got an idea."

"I don't know what it is but I'm sure it's bad."

"Well, I'm sure not going to be able to goddamn swim out there."

"Maybe you could drown yourself in a truck bed."

"It's *right* there," Cait said, unable to prevent herself from pointing at the column. "I'm going to have to go to it. How hard can it be to steer?"

"And you know where to go?"

She pointed at the thing that didn't belong above all other things that were out of place on that beach at that moment. "Stop stalling, Parker."

He thew up his arms and let his hands slap down to his sides. "Fine! And then what?"

"Listen if it'll let me."

Cait waded out to her hips, watching an exotic array of fins and fish swim past, most creatures simply ignoring her and even one another, just all of them in the same ocean at the same moment. Predator and prey relationships had been suspended as everything struggled with being alongside everything else in too small a moment. She pushed out to where she couldn't feel bottom, pursuing a surfboard that rode the surface a little farther out. Moments of exertion and she hauled herself aboard, resting to catch her breath.

Paddle to the boat. Boat to the column. Easy.

The board was orange and painted in ridiculous yellow and black flames that belonged on a hot rod. It bobbed there among scales and fins and churning water. She got three fingers on the board and caught wax and sand ground in like it had been done fresh. Hauling it in, she stepped back to get a good purchase on the top before jumping up to get her belly on the board and start paddling out.

Something slithered around her calf, her exposed ankle feeling muscles covered in frictionless slime. Turning, she saw a purplish tentacle wider around than her arm exploring this strange world past whatever it knew, finally letting go of her in something that felt like disappointment. She sighed in relief, knowing that she couldn't walk away from a fight with just about anything that the ocean could serve up.

"You're crazy!" Parker called from the shore.

"But not insane! And please don't say anything else!"

He watched her and his mouth moved faintly, words trying to get free.

"Another time! I got too much on my mind right now!"

He just nodded and watched her shovel through the water, hand over hand.

The clouds were beginning to break up, but the sky itself was dark and starless behind to the slowly twisting glow at the center of the column all luminescent marble in shades of sapphire and emerald, all coldly alive.

Her hands brushed across tough scales or blubbery skin smoother than glass with the cool seawater being the medium that it all hung in. She caught the texture of something, only half-wet, loose and coarse fibers in a messy sheet. Curious, she hauled it up and only a trickle of water came from it as if had only just hit the surface.

Why not? Everything was happening at once now.

Something flew above her, an arcing streak of light that must have been manmade but moved more quickly than even the helicopter before. She didn't try to name it, thinking instead of the bundle she was setting down.

The bag rustled and there was a name written on it, unreadable. She undid the hastily tied top and cried when she looked in. There were perhaps six or seven kittens, tiny and helpless things, barely old enough to stand. Only some of them moved.

"Oh god. Oh god. Oh god. I got you guys. Hold on."

There was a muted noise of mewling, pinpricks of sound over the gurgling against the board's bow. All the kittens were grey and blue in the half-light.

She kept her heart from bursting out of her chest but only barely. She now kneeled on the board as if supplicant to something bigger and unseen. The bagged kittens wriggled between her knees as she paddled more forcefully now to the circling boat. It was a small-cabin job, maybe a fishing boat. It looked old, but that didn't mean anything anymore in a now that had collapsed past and even the future. She angled the board to parallel the boat's track as it came around once more. One hand on the bag of cats and the other outstretched, she reached for the side of the moving boat and grabbed once she felt it underneath her fingers.

Lurching ahead, almost ripped off the board, she caught herself and brought the bag over the side of the boat, letting it drop as carefully as she could manage. More angry squeaks of angry kittens as they fell to the deck, but at least they were out of the water.

"All aboard," she muttered to herself as she struggled over the side. The wiggling bag rustled before her, more vigorous now. The thought of whoever tossed these creatures to their death was something she couldn't get away from. Then that broadened out to the thought of everyone who died to the water being out there maybe and just as sad and desperate as these little creatures. It brought her to her knees and further. Before she could have struggled against that call, but she had to let go. She lay on the deck and cried at its enormity, a thing bigger than she could imagine made of misery, of the final moments of dying alone.

She opened her mouth but couldn't force her thoughts into voice. She just wanted it to be over. More than secretly, she wanted herself to be over, having stolen from a world over and over, a world she had never believed in but somehow was true anyway. It wasn't that her fiction made it true, but it always had been. All of that and the cries of the chorus filled her for a moment, but that was all she could give it. Any more and they'd take it all.

The column and the Thing That Wants called her now. She picked up the bag and hoped to find a warm place in the cabin. Opening the door, she was greeted by big band sounds, huge orchestras, all-live players, all the current hits of whenever this boat was lost. There was no phonograph, but there was a radio. And a heater blasting at full power. It must've been winter back then. The warmth died past her knees, but that would be enough to keep the kittens going for some time.

Was it even winter now?

She found was a mostly empty wooden crate, slats placed tightly enough to keep even the most determined kitten contained. Right now it held a scattering of tools and a pint bottle of rye that hadn't been cracked open yet. She dumped it all and left the bottle in reach of the wheel in case.

Better to get out of the wet bag at least.

They came out of the bag two at a time and she only needed three trips. A fourth for the last one, who was not only wet but cold. She had to look to make sure for herself. It was little, tiny even, orange and red mackerel-stripes hinted at but not yet grown in. This one didn't wiggle or mewl and Cait couldn't bring herself to give it a name before it passed on. Nor could she give up entirely on it, tucking it between her shirt and skin where it rested like a cold abscess. She was warmer, but just barely. She stripped out of her jacket and placed it over the top of the box to keep the bravest from crawling out just yet. Then she toed the box close to the heating register at foot level, that being all she could do to comfort them.

The wheel was turned all the way to port and she righted it as she saw the column glowing before her. It took a few adjustments to learn the rhythm of guiding the boat, starting out overcorrecting and then again. There was no immediate response, so she had to drive like she wanted to be somewhere in a near but not-yet-there future moment and keep several moves ahead. She got a hold of herself and set the course finally, steering dead on.

She calmed her thoughts, put aside the chugging and shuddering sound of the engine belowdecks and the peeps of the tiny creatures she shared the cabin with. Stepping back from the wheel, she pulled the knife from its sheath.

Cait cut into the air, imagining that each cut was peeling away an obstacle, a barrier, a layer of protection, not to wound but to be able to reach.

She cut away misunderstanding. She tried to pare down to a more direct communication so that confusion would be lost. If this was like anything she was used to, it would take a lot of work. The column of water or sky or both glowed and in that glow, there was the pulse of something alive.

The boat was under a sky that was too big.

Cait didn't dare do more than nudge the wheel now. She saw what must have been the throttle control, but was afraid to go any faster for fear of capsizing. Everything in the ocean was swimming or undulating or steering toward the column as well, called by a song that they could neither hear nor resist. From every direction and degree, life flowed into it. There were other ships on the water too, half-seen in the flickering glow. She could only imagine the menagerie below the surface, occasionally bursting through it with a breach or jostle.

She perceived with the whole of her body, the sweaty salt scent and the uneven lapping surge of flippers, the sensation of being on something un-solid yet physical. Then there was the sight of it, stretching impossibly vertical and growing to fill the horizon before her.

"Hold on, kittens," she murmured. "Hold on, Cait." She pat the warming one next to her but still felt nothing.

The vertical waters were close enough to touch now. The bow tipped into the churning glow, and everything went sideways and stomach-churning. She felt everything turn straight down like a sickening roller-coaster drop. Neither skin nor bones, she was robbed of every bodily sensation as the boat fell up into the bioluminescence. The moment stretched out like with what Lee had done to the car on the pier, pulled out to hours. She had been outside the moment then. Now she was in the middle of it or it was in the middle of her: there was no way to tell.

The world turned sideways and the boat was floating upon it now, bow pointed to what must have been the sky, starless and blanked out. Below the hull was the glowing pulse of the column, not captured sunlight but something generated by a process she couldn't name or understand but could see radiating from below. The wonder of it infected her and she laughed in spite of herself, giddy and terrified. She laughed as she powered ahead. Her hand slipped down to the throttle, finally confident enough and she eased the lever ahead to half speed, clicking past a marker on the control. The big diesels below groaned and growled but obeyed.

There was no way to know what was coming, just the glow and the black sky, stars still hiding in either fear or respect. Behind her, the busy sea looked like hammered glass catching the reflection of the city lights close by, a million chipped glintings. The boat surged ahead, riding now not on water but on something else.

She went back to listening.

All she heard was the rush of a storm from nowhere. Rain pelted horizontally in sheets so loud that it drowned out even the engines below her feet. The boat shook with violence, shuddering as if ground between two titanic millstones. The sound ate everything, forcing Cait to her knees. She doubled over the box of cats, palms pressed to her ears, but that did nothing. Everything was exploding and in the moment she was dragged back to the upstairs room at the Last Prayer Club, the one that didn't exist. There was an instant there where everything was destroyed or rebuilt or it didn't really matter because that place was not a place at all, nor was it a time. It was outside.

There was a final press, hammering waves grating against the boat and everything in it. Cait felt that her bones were being pressed together, that the air was being sucked out of her so she couldn't even scream anymore.

Ricketing across the surface, the boat listed under assault. The curved horizon tilted sideways, revealing geometries of distress as the waters lapped in upon themselves. The dissonant drone of pressure gave way to something else: the sound of water folding and echoing upon itself as the sides closed in, the sound of a wave collapsing from wider to narrower and the air rushing past. Everything became smaller and smaller until the possibility of staying separated from it all was shattered. There was only the sound now as the walls of translucent blue churn came together and the outside was made inside.

The tiny craft disappeared.

CHAPTER NINETEEN

The water was on all sides of it all. Ocean and air had been folded and flattened into a hollow sphere. Every direction Cait looked in showed only liquid hanging at impossible angles, twitching with currents that were not due to wind or gravity but some other hand. Wavelets moved like a flock of birds, murmurations of ripples all guided by an unspoken intelligence, something beyond language or consciousness but undeniable all the same.

"What the utter fuck?" she asked anyone listening.

The only reply was the uneven sloshing of water against the boat's hull, tentative and exploratory as probing fingers.

"Hello!" she called out. She thought she heard an echo of her voice against the waters, but it could easily have been wishful deception. The world just wasn't that big.

There was no sun anywhere, but the place was lit flatly, as if on a cloudy day. Clouds weren't there, though. The light should have filtered jewellike through the captive waters, instead it was omnipresent and deadening.

I'm inside the column. But this looks much too big to be that.

She decided it better to not dwell too deeply on the shortcomings of geometry and perception. The water and the strange currents within it waited. Ripplings swam around the hull not touching it but not letting it pass either. Force gathered into force and became a wave that circled around the boat like a shark, waiting for someone to break and jump overboard.

Any sensation of movement was stilled. Just her and the boat on the water, the bitter sounds of the kittens in their box. The pit of her stomach carved empty. The bristling of soft and drying fur. She knew she had to go into the water. The boat wasn't going anywhere else. She took the tiny and unmoving kitten from beneath her shirt and placed with the others in the box, brushing back the boldest of them clumsily reaching when it saw the cover pulled aside.

"You guys watch this one," she said. "I'll be back..." and left the though unfinished. There was no telling if she could even come back from where she thought was going.

She looked around for an ignition switch, eyes running over unfamiliar controls until she found what she'd wanted, throwing out a quick wish that it started up again when she returned. No need to run out the gas any more than she'd already done. There was nowhere to go if even the water would let her get there.

Other shapes began to move in the water now, but not the creatures and ships and debris of overlapping and collapsing time that she'd seen before. This was something else, waters bending and reforming into the suggestion of sleeping bodies, children, adults and those who were all but skeletal in old age. All of them lay in repose, none alive. There was no use counting them for they were uncountable. The waters had always been hungry. The echoed bodies encircled the boat to the horizon, however close or far away that was, just outside the wave or whatever force was holding the craft where it stood.

The Chorus is right here. The Thing That Wants must be here too. Or I'm in it.

The boat rocked only when Cait shifted her weight upon it, as if there was a balance that could be easily upset. That made her draw within herself, eggshell walking to the railing. She looked at the faces in the water but they were unreadable as Lee's when it had been sheathed in the liquid and bioluminescence. Only hints of pieces could be seen. But what was clear was a spot between two bodies that was empty yet, plain as a crashed car in a swimming pool. Only cobalt blue stirrings lay there in that absence, begging to be filled.

I know what fits into that space.

Cait dashed back to the jacket in the engine room and took the shell from it, carrying it in one hand and the knife in the other. She fingered the shell that she carried, its angles and curves all worn smooth over time. The knife waited in its sheath. She placed both objects into one hand and then made sure the squirming kittens were still alive but not going anywhere. She tucked in the fabric under the box's corners and hoped that some things still had consequence. Then she closed the cabin door tight.

The empty place called to her just like it had the first time she tried to drown herself and at the tub with the gushing bible and the water before the dam. She heard the call but did not fall to it. She would not be led.

WE HAVE MADE A PLACE FOR YOU
WE HAVE MADE A PLACE FOR YOU

It was right there. She could jump to it.
She would lead herself.

CHAPTER TWENTY

Everything went blue. The waters swallowed her as they'd taken the boat and in that those waters there were voices. The voices that she'd heard times before, but now they spoke with a clarity all of a common chord. They called her away in their abyssal loneliness, strong and solid as a rope tied to a weight and dragging. Cait was determined not to surrender to them but instead to pursue them as she saw fit. The pressure built around her, though it grew no darker in these depths.

The voices sang that she would stay with them now. She felt in them the need to be un-alone. She knew the feeling, the hope that there would be just one other person with you in the dark hours, so her pain and fear would at least go recognized. Afraid to ever speak. The voices were not with her but instead trying to drive her. Their unified fear would not stop.

Anguish tugged at her like a heart still beating in a shark's mouth, the meal trying to escape the eater. She let the feeling flow out of her. It wasn't helping now. It wasn't letting her hold on, wasn't giving her anything.

When the last of the fear and isolation of the voices passed through her and she felt wrung out and empty, she worked off the knife's sheath with her thumb and wrestled her hand back. In the water, the knife cut, leaving a thin empty behind wherever the edge led.

All around her, the bodies of the chorus were visible, swirling in the cold blue. They drew closer not hungrily but needily, all of them with arms outstretched. Cait brought the shell before her and then punched the knife through it, through to the other side until she felt it grind against the flat guard. Sensation surged out of the tear, a reversal of pressure flowing past her hands. In the face of that, the chorus pulled back as if from sudden flame.

The absence of water flowed out from the shell and with that, the sound of a young woman's voice singing not of despair or need but of release. Rippling sheets of water parted around her and Cait found herself outside of the waters but also in them, the space solid enough to support her. She could pass through to the waters outside if she pressed hard enough, but had no desire to aside from initial curiosity. The singer had survived apart from the numbing cloy of the chorus, away from Thing That Wants. There was a way out.

The voice sang of being freed and hearing that, the chorus stilled for a moment. When it returned, it was diminished as if some voices had not rejoined. Cait gasped and the echoes rang metallic in the closed space. She plunged the knife into the watery wall surrounding her and cut and peeled more away. Flensed from the whole, pieces fell to the floor of the new chamber and melted back to the waters they had been cut from.

In moments she had sliced out a place enough to take refuge. All around her the chorus slowed and diminished and faded into a pattering of rain or frog song. They were still there but directed elsewhere now, singing a new chant. One not of envy or loneliness but of belonging to another whole.

The girl led them away.

Cait watched as the chorus in all its forms and shapes swam through the water, free in it. She dropped the shell or soul trap or whatever it was to the floor of the open space in which she stood. It fell, not slowed by the transition from air to liquid and continued down and out of sight. The song continued its transition from binding and fear, where each had only reinforced the other. Something freer grew, liquid and open.

She could feel it in her blood, every part of her resonating with it, a song that was older than any single living thing on the planet but playing out through her. Behind the swirling chorus came a weltering of life in a thousand different shapes, powerful reptilian titans and pulsating jellies of rainbow colors, trailing tangled streamers behind them and things that were all eyes and tentacles riding the currents to an alien grace.

The song rose up, not a unison but swarming unevenly around a single note, weaving in and out around it because life itself was not uniform and controlled but organized and so honoring that note, even if only in their own manner. She felt something underneath, finally awoken and stirred into action and perception at this scale. It had only taken the song of the entire chorus breaking free to do so.

Its voice was a resounding basso note that made the walls of Cait's shelter pulse and vibrate before it reached beneath her skin and the hollows of her insides, shivering them in time. She couldn't have ignored it even if she'd wanted to. The sound was everything, her every atom rang with it.

MINE

It was the same voice that had compelled her to leap, compelled her to drown before, tried to compel her into the chorus. This was the voice that bound, that tied, that possessed.

"They're not yours!" she shouted. She was aware of the air leaving her lungs but not of any sound from it. "They're not your prisoners!"

MINE
ALL IS MINE

Thing That Wants shuddered in the below, the waters that had existed before life. Its fury boiled up in shattering waves. The chorus and the animals and that vast parade of life were scattered before it. Cait could only think of those stupid fake houses filled with mannequins, built by scientists to test their bombs and how they shattered into dust when the gates of hell were opened and the bomb laughed at everything that humans made. She held onto thought, imagining riding the shockwave, letting it pass through her, anything to come through this intact.

Her eyes closed when everything went black and she was lurched into a sudden rising, a rejection, bodily and whole from the substance of the water. It spat her to the inner surface where she bobbed to the top in the half-light of the glow inside the column. The geometry of the world had changed again. The sea-plane was flat from horizon to horizon, only the silhouette of the nearby boat breaking the line between water and whatever passed for the sky.

A final membrane, the shape of the shelter she'd carved from the water, stood between her and freedom. Cait sliced it open with a X and pushed through before the water could fill it. The water was choked with bones and skin and remnant, whatever was left of the chorus after Thing That Wants gave its shattering cry. Cait couldn't even cry at it, her guts all but scooped out and put back sideways. She pushed through what felt like miles of flayed skin and scales, a Sargasso of charnel-house drains and floating atrocity. The water was oily with remnant.

GIVE THEM BACK

"They're not yours!" she repeated. "Even if I could, I wouldn't!"

The water surged and the sky drained of light. She looked below her and beneath her feet boiled a nimbus of cold-green twisting veins, overlapping to a fracturing webwork, too large to be seen as a whole. She looked away, afraid of getting lost in it if she stared any longer.

She felt something strange, like time going sick and subjected to whip-lash gravities. All she could do was swim to the boat, hoping for some form of stability. She was lost. Where or when became meaningless. She fought to keep panic tamped down inside her but it fought back with claws.

I'm not lost. I'm here. And now. Even if here is outside space and now is outside time. It's not the first time I've been here.

Like it or not, Ariela showed me the way.

She sucked in a deep breath and stilled herself in the water.

"Thank you, Ariela. I never thought I'd say this, but thank you for showing me what I can do."

Her cheeks went hot for a moment. Shame or tears, she couldn't tell. The stillness within her went big and she held that until she was made strong by it. Strong enough to fight.

"You want someone? Come and take me!" She splashed the surface of the water like she'd slapped boyfriends past, meant to provoke and insult more than anything else. "But you can't have everything!"

The glow intensified and everything was bathed in sickening green that danced and dappled like reflected sunlight, an underwater sun now.

"You better run back! Back to when you had it all!" She slashed the knife in front of her, other hand holding to the lip of the ship's bow. "Go back to when you were King Shit!" She couldn't let go because who knew where the boat would be when she got back.

I WILL SHOW YOU WHO IS KING

The water chattered and jumped with things moving beneath. Gigantic penguins with orange-striped beaks swam under her feet, flapping wings as if flying. Their beaks were serrated and blooded. Schools of razor-toothed fish ripped into the birds. Whales with misshapen jaws ate leopard seals in a bite. Gigantic octopi lashed to the whales while they were set upon by uncounted millions of consuming scavengers. None of them went after her, all consuming one another. They were all old but not primeval, all barely-recognizable as being a part of a world she belonged to. The oldest dance, eaten and eating themselves, becoming food for others.

She would have to take it back farther.

She visualized time in a stream. Even if the thing didn't, she had to work from within herself. That's what she'd done before when she wrote the book that broke the world. She had to do something that made sense to herself first before it could act upon anyone else. Time ran only one way, but in this place, it could be worked upon differently. The Thing lived in a time where all life was just a single lifetime or maybe not even a moment. But it had chosen to relate to Cait on her level. There it could be bound. She could work in its memory.

The river was running backward. The Thing had already taken it back with the hauntings and the things that Lee called. It had showed her a time that was gone from humans but was still remembered. It had to, or it wouldn't have been able to gather power from there.

She had to chase it back upriver.

She prayed the boat would still be there when she finished and couldn't let fear of it being gone hold her back. The surface of this endless sea spread out in all directions, so that any of them would do. Cait took a breath and pushed off the hull, using the knife held vertically in front of her to break the surface like cutting a vast sheet or into a body to find the disease within. The waters broke easily, peeling away from the blade and she felt herself working against the current, not only of gravity and flow but of time itself, digging back into the Thing's reckoning.

YOU CANNOT DO THIS

"Don't tell me what I can't do. Stop me if you're so scared!"

A nightmare of maws flooded to the surface, all of them wet and hungry, ringed with needles or uneven dagger-like teeth and with suckers and lashing tentacles lined with barbs. They threatened but did not eat. She kicked harder into the currents, days becoming anti-days, weeks, years now. Jaws snapped in a cacophony, waters so chopped and frothed that they made a mist. Cait kept moving forward steadily, not slashing or cutting but simply passing through whatever stood in her way. She could feel something be pulled from her, but she'd been so wrung out already there was nothing left. Instead it came off as that feeling of weightlessness when you fly in dream. Even buoyancy didn't matter; it was less even than that.

GO BACK AND CATCH ME THEN

"I've been doing that," she gritted between breaths.

But I figured out why I haven't seen anything really, really old, geologically old. It's scared. Like any living thing that's been burned, it learns to fear.

Chicxulub. That's what it fears. The meteor that ended it all. That had to be a place to start.

She pushed farther back into what she reckoned was time. Mammals grew fewer, mouths were of reptile or fish, birds were forgotten because they hadn't been born yet. The water itself tasted different, felt different because the world was different then, life when it only needed to be alive and not catalogued or reckoned with or understood, free from the limitations and strictures placed upon it by humans or intelligence.

TURN BACK

"Not on your life!" Cait kicked harder even though her legs were burning now.

TURN BACK AND I WILL

"Do what? Spare me? You'll give up?!" She spat the last as alkaline water filled her mouth, more bitter than salt.

The waters went still now, robbed of current. The profusion of life dwindled to only a few and sluggish specimens, laggard filter feeders and slow predators of slower prey. The air smelled like ash and even Cait was made to take pause. There was a sense of everything being hushed and cowed, of the whole of the world holding its breath because it didn't know what was coming next. Unnamable bones littered the waters with no meat attached.

STOP

Cait wanted to yell something defiant at it, but she couldn't. She knew that she was on a vertiginous ledge now.

In for a penny…

She scissor-kicked forward and the waters ahead of her were that of a dead world. The sky was ink black and ash clung to her fingers and clothes and every other part of her. It was falling from the sky. It was in the water. It was the water.

She braced herself for what was to come and took another kick.

The voice pleaded, but it was so small that she couldn't hear it.

Deafening white clouded everything, so much that her vision spotted purple and blue and pink even with her eyes shut. A heartbeat after that was the shockwave that must have come before.

The Thing's scream was worse.

She blacked out before she could take that in.

CHAPTER TWENTY ONE

Cait gagged when she tried to take in a breath but got salt water instead, coughing until she teared. She thrashed in the water, trying to keep
the panic from overtaking her, finally growing so tired all she could do was
to float there and recover.

The sky above had a clarity that was painful, never knowing any smoke
other than that which had been sparked by lightning or forest fire. The air
was rich, making her feel giddy with every breath. She checked herself,
heart hammering as she watched reptiles that hadn't swam the seas in millions of years blithely cruise past her, eyes only for one another in the form
of prey or mate.

She was so in awe that she had to laugh to break the moment, else fall
into it and forget everything that came before.

Creatures as big as houses swam with grace that shouldn't have been
possible. She'd done it. She'd chased it back here, and what? Shocked it
with the memory of its own pain at Chicxulub? The water remembered
everything. She'd only forced it to dig those memories up.

She gulped a deep breath and demanded, "Are you there?!" to the sky.

Nothing. Just the dinosaurs moving through the water and outside any
sight of land. A long-necked creature craned back to look in Cait's direction, chewing thoughtlessly on something. She wished she'd had a camera
with her.

She wished she knew how she was going to go back.

"Thing?"

The surface jarred and jumped, crawling with life and intent, playing
out its anger in waves.

FOOL
I WAS ALREADY OLD IN THIS TIME
I HAVE NO LESS POWER HERE

Dammit.

She kicked with all the strength she could and it felt like kicking wet
concrete. Her strength was further sapped by the thought of how far back
she'd have to go in order to make a confrontation even possible. She was

just… her. And this was something else entirely, not human and maybe not even material.

Roaring sounds churned nearby as creatures in the water took notice now, hungered suddenly or simply just aware that Cait was small and near. A gigantic reptile swiveled its body and swam past her and she lashed in shock and fear it as it did. Dark red flooded into the frothing sea. Flanks the size of billboards, scale and cartilage and bone, shrank from the wound that stretched across them, shuddering gouts of blood with every stroke. That blood was enough to attract others. Cait swam harder, pushing past now, reaching back farther out of the sight of the transitory predator/prey dance. Madness as things slid past her, smelling a large and easy meal but she was already past them. She lived in Thing That Wants' perception now, in a longer time than these reptiles had ever existed.

She wished the chorus was still here to guide her, but they hadn't yet been born and wouldn't be for millions of years. She had only herself and the knife and the last reaches of the thing's memory to plumb.

RUN MORE AND DIE TIRED WITHIN ME

"Not likely," she growled in reply.

She kept focused on the knife blade as it sliced through time and memory in curling sheets like paper too wet to hold its shape. Each moment that passed, the creatures around her changed, bizarre and fevered shapes and arrangements of fins and teeth congealing into more primitive forms, blunted, regressed and fumbling. She blinked a million years at a time.

The Thing That Wants was too strong in the world, rippling through the waters that lapped up and over the lands. It laughed at her, watching her plumb depths yet unable to touch anything of substance.

LITTLE CREATURE STAY WITH ME

It must be weak sometime. Nothing is always strong.

Breath heaved in and out of her lungs like wounded birds. She would have to stop and rest soon, but there was no safe place. Her arms and legs moved only through force of will and she could feel that burning down. She only had millions of years to go.

YIELD AND BE FORGIVEN
YOU HAVE TESTED ME
MORE THAN ANY OTHER
STAY AND BE FORGIVEN

"I don't want your forgiveness."

Something that was neither reptile nor fish but some vast knobby-skinned amphibian brushed against her fingertips in the water. Its flesh yielded uneasily under her touch, even its skin unfinished. Stubby paddle-claws pushed against the water and it dove then was lost. Everything was strange and getting stranger, every last bit of familiarity being squeezed and forced out life until only the weird remained. Segmented crustaceans like aquatic centipedes the size of semi-trucks wriggled through the depths, all chatter and clatter. The seas grew warmer and warmer as she kicked back.

The whole ocean was alive, teeming with energy and alien vitality. Everything had come from this, this strangeness and squirming of evolutionary near-dead-ends, of things so bizarre that they could not have come from design but millions of random shots. Things were climbing back up the tree of time, assuming more and more basic forms, the sturdiest and those unbroken. The water was body-hot, swimming in blood now. Dim orange light pulsed beneath in great veins, squirming and aimless, spreading across the ocean floor. Cait was being boiled, water moving from pleasantly warm to hot to…

She'd have to get out. There was nowhere to go but farther back.

ENOUGH OF THIS GAME

There was fear in the voice now. She could feel it and this gave her strength that surged through her limbs as she clawed through the hot waters of the timeless oceans. Lava spread beneath her, miles below but still hot enough to make her sweat, close to fainting. Fingers of molten rock glowed dully and shrouds of bubbles and steam roiled off them before cooling into rock that was blacker than anything she'd remembered.

ENOUGH

She had nowhere else to go back, peeling back time farther and farther, through the skin of the thing's memories, past the deadened tissue and on to something more alive; more alive and vulnerable.

Salt and sulfur turned every breath into a weak wheeze. The knife was heavy now, a weight in her hand that she could only just barely grasp. The ocean around her was a cauldron, a soup of weird life and its shells, its bones being cooked off.

Much longer and I won't be able to hold out myself.

She kicked through the slackened sea all but dead now. Empty cara-
paces and unidentifiable masses of organic waste bobbed all around her in
a Cambrian wasteland, a necrotic ocean of countless species, which would
never be accounted for by anything other than Cait and the Thing That
Wants, both of them suffering the same withering fate.

Unless she pushed past it.

PLEASE NO MORE
PLEASE NO MORE

"There will be lots more," Cait said. "Until you listen to me."

NEVER WILL I

Cait kicked once, stripping back only a little time. The waters were still
dead. She had no idea how long this period of death had lasted. Surely
something had survived, but she saw no sign of it, nor of any previous life.
It was a dead ocean on a dead world, listless with only a suggestion of current to betray utter stasis.

"Lots more," she repeated.

TAKE ME AWAY
PLEASE

"Okay." Cait pushed back farther, before the point of this calamity, one
which had turned everything to death, mountains of organic matter and
debris left to decay and nourish everything that had come after.

Cait screamed as the cold water hit her skin, whatever time this was
before the greatest death that the planet and its waters. She swam into
the true body of the Thing That Wants, for it could have been no other
place. She lay there letting the heat leech out of her, letting her skin and
flesh drink in the cool swirls of this ocean, one that knew only crustaceans
that swam in bodies twice her length. Thousands of paired legs moved
in waves, turning over and over in the water and they snaked past. Creatures that looked like giant carpets of muscle flapped by, algae-backed,
something from a nightmare puppet show. They were eyeless and huge
and hungry. Giant flaps of skin and meat enveloped crustacean armor and
squeezed until not even shell was left intact, only clouds of plasma in the
sun-streaked water.

This world was so very quiet. No creatures made sounds because
nothing yet lived in the air. Water was the cradle and the prison. Fleshy
feathers of orange and yellow waved in the currents below Cait's feet,

enough of them to be called a forest. Segmented creatures like flattened beetles teemed and swarmed. Their backs were painted in colors that no one had ever seen, into patterns of intricacy and complexity that were hypnotic.

She didn't know how long she watched it, this simple beauty, without assumption or expectation of nothing more than eat and hatch and repeat.

The sun set and the stars above her were upsetting. Their light was millions of years too young and all of them in the wrong place. Any constellation she could have named would have been pre-born or not-yet-placed. Meteorites streaked through the starlight and black so clean and pure that everything would look dirty in comparison. For the first time she understood how far she was away from anything that she'd known. The though wrestled with her, but she couldn't afford the luxury of fear, not now.

"Are you here?" she asked.

The business of life ignored her and willowed through the waters instead.

"Answer me!"

I AM ALWAYS

"Are you through playing games?"

Wind chopped over the water, cutting the still surface into numberless crescents.

FOOL
YOU CAME TO WHERE I AM STRONGEST
LIFE ITSELF IS CHAINED TO ME NOW
AS IT WILL BE THEN

"You have got to be joking," she said with a sigh.

SHOW ME I AM WRONG

There was nothing more to work with. She'd dragged the Thing through cataclysm after cataclysm and it had survived them all. Maybe it was stronger than her and stronger than everything she'd ever know. But she was damned if she was going to give up on that.

It wants to be the only source of life, the only one. But there has to be a time...

She let the thought drop, wondering if it could read her.

STAY HERE
AND I WILL BE SATISFIED
I WILL HAVE ALL

"And still have it in the future?"

OF COURSE

"I'll go to hell first."

She had nothing left now but nerve. She was burning reserves that weren't hers. But it was not simply her life she'd been playing for.

This will have to run to the end, the beginning.

Wearily, she kicked again. She kicked and peeled back time in a butchered tapestry, not flaying them away slowly but aimlessly hacking. The world shuddered at every lashing backward. The headwaters of the river had to be close ahead. That or she would run out of strength.

Mountains rose out of the sea unlike any that Cait had seen before. They were jagged and knife-cut, sculpted by hewing forces that the earth of her time was no longer subjected to but that ran wild here. Geology was unbound and the earth was unsettled, fitful.

And the waters receded.

Cait heard a monstrous gasp of recognition that sucked the breath out of her and everything around. The atmosphere thinned and thinned until it was all but gone.

YOU WOULD NOT DARE

That got to him.

"Watch me!"

The seas, youthful and tentative now, pulled back, revealing more and more of the restive spines of the earth. Knuckled shoals lay exposed and they would not be mountains for millions of years. She peeled them back too, panting from exertion, from the pressure of rushing headlong into a time that she couldn't even guess at. She hoped only that she could breathe there.

Mountains crumbled and she felt her feet brush against solid ground now, rock that would not yield to her touch. The water was heavy, mineralized to an extent as to make even the Dead Sea seem drinkable. If there was life within it she could not see or touch it there.

STOP

Cait stood. The heavy water dripped from her to a surface that was almost slow and elastic. The sun was too bright, obliterating the blue of the sky and bleeding it white. Every rock outcropping was jagged and triangular, cleaved from violent impact or upheaval. There was no smoothness or gentleness anywhere in this place. She could breathe but only barely.

Dust hung in the air, flinders from a huge crater that was evident in regular but erratically carved walls, gouged out of the rock and stone. She looked behind her and the ocean was nowhere to be seen, just a lake, pathetic and aborted. If she'd had half an hour, she could have gone around it, maybe twice.

Cait coughed and a little blood came out with that.

Oh fuck.

She wiped her lip. "I've stopped. You can come out now." Her voice was made strange by the ancient and long-forgotten gauntness of the atmosphere, barely enough to breathe.

no

The voice was small, vibrating weakly through her.

She tried to sit and ended up half-collapsing to the ground, close enough to the shore to put her fingers in the water, which felt tacky and gross to the touch.

"You've got nobody else to talk to. Just you and me."

scared

"Hell, I'm scared too now that I've had time to think this plan through." She scanned the horizon and found nothing that could remind her of a living planet. This was a dead rock in a seething and black nothing, spinning through a void that so clear that it betrayed the thinness of the atmosphere.

don't hurt me

"I never wanted…" She turned her hand over in the water and pulled it out as if expecting something to come nibbling. "I'm not trying to hurt you."

yes you were

"I wanted you to stop. You can't have the world."

want

"Look, humans are fucked-up enough that you'll probably get it all. You'll just have to wait. Probably not all that long a time as you see it." She sighed and rubbed her lower lip, pulling her knuckles back reddened. "I can't stay here long."

stay

"What happens if I go back any farther? Will I be here when the comet or whatever hits? We're standing in a big crater right now, right? That's what brought you."

nothing

"I'm not far enough for there to be nothing."

nothing happens before
scared

"Nothing happens or you just don't remember it? But then I don't know anyone who remembers being born."

Cait eyed the knife and its edge was clean and sharp still. "Well look, you're not alone, right? I mean, I'm going to have to get back, drag my ass all the way back. I'll be there for that long. Which I guess is a pretty long time." The thought of counting years gave her a chill, even in the unfiltered sunlight which burned.

sunlight
too much

She looked at the edge of the water and it was ringed in a finger's width of flaky, scalloped crystals with a rainbow sheen at the right angles. Beyond that, a thinner layer ran almost to the edge of the crater. All that the Thing was, being left behind in this brittle rainbow. She angled her vision to the sun, stopping short of it. The heat rained down, brutal and unrelenting. She dragged her finger through the crystals and up the track to where the water had once ended.

"You're not gonna make it, are you?"

dying scared dying scared dying scared

"You're *not* going to die."

stay dying scared

"I'm leaving. But you have to make a deal with me."

what deal

"An agreement." She kneeled down to her haunches and addressed the dying pool that was all the world's oceans. But only if it survived.

listening

"I'll do what I can to save you, put you somewhere safe from the sun. But you have to remember this and stay Thing That Wants and not try to become Thing That Has."

you stay then
not alone

"No. I have to go back. I can't stay. I don't even know if I can breathe long enough to do this. You'll have to help me get back when I'm done. 'Cause I don't wanna die… billions of years before I'm even born."

The sun beat its unending tattoo on the earth and Cait coughed out a glob that looked like something had died in her.

"You better hurry though."

will stay thing that wants

She could only barely feel its reply.
"That's a promise."

promise

"Say it again."

promise

She stood and made ready to step in. "Once more."

promise

"That's three times. Now you're bound to it. Wish me luck."

Entering the alkaline pool, she clawed to the narrow bottom and felt with her hand, trying to find a good place to begin cutting. Maybe there was water below the surface and maybe not, but getting the water farther down and out of the sun might give the Thing enough of a chance to hold on.

And what? Become everything? The surf that the boys fight over at Zuma? The stuff life crawled out of? I can't keep thinking about this.

She found a narrow seam between jagged rocks like shattered teeth. The knife slid in without hesitation and she slashed across and pulled out stones and rock until her lungs sent her back to the surface. Cough, spit and breathe until she could right herself and then return.

Time lost meaning, but the body kept count.

She continued digging until the trips down were far enough that she could do almost nothing but scrabble once or twice before having to return.

The sun was down and the sky swarmed above with alien stars. They were bright in a way that she'd never seen nor would ever again, skies never having tasted smoke or gasoline or even desert dust. It was as if she'd been staring through mud-caked windows her entire life and they were cleared by sudden rain. Still, the stars were wrong and that gnawed at her, urging her to hurry back to a more familiar time. But she couldn't move, not for the moment. She lay there, crusted entirely with salts both strange and Archean.

Finally she rolled slowly to her feet and cried out at the pain. But she was so close that she had to keep going now.

The sullen and oily surface lapped at her and she breathed as deeply as she could without triggering another coughing fit. It was war between the simmering panic of the shattering sun and thinness of the air and Cait's dwindling physical reserves. She burned in a fire of consumption. She must have given up a pint of blood and tears to this dwindling pool and could only pray that this would be enough because she was on dregs now.

Cait slipped beneath the surface and sank down to the seam she had been working, deepening with careful and deliberate slashes through stone to whatever lay beneath. The voice of Thing That Wants had stilled some time ago. Maybe it was holding its breath, too afraid of the possibility of failure.

That makes two of us.

She dug and dug, slashing away at the substance of the very planet, this dumb and lifeless rock and this trembling lake that was evaporating over days or weeks or eons, however long she'd been in the memory of this thing. Her vision was going red and pulsing in time to her heart. She stabbed until her knuckles were bloodied and numb. The knife was still hungry and ate all it was given.

Then there was a grabbing sensation, something pulling from beneath. The rock wall began to clamber away from itself, caving in as if rotten. She tried to kick upward, to escape the sudden shift in weight and gravity as the whole world fell into an abyss that had been just below her this entire time. The whole of the rock wall disintegrated up to a ledge just above her. Falling into nothing, she fumbled and regained her grip several times, each more tenuous than the last. There was no sound of anything hitting below her, just an emptiness that kept swallowing. Beneath her feet it was black and lightless.

She thrust herself up, reaching past the rush of pressure and alkali water sheeting over her. With her knife hand, she dug in and felt the guard smack against solid stone. Then she turned the blade sideways as much as she could and hung there, hand over hand.

Water cascaded over her and into the dark hole where the world seemingly ended below. She held on, though it felt like standing in a rain of hammers, no longer able to cry or do anything other than cling to that stone.

w o m a n

Cait was unable to speak, conserving every bit of energy into keeping her hands from slipping.

l e t   g o
i s   s a f e
a n d   c o o l   h e r e

She craned her head over into the empty black that was below, all that was below. The last traces of the lake dripped across stones around her before yawning into that deep space. It could have been anything. It could have been absolute nothing.

promise

It could be lying and just wanting to kill me. And I could be so tired that I can't do anything else, either way.

With that, she tugged on the handle of the blade then wrenched it back and forth to pull it free. The rock groaned and sheared and she went weightless, too exhausted to scream in shock. Too drained to do anything but hold her breath and hope that there would be enough when she hit bottom.

Roar of water in her ears and the smash of cold pulled her out of half-consciousness. She struggled to the surface and drank it in, cool and sweet. The salts and grime of the stale alkali washed away. She breathed in and the air was fresh and full, not the lacking thinness she'd had to breathe before. A wracking cough wrestled out of her chest. She felt something come up as she spit a bloody wad into the water where it sank quickly.

Maybe someone will find that and wonder what the hell it was.

Far above her there was a dim and jagged circle, the sunlight so distant that it went cold. Light shimmered on the surface of the subterranean pool, reflecting almost as an afterthought. It was like looking up into the roof of a half-lit cathedral, geometry suggested and sketched out but not whole, only implied. Columns of stone but not stalactite or stalagmite instead formed by some other process, were upthrust out of the water and reached to the ceiling. Cait imagined they had been placed there but couldn't understand how. Regularity was a thing of mercury, craved but poisonous to hold and slippery.

She drank, now that she knew she could breathe here. It was the sweetest water she'd ever remembered tasting, not salty or brackish at all. The first waters.

The liquid beneath and around her moved slowly, pulled by tide or current, but she could not tell from where. She couldn't fight it, so she angled toward one of the columns, to at least stop treading water for a time. Just to rest for a little while.

PROMISE

The voice rang through her every bone, every welt on her knuckles and the scratchiness inside her chest. She wept at the pain of it.

"Too much," she whispered. "I can't…"

YOU CANNOT STAY

The only reply she could manage was a strangled cry.

LISTEN
THIS IS THE RIVER YOU RODE IN ON
MY MEMORY
IT WILL TAKE YOU OUT AS WELL
PROMISE

Her fingers dug into the stone and she cried at the thought of letting go of this solid thing, of yielding to the water and being groundless for another minute much less however long she'd be traveling. The river tugged, insistent and unyielding as every glacier that gouged out every valley and ground down every mountain. Cait wasn't as strong as either one of these.

PROMISE

Her fingernails left scratches in the stone that no human would ever see as the river took her away. All she could do was float and breathe and the last filled her with pain but less now. It was down to feeling like ground glass in her lungs and throat as she swallowed. She drank a little of the water as she went along, just sips, each time thrilling with its purity.

She felt herself borne along by things she could not see. One moment it was the rippling and unfurling of the current and then the sliding plates of a crustacean bigger than a truck a yielding and spongy substance that she dare not look down and see the surge of muscle and smooth reptilian hide and feathers slick with grease and the rasping skin of a shark but spread wide like a ray and thick and waterproof leather finally bristling fur that she glanced at and saw was translucent white between her fingers. The weak blue night of the underground came and went to daylight and dusk to a pulsating turquoise that she recognized as the place she'd come from, billions of years ago or yet to come she could no longer guess.

Cait felt herself being carried along by a carpet of hands and the song wove around her, wordless. There was a new voice with it though, not dominating but underlaying it all, providing a foundation, a steadiness. It was the voice of Thing That Wants; she knew that much. But it was no longer the same. She didn't know what to call it and was too awestruck to ask. Unseen hands in the waters below conveyed her and she opened her eyes to see the boat bobbing where she'd left it on the interior ocean. There were no weird currents around it, no prison, no restraint.

Her hand brushed against the hull and she tried lifting it, her arm only weighing tons now. It took three tries to hook over the gunwale. She tried to pull herself out of the water, but her arm wouldn't respond. Muscles straining, she pulled partway up, tossed the knife carefully over the side and grabbed with her other arm. Maybe there was a surge in the current from beneath that helped her over. She liked to think that she'd managed it herself.

Cait lay on her back, breathing heavily from the exhaustion. At least she wasn't spitting blood any longer. Tiny creature sounds echoed from the cabin and hearing them, she was able to haul herself to her feet.

Woman

The voice's timbre was leavened, without the weight and volume it had used before.

"Give me a minute. Everything hurts."

Why

"Because I'm alive. Why what?"

Why dig
Why help

"I don't know. Maybe nobody should die alone if it can be helped. Maybe I like listening to the waves. Maybe it seemed like the right thing to do."

You could have left
Water still happens
Oceans still rise
Without me

"Look, if you're thankful all of a sudden, then be kinder. The chorus, all those people alone and drowning to death? Show them what I've showed you."

Promise

"Can you take me back to where we started? Back to Venice?"

Straight ahead half will get you there
Just hold tight

"Thanks." She opened the door to the cabin and the kitten noises were insistent and chattering. "Don't worry little guys." She stopped before stepping inside and spoke to the water and sky. "You only ever *thought* you were alone all this time. You know that, right?"

The waters said nothing, perhaps shamed into quiet that she herself could not shake.

෴

Venice beach was deserted, shoreline wiped eerily clean. The storm winds had given up, though the breath of rain hung on the air. The grounded boat lay behind Cait as she took determined steps up the beach, clutching a box full of wriggling kittens and the one that did not. She'd thought about crying over it but couldn't make that happen.

Cait looked in futility for Parker's car but saw nothing. There weren't even early morning fishermen or overnight campers. Maybe she'd only been gone for minutes. Maybe she'd never left at all. She stopped at the little market on the corner and bought a quart of whole milk with a handful of change that had miraculously stayed trapped in her jeans. Or maybe the water had put it there, knowing that she'd need it. The shopkeeper didn't care either way and just said, "You take care of those kitties. They're good luck."

"The best luck," she said as she left and made her way to Vince's apartment. He might even be there.

The streets were shocked quiet and wet, littered with palm fronds stripped from trees like broken umbrellas, lost things cast out of the sea and left to the land.

CHAPTER TWENTY TWO

The kitten was all teeth and claws and orange mackerel stripes, grabbing on Vince's hand with everything it had.

"So much for mister 'Oh I don't want a cat,'" Cait teased.

"Shut up. Can't help it if the little fuzzball imprinted on me." He lifted his hand, and the critter refused to let go.

"I don't think kittens imprint. That's ducklings." Cait stroked the cat's flank and couldn't feel the ribs anymore.

"I know what I'm talking about. Right, Magnanimous?" He brought his hand in and cradled the squirming bundle against his chest. The kitten continued its ridiculous savagery of his limb.

Sun and wind streamed in over the open balcony. Cait just stood in that for a moment. She tried to remember what that first water had tasted like and couldn't remember it now, just the sour salt tang and rank of seaweed in the sun, the car exhaust and smell of civilization.

"Some tough cop. Look at you. The softest dirtbag."

"I'm only human. What kind of monster could turn this face down?"

"And get all the others in her litter homes before I even woke up the next morning?"

The kitten made a sound between a chirp and a purr and swatted at Vince's nose. "You slept for a day and that night, so. And these guys practically sell themselves. We oughta start a business."

"Not a lot of money in it."

Right. I don't have a job still.

"What about…?" she pulled herself short and couldn't even say it.

"What?"

"The last kitten? The one who was dead in the box."

Vince smiled cockeyed and scritched the cat between the ears. "You're looking at her. Carried her in my shirt for a few hours, couldn't bear the thought of putting her in the ground. Maybe she was just cold."

She watched her giant bear of an uncle in the thrall of the tiny creature. It was only sixty years old or so, judging from the bag. Or it just happened to be dropped into a sixty-year-old bag two nights ago.

That was the easier explanation, right? Trager would be proud of my dissembling.

"Did you call my mom? Not every day that your niece shows up with a crate of half-drowned cats and crashes on your couch for a couple days."

"Yeah, that was weird. I called not long after you showed up." Vince didn't look at her, stuck in the blue eyes that stared up from his chest.

Cait braced herself, leaning harder on the balcony than she'd maybe meant to.

Why not have to deal with Hurricane Mom after all this?

"And? When's she going to be here to set me straight?" The beach out in the distance was scattershot with November sunbathers and even a few folks out in the water. The horizon faded from blue into an indeterminate mist out way on the water.

"I told her to trust you. That you turned a corner." He turned to look right at her. "No bullshit."

"If I told you what happened, you probably wouldn't say that."

"Then don't. I'm a pretty good judge of fucked-up. And while all of us roll a little with that quality, I don't see a dangerous amount of it in you."

"That's just 'cause I'm not dressing corporate anymore."

"Left that part out. She survived you in college. She'll survive you making your own choices. Now that you're together enough to make them."

Cait took in a deep breath and got nothing but salt off the water, no Sargasso of flesh, no lost time, nothing but here and now. It had taken her a while to get her senses straight, time-lagged, herself just a bit out of step with her body, not drunk but dissociated.

"I *was* before."

"Agree to no-fucking-way. But yes-fucking-way now."

"You're a poet."

"That and a buck gets me a plain burger down the street."

"Robbery at that."

"Sure, it's not very good, but at least, you get a lot of it."

"Just don't feed the cat any of that. Give 'er parasites."

"Sure thing. You ready to go back to life?"

"Already there, Vince." She reached around him and squeezed him tight. "Thanks for giving me the rope."

"Never thought you were gonna hang yourself with it, kid. For what it's worth."

"A fair bit. You take care." She reached over to pet the kitten. "Bite him, Magnanimous. A lot."

She called for the taxi and waited downstairs in the November that felt like May, but the lighting was all wrong, low and slanting yet still warm.

Cait punched through the waiting messages on the machine, stopping when a lightly drawled voice came through.

"Hey, Cait. Parker. Hope you made it out. Guessing you did since we're not all underwater now. Look, I don't know if you're going to get this or what, but I've got my walking papers. They're letting me stay until Wednesday. I'm seeing some friends of yours off at Union Station at about three that afternoon and then I'll be in the wind. No other cops there, not even make sure I go."

She made her way down to the garage forgetting that she didn't have one now and saw the water trickling across the asphalt before she turned the corner, spreading out in a shape that looked like fingers melting into one another. She was sure there were no pipes in there to burst, but maybe a soaking wet Mercury was big enough to leave a mess like that.

Should have known it wouldn't be that easy to ditch that car. It can remember every fish that ever swam and every wreck that went down, so sure, it could remember that. It probably thought it was doing me a favor.

Unable to face another persistent violation of causality, she made her way back up the stairs and then called Link. Yes, he was available. Yes, he'd drive her to Union Station, lickety-split as he said it.

Link said she looked worlds better and she told him to step on it. He didn't ask what the hurry was.

Cait filtered through the crowds in the station, glanced up the big board of departure gates and found one for Memphis by way of Dallas and New Orleans. Had to be it. The hollow mull of milling people echoed through the high ceilings and off ceramic tile that looked as shiny as the day it had been built. She powered through the tunnel and out to the open concrete departure bays where the Amtrak waited, idling out diesel and farewells.

Parker stood there, smoking a cigarette and shaking someone's hand. It must've been Lee. Sue was standing beside him, taller than her brother and twice as severe. She stood straight as anyone had ever stood, pain in the leg be damned.

"Hey!" Cait shouted. "Hey! Wait!" She ran up the platform quick as she could, weaving and dodging as easily as sea-foam.

Sue said nothing. Lee only half-smiled and Parker finished it for him.

"Even the sea rejected you, huh? Just like Jonah," Parker said. He stubbed out the half-finished cigarette and put it behind his hear.

She took his hand firmly, offering only that. "I'd tell you the whole story, but there isn't time, I guess."

"We have to be going," Sue said, clipped and short. Her face was so tight and controlled that she must have been on fire inside.

Lee looked as if he had a stomach filled with scorpions now.

"I guess it's just goodbye then?" Cait asked.

Sue neglected to respond.

"I thank you, Miss Cait," Lee said. His voice was just a trickling of its former self, played out. "For everything you did for me."

"I didn't exactly do it alone," she replied. "Had help, a lot of it even."

"Some of that comes with regret," Sue said through gritted teeth, still making it sound like sugar.

"Excuse me?"

"Cait, come on. No good gonna come from this." Parker's hand went to her elbow gently.

She shook it off.

"Say what you got to say, Sue. Then buckle up. Come on."

Brake lines on the train hissed close by, kicking up dust and soot from the rails below. It smelled like the death of machines.

"Some costs can't be weighed, Cait. I'm happy that Lee is back and whole. Mostly. But the price was no bargain."

"I don't get you."

"I don't expect you would," she said with a knife twist.

Cait stepped right to her, sure as if someone had been picking a fight on the club floor. "Because I don't go to church on Sunday? 'Cause I had the misfortune of being born in the modern world?"

"I'm glad that I can take Lee home and that maybe I don't have to be the last Whelan to live in Whelan House. But I don't have to like where the help came from and I don't mean just a foul-mouth girl from LA."

"Maybe it all came from the same place."

"I like that answer even less."

Those words ate at Cait, but she didn't know clearly why.

"Now will you please just let us go home? I've got to make my own sense out of this, just as Lee has. And it will not be the same that *you* make out of it."

Cait thought of several different things to say. None of them would have made any of this any better. She settled.

"Okay. You two take care of each other."

"I intend just that." Then she and Lee made their way onto the train, carrying her old suitcase and a couple paper bags filled with supplies and who knew what else.

Cait rubbed tears out of her eyes. "Well, that sucked."

"Think it went pretty good myself. They've been staying with me the last couple days, and you can talk to Sue Whelan, but I don't know that reaching her is possible."

"Hard disagree. She wouldn't have been so angry with me if I hadn't gotten to her. Just wonder if she's pissed that I didn't invoke Jesus when I faced down… whatever it was."

"Was that what happened?"

"Hell no. It was twenty times weirder." She looked for them on the train, but they were already gone. "Come on. Let's go."

"Where?"

"Anywhere not here."

༄

Phillipe's was, as the legend held, the originator of the French dip sandwich, not only in Los Angeles, but every other place as well. It had been standing and open without cease for nearly eighty years, serving everything from beef to lamb between crusty rolls and alongside broth so salty it made patrons sweat. The only thing that had changed in that time were the fashions of the customers and that they didn't layer the floors with sawdust any longer. Noisy throngs of customers gaggled at long common tables where strata of citizenry who'd normally never associate could be found cheek to jowl.

Cait finished her sandwich and looked for more.

"Kittens, you said?"

"Yeah, a bagful of them. Figure someone tried to drown them and at least, I got to short-circuit that." She took a slug of iced tea to cool the hot mustard taste that surged from mouth to sinuses.

"And the rest of it. All of it pret-ty out there." Parker put a dollop of mustard onto the purple pickled egg he'd been holding then bit into it.

"That's why I haven't exactly been beating down Trager's door."

"Oh, I'm sure he'll get to you eventually."

"Great. So are you still in trouble with him, too?"

"I'm never going to be out of it."

"I'm sorry I dragged you down into the mess." she said.

"Truth was I was in it before you came along. Least I got to make your acquaintance this way."

She was too drained to come up with anything clever or disarming or to change the subject. She finished her tea and the ice clinking seemed louder than her own pulse.

"Case is still a mess though, right?"

"It's not nearly as bad as you think. See, that tape that got things so wound up for LAPD? Well, it kinda glitched out. Guess Toretti was one of those cheapskates who just kept taping over the same cassette, over and over, until it all just turned to mush. Couldn't see shit really." He shook his head and laughed. "Rich guys always spend their money wrong."

"Huh. Go figure. Who do I have to thank for that?"

"Toretti of course. Oh, and Sue for identifying the husk of the thing that was left on the beach. I might've hauled it up the shore and took some pictures after you went for your swim. Figured plausible deniability is better than none at all. Not that you could call it a body as such, but you know, weird things happen in this town." His smile was uneven.

"How'd he take that, dumbass?"

"About like you think. But he saw he wasn't going to get anything better. Pretty thin soup, but not all cases close either. Too weird for prime time."

"But *Quest4* and *Easy Street* will eat it up."

"As will the tabloids. Can't stop the press." He glanced down at his watch and back up quickly, haunted. "Hey look, you need a lift anywhere? I mean, Philippe's is nice, but you can't stay here."

"I should be okay."

"Good. Because my car is a hike from here." He fidgeted with the crumpled napkin in his hand. "Bummer that things worked out this way."

Then he pulled the cigarette from behind his ear and rolled it around in his fingers. "But I'm being called back."

"You ever going to be around again?"

"I don't honestly know," he said. "Oh, here. You left this back at the beach." Digging around in his jacket pocket, he came up with the metal cigarette box and weird earphones, if that's what they even were. He passed it over to her, fingers brushing her palm and lingering for almost too long a time.

"Ah, thanks," she said. Then, too quickly "Well, LA's a big city but not *that* big. You could come back around to Los Feliz anytime. I wouldn't tell anyone." She pocketed the box, wires tangling around her fingers as she did.

"I appreciate the offer, but I'm going back home. Farther away than just another precinct."

"I don't get it."

"It's 'cause I didn't throw it out there to be got." He stood and pulled out his wallet and a few more very clean singles, fresh from the mint it seemed. "Let me be a big spender and buy you a French dip and some pickled eggs."

"Not enough money in the world for me to eat those."

"Nobody's making you." He left the bills in a neat pile on the table next to one of his odd packs of cigarettes, only mostly empty. He slipped one into his mouth without thought and left it there.

"That's a sturdy tip."

"Sturdy sandwiches." He got up to walk. She followed, snatching the forgotten cigarette package off the table.

Parker lit up when they got outside, taking a drag that put a toll on the cigarette. He inhaled deeply and breathed out. The smoke lit up like a nimbus in the early evening sun, fingers and tendrils in a flowing halo.

"So long, Parker. Good luck back home."

"Thanks. And thanks for keeping all this" he waved his hands expansively "above water. Got kind of attached to it."

"Not sure I can take all the credit for that," she admitted. "But I got it to keep its promise, I think."

"Let's hope."

They shook hands and Parker was the first to pull away, maybe upset and maybe in frustration. He turned up Ord Street, trailing purplish smoke behind.

When Cait turned the corner and stole up to get a last look, he was simply not there. She watched the street for a moment, trying to imagine where he'd gotten to so quickly or if she was just more tired than she thought.

Cait walked down to the rolled-steel bus stop on Alameda Street, watching the people and cars running their courses, channeled and contained. Color and motion in the dusk, that purpling sky, half-sweet and half-sour on exhaust. The light of Phillipe's flicked on and buzzed, golden cursive arcs somehow reassuring even if you couldn't read the words. So many lives happening all at once in a churning sea of humanity, of time unfolding and unfurling into this very moment then reaching out to a time she couldn't even imagine.

Cait stood there for the first time in a long time, not carried blindly by those currents but steering with them.

AFTERWORD

This book had a particularly troubled upbringing. The writing wasn't so bad. Though it was taking place when the first Covid pandemic was rampaging through America and threw everything into disarray. I was just finishing about the time that people were figuring out this was a long-term if not forever thing. That tempered a few of the decisions I'd originally set out with in the outline. I had enough of stone bummers. You can probably figure out which events got changed, if you put your mind to it.

Like I said, the writing wasn't bad. The editing wasn't bad, once it happened. That took some time. Then deadlines not under my control got missed. Again, Covid, can't be explained. Then lack of communication and finally answers months after I'd been rattling my tin cup against the bars. What I'd thought was certain in terms of publishing was no longer. Which involved not only me but the artist I'd brough on to do the original cover. Yes, it involved the publisher too, but those decisions were on their part and not mine. At least not until I was out of options. So we parted ways and I paid both the editor for his time and the artist for his. Which left a sizable hole to dig out of, mentally, emotionally, not to mention all the ongoing stuff of everyday life.

Then I tried to sell *All Waters Are Graves* to a handful of publishers. That, of course, was a mistake. But I was pretty hungry to have someone not me publish the book (else I wouldn't have put up with half of the delays that caused me and the original publisher to part ways.) That's my own hangup to get over. Which I finally did.

Fast-forward to not long ago and deciding to give Kickstarter a try. If you have this book in your hands, it's likely because of that. For which I'm thankful. Will this book make a splash or even a ripple? Hopefully it does with you, the reader and backer. But coming and going without much left behind is the fate of most books out there today anyways. I'm in good company, only I got the attention of a bunch of folks who thought the project was intriguing and worth their time and money. Which got me an advance better than I would have seen had I stayed with the original publisher (if the book would have even made it out by now.)

Again, for this I'm thankful.

The books will continue, at least the first five or six of them. After that, we'll see where things stand. Hopefully you'll all be around for it. I know I will.

Of course, praise be to the backers. The book would have happened without you, but knowing that you're there and believed enough in me to put up money on this is a very big deal. So, thanks.

Teresa B. Ardrey
Corinna Bechko
David Brothers
Steven Byrd
Ashley Campbell
Don Cardenas
Matthew Carpenter
Laurent Clow
Aleph Craven
Dan Cullen
Mark Davenport
Eric Dodds
Nathan Dryden
Philip Flores
Marc-Oliver Frisch
Paul Fritschle
Ben Gulley
Conrad Heiney
Andrew Hickey
Erik Highter
Alan Hughes
Daniel Johnson
Jared Kahanek
Andrew Kaplan
James Kislingbury
Constantine Koutsoutis
Steve Lieber
Mitch Loidolt
David Long
Ken Lowery
Kyle Marquis

Derek Moreland
Jesse Lawrence Morgan
John Nacinovich
Christopher Nadeau
Kat O.
Kirk Pennak
Chris Reid
Nick Ring
Rhiannon RS
Eric Schuster
Randall Sims
Jimbo Slice
Joe Soares
Tom Speelman
Curtis Square-Briggs
Eric Trautmann
Jeff Treppel
Jason Urbanciz
Tim Utsler
Evan Waters
Mila Webb
Andrew Weiss
Dorian Wright
Jay Wolf

THANKS AND ACKNOWLEDGEMENTS

Too many to name, but I'll make a stab at it. Thanks to Corinna Bechko for paleontological reference info (though I was pretty, uh, liberal in my interpretation of it), and for being an early reader to even see if this book made any damn sense. Other early readers include Jeff Treppel, Costa Koutsoutis and Erik Highter, so thanks to them for putting up with the early draft (which is mostly like what you're reading, or rather have read.) Thanks to Brian Faulkner and Chris Barrus and Ned Raggett for exposing me to a wide range of music from the time back in the day that I might not have otherwise heard. Yes, Vinyl Fetish was a very real place. I probably got a lot of the details wrong, sorry. Thanks always to my wonderful wife Jennifer who put up with my self-doubt and grumbling about such over the course of the writing and failure to publish this book. She is always my rock in this ocean we find ourselves in.

BIOGRAPHY

I was born in California, sometime between the JFK assassination and the moon landing. Lived there my whole life. Learned to drive stick shift in the parking lot of the ziggurat that you see in Roger Corman's *Death Race 2000* and went to school where they filmed all those soft brutalist sets in Battle for the *Planet of the Apes*. I've worked in video arcades and think tanks, been an animator, taught sociology, thanatology and ethnomethodology.

My past writings include work for Blizzard Entertainment, stories in both *Tomorrow's Cthulhu* and *Welcome to Miskatonic University* from Broken Eye Books. Broken Eye was the original publisher for *The Queen of No Tomorrows* as well, recently re-published by Highway 62 Press.

I've self-published a number of books, both nonfiction/commentary and short/long fiction works. I was also the writer and publisher of the weird western comic series *Strangeways*.

Hazeland will be the bulk of my work for the forseeable future. Unless someone wants to pay me to do something else. It's not like there's a lot of money in this. Sorry, high priests of success. It's true.

Sure. I'd love to be on your podcast.

http://highway62press.com
@highway62 on Bluesky, not Twitter
@hwy_62 on Instagram, minimally